The Battle for Badgers Brow

L A Roberts

Copyright © 2024 Leslie A Roberts

All rights reserved.

ISBN: 9798301862908

Cover design © 2024 Nicola Robson

The Battle for Badgers Brow

For Nathan and Joshua.

The Battle for Badgers Brow

"I wrote this for you".

The Battle for Badgers Brow

ACKNOWLEDGMENTS

I would like to express my deepest gratitude to my family and friends for their unwavering support throughout this journey.

A special thanks to my editor, Amy Boxshall, who deserves applause for her insightful feedback and dedication to shaping this manuscript. Her constructive criticism strengthened the book which is greatly improved by her input.

This book would not be the same without the exceptional cover design by Nicola Robson. Her creativity brought the story to life.

Finally, to the readers who embark on this adventure with me, thank you for giving these characters a home in your imagination.

PROLOGUE

"The island is a worthy prize, and its destiny is to be ruled by the Grey. It is rich in history and its folklore tells of ancient deeds of man and beast. With a world of sorcery and magic which are still there to be found, if you know where to find them," said the king's advisor.

"Tell me more. I do like the sound of it, especially the talk of destiny. I take it to mean my destiny, Elder?" asked Slate, the self-appointed king of the grey squirrels.

As he spoke, he stood with his back to his advisor, preening and admiring himself in a cracked, ornate mirror. Vanity was just one of his many bad traits. He was quite small in stature for a grey squirrel, but his cunning made up for his lack of size. Not that that stopped him from filling out his puny frame with his usual attire of a padded, charcoal-grey tunic. Half-a-dozen brass buttons ran down its front, and large gold threaded large gold threaded tasselled decorations on each shoulder to show off his regal status.

Well, he thought, it wouldn't do for the rabble of grey squirrels that called themselves the Grey Army to see their king without his finery. The advisor then continued.

"Yes, sire, undoubtedly, the ancient scrolls foretell it so. And that it shall be conquered by a great leader, and that leader shall not be man but a creature of the wood," he replied with confidence.

Slate then turned to his advisor, finally bothering to stop his preening. The advisor, Oswald the Elder, was a useful kind of creature to have around. First, and possibly most importantly, as a dormouse he was much smaller than the king, and so this made Slate look bigger and braver by comparison. Second, he had a certain set of skills that most creatures didn't. Slate didn't bother to

The Battle for Badgers Brow

pretend to understand most of them, but he was certainly not the simple animal that his small brown body, dressed in a tired brown tunic, would suggest. Oswald's inquisitive eyes then darted around the room. He knew his place, and knew not to interrupt the king so he waited patiently, observing and assessing the king's mood as always.

"Not 'man' you say? For they are to be avoided at all costs, everyone knows this to be true. Are you sure, Elder?" Slate asked, eyeing him cautiously.

"Yes, sire," the dormouse replied courteously. "For man has long since departed the island, its inhabitants being solely animals of the wood and field." Slate certainly liked the sound of that. He turned his attention elsewhere.

"Excellent. Tell me Commander Stone, is my army ready to invade at a moment's notice?" he said to a fearsome-looking larger grey squirrel standing by his side.

Stone was his head commander and he'd got to this lofty position by being ruthless and not showing weakness of any kind to his subordinates. He had been standing patiently while Slate posed and spoke to Oswald. It wasn't the most comfortable thing to do, dressed in the steel armour of the Grey Army. The round helmet and breastplate were heavy, and so was the standard-issue sheathed broadsword which hung from his side.

"Yes, sire, your troop is awaiting your orders and can be ready at a moment's notice," he said steadfastly.

At hearing this Slate's quick temper suddenly flared. "A moment's notice! They shouldn't need any notice at all!" he snapped. "I want them ready to go when I say and not a moment later. Understood?"

"Yes, sire. Of course, sire," replied Stone, trying to remain unflustered and knowing never to question his king. Not if he wanted to keep his command. And his head.

Slate then addressed another.

"Scribe, I do hope you're paying attention in the corner over there and writing all this down," he said to the fourth creature in the room. The brightly dressed weasel looked up fearfully from the notes he was hastily scribbling at his old wooden desk.

"Well, let's hear it then!" barked Slate. "And be quick about it."

"Yes, your majesty," came the hasty reply as the weasel shuffled uneasily in his seat. "Your victory will be delivered, and the island will soon be free—"

"Freed from tyranny by the benevolence of your king. Do not forget to add that, Gutterpress!" Slate thundered.

"Yes, sire. Set free from the dictatorship they currently live under, by your compassionate intervention. Nothing negative, always positive. As always," said

Gutterpress, the scribe, as he continued on with his work, cowering down.

Now satisfied, Slate spoke to his advisor once more.

"Excellent. Now Elder, tell me, is it time to use this gift of yours?" he said as he strutted around the small, dilapidated space. The room was an antechamber of the old abandoned steel mill they called home.

"Do I take the elixir again tonight or is it too soon?"

"No, my liege, enough time has expired since you last consumed the potion and I feel your greatest threat will now be at rest, you can invade his dreams at will. You can enter his inner thoughts again and plant fear into his mind as he sleeps," he said, saying what Slate wanted to hear.

Oswald passed the king a vessel of clear liquid, which the king snatched from him and downed in one. Oswald felt it unwise to be doing this at all, as it may deliver a warning to the island, but the monarch wanted to meddle, and he was not one to be questioned with. Slate then readied to leave.

"Very good, I shall retire now and recline on my bed to visit my friend on this isle. Now, remind me again, Elder, what name does he go by and the name of the island too?" asked the forgetful king.

"They call the isle Badgers Brow, and his name is Rusty, sire. Rusty of the Great Wood."

"Well, Rusty of the Great Wood, rest while you can," sneered Slate. "I'm coming to claim my birthright, and if you stand in my way you will surely fall."

CHAPTER ONE

Rusty the red squirrel hopped easily from branch to branch high up in the Great Wood, as the morning sun began to edge over the horizon like a welcome visit from a long-lost friend. He loved this time of day as it was so peaceful and quiet. Stopping for a second to take in the splendour of it all, the morning light crept slowly across the land, its warming glow casting lengthy shadows, equalled only by the glistening displays of dewy droplets which clung to each surface it touched, each miniscule orb a lustrous testimony to the passing nights blanket of fog. Dressed lightly in a thin cotton tunic tied at the waist with a short piece of rope, he now had just one thing on his mind, to get back to his home in the old oak tree and to be reunited with his resting wife Scarlet. But he saw something which caught his eye.

Far down below there was a sudden movement. What was it? A furtive figure? Being a member of red watch, his local neighbourhood patrol, his interest was immediately aroused. But he had a problem. The rest of the watch had disbanded for the night, their duty to see over their home – the Great Wood – done. He had a decision to make. Find the others and raise the alarm, or investigate alone. The only weapon he carried was a small sword attached to his rope belt wrapped in its simple scabbard. But his decision was made for him as the solitary figure dropped down and disappeared out of sight. Now he felt as if he had no choice but to go and see, for fear of losing sight of the possible stranger. So without further ado, he scampered towards the ground and stopped to take a better look from a vantage point on a lowly branch in a leafy beech tree. Rusty's face broke out into a broad smile.

Rough, the badger, was out and about bright and early with only one thing on his mind; food. Rough had a burly build and could seem quite intimidating at first glance, but he soon won you over with his jovial character and disarming smile. He too was dressed for warm weather in a worn, sleeveless tunic, which showed off his muscular arms.

He was glad he'd risen early, as so far he'd been lucky enough to gather supplies with ease, as his full four-wheeled pull-along trolley was testament to that. Filled with freshly picked fruit to trade, he now eyed another sought-after item.

Buried deep in the bush was a huge chunk of scrap iron. He had seen such things before. It was an abandoned old car, left over from when man roamed the woods. But to Rough this heap of left-over old metal was yet another great find, for not only was he a picker, but he was a blacksmith too, and so the scrap iron would come in great use. In his sett, he could often be heard hammering and banging away, forging his next piece of work. Whether it be a sword or a pot for the pantry, Rough would fashion it to your exact needs.

But just as he reached over to pick up the car's fallen bumper, he heard a noise behind him. He stiffened and felt the hairs on the back of his neck rise. Was he about to be attacked?

His first instinct was to reach for the short sword strapped firmly to his belt. He gripped the blade tightly in his strong paw and spun around, ready to defend himself. Then he let out a huge sigh of relief. It was none other than his old friend Rusty, who was standing there, arms crossed, wearing a bright beaming smile.

"Morning Rough, you're up early. For a minute, I thought I'd caught an intruder up to no good," said Rusty, still smiling.

"Do I look like an intruder?" asked the sturdy badger.

"I'm not going to answer that. It'll only end up getting me in trouble," Rusty quipped, followed by a hearty laugh. He noticed Rough's morning's labour on his fully laden trolley. "Looks like you've been busy," he said approvingly, knowing Rough was always occupied with his work.

"Certainly have. And I'll give you first refusal on this beautiful bounty if you stay on my good side," he said, giving Rusty a playful nudge.

Rusty then made a suggestion that was music to Rough's ears. "Tell you what. Throw in a few of those juicy red apples you've got there and I'll invite you back for breakfast. After all, I promised Scarlet I'd prepare a feast."

Rough's face lit up immediately. "Do you mean a BIG breakfast?" he said, he said excitedly, knowing from past experience that breakfast at Rusty's was a real treat.

"As big as you can manage," said Rusty, knowing it would go down well with his regularly famished friend. Rough immediately reached out to grab the short handle on his trolley with relish.

"Will there be pancakes with syrup, piles of hot buttered toast and lots and lots of tea?" Rough asked licking his lips in anticipation.

"Of course there will," replied Rusty obligingly.

"Well, count me in," said an extremely happy-looking Rough. In a buoyant mood now that food was on the way, Rough decided to have little fun. He deliberately darted behind Rusty to appear back out on the other side, which gained him an inquisitive look from his flustered friend.

"Did you see what I did there?" Rough asked with a grin. "I didn't cross your path. When a badger crosses behind you, it's good luck, but crossing in front, brings bad fortune. Every creature in the wood knows that," he said, in his matter-of-fact way. Rusty just laughed.

"You know I don't believe that," he said waving him away.

"Well, believe it or not, it's true, and one day soon you'll see I'm right," said Rough, as he threw a friendly arm around him.

As they continued to walk along together in the early morning sunshine, they talked about not much really at all, just enjoyed each other's company until they reached Briars Road.

Briars Road was the main thoroughfare through the Great Wood, it ran straight and true surrounded by trees. The wood itself was a home to a variety of creatures: foxes, rabbits, birds and more all co-habited in a close-knit community. And they lived in harmony, well mostly.

After a while, they came upon a most welcoming sight, an old oak tree, which grew in the centre of the wood: Rusty's home. A rope ladder hung from down half its length and at its top was the front door, nestled between the ancient tree's branches.

On their approach, the door swung open and they were both greeted by a most welcoming sight: Scarlet, Rusty's wife. She too wore a simple tunic tied at the waist, and looked really pleased to see them both.

"Morning," she called out affectionately from on high.

"You're both in time to help with breakfast," she added cheerfully.

Rusty scaled the ladder with ease, and gave her a affectionate peck on the cheek. "Morning Scarlet, let's get started, we've got a hungry guest to feed."

They both then went happily inside to fetch the crockery and prepare the meal.

"Well, I must say, I couldn't eat another thing," said a stuffed-looking Rough, as he sat back and loosened his belt and drank his tea from a chipped china mug.

"You sure you couldn't manage another pancake?" asked Scarlet, as she finished her plate.

Rough didn't need asking twice. "I suppose if you insist," he said, reaching over and scooping it onto his plate. "I know I've had six already but I am a growing badger you know," he said patting his round belly with a satisfied smile. It was then he noticed Rusty seemed a little distant and lost in a world of his own.

"What is it, mate? Still having bad dreams?"

Rusty nodded. "When I'm at rest, I sometimes see a shadowy figure standing over me, asking me to reveal all my secrets. I don't understand, I'm just an ordinary red squirrel – I don't have any secrets," he said forlornly.

"I've been thinking. Why don't we go and see the creature they call Willard the Wise? He's supposed to be extremely clever and will help any animal in need of advice, or so the tales go." Scarlet suggested.

"Yeah, my cousin graham told me about him. He says he's an all-wise and powerful warrior who fought in a great battle. He meddles in magic too, helped many a troubled soul, according to our Graham."

This caught Rusty's attention immediately. "Do you really think he can help?" he asked hopefully.

"Can't hurt to try," said Rough, in between sipping more tea. "Bit of a trek, mind. It's up north, across the other side of the Great Wood. You then come to what's known as the Maleficent Meadow, and his home is deep in the forest beyond that. You can be there and back in no time at all, or so Graham reckons." And then with a look of bemusement he scratched his head. "You know, come to think about it, I'm not even sure if our Graham has ever been that way, he is a bit of a home bird after all."

Scarlet, having made up her mind, immediately leapt to her feet. "Well, come on! There's no time to waste, let's get going. We've got a wise one to meet."

But Rough suddenly seemed a little hesitant, as he recalled yet another detail. "I forgot to say. Graham reckons across the meadow is the home of another one too."

"And who might that be?" asked Rusty, as he started to pack the plates away.

Rough swallowed hard and hesitantly replied. "He reckons it's the home of the bogeyman," he said, with a tremble in his voice.

"Oh, come off it, Rough," said Scarlet, having none of it. "Everyone knows Graham is fond of tall tales."

Rough did his best to look brave. "That might be right, but sometimes they do come true." Then his face brightened up as a more favourable thought came to mind. "I don't suppose we're taking a packed lunch?" he asked in hope.

"Consider it done," answered Rusty, which brightened up Rough's day immediately.

CHAPTER TWO

They hadn't been long on their journey when they were noticed by another. A brown rat by the name of misfit, dressed in a black loose-fitting tunic, was lounging idly under a sycamore tree on the lookout for mischief.

Wonder where they're off too? he thought lazily. He shut his eyes again to drift off. But as they strolled by, something he heard made him sit up and pay attention.

"So Rust, all ready for the Lowland games?" Rough asked, loud enough to be heard clearly.

The Lowland games! They were talking about the games! Being a fierce rival, Misfit made up his mind in an instant. He would silently follow them and eavesdrop. He might learn something to his advantage. Now fully awake, he stayed within earshot but out of sight.

"The games? Yeah, we've been practising hard, as well you know. We want to make it three years running that we lift the furball cup," he said proudly.

"Well, it's those rats in the final again, isn't it? Misfit and his bunch. Best show 'em who's boss again, eh?" Rough scoffed.

On hearing this, a livid Misfit nearly fell out from behind a bush revealing himself, but somehow, he managed to stay hidden. "We'll see about that!" fumed the rats' furball captain. Now more than ever, he was determined to listen in as he continued to follow them like an unwanted shadow.

As Rusty, Scarlet and Rough ambled along Briars Road, the morning sun rose ever steadily in the blue cloudless sky. The whole of Badgers Brow was now bathed in its warm heartening glow. Through the gaps in the woodland canopy, the brilliant pinks and oranges of dappled sunlight danced through the trees, creating nature's very own kaleidoscope of colour. It was then that they noticed another creature coming their way, an amiable mole named Melvin.

"Morning, Rusty, morning, Scarlet," he said, doffing his cap, before turning to Rough. "Morning, champ. Still in training I hope?"

Rough stopped and flexed his impressive muscles. "Sure am, Melvin. I aim to be the Great Wood wrestling champion two years running," he said confidently.

Melvin liked the sound of that. "Good to hear," replied the friendly mole. "I'll make sure I put a wager on you!" he added as he went on his way.

Misfit, who was still eavesdropping, was fired up once more. He'd lost a lot the year before betting against Rough, so he still bore a grudge. "I'll make sure I put a wager on you," he said, mimicking the mole with a high-pitched voice. "Well, I'll make sure I won't!" He scowled.

In stark contrast to earlier, Briars Road was now busier than ever, as the resident animals of the Great Wood went about their daily business. The intrepid trio heard many passers-by say 'Good morning!' and received lots of cheery waves from friendly folk.

One was from Vincent the goat off on an errand, another from Roy the field mouse out going blackberry picking. They were amongst many others, just going about their day. As they travelled down Briars Road, they chatted amiably about nothing in particular until the conversation inevitably turned to Rough's favourite topic: food. Not long after, they opened up the packed lunch.

There were sandwiches and fresh fruit, all washed down gratefully with paws full of water taken from a fresh stream. Before long, the food was gone. It was then Rusty noticed an old friend leaning casually against an ash tree.

"Archie!" he called out. "Great to see you." Archie the fox had been a good friend of theirs for years. Dressed in a clean white tunic, he casually glanced up, looking as if he hadn't a care in the world.

"Hey there, what brings you all the way down here? Are you lost?" he quipped, grinning widely.

"It's a long story," said Rusty cheerfully.

"Well then, you'd better come inside and tell me all about it over a drink and a bite to eat," offered Archie, winking conspiratorially at Rough.

The flame-coloured fox indicated a small green door just to the right of the tree, set slightly back off the beaten track. It would have been easy to miss if you didn't know where to look. As he opened the door to his den, a warm glow greeted them, inviting them in.

The three explorers settled into cosy chairs by a lit fire, as Archie disappeared to get something for them to eat and drink. Once Archie had returned, an ever-hungry Rough soon got to work and helped himself to pawfuls of nuts as the squirrels sipped at their cordial.

Rusty told Archie all about the reason for their trip, as the fox listened intently to everything he had to say.

"The Maleficent Meadow you say? I take it you've never actually been there before?" asked Archie, suspecting the answer would be no.

"Can't say as I have," came Rusty's honest reply. "As a matter of fact, I've never left the Great Wood, as I've never felt the need," he freely admitted.

This was true as with most inhabitants of the Great Wood. With its abundance of food and shelter stretching far and wide, they had everything they needed right here, so why venture out? As a result, little was known of life outside the wood as most of them never left.

"Well, it's your lucky day. I'm doing nothing right now so I can show you the way," declared the friendly fox. "Don't worry, I know a short cut. But I reckon once you're there you'll just take one look and turn straight back around." He warned with a grin.

"What do you mean by that mate?" asked a now curious Rough.

"Oh, don't worry, you'll soon see for yourself," said Archie, smiling widely.

"It's this way, not too far," he said, as he began to lead them confidently down a little-known track through the trees. The pathway snaked through the wood, a way not known to many and could easily be missed in the undergrowth of the dense wood. Without Archie leading the way, stopping every now and again to sniff the undergrowth or prod at a tree, they would have been surely lost. As Archie pushed on, he was approached by a troubled Rough trampling noisily towards him.

"Can I ask just you a question, Arch? I know it may sound daft, but have you ever heard of tales of the bogeyman?" he asked, with a nervous smile. "Not that I believe it or anything, I'm just asking for a friend," he added hastily, not wanting to seem scared.

"Well, now you come to mention it," said Archie, turning to him. "I have heard that exact tale. Don't know if there's any truth in it, mind," he conceded.

"But you can tell your, er, friend, that they say the bogeyman lives in a huge cave on the other side of the meadow. To see Willard the Wise you have to go straight past it. No other way apparently. According to the tale, if the wind is blowing in the right direction, you can hear his cry.

"Really?" gulped a now agitated Rough.

"Oh, he's talking nonsense," said Scarlet now catching them up. "He's just having a bit of fun. Aren't you, Arch?" she said, staring pointedly at the affable fox, as she knew what a nervous type Rough could be.

"Well, I'm just telling you what I've heard," Archie said with a shrug. "But there's more. Not saying there's any truth in it, mind," he added. "It's just that animals have ventured up there and never been seen again. Just disappeared without a trace. But don't let me put you off going or anything. I'm sure it'll be fine," he said, trying to play the tale down.

Scarlet shrugged it all off, determined to press on. "Well, I'm sure they're just spooky stories told to frighten the young around the campfire. We've come this far so we're going to find Willard the Wise, no matter what," she said determinedly. Her plucky courage was so contagious that even Rough felt much better now as he plodded along contentedly beside her.

Archie then came to an abrupt halt. "Well, folks, here we are," he announced, glad to change the subject.

As the woods ended, they stepped out into a clearing as three small gasps came as one.

"Now that's how it got its name," said an astounded Rusty.

Standing in front of them was a high barrier of thickets and thorns, with the briar patch extending on either side as far as the eye could see. Archie glanced once more at the resolute trio.

"Well, that's as far as I go. It looks impenetrable to me. They say you can go around it, but I've heard it takes days, maybe weeks," Archie said, as they all took in the size of the formidable natural barrier in their path. Archie then turned to walk away. "Well, I'll be off then, back to my den, but do call for a bite to eat on your way home. Good luck! Let me know how it goes," he said with a wink and a wave.

Archie was sure they'd give up and that they would be knocking on his door before the day was out. When he got to the edge of the woods, he yelled mischievously,

"Say hello to the bogeyman for me, will you?"

Then he walked straight past the hidden Misfit chuckling to himself and whistling a merry tune as he went on his way.

Misfit waited until the wily fox was out of sight and then peered through the undergrowth once more. Surely they'll turn back now? "They'll never make their way through that," he sneered to himself. And maybe he was right, for the Maleficent Meadow had certainly lived up to its harmful name.

CHAPTER THREE

The office that was once the domain of some long-ago chairman, from when man was here, had now become Slate's meeting room. In bygone times there would have been business meetings and frantic discussions, with deals to be made and broken. Now, the room was witness to the rantings and ravings of the King of the Grey. The old, abandoned steel mill was perfect for his requirements. From the tops of the towers and chimneys the whole of his domain, the Kingdom of the Grey, could be surveyed. In the depths of the building, the old foundry rooms, where the metal was once melted and moulded, now made ideal dungeons.

Slate's throne room itself didn't have many original features left but a few remnants of its previous occupant still remained. On the back wall facing the door hung a faded photograph of a grey-haired old man staring down. Standing next to it was an oval ornate Victorian mirror with a long crack running down its length, splitting any viewer's image in two. The brown Regency-leather backed chair behind the desk (which the grey-haired old man had occupied for years) was now tattered and torn, just another remnant of past glories and forgotten plans. But the room's new occupier Slate had plans of his own.

"I can't decide whether to go for military green or khaki brown. Or maybe even my usual charcoal grey. Do I go for something formal or maybe even a casual 'Look at what I threw on first thing this morning' kind of thing?" he mused, posturing and posing in the broken mirror. The great crack zigzagging down the centre of the looking glass appeared to split him in two in a way that many would say was an accurate depiction of his personality. They likely wouldn't dare say it to his face though. The tarnished surface left great splotches of greenish grey across his reflection, but he didn't seem to care, admiring himself all the same.

"Decisions, decisions. What does a monarch wear for an invasion?" he thought aloud. "Well, what say you?" he thundered impatiently, turning to a quaking field vole who stood by his side, with a tape measure in his trembling hand.

The vole had been watching fearfully. Serving Slate was not easy. Speak when you had not been spoken to and you could find yourself on the end of a tongue lashing. Or worse. But fail to answer when he asked a direct question and the result was the same. As the king was prone to talking to himself it was often difficult to distinguish what required an answer, and what didn't.

The vole was wearing a waistcoat made of cheap fabric but it had been well made, and wore a thin nervous smile.

"Well, speak up, I need fashion advice not silence," Slate said irritably. "You're supposed to know, you're a tailor, aren't you?"

"Yes, sire. I've been your official outfitter for years," squeaked the vole.

"Have you? Oh, well, if you say so. What's your name then? Remind me," Slate said dismissively. "And your assistants' names too," he said pointing haughtily with his nose in the air at two more identical-looking voles dressed in similar cheap waistcoats, who were standing as far back as possible. They stared at the floor, trying their best to stay out of the way.

"Bespoke, Nip and Tuck, sire," replied the vole meekly.

"No, you fool! Not what kind of outfit do I require, I asked your names," Slate said, wheeling around and glaring at the impudent seeming vole.

"Bespoke, Nip and Tuck, sire," he repeated even quieter now, shrinking back.

"Am I talking to myself?" asked Slate. "Did you actually hear me vole? I know you're an outfitter, so maybe you do have cloth ears!"

"Ahem," interrupted Commander Stone pretending to clear his throat. The commander was standing nearby with half-a-dozen troops in attendance, trying to catch the king's attention. "It's the voles, sire."

"What is it about the voles, Stone? Well? Speak up!" snapped Slate once more.

"You asked their names, sire. Their names are Bespoke, Nip and Tuck."

Slate was astounded. "Really? Who on Earth gave you those names?" he said, turning to face Bespoke.

"Well, it was our father. He was a tailor too," Bespoke began to explain. "And we're triplets, who followed in the family tradition, so he thought it fittin—"

"Fitting? It's a wonder he didn't call you Needle, Sew and Thread then!" interrupted the king, bursting into fits of laughter.

All of a sudden, the entire room erupted with loud but unconvincing guffaws of fake laughter too. It was an unwritten rule that you too laughed at the king's jokes, especially the bad ones (which they mostly were) or faced his wrath. So the entire room joined in with enforced merriment including Bespoke and his brothers. But as soon as the king stopped the whole room abruptly halted too, as it was most unwise to carry on.

Slate then dithered a little longer before making a final decision. "I've decided the charcoal after all," he declared. "So, you three, off you go and make me an outfit fit for a king. Or you'll be the official outfitters no more. In fact, you'll be dressed in rags and be glad of it. Well, don't dilly-dally, off you go then, shooo!" he said ushering the voles away. They scurried off gratefully as quickly as possible.

The relative calm was broken by the sound of clashing steel upon steel coming from the courtyard outside.

"Is that the sound of combat I hear?" Slate asked Commander Stone, his ears pricking up at the melee.

"Yes, my liege," replied Stone proudly. "Our troops practise daily in the art of swordplay."

"Excellent. Make sure they're trained to kill without question," Slate demanded, his eyes narrowing with pleasure at the thought of it.

"Of course, my liege," bowed Stone.

Slate then dismissed his commander and turned his attention to his advisor, Oswald, who had been waiting patiently in the corner.

"I must say, Elder, your potion worked a treat last night," he said with an enthusiastic rub of the paws. "It felt as if I was actually there on the island. I could smell the red's fear too, it was most exhilarating," he said, lifting his nose to sniff the air, reliving the moment as he paced up and down with excitement. "Can I take it again tonight?" he asked eagerly, paws outstretched like a child wanting more.

"I would advise not, sire," the Elder replied emphatically. "It is a potent draught that must be taken sparingly."

Slate stopped pacing now and fixed his eyes on him. They narrowed with suspicion and anger as he stood waiting for an explanation.

Oswald knew he was now under scrutiny, the king intently listening to his every word, so he chose his next ones very carefully.

"It also makes for a wise strategy most suited to you, my liege," he added cunningly. "It puts fear in the mind of your foe, with him never knowing when next you will invade his inner thoughts."

There was silence in the old boardroom as Slate continued to stare at his advisor. You could have cut the tension with a knife, but where Bespoke, Nip and Tuck had cowered and trembled, the tiny dormouse met the glare with apparent ease. After what seemed like an awfully long time, suddenly Slate's face broke out into a broad grin.

"Ah, I see, a game. Now you see me, now you don't." He then gleefully clapped his paws and looked lost in a world of his own. "Oh, I do love to play games," he said, with his eyes glazed over in joy. As well as he took the king's scrutiny and outbursts, even Oswald was slightly unnerved by some of his odder behaviour.

"Umm, yes, sire, as you say, playing games. But this time with the mind," said the Elder, ignoring the king's peculiar behaviour and tapping his temple with one paw on the side of his head to demonstrate.

"Well, there's one thing, for sure," continued Slate, his mood changing from flippant to serious in a heartbeat. "Once my preparations are in place, the time for games will be over. Then I'll meet this Rusty face to face and I'll make his nightmares a reality!"

"Well, it certainly lives up to its name," gasped an astounded Scarlet, taking in the vastness of the impenetrable-looking obstacle that stood before them. The thicket of bramble and sharp needle-like thorns as long as a man's finger, stretched far and wide, with well-trodden animal tracks leading off in each direction as attempting to pass through it would surely leave you torn to shreds. It was twice the height of Rough and so thick and dense it made for a wild, forbidding obstruction.

"Oh well. "That's it, we've seen it now, might as well turn back as there's no way we're getting through that in a hurry," he said, taking a step back to be able to take it all in. "Even if we had the tools to try to cut our way through, it would take forever and a day," he concluded.

"Well, Archie did say we could go around it, but that would take ages," agreed Rusty, looking left and right at the length of the meadow in dismay.

After a few moments of deliberating about what to do next Scarlet came up with a solution that had been staring them in the face all along.

"You're forgetting one thing," she said to them both. "What's one of the things you're best known for, Rough?"

"Er, well I have been known to enjoy the odd snack or two," he answered beaming. "Are you saying you've brought more sandwiches?" he asked, more in hope than expectation.

"No, sorry, not sandwiches this time," she replied with a light smile. "It's digging of course! I've seen your sett – it's amazing. A real feat of excavation."

"Why thanks, it did win best sett of the year two years in a row," he said with a proud puff of his chest.

"Weren't you the head judge of that, though?" said Rusty with a wink and a smile.

"It was all fair and square, honest," replied Rough defensively. "I can't help it if I'm a master tunneller, can I?"

"I know, mate, I'm just pulling your leg!" joked Rusty, giving him a playful nudge. "Like Scarlet says it's a first-class dig."

"Well, if you're up for it, it's time to put all that practice into action," said Scarlet encouragingly. "After all, badgers are the best diggers of all. If we can't go over it or around it, we can go under it!" she said triumphantly.

"Well, that sounds like a challenge to me," said Rough, straightening up to his full height and stretching. "And there's one thing I know. I never turn down a challenge. I'd advise you to take a step back now and watch how this badger gets things done."

Rusty and Scarlet did as he asked and stood to one side as Rough instantly moved forward and dropped to all fours, and without further ado began to dig ferociously at the foot of the meadow.

Soon, soil and debris flew out from under him as he went at his work at a brisk pace, and before they knew it, a mouth of a freshly dug tunnel began to appear. First his head, then his torso, and finally his legs disappeared into the newly dug shaft.

Rusty and Scarlet looked on impressed at his efforts as the time quickly slipped away. They could still hear Rough digging away furiously in the distance then all at once it stopped. The sound of excavation giving way to silence.

"Rough, are you okay?" shouted Rusty into the newly formed tunnel.

But worryingly there was no reply.

"I do hope he's alright," said a now worried Rusty to Scarlet, as he bent down peering into the hole. But as he stood up and turned to face her, he saw that to his amazement she had mysteriously vanished.

"Scarlet, where are you?" he shouted anxiously, his eyes flitting to and fro searching for her in vain. Then came a shout from above.

"Rusty, I'm up here!" she replied loudly. He followed her voice, and looked up to see she had climbed a huge birch tree directly behind him for a better vantage point. Scarlet stood perched on a long branch, paw over her eyes to block the sun, peering off into the distance.

"Can you see anything?" he yelled up to her.

"I'll tell you exactly what I can see!" she shouted back excitedly. "It's Rough, he's across the other side of the meadow. He's made it!" He's beckoning for us to follow."

She then nimbly scampered down and immediately grabbed Rusty by the paw.

"Come on, let's follow him, there's no time to waste. We've got a badger to catch up with."

And without hesitation she stooped down and led the way in. Rusty smiled bravely and followed her in apprehensively.

Even though he was a red squirrel and had lived in a hollow in a tree all his life, he'd never been happy in unfamiliar confined spaces. He took a deep breath and pushed on as the newly formed dig swallowed them both up.

All this time, Misfit had remained hidden skulking in the shadows, and now seeing the coast was clear came out to investigate. The freshly dug badger-sized hole looked sturdy enough, he thought to himself. Satisfied it was safe to follow, he ventured in. Driven on by his dislike for them, and his desire to know more, he couldn't resist. And after all, *I might learn something to my advantage*, he thought to himself. *Something I can use against them.*

As they scurried along Rusty could feel the loose earth beneath his feet, his tail brush the tunnel roof, and Scarlet's close presence, but the latter gave him little comfort. He just didn't like strange tight spaces. It took all his might not to turn tail and go back the way they had come. Filled with an all-consuming fear, his breathing came in rapid short bursts, and he only mustered the courage to go on because of the nearness of his wife. Then came sudden relief.

"I see light ahead," Scarlet announced eagerly. This urged him on and as he glanced up, he could see the welcoming sight of a chink of daylight. This helped push him on and before he knew it, they were out the other side and he could breathe easy again. As they stood back up, happy to be in the bright sunlight, they gave each other a celebratory hug.

"Are you okay, Rusty?" she said, sensing his unease.

"Yes, I'm fine because after all I've got you to look out for me," he said gratefully.

"And I've got you to look after me," she replied, returning his affection.

All this time Misfit had stayed in pursuit and could hear them scurrying ahead of him in the dark. Moving on as sneakily as possible not wanting to be discovered, he paused near the tunnel exit as he could hear their voices just up ahead.

Rusty and Scarlet now found themselves at the foot of a grassy knoll covered in a blanket of white daisies and yellow buttercups.

"So, where is he?" asked Rusty, looking around for their friend.

"He was up there, on the higher ground," Scarlet replied, pointing up the slope to the top of the small flower-covered hill. "Let's head that way," she insisted, "he can't have gone far."

Misfit's head appeared out of the mouth of the tunnel and seeing them just ahead, he crouched down behind a nearby leafy green bush to conceal himself. He waited a few moments and then when he felt it safe to do so, he continued to follow them, moving from thicket to bush, making sure to remain hidden and out of sight at all times.

As Rusty and Scarlet reached the brow of the hillock they stopped, and to their surprise an even larger hill lay just behind. Half way up the hill was Rough signalling for them to come over. As they approached, they could see something was amiss – he held up one raised claw to his mouth, gesturing them to be quiet. As they reached his side, they could both now see directly behind him, a short distance away, the entrance of a huge cave cut into the hillside. Its dark void gaped like the hungry mouth of a monstrous giant.

"I came ahead to check out the area," he whispered. "Good job I did too. Graham told me he'd heard that there was a big cave the other side of the meadow. Best to be avoided, he reckoned. Says he'd heard it's the home of the bogeyman himself."

Rusty's gaze fell on the cave. "You don't think there's any truth in it, do you?" he asked, his eyes fixed firmly on the darkened cavern, starting to half believe it himself too.

But Scarlet was undeterred. "No, that's just more tales of the forest made up to scare youngsters," she reiterated, trying to reassure them. "But if it makes you happier, we'll avoid it altogether."

She then noticed a whisp of smoke snaking above the tree line. "Look over there! I say we investigate; it may lead us to this Willard."

As they too followed her gaze, they also saw the grey plume drifting lazily skywards, way off in the distance, somewhere deep in the woods that lay ahead. So off they went with their destination hopefully now in striking distance, making sure they gave the ominous-looking cave a very wide berth.

A few moments later a winding path came into view, meandering through the trees in the direction they were heading. The three of them joined the trail immediately. Meanwhile Misfit, still unnoticed, remained within touching distance, determined not to lose his quarry.

Not too long after entering the woods the trio came to a clearing, and a quaint pale blue wooden cottage now came into view. It had a small crooked soot-blackened chimney balanced atop a brown slate roof, where the trail of wispy smoke emitted lazily upwards.

The dwelling had half a dozen well-trodden steps leading up to its pale blue front door, and on the top step was a small dormouse with a perfect sized sweeping brush busily brushing away with a steady to and fro motion. He wore round small glasses and a dark blue waist coat, with small pockets sewn into it for his odds and ends.

"Excuse me, sir," said Scarlet politely. "Is this the home of Willard the

Wise?"

The dormouse stopped his work and looked up from his task, gazing at them quizzically, and then replied.

"It really depends who is asking, and if indeed the request is with good reason," he answered cautiously, whilst pushing his round glasses back up onto his small round nose.

"Oh, of course, forgive me. We don't mean to intrude or seem impolite," said Scarlet courteously. "This is my husband, Rusty, and our friend, Rough.

And I am Scarlet, pleased to meet you." she added respectfully, not wanting to alarm the timid looking dormouse.

"Without a doubt, the pleasure will be all mine," replied the dormouse with a smile, now less wary of the friendly seeming newcomers.

"Please, let me explain our visit. The reason we are here is because Rusty has been having strange recurring dreams, nightmares if you like. And we just don't know why. It's said back in our home of the Great Wood that Willard is wise beyond his years, and is known to give the best advice around, well, so the stories go. We were just wondering if he could help us to fathom why this is all happening," she said hopefully.

The dormouse said nothing for a short while and just looked at them with an inquisitive look on his face, as if deciding what to do next. Finally, after what seemed like an age, he put down his broom and spoke again in his reassuring tone.

"Stories, you say? Well, you have come to the right place, for the tales you heard of advice giving are indeed true. Come, please step inside and hopefully your journey will not be in vain."

He gestured towards the door with an open paw and it creaked open as he pushed it wide.

"Willard!" he exclaimed loudly as he entered the cottage, "we have visitors who have travelled afar for an audience with you." He then disappeared through the door, but not before beckoning them to follow him inside.

Scarlet went first up the steps grinning enthusiastically in anticipation of finally meeting the mysterious Willard, with Rusty and Rough following close behind.

Misfit, having observed from a safe distance, spied a side window that was slightly ajar, and crouched down beneath it, intent on listening in.

Finally, I'll get to hear what this is all about, he thought, pleased with himself for not giving up. He rubbed his paws with glee in anticipation for what he was about to hear.

CHAPTER FOUR

The room they entered was an oddity in itself, to say the least. Sitting in the centre of the space was an old oak table with four different-sized wooden chairs placed around it, all of the same cut and design. They had a crescent moon surrounded by stars carved into them, and the seats themselves ranged from large to small as if to accommodate visitors of all shapes and sizes.

In the middle of it sat a grand candelabra lit with a dozen candles, but the flickering flames seemingly danced to an unheard tune, with ever-changing colours of red, green and blue unlike any shade of light they'd seen before.

To the rear, an open fire crackled and hissed in the middle of a grand fireplace. It looked to be made from intertwining branches of various trees of the forest coming together in an intricate woven design, as if made on a loom.

On the walls hung pictures of woodland creatures in different-sized ornate gilded frames. Owls, hawks, foxes, deer and more stared back at them, their eyes seemingly following their every move.

A bookcase to the left heaved with a mishmash of ancient books, some large, others small, all with shimmering dust covers enticing you to pick them up and browse. On its top were a random selection of odd-sized jars ranging from the size of a cup to a bucket, each with strange things enclosed. There was what looked like pickled eggs in a green ooze in one, frog spawn in another, and yet another filled with twigs and dried weird-shaped leaves.

In the corner on the right was a huge comfy-looking red-and-black plaid armchair, which had stuffing protruding here and there. Sitting in it looking at them with a fixed stare was a big brown owl. He wore a similar waistcoat to the dormouse. The owl's intelligent large unblinking eyes watched them intensely, but it just sat and remained silent.

"I knew it, Rust," said Rough in a low whisper. "Willard's an owl. They're wise aren't they, everyone knows that."

But Rusty wasn't so sure. "Well, Rough, it's just that I don't think he's—"

But before he could finish, he was interrupted by the dormouse waving his arms frantically in the air, making a big fuss and addressing the seated brown owl.

"Screech, what have I told you about sitting in my chair? Now, if you please, go and make our guests tea and cake, they have travelled far and must surely be in need of refreshments."

Screech jumped out of the chair immediately, grumbling under his breath. "I have to do everything around here, it's just not fair,"

he moaned, and went off into the kitchen still mumbling to himself.

The dormouse nimbly leapt into the huge chair and made himself comfortable. He looked tiny in it but also well at ease.

"Come forward," gestured the dormouse. "Do not be

afraid." He leaned forward.

"May I introduce myself? My name is Willard. Willard the Wise. Some say I have earned the title, but that is for you to decide. But one thing I know for sure, and that is why you're here today, even before you explained your reason. For I have been expecting you for some time."

His gaze then fell on Rusty.

"You knew it was I you sought as soon as you set eyes on me, did you not? For my little ruse did not fool you, even for a mere second, is that not the case?"

Rusty was bemused. "I don't know why, but as soon as I saw you, I just sort of knew who you were. And I can't even begin to explain why I'd know that," he said looking bewildered.

Willard then beckoned them closer.

"Well, I will strive to enlighten you. Please all be seated for I shall endeavour to tell you more, and it may take a while."

As the three each took a chair, Willard began. "Now, without delay, I shall reveal what I know to be true.

Unbeknownst to you, Rusty, there lies within you a latent gift.

It is a gift that I possess too, and it is, and has always been, known as the foresight."

On hearing this, Rusty was stunned. "The foresight. What's that? I've never heard of it. Is it an illness?" he voiced in concern.

Willard seeing his distress sought to allay his fears. "No, my friend, it is no malaise but a skill. I must admit at times, it can be perceived differently. Let me try to explain."

Rusty for some reason, felt himself relax a little more as he listened to Willard's calm, soothing voice.

"You see things differently from others. I surmise as a young squirrel you could foresee small events that would happen before they even occurred?"

"It's true, I did," Rusty admitted, slightly taken aback at how Willard could know this, but at the same time beginning to feel strangely at ease, as if in the presence of an old friend. "I knew what the weather would be like days before, and my forecasts were sought far and wide as I never ever got it wrong," he continued. "And once, I dreamt of a falling tree damaged in a storm, and I knew exactly the time it would fall and watched as it did just that, the very next day. There was other stuff too, like knowing when a friend would call in advance, and sure enough they always did. I thought nothing of it, just a coincidence or something."

"And this dream of yours, please, tell me more," said Willard softly.

"Well, it always feels so real. I sort of watch on as a stranger stands over me, threatening me and demanding I reveal all my secrets. It's all so confusing," he said, now with a slight tremble in his voice. "I don't understand. I don't have any secrets. I'm just Rusty, an ordinary red squirrel of the Great Wood."

The others now listened on in silence, enthralled by it all. Misfit was still eavesdropping under the open window, and his ears now pricked up as the conversation began to take a more serious turn.

"You must listen well and take heed of what I reveal to you next, for surely spellcraft is being used," said Willard assuredly. "The creature standing over you, Rusty, is a formidable foe in the making, and not to be taken lightly, for he is in fact one of those who are known as the greys."

Scarlet sat up with a start. "The greys are just a myth, aren't they?" she asked with a frown.

Willard shook his head sadly. "No, not a myth," he answered gravely.

"They are a very real threat, for they are squirrel too but grey in colour, and are bigger and stronger than you. It is said they will take what they can for their very own. No doubt they will see this island through envious eyes with its rich woodland, plentiful food and green acres galore."

Then came another warning.

"Their leader may also be seeking a greater prize, an ancient enchanted sword."

Now worried, Rough decided to speak up. "So they know all about us and seek this sword too?" he asked in growing alarm.

Willard couldn't deny this was true. "Yes, indeed, Rough the badger, it appears they do. But do not concern yourself with such matters as the blade, for there is a more pressing matter at hand. I have felt for some time that they seek to loot and plunder this very island, so we must now prepare."

Willard acknowledged Rough once more. "Rough the badger, come closer, please," he requested politely.

"Me?" replied Rough anxiously. "Why do you need me?"

"Yes, you. There's nothing to fear. Please approach," Willard gently assured him, "for I have words of wisdom which are for your ears alone."

Rough looked slightly confused but did as was asked and warily moved forward.

"Closer, my friend, lean in so you may hear all."

Rough still slightly unsure of this strange dormouse did just that. In one swift movement, Willard reached over and grabbed a tuft of hair straight from the top of his head, yanked it hard, and out came a handful in his tiny paw. Rough didn't like that one bit at all.

"Ouch!" he wailed, jumping back in astonishment. "That really hurt!"

"I apologise if that was the case but I need the fur of a badger," said Willard sincerely. "It is to help ward off the sorcery that is being used, and it must be taken without consent to strengthen the spell. For there are dark deeds afoot as another individual surely helps the grey cause. That is why I took a tuft of badger hair to help break his spell." He then turned to Rusty once more.

"In order for this to work you must wear a bag I have fashioned. It will help to ward off evil. It must include the badger fur inside it along with other items for you to find, and they must be collected soon before the new moon is more than seven days old for the charm to work. There's one slight problem, though, my new friends. The next item you need can only be found in one place. In the cave you have recently passed. The cavern which is known as Ursa's lair."

All three of them now stood there momentarily speechless in the surroundings of the strange cottage while the information they had just received began to sink in.

"If you need a moment to digest that which I have just divulged, I truly do understand. So please, converse amongst yourselves a while and I shall check on Screech and his progress with the necessary delicacies," said Willard, who immediately leapt from his chair and went off into to the kitchen humming a merry tune

"So, what do you reckon"? said Scarlet as they began to speak in hushed tones. "I must admit it all seems a bit strange to me," she said, as she looked around the curious room.

"Yes, I know what you mean. He does seem a bit eccentric," agreed Rusty, as his gaze settled on a portrait of a huge goat whose dark black eyes seemed to be staring back straight right through him.

"Eccentric, what do you mean eccentric"? blustered Rough.

"Well, if you ask me, he's a real oddball. Did you see how he took a handful of my fur without asking? Who in their right mind would do that?" he said rubbing his head vigorously.

"I'm sure you'll live, Rough," joked Rusty. Rusty had also come to a swift decision. "I say we have no choice but to see this through. We'll visit this Ursa's lair. We can find and bring back what Willard said is needed and see if that helps."

"I agree," said Scarlet wholeheartedly. "If there is a threat to the island and bad magic is being used, there is no time to lose."

But Rough had another concern. "Wait a minute, shall we find out more about this Ursa first?" he asked as his thoughts cast back to the tale Archie had told them earlier that day about the bogeyman.

But before they could reply, Willard returned from the kitchen with a little skip and a jump in his step, still humming happily to himself.

"Ah, I believe a decision may have been arrived at," he said with confidence, as he settled back into his oversized chair.

"Yes, sort of. But may I ask first what exactly is the lair of Ursa?" said Scarlet hoping to reassure Rough.

"Er, it's not the home of the bogeyman, is it?" Rough chipped in quickly. "'Cos they say back in the Great Wood, his home is a huge cave," he added, trying his best to look casual and unconcerned, but failing miserably.

Willard smiled. "I can assure you it is not the abode of such a creature," he replied with a slight chuckle, amused at the notion. "Now listen well and I will gladly explain. As you may have well perceived I enjoy my privacy. For it was I who named the meadow Maleficent and the home of Ursa his lair. Grand monikers, do you not think?" he said with a twinkle in his eye. "They are so called to keep inquisitive creatures at bay. Ursa is one of us, an animal of the woods. He is a large brown bear and the last of his kind, on this island at least," he confirmed. "He seeks a life of solitude and chooses his friends carefully, and so visitors are rarely received. We have the badger fur needed thanks to our friend, Rough," he continued, "but for the next part of the charm, you will need to obtain a few glow stones. They are easy to identify for the stones are fluorescent and emit a light of their own. But they can only be found on this isle in his lair, and a handful would surely be enough. But be warned. Ursa holds the stones dearly and won't part readily with them as it is his task to protect them. He may be persuaded to release a small amount, but of this I cannot guarantee. And afterwards you will then need to collect a few special herbs, but one task at a time."

"Well, we've decided that we've come this far and will do as you advise, and collect whatever is necessary for this charm to work," said Scarlet. "Isn't that so?" She looked at the others and received a shrug in return.

"Also, we'd like to thank you for all your help too," she added politely.

"There is no need for thanks," replied Willard. "For I will always help a fellow creature in need. And I do feel this may be just the beginning of a long journey shared."

Meanwhile outside, Misfit had decided he'd heard enough and felt his snooping had been well worthwhile. Forewarned is forearmed, he thought to himself and with that gleefully scurried away.

Back in the cottage a strange occurrence was about to begin. Willard sat suddenly motionless, as still as a statue.

"Is he okay?" whispered Rough to the others, as they stared at his unmoving form.

Before they could respond the door behind them swung open with a loud creak, and Willard himself was standing in the doorway.

"How do you do?" he said cheerfully, before walking straight past them and off into the kitchen, but not before giving a wave to himself sitting in the big armchair.

The three were astounded as Willard, still in his chair, began to move again as his gaze fell upon the bewildered Rusty.

"What you just observed was a demonstration of a simple illusion. You saw what I wanted you to see, another version of me, like seeing a reflection in a pond. I call the mirage my phantom self," Willard told him. "It is something that you, too, can master as the foresight comes into focus. I have so much to teach you, and if you are willing to learn this is only the start of your journey of self-discovery. For now, I feel this is enough information for one day, but any questions you may have can be discussed over tea."

Rusty decided he needed time to think over what Willard had told him as Screech then came back into the room noisily pushing a trolley heaving with scrumptious cakes and tea, grumbling once more to himself.

"I spend all my time in the kitchen and what do I get? More work that's what. I do everything around here, and with little appreciation too." And with that, sloped off still mumbling.

Willard just chuckled. "Thank you, Screech, splendid as always," Willard called after him. "Take no heed of my associate Screech, it's just his way, and I wouldn't change him for the world," he said in way of explanation. "Now, please tuck in, my friends, you must be hungry. There's always more if needed."

They feasted, with Rough eating the most of course, and after discussing the day's events some more, they headed to the door to fulfil their task.

"We'll see you soon then," said Scarlet to Willard, as they prepared to leave.

"Please do, I await your return with great interest. And I wish you luck in your endeavours,"

he added with a small wave, as they headed off together.

"What's the plan, Scarlet? You always come up with a plan." said Rusty, as they made their way down the winding trail back to the bear's cave.

"Well, let's get there and hopefully retrieve the stones without upsetting this Ursa," she replied cautiously. "But Willard did say he wouldn't part with them easily,"

she quickly reminded them.

But Rusty was now full of optimism. "It'll be fine, we'll be back at the cottage before you know it, isn't that right, Rough?" he said encouragingly.

"If you say so, Rust," Rough answered quietly, trying to hide the uncertainty in his voice.

CHAPTER FIVE

Before long, the cave lay directly ahead and they advanced as slowly and as quietly as they could to the cave mouth.

"Maybe no one's home," whispered Scarlet hopefully. "Shall we take a look?"

Rough then stepped in putting his big arm across them both protectively. "I'll go in. You two stay on watch. I've got this, any trouble and I'll wrestle him to the ground," he joked half-heartedly.

"Are you sure?" said Rusty with real concern for his friend.

"It's fine, we'll play to our strengths. I'm by far the biggest, and if need be, definitely the fastest runner," Rough quipped with his bravest smile. "Wait here, it won't take long, I'll be in and out in a jiffy." And with that, he took in a big breath and entered the gloomy cave apprehensively.

"I'm a big brave badger, I can do this," he muttered, trying to convince himself he was unafraid, as he felt his way with a paw along the dank wall in the dark. He continued to trudge slowly forwards, hoping above all the cave was unoccupied. He then stopped for a second to regain his composure, as the darkness completely engulfed him. He took a few more deep breaths and then pushed on into the unknown.

Rough slowly began to make headway, still reaching out into the dark blindly. He was dreading the thought of finding a huge unseen bear with his touch, or even worse, a creature blocking his path: the bogeyman. He was fine with facing an opponent head-on, but it was the unknown that bothered him and the tales of the bogeyman he'd heard since his younger days, played heavily on his mind.

"Don't go across the meadow or he'll get you," they said. But it was the last bit of the story he wished he couldn't recall.

"He'll come and look for you at his favourite time, when it goes dark, and take you back to his cave. And you'll never be seen again." He felt a cold shiver down his spine. But somehow, he found the courage, and not wanting to let his friends down, continued edging forwards.

As he reached out to his side he felt the cave wall, cold to the touch but its firmness gave him slight comfort, for he could now feel his way along into the deep cavern. The hard cool surface helped him to navigate the murkiness and not feel totally lost. Then, he suddenly tripped over an unseen solid obstacle, probably a rock, which sent him sprawling onto his knees in a heap.

"I can't do this," he thought in desperation. "I just can't, it's hopeless, it's too dark."

As panic began to set in, he sat down with his back against the rock wall, and closed his eyes for a short time. He took a few moments to rest, but on opening them again, to his relief, he found his vision had started to become accustomed to the gloom, and he could now make out the boulder that had caused him to fall. Regaining his composure, he stood back upright. "Come on." he thought. I'm not letting the side down, no way! He felt his way around the rock that blocked his path and began to push on.

Meanwhile, Rusty and Scarlet waited patiently outside but were growing more concerned with every passing second.

"Do you think he's okay, Scarlet? I shouldn't have let him go in alone to collect the glow stones," said a concerned Rusty. "It should have been me. I'll never forgive myself if he gets hurt," he said with a disconsolate look.

"I'm sure it'll be fine, dear," said Scarlet consoling him with a hug. "Rough knows how to take care of himself, he's the Great wood champion, remember?" she added reassuringly.

Rusty returned a half-smile, but couldn't hide the fact that deep inside he felt more anxious than ever. Then at once they both felt a presence from behind, as a huge shadow was cast over them. They wheeled around and looked up to see the giant frame of a fierce-looking bear, his face contorted with rage.

"Thieves! I overheard you say you are here to steal my glow stones. Well, you'll pay the price for such insolence!" the angry bear roared.

"So tell me, Commander Stone, is the troop ready for inspection as I ordered?" asked King Slate, as he finished up yet another sumptuous meal while seated at his table, his voice echoing around the big room.

The table sat in the corner of the derelict building, which mostly held long defunct machinery now gathering dust. The low square wooden pine table that once had been man-sized but had been foraged from the long-vacant steel mill factory floor and cut down to meet the king's needs,

it's once long table legs now just off the floor, it's half a dozen matching chairs sharing the same sawed down fate.

"Yes, sire, they are ready. They've been ready for inspection on parade in the courtyard for half a morning now," reported his top commander. The troops had in fact been waiting in the old mill's yard in the heat of a summer's day, much to Stone's utter dismay.

"And er, you did say make it midday, my liege," he added warily, not wanting to upset the king. But Slate just didn't care.

"Midday, did I?" Slate said as he took a big slurp of tea from his cup, his meal now finished. "Oh well, I was famished and this six-course meal won't eat itself," he said, loosening his belt on his tunic as he sat back now feeling stuffed and let out a really large burp.

"And don't forget, Stone, it is midday somewhere, so I'm bang on time!" he quipped, bursting out into hysterical laughter, which Stone was obliged to join along with. "Oh, I do love being me, I'm so funny I ought to sack my court jester as I have no need for one," Slate said holding his sides. "Remind me, I have a jester, do I not?"

"No, sire, you did for a number of years but he failed to amuse you once, so you had him killed," answered Stone stiffly.

"Oh yes, I remember now. Oh well, I don't suffer fools gladly," he said with a smirk. "See, Stone, I'm a natural. No wonder I'm loved by all. Who needs a jester with me around?"

Stone couldn't agree more. "Yes, sire, who indeed," he sighed.

"Very good, do you know what I bore of the idea of this inspection, tell the troop not to bother today."

"Yes, sire. Of course, sire," said the relieved commander finally receiving the order for them to stand down.

"Well, be off with you, Stone. Don't just stand there, my troop has new orders," admonished Slate.

"Yes, sire. Of course, sire," replied his commander and headed quickly for the door.

"Oh, and Stone, before you go."

"Yes, sire? What is it, sire?" Stone replied stopping abruptly, doing his best to avoid showing his annoyance.

"Tell the troop to be ready for inspection midday sharp tomorrow, not a second after. I am a stickler for punctuality after all," said Slate without the slightest hint of irony.

"Yes, of course, sire," said the relieved Stone, tired and just wanting to get away.

Now alone, Slate got up and wandered over to a nearby grimy window, one of many which ran down the length of the foundry, as his eyes stared across the stretch of water between the mainland and the distant isle. *The troop do need to be ready,* he thought to himself as he gazed upon Badgers Brow. *I've the small matter of an island to conquer.*

CHAPTER SIX

Rough began to feel calmer as his eyes began to get used to the dark. He could hear a pin drop from a mile away and smell food in the next valley, or so he always claimed, but his eyesight wasn't his greatest asset, so now being able to make out his close surroundings gave him great comfort. As he looked up, he could now see large previously unseen jagged stalactites giving off a faint lustre, hanging down from the cave roof like the teeth of an angry beast.

He looked ahead and could now make out what appeared to be the rear wall of the cavern, so he pressed on always keeping in contact with its side by touch, so as not to get disorientated. After a few more steps he reached out and touched rear wall. It too felt cold to the touch, but as he looked around, he couldn't help having a feeling of dismay as the stones he searched for were nowhere to be seen. Was Willard even right about this? he thought to himself as he felt his angst return, rising in the pit of his stomach. Now, it was more because of the fear of failure as he would have to report back with no stones.

Then as he looked to his left, the side of the wall appeared different somehow in its consistency, so he decided to edge forward for a closer inspection. Now he could make out a hole in the wall and see that in fact it was an entrance to a small antechamber that was set back and slightly lit with a low flicker of light emanating from within. Once closer he could smell a musky odour of an animal scent he didn't recognise, which sent a cold shiver down his spine. His heart began to pound in his chest as he listened intently for any inhabitants, however heard nothing but the sound of himself breathing hard. I've come this far, he thought, and bravely stepped inside.

To the side of him was a black cast-iron fireplace, its fading embers giving just enough light to bathe the room in a faint reddish glow. He could make out a solid rectangular shape ahead and as he advanced, he could now see it was a large neatly made up wooden bed with two huge pillows at its top. Thankfully it was empty.

This must be Ursa's room, he thought to himself, as he made his way around the edge of the bed. He stumbled across a bedside table nearly knocking over an object, which sat atop it, causing it to nearly wobble and fall.

"Is that what I think it is?" he said aloud in the half-light, before reaching out and picking it up. And as he held it up, he broke out into a big smile. In his hand he held a large-handled brass lamp with a half-used candle sitting inside it. He opened up the glass door at the front, swiftly retrieving the candle and stepped towards the fire place. He held it to the dying embers until a flickering flame could be seen as the candlewick began to burn, and he quickly placed it back into the lamp, closing its door to.

He now felt a feeling of exhilaration as he held up the lamp in front of his face. Now he could finally see at last, as it gave off ample light. All the bear seemed to own in the way of furniture was the bed, the table, and an old wooden chair sitting next to it, but there wasn't a glow stone in sight.

He spent the next ten minutes carefully searching all around the room, even under the bed itself, but to no avail. He sat down on the side of the bed feeling rather dejected. How am I supposed to find these stones in a huge cave with just the aid of candle light? he thought forlornly.

From nowhere inspiration struck. "Wait a minute, what's the only bit of light I've seen since I've been in here?" he said aloud to himself, as his voice echoed and reverberated back from the chamber's walls. He excitedly jumped up and went back into the cavern and with lamp in hand he held it up towards the ceiling.

And there they were, having been there all along, giving off a luminescent glow of red, green and blue, embedded into the sides of the hanging stalactites. The elusive glow stones.

"You crafty bear, who would think of looking up there?" he said to himself, as he gleefully plucked off a pawful. Now with his prize in paw he began to gratefully make his way out, finding his way much more easily with the help of the lamp.

And just ahead there it was, the entrance to the cave getting larger with every step. Once outside, the bright daylight made him squint and he put down the now not-needed lamp to shield his eyes, still grasping the stones tightly in the other.

He could now see Rusty and Scarlet were still waiting for him as expected. But much to his astonishment behind them stood the unmistakable figure of a very large angry brown bear too.

"The audacity! How dare you even attempt to steal my stones!" glowered the huge brown bear as he towered over them, all teeth and claw, his inner fury burning like a raging wild fire, as they cowered down before him.

The colossal bear was dressed in a simple white tunic befitting his no-nonsense attitude, fitted tightly to his huge muscular frame.

"Give me one good reason why I don't crush all three of you, right now!" Ursa roared rearing up to his full height, his arms extended as if ready to strike.

"Please, I know this looks bad," pleaded Scarlet, "but we're not thieves. We're on a mission sent by Willard the Wise himself."

But Ursa looked unimpressed. "A mission, you say? Hah! And I'm supposed to believe such nonsense?" he replied sternly. He scowled at them for a moment or two longer but being a good judge of character, he sensed an honest look in Scarlet's eye, and with his quick temper now cooling, he began to calm down.

"You mentioned the name of Willard," he said warily, still unsure of their motives. "I do trust in him. But it is a trust earned not given. So I have decided I will let you speak, little squirrel. But if I'm not satisfied with your answer, you will rue the day you ever deceived me."

He sat back with a huge thud, much like the sound of a falling tree in the forest, and began listening and watching them thoughtfully, his dark intense eyes looking out from under his furrowed brow.

Scarlet began to retell their tale from the very beginning. She explained the reason for their trek and why Willard had given them such a task, and that the safety of all the creatures of the Great Wood were at stake if they did not succeed.

The big bear listened closely without interruption as she spoke, taking in every word. As she finished, Ursa contemplated for a moment and then he spoke out again, but now in a much gentler way.

"Willard is of good heart and gives his help to those who seek it," he began. "All creatures of worth know this to be true. And if as you say, the Great Wood is truly under threat, I am indebted to help. Therefore, I have made a decision," he said now sitting forward. "You may take a handful of my stones with you, but you must be aware they must return to me. For they have been handed down through the generations of my kin, a task that goes back down the centuries. Listen well, and I will tell you more."

The plucky trio now began to relax as the big bear continued to explain.

"Our duty is to guard and watch over them, you see. One of us is chosen for this task and it is believed to be a great honour. To be the Keeper of the Stones is an important privilege, and so I do not relinquish even a few lightly. They are regarded amongst my own to be sacred and are said to bring peace and tranquillity to the isle, but with you telling me this may be under threat, this has swayed my decision. However, you must promise to return them to me once the danger has passed, to make the collection whole again." He sat back once more awaiting their decision.

"Yes, of course we will return them to you," said Rusty sincerely. "And I promise to guard them with my very life."

Ursa mused for a moment more then broke out into a broad smile. "Very well then," said the big bear now convinced of their integrity, as he introduced himself. "My name, as you probably know is Ursa, and I offer you the paw of friendship."

A relieved Rusty then did the same. "My name is Rusty and this is my wife, Scarlet, and our friend, Rough," he said introducing them in turn. "And we offer you our friendship in return."

"Offer accepted," replied Ursa readily. He then stood up on all fours. "I will now keep you no longer, so be on your way my new friends. I bid you safe journey, for other thoughts now occupy my mind for I grow hungry and have more foraging to pursue."

With that, the three now satisfied with the outcome of their search bade farewell to Ursa and began to head off. Rough came to a sudden halt.

"Tell you what, Ursa!" he yelled loudly. "I like a good forage too, so if I come across some juicy berries, I'll drop you some by when we return."

The offer was returned with a loud roar of approval from the big bear, and with that Rough turned back to hurry to catch the others up.

Before long, they had returned back to the cottage to find Willard sitting on his porch on the top step awaiting their return. Screech was there also and saw their approach first.

"Oh no, they're back already," he groaned, more to himself than not. "Probably wanting more tea and more cake too. I have to do everything around here. Why always me? I do the work of two owls," he moaned before sloping off back into the kitchen to put the kettle on and start preparing more food.

"Ah, my friends you're back. I do hope your quest was successful and Ursa was compliant?" asked Willard hopefully.

"Yes, we've got them alright," said Rough holding out his paw to show off the stones."

Willard looked relieved. "Very good. I feared he would not let any leave from under his watchful eye and split the stones asunder. For without his consent the spell would fail, as the stones must be leant willingly, and your endeavours would therefore be fruitless," said a happy Willard.

"And Ursa's alright once you get to know him. Just a big cuddly bear," quipped Rough jovially. "I even had a good nose around his cave. I bet there's not many who can say that and live to tell the tale," he said merrily, which made Rusty and Scarlet burst out into spontaneous laughter.

"Now Screech has kindly offered, with good grace, to bring refreshments and you can regale us with all your brave deeds," said Willard cheerfully, getting up from the step. "And once you are refreshed you have just one more task to fulfil to complete the charm. You must collect herbs of the forest, which can be found a short distance away from here. But to fulfil this, you will need a trusted guide – someone to show the way. I have sent for her and expect her to arrive imminently. So please, do come inside, I wish to hear all of your tales of valour, no doubt," he said, holding his blue front door open wide for them.

"Come on Rough, you're the hero of the hour," said Scarlet smiling with an outstretched arm as they went in. "You lead the way and tell all to Willard."

Rough felt like the proudest badger who had ever lived.

CHAPTER SEVEN

Willard's table had been put to good use as always. Once again it was laden with Screech's delicious homemade cakes made from the fruits of the forest, followed by lashings of hot tea. The pastries were his speciality and were a delight for the taste buds, with each bite releasing a cascade of summer's sweet delights onto the lucky participant's tongue. When they had all had their fill though Willard seemed a little quiet, seeming a little distant.

All at once, he sat upright and spoke out again.

"I sense our visitors drawing near," he said with a knowing smile. "So let us make haste, there is no time to waste. Let us await outside for their imminent arrival and greet them appropriately." Then without further ado, he leapt from his chair, made his way over to the front door, and pushed it open. He took his usual seat on the top step cross-legged, eyes fixed firmly ahead.

"Come on, let's go and join him," urged Scarlet, not sure how he could know this, but eager to see who these mysterious newcomers could possibly be.

As Scarlet, Rough and Rusty joined Willard on the porch, in the far distance movement could now be seen speeding their way. In the treetops they spied a figure moving swiftly and easily from branch to branch, heading towards them at pace. Overhead simultaneously a raven swooped fast and low above the trees like a speeding arrow. Distracted by the bird, the fleeting form they had glimpsed high in the canopy was lost from sight. Before they could question its whereabouts, the presence instantaneously dropped from above landing gracefully at their feet. It was a pine marten!

"Hello Willard, it's been a while. How have you been?" said the chirpy new arrival with a friendly grin. She was a little taller than a squirrel, of lithe build and clad in a green sleeveless tunic, with a bow and a quiver of arrows strapped firmly to her back. Hands confidently on hips, she beamed widely as the raven landed neatly beside her.

The bird was dressed in a similar fashion minus the bow, and remained silent and just observed them closely, head cocked to one side watching through sharp inquisitive eyes.

"I am fine, my friends, all the better for seeing you both," greeted Willard warmly with arms outstretched, and seemingly genuinely pleased to see them. "And these are the travellers that will need your guidance today," he said indicating to Rusty and the others with an outstretched paw. The pine marten still smiling now turned her attention to the three strangers by his side.

"Hello, my name is Izzy and I'm pleased to make your acquaintance," she said making a slight bow with one arm tucked behind her back. "And this is my companion, Chance, my eye in the sky," she added after straightening up, glancing at the raven by her side. "He's one of few words but as faithful as they come. Once you gain his confidence, that is," she added politely.

The raven stayed quiet just giving a slight nod of assent, but still seemed to be eyeing them cautiously as if weighing them up.

"Hello, we're pleased to meet you too," greeted Scarlet on their behalf. "I'm Scarlet and this is my husband, Rusty, and good friend, Rough," which gained polite smiles all around.

"Very good," said Willard agreeably still sitting cross-legged on his favourite step. "Now the formalities are over, let me explain the reason for your being here." He then told Izzy and Chance about the current situation and the reason their assistance was warranted as they listened on without interruption.

Once Willard had finished his account, Izzy spoke again.

"It would be our great honour to help." Her expression changed from light to serious in an instance. "For after all, a threat to one is a threat to us all," she added defiantly, with a clench of her paw.

"Good, we are all agreed then," said a content-looking Willard as he confirmed his request. "Izzy and Chance, safe passage through the forest is required to collect that what is needed, and there are no better suited to fulfil such a task than yourselves. Therefore, I have drawn up a list of the herbs in question." He pulled a scrap of folded paper from his waistcoat pocket and began to read. "This will include: rosemary, basil, chamomile, bay leaf and sage, if you would be so kind," he said handing over the note to Izzy. She gladly took it, folded it carefully and put it safely in a small pocket in her tunic before speaking to them all.

"Now this journey can be perilous and would be unwise to attempt without an escort who knows the terrain. And of course, that's where we come in," Izzy said placing a confident hand on the raven's wing. "The first hazard we will encounter is the swamplands," she told them, as all eyes now fell on her. "They are notorious in these parts and must be negotiated with great care. But fear not, we know the swamplands well," she said with confidence. "Next, we will encounter a cliff range, which I must inform you is eroding dangerously and we will need to take extra care through there," she warned. "Then finally comes the ravine. The herbs we seek grow in abundance just across the gorge and are accessible by a crumbling bridge. But it'll be fine. Promise." She beamed. "Any questions?"

"I've got one thing to say," said Rusty. "The items needed for this charm to work are meant for me and me alone," he said, before turning to the others. "This all sounds extremely dangerous. Why don't I just go along with our guides and I'll meet you back here?" he insisted.

But Scarlet for one was having none of that. "Absolutely not," she replied adamantly. "I'm coming along too. We can face whatever is out there together. Just like we always do."

"Okay, if you insist," said Rusty, thankful for her support and gave her a grateful hug.

"And you can count me in too, Rust. There's no way I'm missing out on all the fun," said Rough with a grin, along with a firm pat on the back. "Plus, anyway, I promised to find berries for Ursa and I never go back on a promise."

"Very good. That's sorted," declared Izzy, itching to make a start. "Shall we be off then? We've got herbs to collect. If you will, Chance, take to the skies to scout ahead. Keep an eye out for any trouble, will you?"

"Of course," replied the raven, and with a beat of his wings headed immediately skywards.

"Farewell, my friends," shouted Willard to them as they disappeared off into the wood. "I wish you safe journey and a swift return." He continued to sit there for a little while longer still cross-legged on the top step wishing he were joining them, but knowing it was better to stay behind and make plans for their safe return. He was joined once more by Screech.

"I sense you have a question or two my feathered friend?" asked Willard to the owl.

Screech just gave him an unsure shrug. "It's just that I don't understand. Would it not be easier if you and I had fetched the items for them?" Screech asked looking a little perturbed. Willard answered him with a measured smile.

"If it were only that simple, my friend, I would duly oblige. But for the spell to work they must all be found by the user themselves. And introducing them to Izzy and Chance can only create new allies for what surely lies ahead. For I see this journey as a test for them all, and I fear there are many more tests to come."

CHAPTER EIGHT

As they made their way through the dense forest Rusty looked down to see an acorn lying on the ground seemingly waiting there just for him. As he bent down to pick it up, he smiled to himself as thoughts of his younger days growing up in the Great Wood came flooding back to him.

He loved getting up and setting off early with nothing planned, to see how the day would unfold. He'd climb trees just like the ones they were passing now, and leap from one to another getting as high as possible, sometimes with friends, sometimes alone, just for the fun of it. Their favourite game was 'hunter and hunted' where they took it in turns to chase and catch each other. One touch and you were caught. Sometimes pretending the hunter was man, because everyone knows they're to be avoided. Or sometimes, if it was getting late, the bogeyman would come out to play and chase you down, which they all thought was the best and scariest fun of all. And this was how he first met Scarlet.

One morning from on high, whilst waiting in the usual meeting spot for his friends, he spied a stranger to the wood: a young attractive female squirrel he'd never seen before, just sitting up against a tree way down below.

As they continued snaking through the forest in Izzy's wake, he smiled to himself at the memory of how he'd try to impress this captivating new arrival. He had rushed down from the tree eager to please her and held out an acorn he'd found earlier that day, that he had been intending on saving for himself. The acorn must have worked as they hit it off immediately, and giving her an acorn as a gift became their 'thing'.

He knew as he handed the one he'd found today to her would go down well, and he was right. She gave him a kiss on the cheek along with her best smile. Her winning smile as he put it, and reserved only for him.

"Thanks for the gift," she said clutching the acorn tightly, "I'll keep it in my pocket and hopefully it will bring us luck."

"I hope so too," replied Rusty cheerfully. Because for some unknown reason coming from deep inside, he thought they were going to need it.

After a few more minutes, Scarlet decided to catch up with their guide to get know her a little better.

"Hi," she said breathlessly. "I thought I'd come and get to know you a bit better, if that's okay?"

"Hi, and of course it is!" she replied amiably. Izzy was well received by most who met her, as there was something about her you just couldn't help but like. "You're Scarlet from the Great Wood, correct?" she asked, smiling warmly. "I've been there a few times in the past but tend to stick to this side of the meadow as a rule. Have you ever travelled here before?"

Scarlet shook her head. "No, it's my first time in these parts and to be honest, I've never met a pine marten before either. None live in the Great Wood you see."

Izzy looked at her with a gleam in her eye. "Well, there's no need to worry about us, we don't bite!" Izzy laughed. "We pines are a friendly bunch," as long as you don't cross us, we're very loyal. We've lived in this forest forever and a day, so the Elders say," she said as they continued to follow the well-trodden trail snaking through the underbrush.

"The Elders, who are they?" asked a curious Scarlet, eager to know more about her welcoming guide and her kind.

"Oh, in our community that's how the seniors are known. They are treated with the most respect. All pines revere their elderly, for they have a lifetime of wisdom to share, you see."

At that point the pathway led off in two directions.

"See that route to the left?" said Izzy, pointing out a way through the woods. "That's known around here as the pine marten trail and it leads to our home in the pine trees. But our destination lies this way," she said taking the other track.

"So how long have you known Willard then?" enquired Scarlet as they continued on their way walking side by side.

"Oh Willard, he's amazing and we go back a few years," enthused Izzy. "He's helped us many times in the past, including keeping the wild wolves of the north at bay. They're a nasty bunch," she said, with a curl of her lip. "Soldiers of Fortune they call themselves. Mercenaries to the likes of you and me. They'll fight for whoever has the heaviest purse. But luckily the pack has stayed up in their own territory for years now. And Willard, he's amazing, and once you get to know him better, you will find out there's a lot more to him than meets the eye."

Scarlet couldn't agree more. "Yes, he does seem as if he's full of surprises," she said.

Just ahead of them, they came across a clearing in the trees and Izzy raised her paw in a signal to stop. The landscape had changed dramatically as they left the forest and given way to a flat misty marshland cloaked in a swirling fog that stretched as far as the eye could see. Full of thick brown-and-green tall reeds growing out of a thick sludge-filled terrain, the swamp looked impenetrable.

"Up ahead is the wetland I warned you about," reminded Izzy. "There are ancient stories that a pathway can be found through its middle but it's unknown to me," she admitted. "What I can tell you though is many an unwary traveller is said to have been lost and sunk to the very bottom of the quagmire without a trace, never to be seen again," which gained a concerned groan from Rough. "But have no fear, I do know a safe route. Come on, follow me. After all, you've got the best navigator in the region with you, if I do say so myself," she said with a wink and a smile, and with that she skipped off, skirting around the bog with them following close behind.

After a few more minutes of being led now could be seen, jutting out above the fog, a stairway made from stone.

Set in the granite, steps ran up the side of the mire, hewn out of the stone by an expert hand from aeons ago. Now at the foot of them, a confident Izzy went first and began to ascend the man-sized steps vaulting them with ease, having traversed them many times before. She then halted and turned around.

"Follow me, it's fine but do take note, the fog has made it rather slippery in places," she warned them. Taking care, Rough came next. He found it much tougher going as he had to heave his burly frame, one step at a time. Scarlet followed with Rusty taking up the rear. Both being excellent experienced climbers, they skipped effortlessly from one step to the next, keeping a watchful eye on the less agile Rough up ahead.

"You okay, Rough?" asked a concerned Rusty, seeing the badger was finding it tough as he pulled himself up yet another large step.

"Yeah, I'm fine, though I don't fancy finding out how deep that swamp is," he said trying his best to keep away from the edge.

"I know, me neither," replied Rusty as he glanced to the side and could now see the vastness of the wide-reaching misty quagmire far below. Suddenly, he overbalanced and slipped. Losing his footing on the wet stone surface, he felt himself begin to fall backwards, unable to regain his balance as a gasping Scarlet watched helplessly on. As he began to fall away, surely to his certain doom, he felt a firm grip grab him by the arm. It was a quick-thinking Rough. Stooping down, with one strong action, Rough pulled him swiftly back up to safety and out of danger. Rusty let out a huge sigh of relief.

"Phew, thanks Rough. I was a goner then for sure," said a truly relieved Rusty.

"Don't worry, I've told you before, I've got your back," grinned Rough in return. "I've got a soft spot for you Rust, but it's definitely not in that swamp!"

They continued on without another incident and before long the steps gave way to a flat stony pathway at the climb's summit, its short length preceding the long descent down. All this time, Chance had been keeping a watchful eye from above, and seeing them start to make their descent was content to fly on and continue his vigil. Finding the climb down less arduous, and much to their relief, they finally left the last stepway and stopped to take a breath.

"Well done, everyone." We'll take a short break and then continue onwards through there," she said with a glance over her shoulder. Just behind her stood an imposing-looking rock range, its sheer face looked impossible to climb. But cut through its middle was a ravine splitting it in two, as if cleaved with a mighty axe.

"As I've mentioned before, we must take great care going through the pass. Great care indeed."

Misfit was feeling very pleased with himself, very pleased indeed. Being a lazy so and so, he'd decided to take a little nap in the sun after his morning's exertions. Now fully refreshed he'd moved on, and soon found himself exiting the badger tunnel that Rough had dug out under the Maleficent Meadow. He dusted himself down and began to saunter down Briars Road with a self-satisfied smug look across his scrawny face. He gave a nod and a grin to any passer-by he came across, which was mostly ignored but he didn't care a jot. Nothing could spoil the good mood he now found himself in. Then up ahead he spied a furtive-looking pair sitting outside their burrow.

Dressed in unkempt crumpled clothing strewn over their taut sinewy frames and looking as if they'd slept in them, which they probably had, were two brown rats named Pitter and Patter, idly languishing around in the afternoon sun. They were long-known associates of his and were usually up to no good. Just like him.

"Hey up, Misfit, where you been to? Not seen you all day," said a daft sounding Pitter.

"Yeah, what he said," joined in Patter with a big yawn, and a lazy stretch of his arms.

"I'll tell you where I've been, on the other side of the
meadow!" replied Misfit, rapidly hurrying his stride towards them eager to tell all.

"What's the Malif—maluf— err, meadow, and why you been there then?" asked Pitter stumbling over his words.

"Yeah, what he said," joined in the not-so-bright Patter.

"It's Maleficent, you fools," spat out Misfit giving both a disparaging look.

He put up with them more than enjoyed their company, and even though slightly irritated he would not allow his lackeys as he thought of them, to spoil his good mood. After all, he considered that his snooping would pay off later. "I've been on the trail of that pest, Rusty, and his ignoramus pal Rough all morning. It was well worth it," he said gleefully with a rub of his paws, as he paced up and down unable to contain himself.

"He thinks he's so high and mighty, what with his stupid wood watch, pretending to keep an eye on the neighbourhood, more like having a good snoop around," he said with a look of utter disdain.

"And he thinks he's unbeatable at furball too," he snarled with a curl of his lip at the memory.

"Well, his team have won it two years running, Misfit," reminded Patter, who then immediately regretted it as Misfit turned on him.

"Of course I remember, how could I forget? I'm our team captain!" he snarled before quickly regaining his composure. "Well, not to worry. I've heard he's got another foe from across the water, and by all accounts he's paying a visit soon," he said as a sly smile spread across his thin face as a plan began to form in his mind. "And when that happens, I'll be the first to greet him with open arms and help that pest finally get his comeuppance."

After the group had briefly rested, Izzy led them away from the green foliage of the forest towards the imposing-looking ravine directly ahead.

"Now tread carefully," she said quietly as they approached its gaping high-walled entrance, "and please no talking aloud," which gained a silent nod of agreement. The pathway through the ravine was roughly ten metres wide, and boulders large and small were strewn across the floor, evidence of recent falls. Looking up it was easy to see why. Overhead precarious-looking outcrops of rock could be seen seemingly defying the laws of gravity itself. They now made slow and deliberate progress, knowing it was the only sure way to pass safely as any loud noise could reverberate and echo around the ravine walls, bringing sure disaster.

After what seemed an age, they could finally see the exit from the ravine and one by one gladly came out of the other side.

"Phew, that was intense," said Scarlet with a big sigh of relief,

"I know it's dangerous to go through the gorge, but it's by far the quickest route. But don't worry, it's not far now," Izzy said brightly, "our destination is just across the way."

They now found themselves in a wide-open space in a calm meadow filled with buttercups and daisies, their bright white and yellow hue blowing to and fro in the light wind, like ripples on a pond. On each side grew high trees and across the field lay a deep chasm with green hills lying across the other side.

"Welcome to The Vale," said Izzy as they began to cross the grassy flower-filled plain.

"And see over there?" she said indicating an abyss that lay before them in the distance, "once across it, we find the herbs we've come so far for."

"But how do we get across that?" asked Scarlet as they approached the huge drop.

"Oh, that's not a problem," replied Izzy cheerfully.

"We cross using the bridge." As she finished speaking, a rickety old-looking bridge could now be seen that had been previously hidden behind a small copse of trees. It was made from wood and rope, and sagged in the middle. Across its length it had some slats that were missing – long fallen away – so it was obvious to all it had seen better days.

Suddenly from on high, they could hear the distinctive call of a raven. Izzy looked up immediately to see Chance swoop and dive in a prearranged signal to warn her of imminent danger. In the corner of her eye, she saw two shady-looking individuals moving menacingly towards them before coming to a sudden halt. Two large wild boars, named Riff and Raff, stood blocking the path to the bridge entrance. They were clad in well-worn black waistcoats. Izzy recognised them at once.

"Not you two again!" she exclaimed in dismay.

"Unfortunately for you, yes, it is," rasped the seemingly more dominant one, Riff who strode forward, puffing out his chest. "You know the rules, pine," he said with menace.

"We'll take all your valuables and any food you've got if you wanna cross the bridge. Pay the toll or turn back. Simple, isn't it?" he growled.

CHAPTER NINE

"So, what do you say?" roared the beastly boar Riff, as he blocked from moving forward.

"Like I said, simple isn't it? Pay up or move on," he said staring at each one in turn.

"This is our patch and here you play by our rules," he boasted. He then smashed one hoof into the ground in an attempt to intimidate them and make his point clear as the other boar, Raff, stared them down too.

They picked out the biggest amongst the intruders, Rough, and fixed their eyes firmly on him. Standing a head higher than him and both stockily built, they felt they had the advantage. But instead of scaring him, they had achieved the opposite. He felt they had tried to bully him, and if there's one thing a now angry Rough didn't like it was a bully.

"You know what, that sounds like a challenge to me," boomed Rough, "and there's nothing more that this badger loves than a challenge." He might not always be the bravest, but once riled, Rough was a force to be reckoned with. And he hated bullies.

Without thinking too much about it and with the element of surprise on his side, Rough charged forward closing the distance quickly catching the two over-confident boars off-guard. Before Riff knew what was happening, he crashed into him hitting him dead centre and sent him sprawling to the ground. Rough immediately swivelled around and in one well-practised move, dropped down and shoulder-charged Raff hitting him solidly in his chest, sending him crashing backwards too, landing in a heap in the dirt.

"Now pay attention, 'cos that's what happens when you take on the Great Wood wrestling champion!" he boomed with a thump of his chest. He then gave a final warning. "Now it's time for YOU two to back off!" he roared defiantly. Rough now feeling quite pleased with himself, turned around and made his way back to the others contented he'd seen them both off for good.

Lying there Riff felt humiliated. How could a simple badger better them? "I'm not having that!" he raged angrily. In a flash he leapt to his feet and seeing Rough had his back turned, charged head down with his tusks at the ready. In an instant he crunched loudly into Rough's rear with a resounding thud, and sent him flying through the air landing awkwardly in a heap at Scarlet's feet.

"No!" she shrieked looking down at the unmoving figure of Rough. Things had definitely taken a turn for the worse as both the boars were now back on their feet. They both strutted over ignoring the fallen badger no longer considering him a threat.

"Told you," sneered Riff. "He wouldn't listen and paid the price. So you know the deal," he said now standing over them. "Pay up or join him in the dirt."

"Enough!" came a shout. It was Izzy who had swiftly drawn her bow. "Don't make me do it, Riff. Make no mistake, stand down or I will fill you full of arrows. Believe me, you will both fall." The look of intent etched across her livid face left them in no doubt this was no empty threat. She meant every word.

"Woah, take it easy. No need to get nasty," said Riff immediately raising both hooves in the air. "We were only messing with you," he added with a forced smile. "Tell you what, Pine, I've always liked you," he lied. "So today I've decided it's a toll-free day," he said slowly edging away. "Go ahead, cross the bridge, have some fun," he said with a nonchalant wave of a hoof. He turned to leave. "Come on, Raff, I've seen enough. Let's go, we've wasted enough time on these losers." And with that, both boars headed off towards the distant tree line keeping a watchful eye on Izzy as she followed them, her bow still drawn, with them firmly in her sights.

Rusty went to the aid of his stricken friend, who began to stir, shook his head and shakily sat up.

"What happened?" Rough asked still feeling groggy.

"Did I do okay?" Rusty could not have been prouder of his valiant friend.

"Rough, mate, you did better than okay, you did brilliantly as always," he said giving him a grateful hug.

Once at a safe distance and out of range of Izzy's arrows, a dismayed Raff turned to his brother, unhappy at their hasty withdrawal.

"This ain't good enough. We're not letting them get away with that are we, Riff? We've got a bad reputation to keep up!" he growled.

"Too right, we're not," snarled a scowling Riff.

"Don't worry, you'll see, one way or another I'll make that badger wish he'd never been born."

CHAPTER TEN

The troop had stood in line in full armour in the heat of the midday sun sweltering for two long hours before Slate bothered to turn up for the inspection he'd ordered. One or two were beginning to wilt as the hot temperature began to get to them.

On arrival, Slate began to make his way slowly down the company line being sheltered from the hot sun by a big parasol held aloft by a beaver named Billy. He was accompanied by Commander Stone and his advisor, Oswald, who was much smaller than the rest and did his best to keep up, which didn't go unnoticed by Slate.

"Come on, Elder, keep up. We haven't got all day, you know."

A peeved Oswald chose to ignore him and returned a fake smile. Every now and again Slate would stop and ask a trooper his name, say a casual sounding 'Chin up' or something similar, stifle a yawn and then move on.

"They're all looking rather adequate, Stone," he said in a bored-sounding tone as they continued to go slowly side by side in front of the wilting guards as Oswald took up the rear. "But I do love the way I can admire myself in their armour," said Slate suddenly perking up as he stopped and bent over to look at himself in the gleaming breastplate of a startled trooper who didn't dare to move as the king gave a toothy grin right in front of him.

"Well, you did order them to be up at dawn to shine and polish their kit, sire," said an irritable Stone, trying to hide his impatience. He was very proud to be commander-in-chief of the Grey Army and took his responsibilities very seriously. The welfare of his troops was paramount to him, and he didn't take kindly to any perceived mistreatment. All this waiting around had angered him, a fact he had to hide or face the consequences.

"Well, they should look their best for their king," Slate continued pompously, still amusing himself. "Oh, and look, Stone, it makes your face go all funny! "He laughed as he stared at Stone's distorted face in the reflection of the shiny metal. It's just like being in my hall of mirrors, it's great fun! " Slate smirked, referring to an arrangement of old shop mirrors of varied shape and sizes foraged from the old abandoned shopping precinct and placed together to amuse the king in an emptied store room in the mill. But Stone wasn't so sure.

"Er, yes, of course, my liege," he said trying to hide how ridiculous he felt in front of the company, leaning into the next soldier down the line.

"Go on, Stone, give a big smile. It's fun, and that's an order," insisted Slate as Stone smiled weakly, desperately wanting this poor excuse for an inspection to end. At that point the soldier standing directly in front of the king suddenly wavered, rocked to and fro, then fell backwards falling flat on his back with a resounding thump.

"Stone, Stone, what on earth is the matter with him?" asked a bewildered Slate watching in disbelief.

"I believe he may have fainted, sire. It's the heat. They've been here awhile," came the curt matter-of-fact reply.

"The heat? It's barely even warm!" admonished Slate still sheltered from the sun under his parasol. "I can't have insubordination," he whinged. "Have him demoted immediately!" he ordered in a huff, followed by a surly fold of his arms and look of disapproval.

"Er, I can't, sire, he's a private," reminded Stone.

"Really? Oh well, stop his pay for the last month then. That should teach him not to shirk his duty," said Slate with his nose stuck up in the air.

"Sire, he hasn't been paid for the last month. None of them have. Your orders were to make cuts to pay for the impending invasion."

"What? Oh yes, I remember now," blustered Slate as he unfolded his arms and began to move on with the parasol-carrying beaver scurrying to keep up. "Well, tough decisions have to be made and invasions don't come cheap, you know," he went on as Stone fell into line beside him. "Stone, they should count themselves lucky they've got a job at all and me to lead them," he said full of his own self-importance.

"Yes, sire, I'm sure they go to sleep every night counting their very blessings," said Stone with a heavy sigh. At that moment the beaver holding the parasol got slightly out of step with the king and the sun briefly beat down directly down on him.

"Beaver, keep up! Whatever is wrong with you? Is that umbrella too heavy?" scolded Slate with his usual squint-eyed glare. "Shall I fashion you one out of cast iron?" he threatened. Stone knew he meant every word of it.

"Let's see how you'd get on carrying that!"

The beaver was mortified by his stumble. "I'm sorry, sire, it won't happen again," mumbled the beaver quickly doing his best to cover him up.

"Good, make sure it doesn't or I'll have a hat made out of you," he warned, which was another one of Slate's threats he'd carried out on more than one occasion. The king's hat stand was notorious. Many a poor creature who had upset the king had met their demise and had their fur turned into his latest headgear – a fate no one wanted to share. For the first time, Slate took a proper look at the startled beaver. "Are you new? I don't remember you," remarked Slate peering at the beaver closely.

"No, sire, I've been a courtier for years."

"Really?" said Slate now bored of inspecting his waning guard, turning to head back to his converted throne room in the steel mill. "So what's your name, beaver? You have got a name I take it?" he asked. The beaver frantically angled the parasol over his head desperate to keep him in the shade.

"It's Billy, sire," the beaver replied shakily.

"Well, Billy, I don't suppose you're too out of step, unlike the Elder," Slate sneered, which again Oswald did his best to ignore.

Slate then moved on. "You can carry my parasol at all future inspections," he directed. Billy inwardly cringed.

"Thank you, my liege. Most kind," he said whilst doing his best to look pleased, as working so close with the king on a regular basis was the last thing he wanted.

Slate then turned his attention back to Stone.

"Oh, I do love a good inspection of the troops, it so brightens my day. Tell them same time tomorrow. And not to be late, I so abhor bad punctuality." Then Slate halted for a second as another demand popped into his mind. "Oh, Elder, finally caught up I see," he said looking down on the dormouse. "You are to attend later and update me on the invasion. All had better be nearly ready or else you'll be the next for my hat stand," he warned as he began to climb the crumbling stairwell.

Oswald inwardly seethed but was used to Slate's demands. He bowed and walked away, keeping his angry thoughts to himself. For now. Stone then had one last request.

"Ahem, sire, are the troops dismissed?" he asked hopefully.

"What? Oh, those lot? Yes," answered Slate having totally forgotten they were still out there. "And tell them to be quiet about it, it's my afternoon nap time," he said with a dismissive wave from over his shoulder as he disappeared inside with a relieved Billy taking down the parasol and scampering after him.

"Yes, sire," muttered Stone bitterly under his breath as he went back to the guard to give them the good news that they could finally stand down. "Until the same time tomorrow."

As Izzy led the way they approached the rickety old decrepit bridge. It swayed, creaked and groaned as it swung gently in the summer breeze as if giving out a warning to keep away. It consisted of wooden slats held together by rope tied to two wooden posts on each side of the gorge. At each post was more rope running at waist height of an average man, attached to the bridge to provide stability for its users to hold on to when crossing over. It spanned the deep chasm and as they edged forward and stood on the edge of the precipice, they could see a raging river winding way down below. From this height, it looked like no more than a mere trickle and near the bottom of the cliff face, the escarpment was riddled with what looked like a series of caverns that were honeycombed shaped.

"Woah, that's a long way down," said a trembling Rough with a gulp, now rested but still feeling sore after his run-in with the boars. "I wouldn't fancy falling down there." Not a big fan of heights, he stayed a metre away from the drop craning his neck forward getting as close as he dared.

However, Izzy seemed completely unfazed by the great height and stood on the very edge, paws on hips, staring into the void.

"Yes it's a big drop, I'll give you that," she agreed casually. "And look, see the caves? That's where the bats live." She pointed out the hollows far down below. "They're not too friendly a bunch," she added, "but don't worry, they're nocturnal and we'll be long gone before nightfall."

Whilst they had been talking, Rusty had been casting an eye on the rotten bridge and didn't like what he saw. "It's definitely not on its last legs," he noted as the bridge gave out another groan as if to agree with him. He came to a quick conclusion. "Izzy, I say just you and I go across. Alone," he suggested to her. "We don't all need to risk the bridge, and of course you know where to find them."

He next spoke to Scarlet to try to convince her too.

"You know it makes sense," he said gently, knowing she was likely to protest. "You stay with Rough; it'll be fine. We won't be long and there's no point in all of us going." He gave her a comforting peck on the cheek before turning to Rough.

"And I'm sorry, mate, you're way too big for that bridge. It's a job for lightweights like me," he added with a wink and a smile.

"What do you mean 'too big'?" said Rough, pretending to be insulted. "If I am big, it's all muscle," he said flexing a thick arm and then wishing he hadn't as a sharp twinge of pain flashed across his back. Scarlet spotted his discomfort and reached over to console him.

"Rough, you sit and rest awhile. I'll wait with you. As Rusty says, I suppose it does make more sense that way," she reluctantly conceded.

Still feeling sore, Rough gladly took up the offer and gingerly sat back, happy to sit this one out and give his injured back a rest.

"Be careful," Scarlet said to Rusty as he prepared to cross. "No taking unnecessary risks, okay?" she said with a look of concern.

"Don't worry. We'll be back before you know it," he assured her with a confident smile.

"Well shall we go for it, Izzy?" he asked keen to get going.

"The sooner we go, the sooner we get back."

"Agreed, let's get this done," Izzy replied breezily.

"Okay, I'll go first," offered Rusty. "After all, it's all down to me that we're here in the first place." Without awaiting a reply, he advanced and tentatively stepped out on to the bridge, and to his delight, it held firm.

It swayed and creaked gently a little but seemed fine, and so he carefully started to make his way across. Some of the bridge's slats had fallen away with time, creating gaps to avoid and skip over, and he could see that the rope had deteriorated with age too. Its thickness had frayed away in places, being held together with just a few strands, but being a nimble squirrel, he darted and skipped his way across the divide and in very little time, he was back on firm ground across the other side. "It's okay, Izzy. Be careful, but it's fine. Make your way over," he yelled back to her, his voice echoing loudly in the chasm below. Izzy then began to cross too and hopped, skipped and jumped her way across quite easily with no bother at all.

"Dunno what the fuss was about," joked a watching Rough with a playful grin. "If I was fit, I'd be across in no time at all."

Scarlet, relieved to see they were safely across, joined in the fun too. "I'm sure you would, Rough, in one leap and a bound," she added gleefully.

Meanwhile across the other side, Izzy had led the way up a small embankment to where a multitude of different species of multi-coloured plants grew in abundance. "Here you go, Rusty. This is what we've come looking for and I know the right ones to pick so follow me," she said with confidence. They went about their work. Within a few short minutes, they had picked the herbs Willard had requested and she busily packed them into a side pouch on her belt. "Mission accomplished." She beamed as she packed the last one away. "Come on, let's get back to the others. If we hurry, we can get back to the cottage in time for supper," she promised. And with that, she again made light work of crossing the bridge once more and leapt off the last slat with an effortless bound.

Rusty was delighted to see Izzy had made it across safely and smiled to himself watching her greeted warmly by the others. "Now my turn," he said to himself. He was just about to cross when suddenly he heard a noise directly behind him. It was the unmistakable sound of the snap of a trodden twig. An unwanted shiver ran down his spine. He spun around immediately to be faced by a most fearsome sight. Standing before him was a large, pale creature glaring wildly at him. It was much taller than him, its long white straggly hair hanging over a gaping hungry-looking mouth.

Then, with one swift movement, it reached out quickly and gripped him tightly in its mighty grasp. Snatching him up easily, it then turned and carried him off snarling and growling as it went, as the others watched on helplessly and a horrified Scarlet was left frozen in shock.

"What. Just. Happened? What was that?" she cried in alarm.

"I'm afraid that was trouble I was hoping to avoid," Izzy replied solemnly. "It's a creature that lives high in the hills. The inhabitants of the pine trees call it the spirit of the woods. But I believe in the Great Wood, you know it by a different name. You know it as the bogeyman."

CHAPTER ELEVEN

"I just don't get it," said a now-flustered Izzy. "The spirit never comes this far south, it's only ever been sighted up in the hills before, and scant sightings by a few spooked animals aren't a reliable source, are they? That's why I didn't warn you about it because before now, I wasn't sure it even existed," she said with a downcast look.

"It's not your fault," insisted Scarlet, reaching out to console her. "We've heard the strange tales too." She was trying to stay strong as tears welled in her eyes. She took a moment to compose herself, wiped away her tears and firmly said. "I'll go after him. After all, that's what he'd do for me." But Izzy had different ideas.

"Scarlet, you can trust me," Izzy said turning to her.

"It must be me who goes, and goes alone. I travel quicker by myself and I'm the best tracker in these parts. Go with Chance. He'll take good care of you both and escort you to our home. You'll both be safe there amongst friends until our return. And it will give Rough time to recuperate too," she reasoned sensibly. Scarlet mulled it over for a second before coming to a swift decision.

"Alright if you insist," she agreed reluctantly, knowing Izzy's plan made the most sense and had the best chance for success. "But I promise you this. If any harm comes to either of you I'll seek revenge, on that you can be sure," she said firmly.

"I'm sure you would," replied Izzy. She hadn't known Scarlet for long, but it was enough to know she truly meant it. Now in agreement, Izzy turned to face the bridge again.

"Well, I'll be off then," she said chirpily. And with a final 'see you soon,' immediately sprang into action and being fleet of foot, was across the bridge, again in no time at all.

"Good luck and safe return," Scarlet called, not sure if her echoed shout was heard, as Izzy disappeared quickly out of sight into the underbrush and beyond. She delved into her pocket and fished out the acorn Rusty had given her earlier that day. She gave it a tight squeeze and put it back for safe keeping, hoping that it would bring them good fortune and bring him back safely to her.

Meanwhile, Izzy had picked up the trail with ease as the beast's big tracks could be seen heading away up the hill. She immediately set off in swift pursuit.

Rusty hadn't moved for quite a while now as he tried to make sense of what had happened. He knew that he had been abducted by a brute but why, and for what reason? The thought had crossed his mind that he was about to be killed and eaten, and he knew he had to keep his wits about him if he had any chance of survival at all. Initially, he'd struggled with all his might to try and break free from his captor but all this had earned him was a hefty strike and an angry growl. The creature suddenly came to a halt and held him even tighter now, before force-feeding him a strange sweet-tasting liquid from a small bottle by forcing it deep into Rusty's mouth.

Rusty gagged on it at first and held his breath, trying not to swallow for fear of being poisoned, but he had little choice in the matter as the brute held firm, so he gave in to his demands and swallowed hard taking in air and the liquid in equal amounts. The beast now seemed satisfied as Rusty's body went limp and marched determinedly on. Rusty tried to take in his surroundings hoping to remember the way back to the bridge but it all became a blur as the world began to close in on him. And then the realization of what had actually happened sank in. I must have been drugged or worse were his final thoughts, before his whole world went dark.

Rusty awoke with a start. Where am I? he thought as his confused gaze fell on a darkened ceiling. Looking around, he could see that he was lying on a bed of filthy straw. He shook his head in an attempt to clear it and slowly sat up. To his disbelief, he found himself in a small dark space and in front of him bars ran from wall to ceiling, caging him in. Then the smell hit him, the stench of a place that had not been cleaned out for weeks. He was lying on his front and as such, could not see a great deal so steeling himself, he unsteadily got up and edged towards the cage bars. Peering through them, he could now make out he was in a blackened room and in the distance was a solitary door with an edge of daylight creeping from under its length.

As his eyes began to slowly clear he could see that all around him from floor to ceiling were other enclosures identical to his, stacked on high, running the length and breadth of each wall. Each one had bars like his with a hinged door at the front fitted with identical big padlocks. It was then he realised that he was not alone.

Each enclosure was filled with various animals of the Brow. Rabbit, fox, mouse, hedgehog and more, all caged just like him. Then he saw the cages on the back wall were filled with birds. Crow, raven, blackbird, starling, geese, thrush and many others. all locked away too. But the oddest thing of all was they all stayed strangely silent, just staring blankly from out of their terrible captivity. Then the beast appeared.

The only door to the room swung open with a crash instantly bathing the room in daylight. The brute stood there for a second, its menacing silhouette made all the creatures shrink back in their cages. Advancing forward, it spoke.

"What's the matter, little squirrel? Never seen a man before?" he growled.

Rusty could see him properly for the first time. Fear ran through him. Even though it was not the bogeyman that stood before him, the situation was still dire. He was in the dwelling of a man. The first man he'd ever seen in his life. The man was tall and wiry dressed in little more than filthy rags. His long straggly unkempt grey hair and beard framed a gaunt hollow-cheeked hostile face.

The man leaned in closer and broke out into a wide grin showing off his badly yellowed teeth, and a rancid odour, which hung in the air could only have come from not having washed for months.

"Well, I might as well introduce myself," he said staring into the cage intensely, as if never having seen a squirrel before. "My name is Finnegan." He straightened up and began to pace up and down the room, his eyes darting madly to and fro as if seeking the company of others. "I suppose you're wondering why I'm here, little one," he said, his mad gaze settling back on Rusty. "Well, I'll tell you. I'm from the mainland, you see, but I couldn't take being amongst the presence of the rest of them anymore!" he spat in disgust. "What with their greed, arrogance, selfishness and love of war, I'd had enough!" he continued, flailing his arms around wildly. "I had great ideas and dreams, you see. But would they listen? No! They just wanted to steal them. Steal them and my riches, all for themselves!" he ranted. "They even locked me up and accused me of being insane. How dare they!" he bellowed, his bloodshot eyes bulging wildly. "So on my release, I came here by boat to live alone, and built my secret hideaway to continue my work in solitude away from prying eyes, and let them get on with it. To self-destruct. And oh yes, they did a good job of that too, the fools!" he said shrieking with laughter.

"Man's inhumanity to man, eh?" He then seemed a little less agitated as he came to a halt once more. "I suppose you're wondering why I brought you here. Well, my little friend, the outcome will be up to you. Behave, and when I leave this place a rich man and finally go home, you can be a part of my collection, have a new home in my private menagerie. But cause me trouble, and you'll end up on the menu!" he snarled, getting angry once more and pointing out a large old stained cooking pot which stood in the centre of the room. He threw his hands in the air in a show of frustration.

"Pah! Why am I wasting my breath talking to a dumb animal like you? You obviously don't understand a word I'm saying," he said feeling vexed with himself. He stopped in full flow and his face lit up as a new thought entered his mind. "Hmm, time for a little fun," he sniggered. "I've heard that reds don't mix well with others of your kind. Well, there's only one way to find out!"

He abruptly reached down and unlocked a cage underneath him with a key which hung from a bunch around his neck. He reached in and pulled out the animal that was kept within. Straightening up, he briskly unlocked Rusty's cage and threw it in. "Now then, you two behave or be in my next stew!" he threatened and left the room cackling loudly.

An alarmed Rusty took a long look hard look at the new arrival that was now sharing his space. It was another squirrel. But much bigger than him. And it was a grey.

CHAPTER TWELVE

Rusty instinctively backed away from the new arrival. He couldn't quite believe it. Not only had he been abducted by a madman, he was now sharing his captivity with a real-life grey! The newcomer was taller and bigger than him, his tattered tunic hanging loosely from his malnourished large frame.

He came over to Rusty, slowly closing the gap between them and seemed to be studying him closely through dark intense eyes. Was he making a judgement call? Does he want to fight me? If that was the case there would only be one winner, thought a bewildered Rusty, still groggy and therefore unable to defend himself.

The grey came within touching distance and stood over him, his intentions impossible to read. Then all at once, he stuck out a welcoming paw along with a huge grin.

"How are you? Pleased to meet you," came the friendly greeting. "My name's Ash. What's yours?"

Without thinking too much about it, Rusty held out his own paw and felt the firm grip of the newcomer as he shook it vigorously.

"I'm Rusty," he heard himself saying, still feeling not quite himself.

"Well, I suppose you're thinking, what am I doing in these parts?" asked Ash, as he walked away and peered through the cage bars checking to see if the coast was clear.

"I suppose I am," Rusty replied slowly still trying to shake off the stupor he was in.

"Well, I'll tell you then," said the larger grey eagerly. "For after all, we've got all the time in the world. I'll start at the beginning. I'm from the mainland," he began, looking visibly more relaxed seeing that Finnegan was not in the vicinity.

"I'm an adventurous type, you see, and I'd heard tales of this island all my life. I'd seen man's boats head out on the water coming this way on many occasions. So one day I spotted an opportunity that I just couldn't resist. It was a small sailing ship that surely seemed to be going in the right direction so I hopped on board, stayed unseen, hidden away, and waited till it got near, then leapt over the side and swam the last bit. I'm a good swimmer, see?" he said assuredly as Rusty watched and listened to give him time to assess his new cellmate. But he had determined one thing already. He couldn't be a danger after all. Surely if he was going to attack, he would have done it by now? he reasoned, as Ash continued his tale.

"I'd only been here a few days and was just finding my way around when I got captured just like you must have been," Ash said with one eye still watching out for Finnegan.

Rusty then broke his silence. "How long have you been here for?" he asked curiously.

"Too long," replied Ash with a sigh. "Maybe half a year or so."

Rusty was aghast. "Half a year, that's forever!" he wailed raising his paws to his face in disbelief. He felt panic welling up inside him. "I can't stay here. I've got a family and friends to get back to. They also need me to succeed because—"

He quickly stopped himself from saying more about his reason for being here. It wouldn't be wise to tell all to a stranger he'd only just met. But one thing he did know for sure, he wanted freedom. "I need to escape," he then added defiantly.

Ash noting this made his way over to his side. "A word of advice, my friend. You need to take care. I've seen a few like yourself, keen to get out," Ash warned. "They ran alright, but he's crafty and caught them all. Yes, they escaped alright. Straight into his pot! He lays traps, you see. And they're caught, just like that!" he said dramatically with a sharp clap of his paws to demonstrate.

Rusty, his mind now beginning to clear, shuddered at the thought of their grisly fate.

"Oh, and another thing, don't drink the water," Ash said pointing to a container filled with liquid attached to the cage door. "He puts something in it. Makes them less rebellious, more compliant," he said with a glance at the rest outside. "I took one taste on day one, knew it didn't taste right being so sweet. So I took one look at our captive friends to confirm my suspicions and made myself sick. He's brought me fresh rain water from then on. Doesn't like to lose his collection you see, unless he deems otherwise. Because of that I'm the only one here who knows what day it is," he said with a wink and a tap to the temple.

To Rusty it now started to make sense. "That explains a lot. He forced me to drink it on the way here," he conceded.

Ash simply nodded and then grasping the bars, took another look outside before continuing. "You've probably noticed the vagabond is always talking to himself in 'man babble'. Too much time alone without his own kind, if you ask me. I have no idea what he's saying, it's all gibberish to me," he said with a shrug of his shoulders.

"His name is Finnegan," replied Rusty without thinking.

"What? How do you know that? Have you met him before?" Ash asked wheeling around in astonishment.

"No, he told me. He told me his name."

"You mean you understand the babble? How can that be?"

"I don't know. I've never heard a man talk before, but I understood every word he said. Don't you?"

"Listen, Rusty, can I call you that?" Ash asked with a look of concern. Rusty nodded. "I've never met an animal who can understand man before and I don't get why you can, but I wouldn't tell the rest, they're already scared enough. They don't need anything else to worry about and some are a superstitious lot you see. They believe in witchcraft and other such things. I've heard some of them talking, best not to worry them more."

Rusty quietly agreed. He knew Ash had survived on his wits for months now so listening to his tips for survival were important if he wanted to escape. Ash still on the lookout then spoke again.

"A word of warning. Don't let this Finnegan know you understand him. He's dangerous, a loose cannon, the less he knows the better. Got it?"

"Yes, I understand completely," Rusty replied solemnly.

"Good, hopefully I've helped you survive a bit longer in here." Ash smiled before looking edgy once more. "Listen, he's a creature of habit so he'll be back soon as it's time for his usual afternoon nap. Best not make a fuss, he's got a short fuse, real bad-tempered as you may have noticed. And he tends to wake up hungry. Hopefully he's got fresh meat from his traps when he returns," he added optimistically. And then, just as Ash had predicted, on cue, Finnegan re-entered the room as Ash retreated to the back of the cage in fear.

"You lot, not a noise or you'll regret it!" he growled before stretching out on a bed of straw and within seconds fell fast asleep snoring loudly.

"Did you notice?" whispered a worried Ash into Rusty's ear.

"Notice what?" came the confused reply.

"He came back empty-handed. I've told you he's a creature of habit," said a fearful Ash. "He always wakes up hungry. And that can mean only one thing. One of us will fill his pot tonight."

CHAPTER THIRTEEN

Rusty felt a wave of despair wash over him. Reality began to sink in as Ash stayed on watch. He surveyed the sea of desperate faces staring blankly from their captivity with growing concern. They've been here for goodness knows how long now. And now I'm going to share their fate, he thought forlornly. I may never see Scarlet again. And what about the Great Wood? That's under threat too, he reminded himself as he sank back with his head in his hands in despair.

In desperation he instinctively reached for his short sword on his belt, but to his dismay it was gone, surely confiscated by the madman. Suddenly from above the cage, he heard a noise like the tip tapping of little feet and a figure appeared, hanging upside down, gazing bright-eyed into his enclosure. He recognised immediately who it was.

"Izzy, it's you!" he whispered excitedly. "How did you find me?" he gasped with shock.

"Oh, it's easy when you're the best tracker on the island, or so they say," she replied quietly with a cheeky grin.

Meanwhile Ash observed her warily. He'd had a previous encounter with a pine marten back home. They'd come across each other one night in the woods. Ash, accused of trespassing, got into a squabble with the pine and came off second best. He'd found they were ferocious fighters and he didn't want a repeat of that, so edged away from the larger new arrival.

"It's your lucky day, I'm here to break you out," Izzy declared brightly. She swiftly spun around and began to study the sturdy padlock on the cage door. But she was immediately disappointed. "I won't be getting this off in a hurry," she said softly after scrutinising the lock.

"I don't suppose you know where the key is?" she asked more in hope than expectation.

"Well, there's good news and bad news," Rusty replied truthfully. "The good news is there is a key, the bad news it's hanging on a chain around our host's neck," he said pointing out the sleeping figure of Finnegan, still snoring loudly flat on his back.

"Oh him? I spotted him as soon as I entered the room," she remarked with a look of indifference. Rusty couldn't tell if this act of not caring was for bravado or not, but he did know one thing for sure, just being in her presence certainly helped lift his spirits. Izzy then looked down, spied the set of keys, and made a quick decision. "Don't go anywhere. I'll be back in a jiffy."

With that, and without further ado, she flipped acrobatically and with an impressive mid-air somersault landed silently at the sleeping man's feet as the rest of the room watching on in awe, transfixed at the drama unfolding before them. Even though they were still under the influence of the sedated water, this was the most alive they had felt in months.

Izzy carefully edged her way around his sleeping form, knowing waking him would be a disaster, with every animal's eyes in the room firmly fixed on her, silently willing her on.

Finnegan, still lying flat on his back, was out to the world with his chest heaving in and out with each noisy breath. As the keys that hung around his neck had slipped to the side and lay tantalisingly close, Izzy studied them closely. She could see they were made from wrought iron with a looped bow at one end and a three-pronged bit at the other, in order to release the mechanism of the padlock. It's now or never, she thought. She turned quickly, gave Rusty a paws up, took a deep breath, grabbed them and slowly began to lift the bunch as the whole room held their breath as one.

She began to edge the keys upwards, slowly, ever so slowly along the chain in order to get them over his sleeping head. She was making good progress with the keys lifted up just past his nose, when he stirred and gave out a loud groan, as his eyes fluttered like the wings of a butterfly. She froze to the spot. Was he about to waken? She didn't dare to move for what seemed like an eternity with the keys held firmly in mid-air. She was strong but they were heavy too. How long could she keep this up? she thought, as her arms began to tire. Then he again began to breathe slowly, settling back into a deep noisy rhythm.

Phew, thought Rusty watching the drama unfold from on high. "Come on, you're nearly there," he urged under his breath.

"There's one thing I'll say," said Ash standing next to him watching on with growing admiration. "Your friend's one brave girl, I'll give her that."

Down below, Izzy made one last almighty effort. She pulled and tugged and finally lifted the keys over his head with a triumphant smile. Izzy nimbly clambered back up to the cage holding Rusty and Ash. On the bunch there were six identical-looking keys. She tried the first one but to no success, it didn't fit, it was the wrong key. She tried a second, and much to her delight, success. It opened!

She flung the door open and stood their smiling happily. Rusty had never felt so relieved in all his life.

"Izzy, I can't put into words how I feel, but thank you. Thank you so much!" he said gratefully.

"Oh, don't worry about it," she said delightfully, brushing him away. "It was no problem at all." She urged them on. "Come on, let's make our escape!" She was eager to head back the way she had come. But Rusty hesitated.

"One minute," he said gravely. "What about the others? Finnegan won't take this lightly. I've seen his temper. They will all pay a terrible price."

"He's right," agreed Ash readily. "We can't leave them behind. Not like this."

Izzy knew deep down inside they were right and drew up a quickly thought-out plan.

"Rusty, come with me. One by one we'll free the captives. Ash, wait by the door. Once all are free, give a signal. A raised paw will do. We'll instruct them all to wait for that."

So Rusty and Izzy did just that as Ash took his place. Going from cage to cage, they undid each lock one at a time informing the captives to remain calm and quiet until everyone was free.

Finally, after what seemed like an age, the last door was opened. Ash waiting for that very moment, then gave the signal. It had all gone smoothly up until now. But then there was a problem. A big problem.

CHAPTER FOURTEEN

All thoughts of leaving in a quiet and orderly fashion vanished quickly into thin air. With their adrenalin now in full flow, one, then two, and then a third animal, after feeling the first taste of freedom in a long time, panicked and bolted for the open door. One large hare in particular leapt down and landed firmly from on high onto Finnegan's sleeping chest with a thump, before bounding off to freedom.

Finnegan sat up with a start, shaking his head with confusion. More of the jailed occupants, now realising it was a free-for-all, filled the air with screams and shouts as they all fled for their lives.

Pandemonium reigned as the room became filled with clouds of dust, feathers and escapees.

"No, my beautiful collection!" Finnegan wailed as he leapt to his feet. He tried to grab a fleeing goose but it managed to evade him and dance away with glee. He quickly whirled around and saw amongst the mayhem Rusty and Izzy side by side, standing in the doorway of the last cage to be opened, urging the remaining frightened few too scared to leave to flee. As the stragglers, two field mice, finally made a run for it now was the time to make their move.

"Go, go, go!" yelled Izzy, spying Finnegan had spotted them, and frantically grabbed Rusty by the paw. But it was too late as he swiftly slammed the door on them and began fumbling at the lock.

"It was you, pine marten, you're not one of my menagerie. You set them free!" he raged, seeing the keys lying at her feet. He held the door firmly shut with one hand trapping them both inside. "Play nice and I won't hurt you, I promise," he cackled. Ash looked up and seeing their dilemma, leapt straight into action. Without any thought for his own safety, he ran forward, bared his teeth, and bit down hard on Finnegan's ankle.

"Ow, Ow, Ow!" he wailed in self-pity, and spun around to find his assailant, taking his hand off the cage door as he did.

"Now! Let's go!" urged Izzy, kicking the door back open, taking Rusty by the paw once more, and leaping down. They hit the ground running and ducked smartly between Finnegan's legs as he reached out in desperation, grabbing only thin air.

"Get back here!" he demanded as his grasp missed them by the smallest of margins, but without looking back, they sprinted out of the door as fast as their legs could carry them. Finnegan was now fuming and rushed out after them as creatures darted off in all directions, with the birds taking to flight, off into the air and away to freedom.

"Come on, this way, through the trees!" urged Ash as they scampered off, trying to put as much distance between them and Finnegan as they could. But seeing this, made Finnegan's heart soar.

"That's it, my beauties, head straight for my traps!" he exclaimed in glee. But Rusty heard it all.

"Stop, immediately!" he cried putting his arms across them.

"There's danger ahead!" He could see directly in front of them lay a tripwire and snare craftily hidden in the thick green foliage. Barely visible, but luckily he'd seen it thanks to Finnegan's rant. "Let's go, straight up into the trees, now!"

Finnegan stopped dumbfounded in his tracks as he observed Rusty's actions. "Wait a minute, you understood me didn't you, little one. But how. How could that be?" he said throwing his arms up in despair. "If that's so," he went on, "you're special, really special. The pride of my collection and I'm not losing you, not for anything!" He then began to make chase after them.

High up above, the three were easily making headway with Izzy remembering the best way back and before long, they spied the old bridge directly below.

"Come on, follow me. There's no time to waste!" she urged as they descended down quickly. Once on the ground, and without hesitation, they scurried quickly across as the bridge swung and groaned dangerously beneath them. Once across, they all stood and embraced each other and then turned to see the hapless figure of Finnegan standing there breathless, hands on hips on the other side. He called out across the void.

"Tell me, little one, do you really understand me? Don't worry, you win, I give up," he said lifting his hands in defeat. "I just need to know. Raise one paw if so."

"What's the man babbling on about now?" asked Ash to Rusty. "Oh, it's nothing really, he's finally given up the chase,"

came the relieved reply. Rusty then looked across at him for one last time as a new emotion swept over him like an incoming tide. Instead of fear or loathing, he now felt sorry for him. Finnegan looked a sorry sight, standing there in his abject misery so Rusty did as he asked and raised one paw in a wave of goodbye.

Finnegan was stunned. "What! I don't believe it. You do understand me after all!" he called out in shock. "No one will ever believe me back home," he moaned. He then made his move. "Get back here you, you're mine!" he screamed out in pure desperation. Determined to regain his prized asset, he rushed headlong across the failing bridge.

"No, get back! It's not safe," Rusty implored as the bridge rocked and swayed dramatically. But Finnegan wasn't in the mood to listen, his face now reddened and contorted with rage. He made it halfway across before it gave out one final despairing groan as if saying goodbye to the world.

The bridge then snapped and broke fatally in two. It fell away at once leaving Finnegan floundering, his arms flailing madly, clawing at thin air.

"Nooooooo!" he cried out in vain, but was lost, falling down into the deep chasm below and to his certain doom.

CHAPTER FIFTEEN

Izzy marched on heading for the pine marten trail and before too long, they came to a natural clearing where a small group of figures sat around a camp fire, warming themselves in the welcoming glow of the flickering flames. As they got closer, Rusty could now make out the unmistakable figure of Rough sitting next to Scarlet and Chance amongst them. The rest of the gathering were pine martens, all clad in green, enjoying an evening meal, busily chatting amongst themselves, including Izzy's best friend Tricky.

Scarlet looked up first. She saw their approach, leapt to her feet, and immediately ran over to Rusty and gave him a huge hug.

"You're safe!" she cried in delight, squeezing him joyfully like she'd never let him go.

"Yes, and I'm fine, honestly," Rusty replied, so relieved to see his wife too. Scarlet then turned to Izzy.

"Thank you for rescuing him. How will I ever repay you?" she asked gratefully.

"Oh, it's fine, don't worry about it. It's all in a day's work," Izzy replied merrily. Rough had now joined them too, but his eyes were fixed firmly on the stranger, Ash.

"Hi Rust. Glad you're okay. What's this trouble I see?" he said with a grimace.

"Stand down, Rough. It's fine. This is Ash, he's a friend and without him we would never have got away," assured Rusty.

"Okay, Rust, if you say so," replied Rough, reluctantly giving him the benefit of the doubt and trusting his friend's judgment.

Izzy, sensing the tension between them, made an offer they couldn't refuse.

"Come on over to the campfire, you're more than welcome. There's always enough food to go round at a pine marten spread," she said cheerfully.

"You don't have to ask me twice," replied Rough forgetting the newcomer immediately, as he hurriedly retook his place and refilled his plate.

After feasting on homemade crumble with the thickest crust they had ever seen, followed by a huge sponge cake filled with jam, and finally a delicious trifle, they sat around drinking lots of hot tea feeling really stuffed. As they relaxed by the fireside, Izzy regaled them all with the tale of Finnegan's den.

She began with their escape and helping all the others to go free, through to his final demise at the bridge, as they all listened on in silence. And then, as she finished, they all broke out in cheers and wild applause. She hadn't quite expected that, but the adulation certainly felt good.

"Well, after hearing that, I can't say I'm sorry he's gone," said Rough emphatically after the cheering subsided. "He sounds like a nasty piece of work that got his comeuppance if you ask me," he said before reaching for a last piece of pie. His opinion was met with a murmur of approval, and even Rusty couldn't disagree.

The day was nearing its end now as the sun began to sink on the horizon in a haze of brilliant red and orange, Mother Nature's work at its stunning best.

"I insist you all stop for the night," offered Izzy as the light began to fail. "It's getting dark and the bats from the ravine will be out soon," she said with a look of concern. "They've been acting a bit agitated of late, so it's best to avoid them if possible."

"Thanks, that's very kind of you," replied Scarlet graciously. "But what of Willard? He'll be expecting us and may worry when we haven't returned."

"I can go there and inform him," said Chance, brief and to the point as usual. And it's a good excuse to see my old friend Screech, he thought to himself, smiling inwardly as he prepared to fly away.

The pine martens' homes were located high in the trees. With the help of local beavers, they had built small wooden cabins way up high in the canopy. You could reach them by long rope ladders, which they hauled up at night for safety from any possible threat, although any would be interloper would be foolish to take on the pine martens in their own domain.

The cabins were well constructed as beavers made the best carpenters. They were uniform in design and had slanted roofs with two small windows either side of a stout front door. Inside there was hand crafted furniture for dining and entertaining, and hammocks hung from the ceiling where the pines spent the night. Each cabin always had an extra hammock or two for guests, as they were well-known in these parts for their hospitality. It was also known that if you made a friend of them, it was a friend for life. But make an enemy and the same would also be true.

After an uneventful night, they were up early and were soon tucking into a big breakfast of porridge oats and toast, with scrumptious homemade jam and of course lots of tea.

"Before you leave," Izzy said to them "I'd like to show you something that I'm sure you'll find of interest. It's a cave. It's not far and it won't take long. I'll explain it all when we get there," she said mysteriously.

They finished their meal and were now intrigued to see the curious cavern, so at mid-morning, they set off and before long approached a cliff wall jutting out from a nearby hillside. Cut into its face like a huge jagged scar was a fissure, large and black, running vertically through it.

"Come on, follow me. It's this way," said Izzy and squeezed in between the gap in the rock. Scarlet, Rusty and Ash came next, squeezing in through the darkened void.

"Hold on a minute, wait for me!" said Rough who being the widest by far, had to turn side-on and breathe in deeply.

With a lot of effort and much grunting, he just about managed to get through, luckily without getting stuck.

"I made it, though it's not exactly a badger-sized gap," he grinned as he appeared out again on the other side.

He found himself standing in a large cavern. The cave had high walls, its ceiling lost in the inky darkness. It was compact and roughly square in size and was illuminated by a lantern held by Izzy, which she had picked up by the entrance, which was always left there for the use of any visiting pine.

"If you're wondering why I've brought you here, I'm sure you'll find it fascinating, so please all step this way," she said and headed over to the nearest wall. She then held up the lantern and it lit up the cold black surface.

Previously unseen images now flickered into life, strange paintings the likes of which they'd never seen before in their life. Before their eyes they could now make out images of men painted in deep ochre carrying spears, hunting down a large furry horned animal.

"Our clan has been visiting this cavern since time immemorial," explained Izzy, "and therefore the paintings you see are special to us." She then lifted the lantern higher. "As you can see, ancient man is chasing down its prey. I believe the creature to be an elephant," she said. "The migrating birds talk of seeing them in far-off lands, but this one seems to have fur for some unknown reason."

She then moved on further down the length of the cave and held up the lamp to show more of the same: scenes of men hunting various other animals, bears and deer, now painted in ochre and white. As they reached the rear wall, more artwork came into view. Running down its length from left to right was a line of white painted man-sized hand prints, left by artists now long departed.

"Now let me show you more," she said as she held up her lantern once more. Again, it showed men with weapons drawn in what at first appeared to be yet another hunting scene. But as more of the mural came to light, they could now make out it was a battle scene that played out before their eyes. Man against man in mortal combat.

"As you can see, they are war-like, destructive and cannot live in harmony, even with their own kind," she said ominously. "It was Willard himself who personally asked me to bring you here and show you all this final work." She turned to the portrayal on the wall behind her. It depicted another great conflict but this time it was not man in battle but animals of the wood and field with weapons at the ready, including sword and bow, bearing down on each other.

"We don't know who painted this final scene," she explained, "as it asks more questions than answers. Is this a vision of the future?

The Olde ones of our clan have always thought so. If correct, it seems that our destiny is to be no better ourselves," she warned.

Later that day, Willard sat cross-legged waiting patiently on his porch on the top step. He felt quite content knowing that the quest had been a success. Chance had delivered the message, but the foresight had already told him so. So now he felt at ease. He had been concerned for their welfare. He couldn't help it, it was in his nature to worry.

"You're a born warrior," Screech had told him in the past.

"Don't you mean worrier?" he'd joked in return.

He knew what loss felt like. He'd lost friends and loved ones before in previous struggles and didn't want a repeat of that. Rusty had sought his advice true, but it was he who had sent them on a journey. So he began to relax now sensing that Rusty and the others drew near. And sure enough, as he sat sipping his tea, he saw their approach as they came into view through the trees. A welcome sight indeed, which pleased him greatly.

Screech standing in the doorway just behind him spotted them too and gave out a loud groan.

"Oh no. Before you ask, I'll go and fill the tea trolley again. I do everything around here," he moaned, and sloped off back to the kitchen, hunched over mumbling and grumbling as he went.

"You know your tea trolley is always a delight for all to see," Willard called after him as he knew Screech didn't mind really. He just enjoyed 'a good old-fashioned grumble', as Screech put it. He then turned his attention back to the tired-looking travellers Rusty, Scarlet, Rough, Ash and Izzy.

"I take it your enterprise was a success and hopefully not too trying?" he asked with a sincere smile.

"Hi Willard. Yes, we got the herbs you asked for but I've got to say, it wasn't easy," admitted a weary-looking Rusty, glad to be back at the cottage.

"Yeah, you might say we've had an adventure or two," added Rough with a grin.

"Ah, very good. I knew you wouldn't fail. And I must say your timing is impeccable as you're just in time for refreshments," came the well-received reply.

Just on cue the unmistakable trundle of Screech's freshly laden tea trolley could now be heard.

"You must be hungry after your endeavours," said Willard. "Please, join us for refreshments and tell all of your expedition. Come inside, I insist. Chance is already seated and awaits us to join him," he urged as he got up from his seat on the top step and waved them in.

Rough led the way eagerly with the rest following in his wake, rushing to take a seat at the dining table.

"I don't need asking twice," he said gleefully rubbing his paws in delight at the thought of the mouth-watering treats that were to come.

"Well, I must say, Screech, that was top quality as always. The best on the island, without doubt," said Willard, as every last morsel had been consumed.

"Well, I'm not surprised really, I get plenty of practise don't I?" muttered Screech pushing the empty trolley away. Now out of sight he smiled to himself secretly satisfied his food had gone down a treat. As always.

Willard then stood and raised his tea cup to make a toast.

"I'm pleased to hear of your success and would like to extend my gratitude to Izzy, Chance and Ash too for their endeavours and fortitude. Well done, one and all!" They all smiled gratefully. Willard seemed distracted and put down his cup, heading for the open fire that had been set that morning. He was very particular about it. Even in the summer months when receiving guests, which didn't happen that often, he always insisted on a freshly lit fire. 'It gives off a welcoming aura', he always said. Willard tutted to himself as he noticed its glow diminishing, and threw on another log.

"Hah, much better," he said to no one in particular, as the flame rekindled and burst back into life before turning back to his visitors.

"Now, please hand over the herbs you obtained, if you will," said Willard as he made his way over to a side cabinet.

He opened the top drawer and pulled out a brown backpack that lay within, along with a small brown paper parcel tied with string. The bag had been sewn together in their absence by Screech, another one of his many skills. It was handmade to squirrel size from spare fabric, with a buckle fastening for the flap of the back compartment, and two looped straps to fit over the shoulder.

As he returned to the table, Izzy reached into her side pouch hanging from her belt and produced the foraged plants and handed them over to him. Willard thanked her with a smile, and proceeded to place them inside the bag. He then opened up the small package which contained the other items he needed. He took out the badger fur taken from Rough, and the glow stones from Ursa's lair, and placed them inside.

"Rusty, you must wear this or keep it by your side at all times," he insisted. "It will surely ward off the spell that has been cast and deter any more interference and infiltration from afar."

Rusty took the bag gratefully and placed it over his shoulders.

It was a nice snug fit.

"But beware, you must stay vigilant, for I fear the threat is far from diminished. You have witnessed the cavern and the paintings within?"

"Yes, we did," confirmed Rusty. "Though I'm not really sure what to make of them," he freely admitted.

"My friend, it's a mystery that transcends the years," Willard began to explain. "Do the paintings tell of a certain prophecy of turmoil and unrest? And if so, who will rise to the challenge and lead the way to resist. Who can say?" he mused. "One thing is certain. The island has a history of upheaval, old and new, of which I myself know all too well." He sighed. "So please know this. We must be ready for all eventualities," he warned. He then turned his attention solely to Rusty.

"I know there are more questions to ask, such as why you understand the tongue of man," he conceded. "But this and more will be revealed to you all in good time."

Before Rusty could ask more, Willard rose again and began tending the fire with an old iron poker.

"And do forgive me as I have a tendency to go on at times. Visitors are a rarity you see and I enjoy the company. Hopefully they enjoy mine too." He laughed. "Now I insist you all stay for the night. We have blankets and pillows to spare. Continue your journey home on the 'morrow. It will be much safer that way."

"Great stuff, but I've got one question." said Rough.

"Please my friend, ask away."

"I don't suppose there'll be a big breakfast going in the morning will there?" Rough asked hopefully.

They heard a familiar huge groan coming from the kitchen.

CHAPTER SIXTEEN

Slate slumped back on his throne staring out dismally through the huge cracked window of the abandoned mill with its view across the bay. The sky outside was leaden grey. A storm was brewing which matched his mood. In the distance, the Isle of Badgers Brow could be seen. So near but yet so far. Just out of reach as if it were taunting him. Look but don't touch. Slate wasn't known for his patience. Far from it. Of which he had made himself abundantly clear on countless occasions. He was used to always getting his way, and he wanted it all and he wanted it now. And his patience had finally run out.

"Well, where is he? I sent for the Elder ages ago and he's not here yet!" he yelled kicking over his footstool sending it flying across the floor. The nervous minion in attendance named Cadet, dressed in the standard cheap cut grey tunic with his head bowed, answered him timidly.

"He's been sent for, sire, but he lives in a hovel in the poor part of town and has no means of transport," he said before shrinking back.

Slate was less than impressed. "Don't be so impudent! No means of transport?" he raged. "He's got tiny legs, hasn't he? Why can't he run? He'll be running from the wrong end of a sword if he's not here shortly!" bellowed Slate clearly getting more agitated by the minute.

He rose from his seat and began impatiently pacing up and down with his arms tucked stiffly behind his back, cursing to himself under his breath.

Another servant, Pewter, flung open the door and burst into the room breathlessly and made an announcement.

"Ahem your majesty— Sorry to intrude," he gasped. "Your chief adviser, the Elder, has been found—"

"About time too. Otherwise, he'd be needing advice of his own. The advice of my physician!" seethed Slate.

"Yes, sire, of course," replied Pewter backing away, looking at the floor anxiously.

Slate then stopped pacing up and down and turned to stare out of the window again. At that point, the Elder finally stepped into the room wearing a worried frown. He knew it was unwise to keep the king waiting even though this was no fault of his own.

"Apologies, my liege, but I was busy concocting elixirs and potions," he said to Slate, who was standing stiffly with his back to him watching his approach in the glass pane. "The ingredients required are scattered around your kingdom and it can be rather time-consuming," he added before giving a slight bow.

"Well, that's a waste of time, Elder!" Slate spat out angrily. "Because I've got news for you, the potion you gave to me is useless. I've lost my connection with the red, it's gone! there's nothing, nothing at all," he simmered.

Oswald, taken aback, had seen this mood before and knew he had to tread carefully or face the consequences.

"I see, my liege. Now that's an interesting development, which we can use to our advantage," he said in an attempt to placate him. "They have let their guard down foolishly and revealed all. I conclude they must have outside interference."

Slate didn't answer straight away as if digesting the fresh information, and after what seemed like an age he spoke again. "Well don't just stand there, dolt. Find out who is helping

them!" he demanded. "And before you do, may I remind you I was promised you'd make my new found power permanent?"

To Oswald, he still seemed angry and still had his back to him. More work needed to calm him, he thought quickly.

"As I have previously explained, your highness, the elixir I gave you is but a temporary measure and must be taken sparingly or it will cause long-term ill effects. For after all, your wellbeing is of the utmost importance."

The king gave a slight nod. An improvement in his mood?

"Well, you seem to be able to play a trick or two without any bother, why can't I? Are you keeping something from me?" questioned Slate.

Oswald could see his eyes narrow watching him in the reflection of the glass window. The atmosphere still tense he knew he still had to pacify him. "Sire, forgive me, I'll elaborate. I have a gift from birth. It is known as the foresight. But give me more time and I will surely find a way to bestow it on you, for the elixir, my liege, is but a short-term measure."

He saw a slight shift in Slate's posture, a slacken of the shoulders. A good sign at last.

"I like the sound of that, Elder, make it happen sooner rather than later," he said his tone now less threatening. "And you mentioned interference, explain more," he insisted.

"Indeed, I believe I can, my liege. My conclusion is it can only be one who has meddled. He too has the foresight, along with Rusty the red, who is a mere novice. This Rusty must have sought him out. It's the only answer. His name is Willard the Wise."

"Never heard of him," Slate snorted still facing the window. "Tell me, Elder, can this Willard be bought out?" he asked his curiosity now piqued.

"Unfortunately not, your highness, he is boringly beyond reproach."

"Are you sure? I've never met anyone yet who has turned down the king's purse. Especially you, Elder, you didn't take much convincing at all!" Slate let out a light laugh.

A definite improvement, thought Oswald.

"Yes, sire, I am definitely sure, for I know him all too well. He is of my kind, a dormouse. In fact, we share the same blood. For Willard is my younger brother, and we have crossed swords before."

With that news, Slate spun around.

But to Oswald's great relief, he was grinning widely.

"Your brother, you say. And you fought? That's interesting. A bit of sibling rivalry, eh? Who doesn't love a good old fashioned family feud?" he smirked.

"Well, if he can't be won over, you have my permission to finish him yourself."

"Yes, sire, consider it done. It would be my utmost pleasure," said Oswald with a sly smile.

Slate had one more question. "The invasion. The plans at an advanced stage I take?"

"Indeed, sire. Your army is on a war footing as we speak."

"Excellent news. Soon, Elder, we can kill two birds with one stone. You can settle this score with your brother, and I can finally take what is rightfully mine. And let no creature dare stand in my way!"

The following morning duly arrived and much to Rough's delight, Screech had risen early and delivered up the requested big breakfast. It consisted of pancakes with syrup, porridge oats and as much jam and toast you could manage. Of course, this was all washed down with lots and lots of tea. After they had all had their fill, Willard addressed them once more.

"Well, my friends, all visits sadly come to an end and it's time you journeyed back to the Great Wood."

He then spoke to Rusty directly.

"If you seek advice, just think of me and I will be there, that I promise. The foresight will show you the way. Now do not let me delay you any longer. Screech informed me you have an annual event which needs your attention?"

"Yes, with all the excitement I'd almost forgotten, the Lowland games draw near," admitted Rusty, as a look of concern shot across his face. "We will have to double our guard and stay alert, but we can't let the islanders down, they've prepared for it for so long."

He paused for a moment and then had an exciting suggestion. "Izzy, why don't you attend? We're always looking to broaden the events," he offered genially. "We could hold an archery competition. It will be a real crowd pleaser and I'm guessing you pines might be quite good at that!" He beamed.

"You know what, I think we will," said Izzy enthusiastically. "It sounds like fun. I'll gather my kin and bring them along. Consider it done," she said with a smile.

Rusty then placed a friendly paw on Ash's shoulder.

"Ash, you join us too. We owe you. I wouldn't have escaped without you. Come along see what the Great Wood has got to offer." Ash paused for a moment and then replied.

"Well, if you're sure," replied Ash happily. "I'd like that, I'd like that a lot."

And so with that settled, they bade fond farewell and went their way, promising to stay in touch.

"You know, Screech," said Willard to his faithful companion as they both sat alone again in the now quiet cottage. "We will be seeing them again very soon. Very soon indeed."

The brown owl agreed, for he knew full well that Willard was rarely wrong.

CHAPTER SEVENTEEN

Mid-morning had arrived at the Brow and the weather had changed dramatically for the worse. Dark ominous-looking clouds now chased away the early promise of a sun-filled day as a summer storm began to roll in. Seeing that, Rusty and the others hastened their way home. After leaving Willard's cottage behind them, they again faced the imposing natural barrier of the Maleficent Meadow. But much to their relief the tunnel Rough had dug out remained solidly intact.

"Never in any doubt," Rough remarked proudly.

As quick as they could, they made their way through the excavation to emerge happily on the other side. The dark clouds were now moving in fast as the sky turned leaden grey as Scarlet urged them to hurry back before the tempest hit.

"We'd better get a move on if we don't want to get soaked," she warned, glancing up at the angry sky. So they hurried along and as they headed down Briars Road the group received lots of inquisitive looks as the animals of the Great Wood hurried by, desperate to escape the incoming weather too. Low whispers and heads came together as no one had ever seen a grey squirrel before.

"Look, it's true," whispered an elderly hedgehog named Wilf. "It's not a myth, they do exist after all." His companion, a young vole named Belle, nodded her head in silent agreement never taking her eyes off the stranger.

Next they came across Archie the fox who was sitting outside his den in his usual spot with his feet up on a stool. He gave them a leisurely wave and then hailed them.

"You took your time. Thought you'd got lost," he remarked gaily. "I was just about to send out a search party," he joked accompanied by his trademark big smile. Rusty laughed and returned the wave.

"There was no need to worry, though we have been on a bit of an adventure," he admitted. He had a lot of time for Archie. Always there when you needed a good friend. "It's a long story. Call round the house, the first chance you get," offered Rusty. "We want to get back before the storm hits," he said, casting a watchful glance at the darkening the sky. "I'll fill you in then. Promise."

"Okay, will do," came the light response.

A still curious Archie had one last question though. "I don't suppose you met the bogeyman after all?" he called out after them.

Rusty smiled. "Let's just say the mystery of the bogeyman is well and truly solved," he said before moving away, leaving Archie more confused than ever. He was definitely going to drop by as soon as possible.

Misfit, Pitter and Patter were lurking around as usual too.

"Look," grunted a startled Patter. "A grey. They've got a grey with them!" he remarked, before giving Misfit an unwanted sharp nudge in the ribs with his bony elbow, which only earned him an indignant glare.

But Misfit was now intrigued. "Very interesting," he said shiftily. "Pitter, I've got a mission for you. Prove your worth. Stay low and follow them. Report back anything out of the ordinary. You got that?"

Pitter scratched his head as he wasn't the brightest. "How will I know if what they're up to his ordinary or not?" he asked with a vacant slack-jawed look.

Misfit was exasperated. "I was going to ask are you stupid? But just one look at you tells me that!" he fumed. "Look, I'll make it simple. Just be a sneak. Got it?"

Pitter's face then immediately lit up because being a sneak came naturally to him.

"Righto, will do," he said desperate to impress. Pitter then made his move. He began to saunter along as if just out for a casual stroll, which was at odds with everyone else who scattered willy nilly as a huge clap of thunder echoed across the stormy sky.

They were nearly home when another regular of the Great Wood approached them coming the other way. He was a red squirrel too. His name was Brick and Rusty knew him well. Tall for a red, he had an air of confidence about him, and over his sturdy broad frame he wore a simple white tunic.

"Alright, Rusty?" he asked always glad to see his friend. His gaze then fell on Ash. "So who's this then? Picked up a stray?"

"Brick, this is Ash. Trust me, he's alright," assured Rusty. He looked at Brick with purpose. "Listen, I've important news to share but it's best to tell everyone at once. I'll fill you in tonight on the details," he said. Brick was now bemused.

"Yes, okay, Rust," he replied uncertainly. Brick was intrigued to know more but was willing to wait. Then another loud rumble could be heard. It was much closer this time and now accompanied by the inevitable big drops of rain as Brick glanced up to the heavens.

"This lot should blow over by tonight," said Brick. Rusty smiled. He knew for a fact it would just do that; the foresight told him so.

"The wood watch will go ahead as planned," Rusty assured him before turning to Ash. "The wood watch is an evening patrol. We take it in turns to keep an eye on the neighbourhood."

"Makes sense. You never can be too careful," agreed Ash.

Brick then moved off. "See you later, same time, same place," he said before hurriedly heading off, wondering exactly what would be revealed later.

The rain now fell heavily as Rough said his farewells too.

"I'll see you at furball training tomorrow," he said cheerily as he went on his way.

"Yes, okay, mate," replied Rusty. "And thanks for everything," he said with a broad smile.

Rough smiled back. "Wouldn't have missed it for the world. Rough beamed and went off with a skip and a bounce, not minding the rain at all, for his mind was on far more important matters. (Like what he'd have for his well-earned evening meal.)

The rain was now incessant and falling harder than ever, leaving them soaked to the skin. Then at last came the welcome sight of the old oak tree as the thunder was joined by a streak of lightning flashing across the noisy sky. Beckoning Ash to follow, they hastily climbed the steps and flung open the door to take welcome refuge from the rain.

It was only a small hollow in the tree, and they didn't own much in the way of furnishings; just a large bed, two cupboards and a set of chairs for entertaining, but to Rusty and Scarlet this was their home. After stoking up the small fireplace and drying out in its warming glow, Ash received an offer he found hard to refuse. A bed in the spare room until he got settled.

"If you're sure? I don't want to be a burden," Ash replied humbly.

"No, it's fine. Honestly. It's the least we can do," they both insisted.

Later that evening, Rusty had been proven right and the storm had abated, leaving behind a serene-looking crimson sky as the watch began to gather as usual at the allotted time. They met in the village square, which was really just a big clearing in the woods. It contained one large low-roofed wooden building on the edge of the green, which was regarded as the town hall.

In attendance were the usual group of volunteers who consisted of Rusty, Brick and three more red squirrels. They were Chilli, Madder and Cornell who were all members of the furball team too. Chilli was the eldest of the three. With an athletic build and assured look, he was a valuable member of the group. Madder and Cornell made up the rest of the crew. They too loved to keep active, their wiry frames a testimony to this, and were as loyal as they come. Now together Rusty wearing his new charmed bag, told Ash more of about what they did.

"Red watch is the squirrel branch of the local wood watch," he began. "The other watches are blue, green and yellow. We all patrol on a rota and tonight it's our turn to go out," he told the listening Ash. Rusty then spoke to the watch. They all listened in silence as he recalled the last few days. From seeking Willard's help to escaping Finnegan's den, and their arrival back home. "As you can see," he went on, "Ash has more than proven his worth. So with your consent I'd like to swear him in to red watch."

Everyone present knew the procedure. A new would-be member of the watch would have to be accepted by all and a show of paws was needed, and this had to be unanimous. One by one they all duly raised their paws leaving Brick the casting vote. He was swayed by the vote of confidence showed by Rusty and slowly lifted his too.

"Okay, good. That's settled then," said a happy Rusty. He turned to Ash and began to recite the pledge of allegiance.

> "We promise to protect all we hold good.
> And watch over the neighbourhood.
> Whether creature big or creature small,
> to lay down our lives to protect them all.

"Do you agree to this Ash? If so, say aye."

"Aye," Ash repeated at once, which was met by a resounding round of cheers.

"Right, now that's settled, tell us more about this threat. Should we be worried? Is it imminent?" questioned Brick.

Rusty answered at once. "Well, that's to be determined. But one thing is for sure. We all must be extra-vigilant that's for sure."

"I've got a question. Will this affect this year's games?" asked a concerned Chilli.

"No, not at all," said a determined Rusty. "The games must go on. Everyone has worked so hard to prepare for it so we can't let them down. If all the watches keep a sharp look out, I'm sure we will be alright."

The sun began to set in the distance behind them announcing the beginning of the end of another day. Brick prepared the brief for tonight's watch, and as captain of red watch it was a duty he was extremely proud of. He considered it to be a prestigious role as it was voted for by the other members of the watch, and so it was a duty he took very seriously. And as Brick was very particular, he liked to get every detail just right. As they stood patiently in line in front of him, he cleared his throat threw out his chest and began.

"Rusty has informed us of a possible threat," he said gravely,

in his deep gruff voice. "So we need to take it seriously and be extra vigilant from now on. Keep an eye out for anything odd or out of the ordinary, even if it seems trivial," he insisted. "Nothing can be overlooked." He paused, then walked up and down the line, like an officer inspecting his troops, making sure he'd got their full attention. Now satisfied he had it, he stopped at his original spot and continued.

"We can't be too careful, not if the safety of the Great Wood is at stake," he said as they all listened and watched him without saying a word, but all were in silent agreement, for he had their full attention. With a firm but friendly manner he had their total respect.

"I've decided we'll split up, that way we can cover more ground," he said. "Stay within sight of each other at all times and report back here." He turned his attention to Rusty. "Take Cornell with you to the north of the Wood. It's a narrow stretch there and so not too much distance to cover. Once clear, head east. Chilli, Madder, you take the south. Keep an eye on the coast line too, understood?"

"Yes, captain," came the quick response.

"Good. Ash, you're with me. We'll take the west. Stick close, I'll show you the ropes, got that?"

"Yes, no problem, captain," he promptly replied. "Like I've said, I'm here to help."

"Very good. We all understand what's needed so come on,

let's do this," said Brick with an enthusiastic clap of his paws to spur them on. Now with their new instructions firmly at the forefront of their minds, they quickly dispersed in different directions into the night.

"Right, stay close and follow me," Brick ordered and quickly headed off towards the west of the Wood with Ash keeping pace closely behind.

All this time, Pitter the brown rat had been following Misfit's directives to the letter. He had watched and listened from afar, trying to remember every detail, and already some of the conservation began to get muddled in his tiny

The Battle for Badgers Brow

mind.

"Nevermind, I'll make up what I can't remember. Misfit will never know," he mumbled to himself. Now who to follow? he thought, as they shot off separately. The decision was quickly made for him as Brick and Ash swept closely by. To his great relief, he remained unnoticed, and he waited a moment or two until he could hear Brick's deep voice far off enough in the distance. He then skulked after them.

Overhead a full moon could now be seen rising in the cloudless sky drenching the woods in its soft lunar light making things much easier to see.

"Let's head upwards," Brick said, as Pitter observed him quickly clamber one tree, then Ash another. Then, just as Pitter was about to sneak forward for a closer look, something odd happened. Ash reappeared quickly descending from his viewpoint and bolted off away from him through the trees. Pitter, taken aback at first, quickly recovered his composure and took chase, making sure to stay hidden.

After a few seconds, the woods gave way to a glade of open grass at the foot of a hillock. Ash stopped. He looked around as if to check no one was watching, and then preceded to scamper up it. At its small summit, he halted and reached into his pocket and pulled out a small object.

"What's that he's holding?" mused Pitter, too far away to see. Ash then lifted it to his mouth and blew. As the sound of birdsong filled the air, Pitter's eyes lit up. He'd seen this device before. It was a bird whistle. He's calling a bird! he thought excitedly.

Ash waited a little, then repeated his actions, and then the beat of wings could be heard. He was joined by a grumpy-looking pigeon in a short dark robe. The bird landed softly at Ash's side and they began to converse in hushed tones.

Pitter, out of ear shot, dropped to the floor and edged ever closer, desperate to eavesdrop.

"You're a difficult one to track down," he heard the pigeon say dismissively. "I've searched high and low. Nearly gave you up for dead."

"My apologies, Paulie," Ash replied. "But I was somewhat tied up."

"And what exactly is your message?" asked the pigeon tersely, still aggrieved at the long wait.

"Tell King Slate all is well and make haste his preparations. They are ill-prepared with few defences. Invade at will, the island is set for the taking," Ash informed him.

The pigeon said no more. He smartly turned away and immediately took flight, heading back to the mainland. Ash then hurried back to join Brick and make sure he'd not been missed.

Pitter was overjoyed. Not only had he remained undiscovered he'd surely have news to impress Misfit. *We have a spy in the camp!*

CHAPTER EIGHTEEN

Paulie the pigeon flew straight and true and before long, the formidable stone structure that was the residence of King Slate lay dead ahead. He could now see the familiar white large letters, still emblazoned across the front, the paintwork now faded and peeling, but still legible in metre-high print.
STEEL MILL
The abandoned workplace loomed ever closer, the machinery now silent, the workmen long gone. He landed on a crumbling brick wall to be met by two heavily armoured grey squirrels with crossed spears and serious expressions blocking his path.

"What's the password?" the one on the left grunted.

"Oh, come on. You know it's me, Paulie," the pigeon said impatiently trying to brush past them.

"I said password! You know the drill. Commander Stone insists!" growled the one on the left louder, now raising and pointing his spear at Paulie's chest. Paulie knew there was no point in arguing with him and raised his wings obligingly.

"Alright, alright," he conceded. "The password is—"

And the answer was lost on the wind.

"Correct, you may enter," the one on the right grumbled as they both stood down to let him pass. Behind them stood two old wooden doors. The guards pushed them open with much grunting and heaving, as they creaked loudly on rusty hinges. They stood aside and Paulie went in. He then entered a long candle-lit musky-smelling corridor. Damp ran down its walls through the unrepaired ceiling and puddles of rainwater gathered on the floor. Old ornate paintings of men and women, sitting and posing in their finery, were left hanging to gather dust and mould on each side of the corridor, like images of ghosts of the past.

At the end of the passageway stood two more identically dressed armed guards standing either side of another grand old door. The one on the right knocked three times on a centre wooden panel and it was immediately opened by a servant named Cadet who nervously stuck his head around the door.

"Tell the king his messenger has arrived," said the guard brusquely. Without further ado, Cadet disappeared back inside. Paulie waited patiently outside now. He knew the king was not one to be rushed and an audience with him took as long as the king decided. To his amazement, he was only waiting three hours before Cadet reappeared and ushered him In.

This wasn't Paulie's first audience with the king, far from it, but each time he entered the king's chamber it was a daunting experience as you just never knew what mood he would be in. One wrong move or word may prove to be your last.

The room itself was huge with high-walled ceilings. On its floor, old unused machinery and tools lay scattered about. Along its length stood tall windows on either side, some broken, others stained and cracked, just clean enough to let in the suns dappled light.

At the rear of the room, Slate sat staring imperiously at him perched on what used to be a boardroom chair, now his throne, the previous occupier no longer needing it, and the elite royal guard lined the route either side dressed in battle-ready armour, headed by the imposing Commander Stone standing at Slate's right-hand side with Oswald the Elder to the left.

"Well, come on then, you fool. You've kept me waiting long enough. Approach now with good news or I'll make pigeon pie out of you!" thundered an impatient Slate, as his voice echoed ominously off the high-walled room. Paulie gulped, took a big breath, and approached between the line of elite on what always seemed the longest walk of his life.

Oh, I do need to get myself another job, one with better long-term prospects, he thought to himself as he approached the throne.

"Well, come on, bird. Spit it out!" yelled Slate impatiently.

"Y-y-your highness, my deepest apologies," stammered a terrified Paulie. "I know you have been awaiting news from your scout A-a-sh, but he was apparently detained."

Slate was fuming. "Detained! How dare he be detained without my permission. I've got plenty of room in the dungeons for that!" Slate thundered. He then glared furiously before continuing. "Go on, pigeon, tell all, and it had better be good!" he demanded.

Paulie then nervously cleared his throat. "Ahem. H-h-he says all is well and to make haste. The island is ready to invade and they are ill-prepared," he said before lowering his head.

"Make haste, make haste! How dare he suggest that I should make haste! I've been awaiting half a year for this news and he tells me to hurry up!" Slate roared, banging his paws on the arms of the old chair sending dust flying into the air.

Paulie shrank back in despair. This is it, I'm on the evening royal menu now for sure, he thought as he closed his eyes awaiting imminent arrest.

All then fell silent for a moment as a hush came over the room as no one dared to move. And then Slate began to rock backward and forward laughing hysterically loud.

"Ha, ha, ha, hee, hee, hee!" he chuckled, still thumping his paws up and down but this time in glee. The whole room now broke out into fits of laughter too. No one knew what was so funny, but joined in regardless. It was safer that way.

Paulie still cowering down, dared to open one eye to peek, still unsure of his fate. And then Slate stopped laughing abruptly and silence immediately fell on the gathering, as no one ever laughed longer than he.

"Excellent work, pigeon. You have pleased me. You may now go, you live to fly another day," he said to the now frozen Paulie, too scared to move. "Well don't just stand there, off with you, shoo, shoo ,shoo! Go!" he said ushering him away.

A relieved Paulie gladly backed off, and not daring to turn his back, nearly fell over in the process. Slate, bored with the pigeon, now turned his attention to Oswald.

"It seems the prophecies of the scrolls are true then, Elder," said Slate turning to his advisor. "Now let me recall what you told me," Slate said with a rub of his chin. "Ah yes. The island is ripe for the picking, and my destiny, my birthright to rule, shall soon come to pass, and that my domain is as far as the eye can see, therefore the island is truly mine. Correct, Elder? "

"Yes, indeed, sire. That is correct," agreed Oswald, with a slight nod of acknowledgment.

Slate then gave him a hard stare. "These ancient scrolls you speak of, why have I never seen them?" he asked abruptly.

Was that suspicion that Oswald read in his eyes? He knew now he had to tread very carefully, and to now think fast, as no such scrolls had ever existed.

"My liege, they are back at my cabin which lies in the poorest part of town. They are too delicate with age to bring to the palace, but of course a royal visit to view them would be my greatest honour," he said meekly.

Slate stiffened at once. "I think not, Elder," he said sniffily.

Oswald knew only too well that Slate never entered that part of the kingdom, and smiled inwardly at how easily his ruse had worked.

Slate then sat and brooded before coming to a swift decision. "Elder, ready the troops," he'd decided. "No more dilly-dallying. We will strike at dawn. After all, I've got nothing else planned for tomorrow," he added haughtily.

But Oswald thought this too soon. He had to be ready.

"Well, your majesty," said the Elder, now picking his words very carefully. "May I suggest a slight delay? The omens would be better that way. This gained another hard stare from Slate, but he knew Oswald was learned and wise in such matters and so decided to hear him out.

"Go on then, Elder, advise me," he ordered snappily.

"A new moon is soon to rise, a blood moon my liege. This signifies new beginnings and will align with the prophecy from the aforementioned ancient scrolls."

Slate broke out into a broad grin. "And what prophecy exactly is that, Elder? Remind me again.

I do so love to hear it," he said sitting back with a smug look on his face.

"That victory without doubt will surely be yours, sire. And soon you shall claim the isle for your own."

CHAPTER NINETEEN

The furball pitch had been cut down to perfection by Vincent the goat, the groundskeeper every year now for the last ten years running, but this year he felt he'd surpassed himself. He stood there in his worn once pristine tunic, now an off-white grey, and studied it and smiled, feeling rather satisfied with the results he now saw before him.

It was hardly a tough task for him and his team of goats. Eat the grass and keep it short, or so it would seem to the casual observer, but he knew there was much more to it than that. Rain was important, but not too much. That made it muddy, so good drainage was required. Too dry made it parched and ruined the grass. So keep it watered. It had been extremely dry recently, with the exception of the recent storm, so he and his team had been busy watering the green with their watering cans to get it to grow and then nibbling away to keep it down. It had to be just to the right length for the upcoming games, and he felt he'd achieved just that. The pitch was marked out with very straight chalked white lines, and being a perfectionist, they were as straight as the crow flies. Yes, Vincent was very happy with his efforts, much better than last year. Even though last year's pitch was deemed perfect by all.

It was the last match practice before the big day, and Rough being the coach, wanted to put the team through their paces for one last time. Rusty had turned up a few minutes earlier than the rest with Ash, to show him around. He'd also offered to let him train with them as they were a player down. Garnet, the sixth member of the team, was injured and convalescing at home and therefore out, and fortunately Ash had turned up and was eager to try out.

"Anything to help," he repeated obligingly.

Rusty wore the team strip of red-and-white vertical stripes, with Ash wearing a borrowed spare top that had always been a little on the large side for Rusty, but fitted him just fine. Over his shoulders Rusty wore his new constant companion, the backpack Willard had made up for him. Since receiving it, much to his delight, the bad dreams had been kept at bay, and less troubled thoughts filled his mind. That feeling of a distant menace no longer hung over him. Well at least for now.

At the meadow there were two furball pitches, and just behind them an expansive open glade used for the other events. At the side of the greens stood a solitary large wooden cabin. Used mainly as the town hall normally, but for the duration of the games it would be where the judges resided for the day and a place where any injuries could be tended to.

It was stoutly built from timber from the Great Wood expertly constructed by the beavers. It had a tiled sloping roof and neat square windows, each side of its well-used oak front door. After showing Ash inside, they made their way over to the main field of play. Rusty spied Vincent and gave him a wave. He was busy pushing along a hand-held roller.

"Team practice, is it Rusty?" asked Vincent, looking up from his work with a smile.

"Yes, Vince, and don't worry, I know the rules. No training on the main pitch, keep off till match day."

"I know you do. Rules are rules," came the friendly reply. "Good luck in the game tomorrow," Vincent then said cheerily as he went about his work. I've so much to do, he thought, having spotted a very small bump to flatten, which most eyes would have definitely missed.

The practice pitch was just behind the main one, and as always Vincent's attention to detail could be seen, as they both looked identical to each other. Vincent wouldn't have it any other way.

"The others will be here shortly, but it'll give me just enough time to just go through the rules with you," said Rusty helpfully.

"That's great," agreed Ash. "I'm eager to learn."

"Well, the rules of furball are as follows," Rusty began to explain. "First of all, let me tell start at the beginning. Furball has been played on the Brow for years, and the name of the game is taken from the ball itself. It's stuffed with donated animal fur from a chosen few you see. It's seen as an honour to have your fur used to fill the match ball, and so we draw lots to see who is lucky enough to win. If you're drawn out, you and your family get to collect enough fur to fill it. This year it's made from fox fur and the fortunate winners will be guests of honour. It's Archie the fox and his clan who got pulled from the hat. You remember, we met him on Briars Road?"

Ash recalled the moment and smiled. "It might seem odd," Rusty went on, "but it creates a lot of excitement, believe me. The ball once filled, is stitched together by our groundskeeper Vincent. The game is played by most of the animals and this year we face off against our fierce rivals, the rats, in the final again." Rusty cast his eye over the pitch as Ash followed his gaze.

"The opposing teams start at opposite ends of the pitch, which is divided evenly down the middle with chalk," he continued, pointing out the dividing line to Ash. "At the start the ball is placed on the centre line by the referee. When the whistle is blown, the opposing teams race to the ball, with the exception of one player. He's known as the back stop, and guards the rear line. The aim of the game is to get the ball over the opponent's line. You can carry or kick it, whatever works best at the time. Of course, the opposition's aim is to dispossess you, and start an attack of their own. Tackling is part of the game, and if you are grounded the ball is lost.

Fouls include: tripping and dangerous play, or causing deliberate harm to your opponent. Once over the line, you sit on the ball and a goal is scored. That's when the crowd would cheer furball! Got all that?"

Ash was a quick learner. "Yes," he replied. I think so."

"Don't worry, it's a lot to take in, so just ask any questions anytime you like," said Rusty, with an encouraging pat on the back. And as I've invited you along to join in there's no pressure, we'll just see how it goes," he said encouragingly. Just then the rest turned up. It was Chilli, Madder and Cornell, all keen to get started.

"Right, you lot, let's put you through your paces," came the jovial shout as Rough ambled over to join them. He always took charge of proceedings and oversaw all the training. He loved furball but even he admitted he was a little too slow to catch a speedy opponent, especially a furtive little rat.

Rusty placed the backpack Willard had given him to wear on the sideline, as it would be considered a safety issue to keep on during a game. I'll concentrate on furball and block all other thoughts from my mind, and surely that will do, he assured himself. Rough was an excellent coach, and quickly started the drill, which included sprints and a game of catch tail. This was where a scarf was tied to a tail and you had to catch your quarry and take the scarf. Then it was attached to you and off you go again.

"Come on, let's get some speed up," barked Rough encouragingly, but it was difficult to shout and eat cake at the same time. He did his best. "Those rats will want the trophy back, so let's show 'em!" roared Rough, pushing them on. Finally, a short game of furball was held, which was three a side.

"Don't forget. You can run with it or kick it, just get it over the line!" Ash did really well and scored twice for Rusty's team, winning the practice 3–2, with Rusty getting the winner. "Well done all," said a pleased-looking Rough at the end to his exhausted team, as they stood in a circle catching their breath. "You worked hard and there's a place on the side for you too, Ash. I was very impressed. You're a natural," he said praising the breathless grey, which received a thankful smile from Ash. "Come Saturday, we'll send those rats home with their tails firmly between their legs!" roared a passionate Rough. Vincent had watched from afar with great interest, as he was a big furball fan too. Who wasn't? But more importantly he was glad the evening's training had been on the practice pitch and not the main ground. Oh no. That had to be saved for the main event because after all, Vincent was very particular indeed.

CHAPTER TWENTY

Today was the day that the whole of the Great Wood had looked forward to all year round, the annual lowland games. There were various events today lined up for their entertainment including running, throwing, wrestling, aerial displays and much more. And of course, furball. Rusty, Scarlet, Rough and Archie were the main organisers of the day, and they did their best to keep it running smoothly.

Rusty and Scarlet took care of crowd control, ushering the animals to their seats. Rough had two tasks. First to make sure the competitors knew what order the events ran in and where to go. Secondly, and the one he enjoyed the most, organising the catering.

All attending brought along the best food they could muster to be eaten during the day and Rough insisted on trying a few samples of the fare. Just to make sure it was all of the highest standard of course. Archie's job was to sell the programmes. They were handwritten on foraged paper by a self-taught to read hare, named Alf. He knew most of the animals could not read or write, and so, being quite an artist he made sure he added lots of illustrations and left the rest to Archie. This was where the wily fox came into his own. Being a bit of an extrovert, he didn't shy away from the task at all, and he could be heard loud and clear with his shout of,

"Programmes, programmes get your programmes!" echoing all around the glade. There was no actual currency on the isle and bartering for goods was the order of the day. One piece of fruit or veg, or even a nice pie would suffice. He was more than happy as he did a roaring trade too, with all produce donated going to the after games feast. And his family being guests of honour made the games extra special this year.

The grassland was surrounded by a natural embankment, which made for a great viewing platform, and lots had turned up early to get the best seats. Foxes, rabbits, moles, hedgehogs, squirrels and more, all sat next to each other, with some bringing picnics, as it was a day-long event, and the glade was filled with lots of excited chatter. The treetops gave a great view too, and birds of all varieties filled the branches awaiting the fun and games.

"It looks busier than last year," said Scarlet excitedly, as she scanned the building crowd.

"Yes, it's great to see such a great turn out," agreed Rusty, enjoying and soaking up the great atmosphere. Then, a deer dressed in a calf length white tunic, waved and smiled to them from across the field. Her name was Dr Titch. She and her team of deer were on hand in case of any medical needs. They were well respected and trusted by all, a great asset to the Great Wood, so all knew they were in safe hands.

A panel of judges sat on a long table at the edge of the green too. A variety of animals from the wood, chosen by their peers, and ready to keep scores and hand out trophies. In the middle of the group sat an elderly white owl named Mildred. Wearing her best straw hat and a crimson cape draped over her shoulders, she was head judge. She had presided over the games for years now with a respected authority, and looked on impassively, peering over her half-moon glasses. If any event was too close to call, she had the final say and her impartial judgment was readily accepted by all. As Rusty and Scarlet busied themselves, they spotted a welcome figure striding over towards them.

"Hi folks, told you we'd accept your invitation," came the cheerful greeting. To their delight, Izzy had joined them, accompanied by half a dozen pine martens.

"Izzy, great to see you," said Scarlet, and gave her a huge hug.

"I didn't doubt for a moment you'd fail," said Rusty brightly.

"In fact, I was so confident archery is the first event of the day". He knew this would be a crowd pleaser as new events always created a buzz, and a ripple of excitement went through the crowd at the sight of the arriving archers.

"We've set up targets ready for you," he said pointing out a corner of the field, where sets of three wooden blocks stood spaced out a few metres apart. Each block went down in size, and had a white 'X' painted in the middle. Behind them stood bales of hay for safety.

"I see," said Izzy eyeing the targets. "Hit all three, closest to the centre wins."

"Yes," replied Rusty." A point scored for each strike with a bonus given for best shot."

"This looks fun," said Izzy with a grin of approval, and soon the pines were delighting the crowd with their marksmanship. They were all excellent shots but after counting up the scores, two remained in the final. Izzy and another pine named Havoc.

Havoc went first, easily hitting the first block. He followed that by again hitting the middle target. The crowd watched on in silence as he aimed at the smallest. He fired, and it narrowly missed, fizzing by hitting the haystack behind. He turned in dismay as Izzy took aim. In a flash, to the crowd's joy, one target was hit, then another in quick succession. The audience held its breath as she aimed at the much smaller third 'X'.

She let fly, and the arrow hit dead centre. The crowd loved it and all stood and roared as one. Izzy smiled and bowed, enjoying the rapturous applause, as Scarlet declared her the winner.

"A big cheer for Izzy. The first to win the archery cup!"

As the applause subsided, Izzy then received the trophy from Chief Judge Mildred, and held it aloft to the delight of all to see.

Various activities were now taking place, including the fun event of badger bothering. The badgers had to stand in a line and raise their arms. Their opponent then had to make them laugh or give up by tickling them with a long stick with bird feathers attached. Rough was rubbish at this and came last, only lasting three seconds before laughing out loud. The eventual winner was his cousin Graham who just stood there impassively until Rough gave up and dropped his stick in a huff.

"That's not fair," groaned Rough. "How can he not be ticklish?" Next came the 100-metre dash. The aim was to walk and not run, as fast you could to win. This was Scarlet's best event and she romped home a few quick paces ahead of the rest of the field, much to the delight of Rusty, who whooped and clapped with joy.

Meanwhile, high above, various birds put on a brilliant aerial display. There was much swooping and diving gaining oohs and aahs from below, with the most impressive routines winning the day. The atmosphere was now electric, and left Rusty and Scarlet filled with pride.

"This is definitely the best tournament ever," she said beaming widely. The next event was the wild wood wrestling. This was a crowd favourite and they all waited patiently for its start.

A circle of chalk was drawn on the grass. Two opponents then faced off. The rules stated if you were knocked out of the circle twice, you lost. If you were lifted and held up off your feet for a count of ten you also lost. Also if you shouted enough, again you lost. Rough was favourite, and rightly so. He'd won it twice in a row and three would be a record. He stood in the middle of the circle and roared loudly.

"Are there any challengers today brave enough to take me on?

He flexed his muscles as the crowd as they chanted merrily, "Roughy,

Roughy, Roughy!"

He waved back grinning as a ram strutted towards him. His name was Rod.

"I'll accept your challenge!" Rod declared defiantly. Again, the crowd roared, loving every moment. Then they met in the middle with Rusty as the referee.

"Okay, you two, keep it clean and stick to the rules."
He then turned to Rod pointing at his horns.

"No head butting. Got it?" he said firmly. Rod nodded and off to their corners they went. Rusty could see they were now ready. "Okay. Wrestle!"

The two rushed each other, Rod hoping to knock Rough out of the circle. But Rough was too quick and side-stepped smartly, grabbing the on-rushing ram in a clinch from behind.

"Ooh, he's in trouble now," said an excited Archie sitting at the front next to a watching mole named Melvin. "He's got him in a clinch." Rough had him around the middle now and wasn't letting go for anything. Rod wriggled but to no avail as Rough was far too strong. And as his grip got even tighter, Rod had no choice but to give up.

"Enough!" wailed the ram, and Rough let go to a huge cheer. The two parted amicably and then Rusty held Roughs paw up on high.

"And the winner is Rough!" After a short rest Rough again stood in the middle.

"Any more challengers today or am I Great Wood wrestling champion for the second time?" The crowd roared in appreciation and then a shout came from the rear as a burly figure pushed them out of the way, forcing his way through.

"I'll take you down, badger. I've done it once, I'll do it again!"

Rough recognised his challenger straight away. It was the wild boar from the bridge, Riff. And he looked like he meant business.

You could now feel the tension in the air as the crowd sensed a grudge match in the offing. At Riff's side was Raff, and he leaned into his fellow boar and whispered slyly in his ear. "Listen up. First chance you get, grab him in the boar hug. He thinks he's got a powerful grip. We've practised it long enough. Show him who's boss. And squeeze the last breath out of him if that's what it takes to win," came the wretched advice.

Riff smirked and advanced to the middle of the circle where Rough stood waiting. The two then went snout to snout staring each other down, with Riff being much bigger bearing down on him as Rusty began to give his instructions.

"I want a fair contest. You know the rules," he ordered. Rusty then made a point for all to see of picking out Riff's tusks. "Keep your head up at all times," he said firmly.

"What do you take me for? A cheat!" retorted Riff angrily.

He then turned yelling to the crowd.

"You're going down badger!" He raised his hooves quickly pushing Rough unexpectedly in the chest. Rough was caught off guard and was forced back briefly by his larger rival, but immediately regained his balance.

Archie on the front row saw this and stood up shouting encouragement. "Go get him, Rough! He's nothing to worry about. He's just a big bag of wind!" which raised a big cheer and howls of laughter from the crowd, and a snarl from Riff, who turned and shook a hoof at the gathering.

"Boooo!" they jeered at the disgruntled boar as he waved them away dismissively.

They both made their way back to the perimeter as Rusty again addressed the throng.

"Are you ready to see some wrestling?" he cried, which was met with wild whoops and cheers. Now seeing they were ready Rusty started the show. "Okay, let's wrestle!" he yelled over the din. The contestants both began warily stalking each other around the edge of the circle, neither taking their eyes off each other, both seeking an advantage and seeing who would make the first move.

As they circled once more suddenly Riff decided to go for it. He charged straight at Rough, hooves high, ready to crash into him. But Rough was alert to the danger and retaliated in kind. They collided with a huge thud grappling in the middle, hoof to paw as they both pressed hard, neither wanting to give ground. They grunted and groaned with the effort, with the crowd hooting and cheering loudly as Rusty kept vigilant.

Keeping his distance, he circled the edge, checking there was no foul play. Then, with one huge effort, Rough dug deeper and somehow forced Riff back a few metres. But Riff rallied. He dug into the soil beneath his hooves and just managed to stay in the ring. Rusty shifted position to try and gain a better view of the action and as he did Riff saw his chance to cheat, and took full advantage. He broke free of Rough's grip, dropped down, and headbutted him solidly in the centre of his chest. The villain sent Rough flying out of the circle and onto his back.

"Cheat!" cried Archie rushing to his feet. "That was a definite head-butt!"

But Rusty was unsighted and didn't see it.

Riff raised his hooves above his head, grinning as the crowd responded with boos, jeers and whistles.

Rusty rushed over to the fallen Rough to check his condition.

"It was a head-butt," gasped an unsteady Rough.

"Sorry, I didn't see it," replied Rusty remorsefully.

"Are you okay to continue? If not, just say so."

But Rough was determined to go on. "No way. I'm not a quitter," he replied with a cough and a splutter before rising slowly up. "I'm fine. Just let me at him." He shook his head in an attempt to clear his senses.

"Okay, if you're sure," said Rusty. "But leave the ring again, you lose. Got that?"

Rough nodded. With his head slowly clearing, he gave the crowd his rallying cry.

"Rough by name, Rough by nature!" he roared with a paw pump to the air. Hearing this, they stood up cheering and chanted back louder than ever.

"Roughy, Roughy, Roughy!"

The two combatants readied themselves once more facing off again.

"Okay, let's wrestle!" yelled Rusty.

Riff attacked immediately, in an attempt again to catch him off-guard. He charged straight at him, but Rough was ready, smartly side stepping away. Riff was stunned by his speed. Grasping at thin air, he just couldn't stop. Fully expecting to smash into Rough, the forward momentum instead saw him leave the ring, ending up in the front row of the crowd in a heap leaving him furious and humiliated.

"What happened there, Riff?" called out Rough loudly, playing to the crowd. "Lost your way! Need a map?"

The audience loved the banter and roared appreciatively relishing every second of this great match-up. Riff quickly regrouped and re-entered the circle, his face now contorted with rage.

Again, they rushed each other, but Riff twisted his body at the last second and grabbed Rough around the shoulders and behind the neck in a firm hold.

"Go on. It's the boar hug," squealed Raff excitedly. Crush him!" Riff, who now had him firmly in his grip, squeezed as hard as he could with fiendish delight. Rough, trying to prise him off, clawed away desperately, trying his best to break the hold, but was powerless to stop him. He'd never felt a grip so strong in all his wrestling days.

Rusty seeing Rough was in distress asked the question again. "Enough?"

Rough grimaced and shook his head stubbornly. "Never," he grimaced.

Riff now sensing victory was in his grasp squeezed ever tighter. Then somehow, from the brink of defeat, Rough rallied and summoned up his last ounce of strength. He managed to draw back his arms and smashed both his elbows as hard as he could into Riff's unprotected ribs.

Riff winced. The pain shot through him like a lightning bolt,

he let go at once, grunting and holding his sides. Rough reacted first. Bracing himself, he moved forward and grabbed the stricken Riff by his tunic and with all his might threw him head-first over his shoulder. Riff flew through the air before landing hard in an untidy heap. Still in the circle, Rusty rushed over, leant down, and spoke loudly and clearly.

"Enough?" he asked.

"No chance!" barked Riff. He got back up, grimaced, stared back and roared. "Raaaaaaargh!" He pushed Rough with both hooves, forcing him back to the very edge of the circle, with pure adrenalin forcing him on. Rough clung on, knowing one slip meant it was all over. Rusty rushed to check the chalk line. He was still in.

"I've got to push back!" cried Rough.

With a huge effort Rough gained ground, one step, then two. With Riff grunting defiantly, Rough pushed harder still gaining another metre. Up close, for the first time he could see doubt in Riff's eyes, and this drove him on. Then, in a surprise move, he spun behind the boar and with an almighty effort, lifted Riff up off the ground and onto his shoulders. This brought the crowd to their feet. They knew if Rough kept him off the ground for a count of ten he'd win.

Rusty raised his paw and started counting.

"One...two...three..."

Riff tried to break out of the hold and fought back hitting Rough violently on the arms, but Rough held on stubbornly for dear life.

"Four...five...six..." continued Rusty.

The crowd were now all on their feet chanting the count too. Riff fought on even more desperately now, lashing out wildly. Rough was starting to tire. He's too heavy, he thought. I can't do this, and dropped to one knee. Riff knew he only had to touch the ground with one hoof and Rusty would stop the count. He reached an outstretched hoof. Rusty got down on all fours to check. With a raised paw he signalled no contact. Just. So the count continued.

"Seven...Eight...Nine..."

Rough delved even deeper, the will to win driving him on. With one last almighty effort, he stood triumphantly back up onto his feet and lifted Riff high up in the air.

"Ten. It's over!" shouted Rusty, waving his arms over his head. Rough, sweaty and exhausted, put Riff down and Rusty rushed over and raised his paw high.

"And still the Great Wood wrestling champion is... Rough!"

The crowd erupted, everyone on their feet now, cheering as one.

"Roughy, Roughy, Roughy!" they chanted as a washed-out Rough waved back gratefully.

"Are you okay?" asked a concerned Rusty, seeing his friend looked a little unsteady on his feet.

"Yeah I am. He was no problem. I was playing with him all along," gasped a tired but happy Rough.

"Of course you were mate," replied a relieved Rusty.

Rough then went over to Riff who was being consoled by Raff in his corner.

"Bad luck. Maybe you can try again next year," and held out his paw to shake it. But Riff refused point blank and just glared back at him.

"I don't how you won. I never lose," he spat before stomping moodily away with Raff close behind, with the jeers of the crowd still ringing in their ears.

CHAPTER TWENTY ONE

It was the final event of a fantastic day of sports and the crowd began to settle down after the excitement of the wrestling match. A feeling of euphoria filled the air as they chatted excitedly amongst themselves awaiting the finale, the big game itself, and they were evenly split who would come out on top.

"I fancy United again," said a rabbit to a hare sitting at the front.

"What, the squirrels? Nah. I'm going for Rat Rovers. Seen all their games this season, they're unbeaten," the hare responded. "They look up for it too," he said with confidence, fully dressed for the occasion in his Rovers replicate kit of white tunic and black hose.

"Yeah, it'll be a tough one, I'll give you that," admitted the rabbit, with his red-and-white scarf tied loosely around his neck. "But may the best team win, eh? As long as it's United!" he added with a friendly pat on the back.

Meanwhile, down at pitch side, a slightly concerned Rusty sought the advice of the physician Dr Titch.

"So is Rough okay to manage the team? He looked a little dazed to me after the bout."

"Yes, he's fine. He's got a few bumps and bruises, but I've checked him over thoroughly and he's good to go," she said as her gaze drifted over to Rough. "And as you can see, it's certainly not upset his appetite." Rough sat nearby demolishing another big piece of homemade pie with relish.

"Thanks doc, much appreciated," said Rusty before going over to his team with the good news. They had been stretching and warming up on the sideline as Rough, full for now, joined them.

"Gather round," Rough asked as they came together, heads bowed, listening intently. "Well, we're here again in the final," he began. "It's a been a tough old season but the reason we're standing here today is down to you lot, and all the hard work you've put in. "

"You too, Coach" Madder insisted. "We couldn't do it without you." Rough was flattered.

"Nice to hear," he said puffing out his chest proudly before getting back to business. "Now, listen carefully, here's today's play. Brick, take your usual position, backstop. Stay on our line and defend it at all costs. Chilli, I want you on the left, Madder, you stay right. Cornell, go centre for me. Rusty, up front."

He then turned to Ash. "You're our spare, so be ready.

I may call on you at any time, okay?"

"No problem coach," Ash replied readily.

"Stick with our usual game. Remember we win or lose as one. But today we win!" roared Rough, gaining resounding cheers all round.

Across the pitch, the rats were also huddled together in deep discussion.

"Listen to that lot," Misfit fired angrily, "anyone would think they'd won this already. Well, we'll show 'em, eh?"

The team regulars of Pitter, Patter, Hugh, Hugo and Huw agreed wholeheartedly. Just then, a grumpy-looking hedgehog made his way over. His name was Spike and he was their team coach. He was wearing his lucky chequered cap, his long coat and a sour expression. This cap was lucky because whilst wearing it they remained unbeaten.

"Listen you lot, I'm not saying it twice," Spike barked impatiently. "Losing is not an option. No one remembers second place so don't let me down. Do whatever it takes to win, got it?"

"Yes, boss, whatever it takes," they chanted in unison.

Now satisfied, Spike gave his orders. "Hugo backstop, guard the line with your life," he growled. "You," he said looking at Pitter, "go on the left."

"Who? Me?" said Hugh with a look of confusion.

"No, not Hugh, I mean you!" he shouted angrily. "When I said 'you', I meant you, not Hugh," picking out Pitter, which gained more confused looks. Spike threw his paws up in despair. "Oh, never mind, usual positions!" he ordered impatiently, before pulling Misfit to one side.

"Misfit, a word before you go. Listen up," he said in his ear. "Stop that Rusty and they'll fold like paper. Here, wear these," he said, handing over a black pair of gloves. "They're weighted with a nice iron lining. Give him a little dig in the ribs, that'll slow him down for sure."

Misfit's eyes lit up at the thought of the deception. "Yes, boss," he said with delight. "Whatever it takes to win," he repeated as he donned them.

Melvin the mole was the referee and he stood in the middle and called the captains over.

"It's time to choose the button," he told Rusty and Misfit.

This was a practice in which ends were chosen. He held his clenched paws out from his body, with one containing a button. Misfit moved fast, his intuition saying the left paw. He wanted to win this badly. Melvin turned his hand over and opened it and there it was, the coat button.

"Correct, you choose, captain. Which end will it be?"

"We'll stay this end," said Misfit firmly with a look over his shoulder, and turned and loped back to his team.

"I won 'Find the button'," he said gleefully. "Come on! We've gained the advantage, the sun is in their eyes." This went down well with the rats and they started to take their positions, already feeling one step closer to victory.

"They won the end, but let's make it the only thing they win today!" yelled Rusty on his return. He then carefully removed his backpack, made his way over to the sideline and gave it to Scarlet for safe keeping.

"Go, win it!" she said as she kissed him for good luck, and then took her seat next to Izzy on the front row. The two coaches then went to opposite sides of the pitch and acknowledged one another from afar with a slight nod.

Ash took his place on the sideline as Patter jogged past him, as if to warm up. He stopped just behind him and leaned in to whisper slyly in his ear.

"We know your little game," he sneered, and jogged away, turning to see Ash glaring back at him.

With everyone in position the crowd hushed as Melvin placed the ball on the spot.

"Are you ready?" he called, as both captains raised their paws to signal yes. He then raised his whistle to his mouth and blew down hard. Rusty reacted first. Swiftly off the mark, he ran hard and fast to his target, the furball. Misfit didn't hang about, and closed the gap rapidly. The others set off across the pitch too, with only the backstops staying on the line. Rusty was the fastest and got their first, deftly knocking the ball to one side. Misfit dived in but narrowly missed, and ended up face down in the dirt. In dismay he looked up to see Rusty pick up the ball and start to run towards their line.

Misfit got up and yelled out in desperation. "Don't give him space, tackle him!"

Pitter was closest and closed the gap first. Then Cornell, with a nice piece of teamwork, ran alongside him as Rusty threw the ball to him. Cornell then carried it forward and he easily jinked past the stuttering Huw, much to Spike's dismay, who threw his lucky cap to the floor in temper.

"Useless!" he screamed. "Why did we do that?" Then Hugo the backstop moved over in a vain attempt to intercept, but was far too slow and cumbersome, as Cornell crossed the line easily, and promptly sat on the ball.

"Furball!" yelled the red-and-white section of the crowd in excitement as Melvin signalled a goal with a paw to the air, as a disgruntled Spike kicked a water bottle, sending it flying through the air in disgust.

"Why did we do that?" he repeated as he called Misfit over. "Come on you, fool, do you want to lose again? Sort it out. I told you to take Rusty out!"

A smarting Misfit without saying a word went immediately back to the line.

The next fifteen minutes after the early goal was nip and tuck, with each team winning, then losing the ball, the ebb and flow of the game making it a thrilling even match.

United had possession of the ball with Rusty making headway. Then suddenly, the sun broke out from behind a cloud. It's bright glare momentarily dazzled him and Misfit spotted his chance.

Flying in, Rusty didn't see him until the last second, as he tackled him hard. As they came together, Misfit drew back his arm, bunched his weighted glove, and punched Rusty fiercely in his side. Rusty at once lost control of the ball and doubled up in pain, as Misfit took full advantage of his plight. He grabbed the loose ball and kicked it high and long to Hugh, who collected it neatly and ran the last few metres, sliding triumphantly over the line to score, and sat promptly on the ball as the rats' fans whooped in delight.

A watching Spike, having retrieved his lucky cap, threw it in the air and did a little jig of delight. Melvin then blew his whistle loudly for half-time as a worried Chilli came rushing over to Rusty's side.

"What's the matter, mate?" he asked spotting his discomfort and throwing a consoling arm around him.

"It was... Misfit. He threw a punch," he gasped. As he was led off the pitch by the team, Dr Titch immediately came to his aid. An interested spectator made his way over to Rusty's side. It was none other than Willard himself!

"How are you? You seem to be in some discomfort," asked Willard to his injured friend.

"It's fine, I'll live, thanks," Rusty replied, putting on a brave smile. He was a little surprised to see him there.

"Tell me, what exactly occurred? Was it foul play?" Willard asked in concern. "Yeah, it was Misfit, he hit me hard and low, the cheat," fumed Rusty. "The doc says nothing's broken though, so I'll rest a little, but I'm hoping to get back on for the second half and make him pay."

"That, my friend, would be most unwise," Willard advised.

"You need to replace the charmed bag I gave to you. What you see before you is my phantom form, as my true self lies back at the cottage with Screech, for I was drawn here by another," he said scanning the crowd. "It's most disconcerting, I sense a presence of evil, hence my appearance. Therefore, you must retrieve the bag to restore the power of the charm. You too would then be aware of the intrusion, and then surely the danger will pass. For now, at least," he reasoned.

Rusty could see this made sense but with the match finely balanced he faced a dilemma. "But what about the game? They need me out there," he said giving an anxious glance over to his resting teammates.

But Willard was unmoved. "Trust me, my friend, some things in life are more important than games," came the honest reply.

"I know you're right," Rusty conceded. "And you spoke of evil. Is it even safe to continue?" he asked, following Willard's watchful gaze into the crowd. Before Willard could answer him, Scarlet appeared by their side.

"Hello, Scarlet. I hope you are well," said Willard greeting her warmly. He re-explained the reason for his visit as Scarlet listened on. Once finished, she reached for the bag.

"Here, Rusty, take the backpack," she said handing it over.

Immediately the essence of Willard seemed calmer as he spoke to Rusty once more.

"With the charm back with you, I sense the peril receding. Therefore, I shall return to my home and rest. Projecting my image this distance is a most taxing event," he conceded. "I shall keep on my guard and so must you," warned Willard as he began to fade away. "Good luck with your games, I shall contact you soon." And with that he was gone.

Nearby the watching spirit form of Oswald the Elder, now fearful of being detected, disappeared into thin air too. His purpose served, he felt like he had seen enough. For now.

"Right, team, Rusty's not coming out for the second half," Rough informed the squad. "I've spoken to the ref and he didn't spot a foul but Rusty tells me differently so I've insisted he check Misfit's gloves."

He leaned forward looking them each in the eye individually. "Don't take any nonsense out there, and I've had stern words with Spike too, don't you worry about that," he assured them. He turned to Ash. "You're on. Take Rusty's place up front. You did well in training so just do your best. Are you ready?"

"No problem, Coach," replied a confident-looking Ash. "I was born ready."

"Now, that's an attitude I like," replied a satisfied Rough.

"Keep an eye out for more dirty tricks and don't let 'em put you off your game. We're the stronger team. Trained longer and harder, put the extra hours in. We've got this. Okay United, let's win this thing!"

Meanwhile Spike was holding court too. "You weren't great to start with, what you were thinking?" he said glaring. "But you came back strong, so keep that up. Push on, finish 'em off," he growled. "Misfit, did you ditch the gloves? That nosey ref has been sniffing around."

"Yes, Coach. Dumped 'em in a bush where no will find 'em."

This pleased Spike. "Good. Now let's get out there and bring that trophy home!"

Everyone took their positions again as Melvin placed the ball down in preparation for the second half. The crowd were still cheering loudly as the whistle was blown. Ten minutes passed by and both teams came close to taking the lead with some great play, but the backstops thwarted them at each turn, with Brick and Hugo doing a great defensive job.

As the half slipped away Spike was now getting more and more anxious, yelling desperate instructions that seemed to go unheard, as he vented his frustration on yet another water bottle. He then noticed that Madder was starting to make a run for United down the wing, not seen by his flagging team. He bellowed fresh orders.

"Huw, what are you playing at? Wake up, mark him!"

"Who me?" replied a muddled Hugh.

"No, you fool. Not Hugh, Huw," Spike cried. But his demands were met with utter confusion, the end result being both teammates crashed into each other in a comical heap, making the United fans leap up and roar with laughter.

Spike threw his lucky cap on the floor once more and jumped up and down stamping on it in frustration. "Why did we do that?" he squealed.

Madder, now taking full advantage of the mayhem, ran speedily towards their line. Having spotted the danger, Hugo manoeuvred himself ready to intercept. Madder, though, with quick thinking at the last second, side stepped him and the cumbersome Hugo reacted too slowly. Desperate to stop him, he stuck out a leg and tripped him up. Hoping to get away with it, he immediately held both paws up in the air feigning his innocence. But Melvin the referee was having none of it and blew his whistle straight away indicating a penalty.

"No way was that a foul!" shouted Misfit, clasping his paws to his face in mock disbelief. "He dived," he pleaded as the other rats surrounded the referee to complain.

Melvin was in no mood for nonsense and immediately waved them away before walking over and placing the ball on the mid-way spot.

But Rough had a problem: his usual penalty-taker, Rusty, was injured so he made a quick decision.

"I need a volunteer to take it," he called from the sidelines as his players all gathered in the middle. Ash didn't hesitate for a second.

"I'll do it," he offered, and at once made his claim and stood over the ball.

An impressed Rough came over and put an arm around him. "Well done for stepping up. Now, let me just go over the rules once more. It's just you and their backstop now, one-on-one. Got that?"

Ash nodded.

"Good. How long, ref?" shouted Rough turning to Melvin.

"There are two minutes to go," came the steady reply.

Rough acknowledged him and then spoke to Ash. "It's not only them who can play games." He grinned. "Watch me as I wind them up." He winked, then turned and ambled over to the opposite end. He then walked blatantly in front of Hugo before making his way slowly back.

"What's he doing?" asked a mystified Huw.

"I'll tell you what he's doing. He's crossing Hugo's path, bringing us badger bad luck," moaned Misfit loudly enough for the ref to hear.

"Superstitious nonsense," insisted Melvin as he ushered the complaining Misfit away. He then readied himself, raised his spade-like paw, and blew down hard. Hugo was away first. Trying to take the initiative, he rushed off his line roaring aggressively in order to intimidate his smaller opponent.

But Ash was ready. Seeing the oncoming Hugo thundering towards him like a raging bull was a frightening sight to see, but he used his fear to galvanise him. He scooped up the ball and faced him head-on, racing courageously towards him. As the gap between them closed and a collision looked inevitable, Ash at the last second drop-kicked the ball over the on-rushing larger rat's wide shoulders.

He smartly body-swerved him, leaving the bewildered Hugo floundering. Now wrong-footed, the big rat went for the same trick and attempted to trip him up last-minute again

But Ash was alert and easily vaulted over the outstretched limb. He got past him, collected the ball, took it over the line and sat on it triumphantly, yelling one word.

"Furball!"

Almost immediately, Melvin's whistle sounded meaning the end of the match. Rusty at once turned to Scarlet in delight as they hugged and jumped up and down with joy.

The whole ground erupted with the thrilling shouts of "United, United, United!" filling the air.

A disconsolate Spike sat down with his head in his paws as the United players all ran over to Ash. They lifted him up into the air and carried him to the cheers of "Ash, Ash, Ash!" He laughed and waved back to the crowd, enjoying every single moment.

A few minutes later, the team lined up for the trophy being given out by the head judge, Mildred.

"And I duly declare Red Watch United furball champions," she trilled, as Rusty lifted the cup high up to rapturous applause. Moments before the rats had received their losers' medals and trooped off looking dejected.

"So, what happens now, then?" groaned Hugo, still smarting from the humiliating defeat.

"I'll tell you what happens now," Misfit spat angrily. "We get that grey, Ash, alone and find out exactly what he's up to because I know one thing, for sure. He'll tell us all or regret the day he was ever born!"

CHAPTER TWENTY TWO

The evening following the tournament was always an event in itself as everyone was invited to a huge post-games feast. This year was hosted by Rusty and Scarlet beneath the old oak tree. All attending knew that it was expected that they should bring food along to share and enjoy, so there was always enough to go round, and this year it was a sumptuous sight to see.

Laid out on half a dozen placed-together tables were various delicious homemade pies and stew, alongside baked potatoes with lashings of scrumptious toppings. This was to be followed by toasted marshmallows from the campfire, and a delectable selection of mouth-watering cakes of all shapes and sizes to be washed down with lashings of hot tea.

This year's gathering seemed to be the best attended yet, and they all sat around the camp merrily chatting and sharing their favourite tales of the previous day's activities. Rusty and Scarlet sat next to each happily at the head of the tables listening to the banter and chatter that was going back and forth between friends old and new.

The pine martens sat nearby making new acquaintances with the residents of the Great Wood, as strangers rarely visited, and so they found themselves in great demand with questions like, 'What's it like up north?' and 'Do bogeymen really exist?'

Archie, as he loved to given half the chance, regaled them with merry campfire songs of old, encouraging others to join in and sing along too. He wasn't the best singer in the world or even in the wood for that matter, but that never stopped Archie bursting into song at the drop of a hat, and even though sometimes off-key, he certainly made up for it in enthusiasm.

"It's a great atmosphere this year, dear. Don't you think?" said Scarlet as Archie took his seat to much applause.

"Yeah, it certainly is," Rusty agreed readily. "I think most had fun today but maybe not Misfit and his Rovers," he quipped merrily, making Scarlet laugh out loud.

The evening continued in the same jovial manner when a thought suddenly occurred to Scarlet.

"I've not seen Misfit and his crew all evening, have you?" she asked.

"I can't say I have," admitted Rusty. "But as you know, it was an open invitation to all so I suppose it was up to them if they wanted to stay away." He shrugged.

He was interrupted with a shout from the rear.

"Hey there, Rusty, you scoundrel. I do hope you've saved a morsel or two for a returning hero."

Rusty broke out into a smile as he turned to see the unmistakable figure of his good friend Sebastian, a stoat, the captain of blue watch approach. He was striding gainfully towards him from the depths of the woods, dressed in an indigo tunic, to indicate his watch, and armed with a deadly slingshot.

"Hi Seb, was everything okay out there tonight on your evening stroll?" asked Rusty cheerfully as he made his way over to greet him.

"Of course it was," replied Sebastian cordially. "You do know the best watch in the wood was on guard tonight while you lot stuffed your faces?" he chortled. "But now we're back it's all downhill from here. Folks won't sleep well in their beds tonight knowing it's red watch's duty this evening," he said with a playful slap of the back, accompanied by a broad grin. "And I do hope you've saved us some food and not scoffed the lot, this patrolling malarkey his rather hungry work," he added casting a ravenous eye over the spread.

They were joined by ten other agile stoats, descending swiftly from the trees. "Don't worry, there's plenty left to go around. Help yourselves even though you've not earned it," said Rusty with a jovial wink.

"I don't mind if I do." Seb beamed as he and the famished stoats brushed past him and eagerly joined the rest. As they took their seats, the members of red watch finished up, said farewell to their partners and companions, and readied themselves to do the next patrol.

"We aren't all present," said Brick tersely as he scanned the assembled watch. Rusty, Madder, Chilli and Cornell were present, but Ash was nowhere to be found.

"We seem to be missing Ash. Anyone seen him?" snapped Brick, annoyed at his non-attendance.

"Well, he was at the meal earlier. I saw him taking to Havoc, one of the pine martens, but I've not seen him since," admitted Chilli.

"But that was a while ago," he added quickly.

"Right, okay. Well, we can't hang around for a no-show, we've got a watch to cover," said Brick impatiently, keen to get them started. He went on to give his instructions for that night's patrol but Rusty was only half listening as his mind began to wander elsewhere. A feeling of foreboding he couldn't explain began to rise from deep inside. Something was definitely amiss; he was sure of that.

Earlier that evening, Ash had indeed been at the meal and having chatted, eaten and mingled, became restless as a pressing matter came to mind. It was getting closer to the pre-arranged time that he had made to meet the messenger pigeon, Paulie, for an update.

Contact had been re-established and now wasn't the time to seen to be failing the king. And so, the first chance he'd got, as everyone was busy watching Archie sing, he slipped away unnoticed, and was now making his way through the woods to the designated rendezvous point. He had made steady progress when suddenly up ahead he thought he saw movement in the shadows.

He stopped in his tracks listening intently. Are my eyes deceiving me? he thought to himself as he surveyed the gloomily half-lit track ahead. And then as if from nowhere, he found himself suddenly surrounded on all sides as Misfit and his associates stepped out from their hiding places in the bushes.

"Hello, squirrel. Or should I call you a sneak?" sneered Misfit as he stood leering at him. "I think you and I need a little chat. You know, a friendly conversation to clear the air. It's cards on the table time. Start from the beginning and leave nothing out. Got it?" His first thought was to run but being surrounded on all sides, Ash quickly decided to change strategy and bluff his way out.

"Okay, Misfit. I don't know what you're up to but I must remind you I'm a member of red watch. I'm on patrol and you're stopping me from performing my duty," he said with as much authority as he could muster. But Misfit was having none of that.

"Pah, nonsense!" sneered Misfit. "Let's cut to the chase." He moved closer and stared him straight in the eye. "Look I know you're a spy. Pitter overhead you plotting with the pigeon, so don't bother denying it. He heard it all!"

Ash knew the game was up so he said nothing, and waited to see how this played out. Misfit was now in his element, and began to pace excitedly to and fro, enjoying the feeling of being in control. He stopped and got straight to the point.

"I know you've got a master that awaits across the water and he plans to invade, so don't deny it."

Ash still didn't respond.

"Oh, it's the silent treatment," is it?" rasped Misfit as he now circled the unmoving Ash. "Well, I'll do all the talking then. Tell your master I'll be his ally. I can't bear that Rusty and his cohorts, and his preposterous watch. He thinks he's so righteous and runs the place."

"And he's too good at furball too," interrupted Patter, who received a piercing glare from Misfit for his trouble. Misfit then fired a sly smile in Ash's direction.

"Give him this message, will you? Word for word," he said, his tone now decidedly warmer. "Tell him I await his arrival eagerly. I know the lay of the land, and I'm sure I can be of great assistance. I'll greet him as an equal, as I'm sure this will benefit us both. That is all."

He stepped aside.

"Well, go on, then. Go to your not-so-secret meet."

Ash gave a half smile and continued to move off as Misfit called after him.

"Don't forget to report back to me soon. I can make it worth your while too," he said waving him off with a smile.

Ash said nothing, and walked away without looking back.

You're a fool, rat, he thought to himself. You think you'll be treated as his equal? You just don't know who you're dealing with.

CHAPTER TWENTY THREE

"Tell me I heard you correctly. A common rat thinks he's my equal?" scoffed Slate in utter disbelief.

"Er, yes, your majesty," Paulie replied meekly, not wanting to incur the king's wrath once more.

Slate then sat forward on his throne, uncomfortably close to the pigeon for his liking. A trembling Paulie could feel his eyes boring through him, but just stared at the floor fearing being made into a pie. Then Slate sat back and roared with uncontrollable laughter.

"Ha ha ha! I've never heard anything so ridiculous in all my life," he said rocking to and fro holding his sides. The rest in the room forced laughter too, knowing it was unwise not to.

"Oh, that has so amused me," said Slate, as he wiped a mirthful tear from his eye on his sleeve before regained his composure. He then reached for a bunch of grapes from a bowl by his side and noisily ate a handful. The room then fell silent as he spoke to Paulie again.

"Pigeon, I'm done with you. You may leave," he said with a nonchalant wave of his paw, much to the great relief of the trembling bird. He then turned his attention to Commander Stone standing motionless at his side.

"Are the garrison and carrion crows primed and ready to go at a moment's notice, Stone?" he asked bluntly.

"Yes, sire. I've trained and readied them personally myself," Stone assured him.

"Excellent. So if I'm disappointed I know who to blame," he hissed, giving his commander the evil eye. Slate turned his attention to another of his many lackeys sitting in the corner of the room busy at work, his head bowed.

"Scribe, I hope you're taking appropriate notes?" Gutterpress, hunched over a small wooden desk, looked up timidly. Dressed in his latest garish multi-coloured tunic and bright blue hose, he stopped scribbling at once with his quill and nervously replied.

"Yes, sire. Of course, sire. Nothing negative, always positive.

As always," he whimpered. "Everything you do is beyond reproach and all for the greater good."

Slate gave a curt satisfied nod.

"Excellent. I've a hard-earned reputation to upkeep," he replied haughtily. He turned to his left with a look of disdain at Oswald the Elder, who waited patiently by his side.

"What news have you, Elder? You promised a return of the visions to me," he spat out impatiently.

Oswald knew he had to tread carefully. "As you know, your majesty, you weren't gifted the foresight from birth," Oswald began to explain hesitantly. "And the elixir I gave you must be, for now, taken sparingly. Too much for the untrained mind can lead to madness."

"Hah! Well, we can't have that can we, Elder? A mad king? No, that just wouldn't do at all," he retorted.

"Of course your majesty," Oswald continued. "Soon enough, I'll perfect the potion and make it completely safe for you to use at will. From then on the gift will be yours for forever and a day," he promised falsely.

This seemed to please Slate at least for now, as he munched loudly on another helping of fruit before asking Oswald another question.

"And what news of the wolves from the north, your former allies?" he said noisily, through an open mouth half-full of food.

"I've already ordered a message to be sent with the bird Paulie. He is to inform the wolves to ready themselves for my return as we attack within the week.

"I presume this pleases you, sire?" he asked submissively.

Slate, appeased for now, let out a large belch before turning his attention back to Gutterpress.

"Scribe, take notes," he instructed.

"Of course, your majesty," replied the scribe nervously, head down, pen in hand again.

"Soon we will rise up as one and take what is rightfully your king's. The taxes you have paid will go to good use. The sacrifices and the hunger you feel in your bellies will soon be replaced by another desire. The one for victory! Oh, that's rather good I think, straight off the top of my head," he bragged sitting back paws behind his head, wearing a self-satisfied grin. "Oh, and one more, thing scribe. Make sure you get it all printed by tonight by my minister of misinformation, Bliss. I know he won't let me down," he said raising a rare smile. "He's one of my most loyal and trusted subjects. I ask once and he gets things done. I do so wish I had more just like him."

Rusty awoke early from a restless night's sleep, the worst night he'd had since the nightmares had stopped. He glanced to see the furball cup gleaming on the dresser by his side, which brought a fleeting smile to his face.

But the tight ball of anguish he felt in the pit of his stomach soon returned. He got up and dressed quietly so as not to wake Scarlet, who slept peacefully still. The door to the spare room was ajar and he popped his head around hoping to see if Ash had returned, but much to his dismay the bed remained unslept in. He picked up his backpack hung on the foot of the bed, slid it on and silently made his way down the ladder. He sat on the bottom step lost in deep thought just as Rough came into view ambling down the lane.

"I thought I'd find you out and about early," he said chirpily before noticing the worried frown on Rusty's face. "Still no sign of Ash?" he guessed correctly.

"No, it's a mystery," Rusty admitted. "He's just disappeared into thin air."

"Yeah, that is odd," agreed Rough, trying to make some sense of it all. "It doesn't add up, to just go missing like that."

"I know, you're right," Rusty replied anxiously. "It makes no sense at all."

CHAPTER TWENTY FOUR

As the day turned to night, the large, blood-red moon that Oswald had promised would appear as a good omen, hung high in the night sky over the distant island. The once-flat grey-white disc had moved across the heavens, first deepening to a yellow and orange, and now a dark red. Some would say it was a sign of a change in fortune, either good or ill. The Elder had said the blood moon would be there to guide the way and he was correct, which pleased the king greatly, and he grinned accordingly as he stepped out onto the moonlit beach.

Along the shoreline standing before him were one hundred of his elite troops looking resplendent in their shining armour, standing stiffly to attention staring impassively ahead awaiting their orders. In front of each trooper waiting patiently was a carrion crow. Each had a saddle and harness attached to its back. They would be the Grey Army's transport to the island. Once there most would disembark. They were the infantry. The foot soldiers. The rest would stay in their saddles. They were known as the crow riders, the air-borne division of the Corp.

Slate stepped out in front of the assembled force, accompanied by Stone, inspecting the troop with a critical eye as each stood motionless as he passed by. He'd stop occasionally to get Stone to adjust the odd helmet strap or straighten a soldier's stance, but all in all for once he liked what he saw. A larger-saddled crow named Wolfram stood waiting impassively away from the others alone at the front. He was the king's ride. Slate now satisfied with the turn-out halted mid-way down the line to address the troops.

"Today is a day that will go down in Grey history!" he bellowed. "For the time has come. A time of destiny. Our destiny. We will finally remove the red scourge from our door step. For too long they have taunted us, threatening to kill us all in our beds!" he lied. "This can and will not be tolerated!" he roared as a murmur of approval went through the ranks. The troops now stirred; he went for the big finale. "Your offspring and their descendants will sing of your valour, for now and forever more! For victory will be ours!" A moment's silence came next before Stone yelled loudly.

"All Hail Slate!"

Slate stood to attention. The troops as one then punched two clenched gloved paws straight out on high in front of them, giving the Grey Army salute.

"Hail Slate! Hail Slate!" came the fevered cry.

Oswald had joined them too, but stayed purposely in the background. "Let the king have his moment," he said quietly to the large saddled hawk at his side. His name was Talon.

Talon remained silent and surveyed the scene impassively with his piercing black eyes. He knew his job. Fly with Oswald at a moment's notice. Obey his every command. Nothing more. As the furore abated, Slate noticed Oswald and beckoned him over.

"Elder," he said quietly in his ear. "Have you cast your spell on the subordinates? Will they blindly obey my every command?"

"Fear not, sire. The sorcery I have used tonight will ensure their total obedience," he replied softly.

Slate certainly liked the sound of that.

"And if required, they will give their very lives for you without hesitation," Oswald assured him.

"Excellent, truly excellent," The king smirked. Slate hesitated before he mounted his bird. Not a keen flier, he took a deep breath, then sat astride reluctantly.

"Squadron, mount up!" came the order from Commander Stone as the troop obeyed instantly.

"Wolfram, take flight!" Slate commanded uneasily. The bird did as he asked and with a flap of its mighty wings, took off effortlessly into the starry sky with him hanging onto its reins with fear, whilst also doing his best to hang onto his evening meal.

The crows followed suit at once in formation. Last of all, Oswald mounted Talon and also took flight. The still night was now filled with the steady rhythm of beating wings and within a few brief moments, they had left their home land far behind.

Now as the moon light glistened over the placid sea below, they flew low over the water, like an incoming black cloud of menace. In the distance, the darkened silhouette of the isle grew ever closer. Then, in the dark, a faint

The Battle for Badgers Brow

flickering light could be made out on the shoreline. It was the prearranged signal that Slate was looking for and now spotted, he headed straight for it. It was Ash.

He stood there on the beachhead, waving lantern in paw, guiding them in. Slate arrived first, and Wolfram dropped out of the night sky and landed in front of the waiting grey. The crow squadron arrived simultaneously and the well-drilled army swiftly dismounted. The riderless birds, knowing their predetermined orders, awaited in the trees for further instructions. The crow riders, with orders of their own, stayed air borne, for now.

Oswald was the last to arrive, and once dismounted, Talon headed for the treeline too, but chose a solitary vantage point away from the others. He liked to be alone. Slate now on foot, feeling queasy but glad to be back on firm ground again, gave his first order.

"Scout, you may approach and kneel before me," he ordered. Ash obeyed instantly, hurried over and planted a knee in the sand and bowed his head.

"Your highness, I am yours to command."

"Of course you are," remarked Slate, before drawing out his short sword in a flash. Ash remained still not daring to move, thinking his unexplained disappearance at the hands of Finnegan had brought about his premature death. He accepted his fate, closed his eyes and awaited the fatal blow. It was a blow that never came. Slate raised his sword and in one swift movement touched one shoulder and then the other.

"Arise, sir Ash, for you have served me well," he pronounced. The relieved Ash rose shakily to his feet, in shock from the reprieve of his perceived execution.

Slate then faced his troops. "Let this be a lesson to you all. Serve me well and you will be rewarded. But fail me and it will be your final undoing!" He placed a paw on Ash's shoulder.

"Now sir Ash, walk with me a short while, I insist," Slate said, allowing him to join him at his side, along with four of the elite guard.

"Sir Ash, you are cunning and oh so deceitful," purred Slate as they began to stroll together. "They are things I commend you for. Attributes I admire."

"Thank you, sire," replied Ash, still a little stunned at the turn of events, not quite believing he was still alive.

"You do so remind me of a younger me," added Slate with a sly smile. "Now walk with me, we have much to discuss," he said as they walked the shoreline, with the waves lapping at their feet. "Tell me their strengths and weaknesses. But first of all, one thing."

"Yes, my liege, what is it?" replied the eager-to-please knight.

"I want to know where I can find the home of this Rusty the red. I do so wish to pay him a visit, in person this time. As soon as possible." Oswald scrutinized the scene with the newcomer Ash with little interest. Later, he would make his own move.

CHAPTER TWENTY FIVE

"Are you not impressed, sire? Is this not a rich and bountiful land? Did it not all unfold as I foretold?" said a smug-looking Oswald to his king, as he and Ash stood patiently by his side.

Slate didn't answer immediately as he played back the last few hours in his head. The landing had gone to plan without any opposition. True. He'd slept well in his marquee tent for a few short hours set up near the shoreline, and had his fill of a hearty late-night feast. Also true. And he now in the dead of night he surveyed what he could make out of the rich woodland spread out before them with a pleasing eye.

"Yes, Elder," he responded at last. "You have done well so far," he admitted, sounding possibly pleased. "Your advice has been sound; I'll give you that."

Then he stiffened, his tone changing in the blink of an eye. "But let's not get carried away just yet, shall we. You think your work is done? Well, think again," he said scathingly. "For is this not just the beginning? We have a foothold yes, but the day is not yet won. Only a fool would believe otherwise," he said, shooting Oswald a sudden withering look of disapproval. "The reds have yet to be subdued, and we have an island to pacify," he continued.

"Or have you forgotten these facts already? Has scant success gone to your tiny little head? "

Oswald could have been forgiven for being angry at the king's perceived ungratefulness. And deep inside he was. For after all, his guidance had been outstanding. The surprise attack and its timing after all, had been down to him. His sorcery had been exceptional in its use. But he knew it would be unwise to rise to the bait and just replied with a simple, "I always try to please your majesty," adding a slight bow.

The king seemed to dwell on his response for a second or two before a smile flitted across his face. Seemingly appeased by the deference of his advisor, his posture became more relaxed.

"Now remind me, what is the island's so-called name again, Elder?" asked Slate.

"It is known as Badgers Brow, sire. And has been for aeons," replied Oswald humbly, eager to change the subject.

Slate looked unimpressed.

"Well, that's about to change. I don't like it one bit," he barked along with a disapproving shake of his head. He then seemed lost in thought. "Yes, it needs something more appealing," he mused, stroking his chin. "Come on, Elder, don't just stand there, advise me!" he insisted. "It's not every day you get to name an island, you know. Well? Speak up, don't keep me waiting."

For once, Oswald was lost for words as he racked his brain searching for an adequate reply, not wanting to seem foolish.

"May I suggest something, sire?" Ash asked modestly.

"Yes, of course. What is it Sir Ash?" responded Slate.

"Does the name the Isle of Grey please you at all, sire? " Ash asked.

Slate didn't answer for a few seconds, and then his face lit up.

"Excellent work there, Sir Ash," he said, patting him on the back. "The Isle of Grey! Oh, I do like the sound of that. It's got a nice ring to it. And it's so appropriate. See, now that's what I call initiative. You'll go far, Sir Ash," he said sounding genuinely impressed. "Do you not agree, Elder?"

Oswald was fuming but hid it well. "Indeed, sire, I do," he said reluctantly, as he gave Ash a withering glance for stealing his thunder.

Unnoticed by Slate, Ash glared back at Oswald.

Slate, Oswald and Ash then gathered round an ancient map spread open on a tree stump, carried here by the Elder himself, and began studying it closely by lantern light.

"So, Sir Ash, their defences are pitiful and they send out but a handful to patrol, with a so-called watch. Correct?"

"Yes, sire, that's always the case. Search the treetops and you'll surely find them there," he said pointing towards the Great Wood.

"Very good, Sir Ash." Slate beamed. He picked out a large darkened square on the map. "Elder, tell me. What is that? Is it a cause for concern?"

The small dormouse craned his neck to look. "Oh no, sire, it's just an old abandoned mine. But it is important I gather much-needed supplies from there." he added quickly.

A now-satisfied Slate called his commander. "Stone, come here, immediately!" he barked.

The commander rushed over immediately to his side.

"Take Sir Ash with you and bring me back this so-called watch. Not all of them of course. I'll need only one alive for interrogation. Got that?"

"Yes, sire," replied Stone with a double-fisted salute. "You, you, you and you, with me now!" he ordered, picking out four of the troop. Without further delay, they set off, accompanied by Ash, into the darkened woods in search of their quarry.

"Oh, this is so exciting! Don't you think, Elder?" Slate grinned and clapped his paws together in excitement. "Oh, I do love a good old-fashioned hunt. Makes me half wish I was going myself. But I'll nap instead. Invasions are so tiring," he said with a stretch and a yawn. "I think I'll rise on their return."

Just before dawn, a sudden commotion could be heard coming from the woodland. It was Stone returning with his party and they had someone with them. It was the beaten and bloodied figure of Sebastian, the blue watch captain. He cut a sorry sight as he staggered along with his paws bound behind him surrounded on all sides by surly greys.

Stone, a few metres now before the risen king, planted his foot squarely in the stoat's back sending him sprawling at the king's feet.

"Oh, so what have we here, then?" scoffed Slate unpleasantly. "Have you brought me a prize?"

"Apologies, sire, the pursuit took longer than expected. And this one was particularly elusive," Stone growled, accompanied by a nasty kick to the ribs of his captive. "He was one of the islanders we caught on lookout," reported Stone stiffly. "The others were no match for us and were swiftly dispatched, sire, but this one seemed to be the leader so we brought him in. Under interrogation, my liege, he refused to talk," Stone reported.

"Really, not feeling chatty, eh?" Slate scoffed with a contemptuous curl of the lip. Sebastian remained silent.

"Is your tongue tied along with your wrists too?" he sneered, leaning into Sebastian, staring him straight in the eye. Again, there was no response, just a look of stern defiance. But as Slate straightened back up, Sebastian spoke out defiantly.

"You'll get nothing from me, you vermin!" he fired back angrily, before turning to Ash. "And as for you, you're nothing but a coward and a traitor!" he hissed in disgust.

Slate let out a huge yawn. "Oh, do shut up, you're such a bore. And don't worry, I've met your kind before. Braver than brave, or so you think. As stupid as the day is long, if you ask me." He turned to his commander. "Stone, take him away. You say he won't talk? Well, let's make that a permanent arrangement."

"Yes, sire, it will be my pleasure," growled Stone as dragged the wretched figure of Seb away.

"Again, you've done well, Sir Ash, and continue to impress," enthused Slate to his new knight. "You'll rise through the ranks quickly, of that I am sure."

Then he turned his attention to the Great Wood itself. "Now, there's more work to be done. Let's drag these reds from their nests. Oh, I do love a good old-fashioned raid," he said gleefully. "It so works up an appetite."

CHAPTER TWENTY SIX

The sun was yet to rise as Ash led the way through the silence of the Great Wood with an advance party of greys, with Slate now going on his first raid, bringing up the rear. As always.

Ash had urged caution. With blue watch now taken care of they may encounter another patrol if they had been missed he warned. But so far, nothing seemed amiss as the rest of the Grey Army moved into position behind them, ready to stifle any further opposition.

They moved as silently as possible, and with this being the elite guard —well-practised in stealthy pursuits – they hardly made a sound at all. Before long, Ash stopped and picked out the old great oak, its ladder leaning against its side invitingly. Slate caught up and joined him by his side wearing a huge grin.

"I know this place from my dreams, it's the red's home," he whispered to Ash excitedly, and silently beckoned Stone over.

"Commander, their ring leader lies there," he said in muted tones, pointing out the tree. "Lead the way in, but leave him to me."

"Yes, sire, don't worry, no harm will befall you," Stone assured him.

"I know, Stone, you fool, because you'll get in harm's way first! Don't you worry about that!" he rasped with a scathing glance. "Now, off you go, I'm right behind you," he said ushering him away.

Stone did as he was ordered and crept forwards. Once he'd reached the foot of the ladder, he stealthily started to climb. At the top he turned to see Slate peering up, urging him to go on, so he reached out, turned the handle and slowly opened the door.

As it fell open without a sound, he could now see Rusty and Scarlet fast asleep side by side in their bed. He drew out his sword, crept over and waited silently by Scarlet's side. Slate appeared, peeking around the doorway. Once he was satisfied there was no imminent danger to himself, he strode over without a care, the need for secrecy now gone.

Rusty stirred from his sleep by the intrusion, awoke with a start and sat bolt upright in his bed to be met by the terrifying sight of Slate leering at him.

"I've waited a long time to say this, red," Slate purred slyly. "It's all mine now!"

As Rusty stared helplessly into Slate's intimidating black eyes, he wasn't sure at first if this was yet another nightmare. Surely this couldn't be real and he'd wake up safe and sound in his bed in a moment. Then reality struck home as Slate spoke out once more.

"So, finally we meet at long last, even though I feel as if I already know you oh so well", he sneered.

Rusty still in shock, couldn't quite believe the surreal scene playing out before his very eyes. He glanced over to see the fearsome figure of Commander Stone looming over his astonished wife, sword in hand, as if ready to strike.

"What is it you want?" he gasped, still shaken but trying to appear brave, and hide the tremor in his voice. "If it's me, then let Scarlet go," he implored.

Slate studied him for a minute and then straightened up. He began to pace up and down the small room with his little paws tucked firmly behind his back.

"What do I want?" Slate said. "Isn't it obvious? I want it all!" came the odious reply. "Does that not answer your question?" He wheeled around and spoke sharply to his commander. "Stone, you may now leave the room. You are no longer required," he said waving him away brusquely.

"But, your majesty, I'm here to protect you," Stone protested.

"Leave the room, you imbecile, and never question your king again!" he thundered, shaking his paw at him.

At that Stone bowed, aggressively resheathed his sword and headed towards the door. He scowled at Rusty as he closed the door behind him.

"My apologies for that, you just can't get the staff nowadays," said Slate with a dismissive wave. He continued to pace up and down again, seemingly lost in thought.

"Now, where were we? Oh yes, my desires. Well, not to state the obvious but to rule this island, of course. It has been foretold and it is my destiny!" he crowed loudly, as if addressing a crowd.

Rusty, with anger now replacing fear, responded. "I don't see a leader before me, I just see an uninvited guest!"

Slate threw up his arms in fake shock. "Now, there's no need for that, where are your manners?" He broke out into a broad grin, leant against the foot of the bed and glanced around. "It's a nice little hovel you have here," he said disparagingly. "A little sparse and cheaply furnished, but you can't have it all. Unlike like yours truly." He leant closer still. "It doesn't have to be this way, so listen carefully, for I have a proposition, a once in a lifetime opportunity," he purred. "We're both squirrel, are we not? Even though you're an inferior red, I suppose in time I can try to overlook that," he added haughtily. "Join me, you have the beginnings of this gift, I believe. I too will possess it soon, you know." An envious look appeared in his eyes. Rusty watched on unmoved and stayed silent, still assessing this new threat. Seeing this, Slate decided flattery was the next best course of action to try and win him over. "You're a born leader too, I can sense that, and you have the respect of your peers, no doubt. Just like yours truly." His sly face hardened as he continued to talk. "Come and work for me. Control your kind, it'll be easier for them to have one of their own in charge, and I'll make you rich beyond your wildest dreams. I'll even let you keep this little nest of yours, if you wish, and you can adorn it with only the best, and throw away all these cheap and nasty belongings you own," he said glancing around once more.

"Yuck, this place is so distasteful and in desperate need of a makeover, "he said with a look of disgust, as if he'd got a bitter taste in his mouth. "But luckily for you I can get my top designer over from the main land and sort out this mess in a jiffy. So what say you, my little red friend, do we have an agreement? Shall we shake on it?" he asked, standing back with an outstretched paw.

Rusty got up at once. Striding over to him, he ignored his offer and instead stared at him straight in the eye.

"I'll tell you what I think," he glowered. "We may both be squirrel, you're right about that, but that's where the comparison ends. I'd rather die right now than collaborate with the likes of you!"

Taken aback, Slate retorted, "Now there's no need to get nasty!" Seeing the anger in Rusty's eyes, he backed away to the door. "Stone! Come here, right now!" He barked.

A moment later, his commander burst through the door.

"These two now bore me. Take them with the others for detainment in the labour camp. They can be put to work for the grey cause, like the rest."

"Yes, sire, immediately," replied Stone, as two more guards rushed into the room and grabbed Rusty and Scarlet before forcibly bundling them away.

"Oh, well," said Slate, talking to himself in the now empty room. "He can't say I didn't ask nicely."

"Well, Elder, my plan was well executed don't you think? With no casualties, well for us at least." Slate grinned as he reclined on a couch in his newly erected marquee.

"Yes, sire, indeed it did. The omens were true and the wait for the blood moon was truly justified," replied a smug-looking Oswald, standing attentively nearby.

However, inwardly he was seething. It wasn't your plan at all! he thought angrily. But he remained a picture of calm as always, as Slate nattered on.

"And a few of the reds will be put to task on the abandoned mine that you say lies nearby, so that you may perform your duties. Correct?" he asked before quaffing his tea even louder, much to the annoyance of Oswald.

"Yes, sire. The ingredients I require for my spells to be carried out can be found in there. And maybe they will unearth a long-lost artefact too, who knows? It's of little interest to most, a mere trinket of the past," he added dismissively.

With Slate it was difficult to tell half the time if he was even listening. He could seem so indifferent to the world at times, and now seemed to be more interested in slurping his tea and eyeing more cake. But Oswald pressed on regardless.

"And needless to say, once the materials are found, I can provide you with the gift of the foresight you so desire," he said. He saw that this had definitely caught Slate's attention as he began to grin inanely at the prospect, and at the same time reaching for another large slice of gateau from a nearby cake stand, before shovelling it in all at once.

"Elder, what say you on the red ringleader? He possesses the gift too. Is he not a danger and better off eliminated?" Slate asked through a mouthful of pastry.

"Sire, worry not, for I have sensed his presence for a while and watched him from afar. He is nought but a weakling," Oswald told him. "Be assured, I will watch him like a hawk. Some say it's wise to keep your friends close and your enemies closer, sire.

"Fine, he lives for now if that's your counsel," Slate replied, burping loudly before turning and looking him directly in the eye. "Now, tell me counsellor, is that what you do with me? Keep me nice and close under false pretences?"

Oswald knew he now had to tread carefully.

"Of course not, your highness. I hold you with the highest esteem and only live to serve," he responded, doing his best to look shocked.

This amused Slate greatly. "Ha, ha, fear not. I jest with you dormouse!" he hooted with laughter. "As if you'd dare to even contemplate betraying me. And who knows, once I own this gift, one day maybe I'll even pay you a little visit in your dreams too," he sneered. "Now tell me, what news of your brother? He too has the gift, is he not a serious threat?"

"Do not concern yourself with such matters, sire. I have hidden our very existence from him easily with a simple hex and if he does emerge from under his rock, you'll surely crush him like a bug," he said, demonstrating with a stamp of his tiny foot.

The answer seemed to satisfy Slate as he continued to recline lazily, mug in hand.

"Oh, one more thing, Elder, you mentioned the mine may hold an artefact. Explain more," he said, finishing his drink with a smack of the lips.

"Oh, it's nothing, sire. And not worthy of your attention. Just a broken sword, a thing of fancy."

"Well, what would I need of that when I've got an armoury full of brand-new weapons?" Slate scoffed scornfully before dismissing it once more. "Elder, for your loyalty, if you find this worthless thing, keep it for yourself," he said before waving him away. "Now be off, you have a victory banquet to prepare, do you not? It's time for my next nap," he added with a large yawn. "Leading Invasions is extremely tiring you know."

"Yes, sire," replied Oswald, backing out of the tent bowing and scraping as he went. "All will be prepared and readied. I will make it my top priority, sire," he fawned as he closed the tent flap.

Straightening up, he marched away glowering angrily, and mumbling under his breath.

"I have no intention of sharing such a great prize with a buffoon such as you!" he hissed.

CHAPTER TWENTY SEVEN

What followed next would go into island folklore as The Day of Infamy, its darkest hour, or The Day of Freedom, depending whose story you listened to. For the islanders, it was a day of misery and mayhem. All of the red squirrels, around forty in all, were rounded up, dragged from their beds and taken to the furball pitch, where they found themselves surrounded by the grey guard.

Branches had been hacked down and made into a make-shift barrier which surrounded the pitch to keep them imprisoned. The captive reds were still in a state of shock and could not quite believe what had occurred. They huddled closely together for comfort and spoke in low murmurs as fear filled the air.

Rusty stood by the perimeter fence with Scarlet trying to appear brave but inside he felt scared, the most he'd ever felt in his life.

"It's the premonitions I had," he said quietly to her holding her paw. "It seems they've come true, and I feel I should have known done more, somehow, to try and stop this."

Scarlet pulled him close. "Rusty, don't be silly. How could you have known? It's no one's fault," she assured him. "We just need to stay calm. We'll find a way to get out of this, I know we will," she added reassuringly.

Outside the compound. the guards suddenly stopped patrolling and stood to attention. Striding towards them at a pace came Stone, and as he got up to the fence, they gave him the grey two-fisted salute.

Stone saluted back and then he turned to address the captives.

"Reds, listen carefully!" he bellowed. "The king has summoned you all to a victory speech. It will happen here today. That is all!" Then he did an about turn and marched away as the guards continued their patrol. The captives began to talk again in hushed tones still trying to make some sense of it all.

"So, this so-called king is making a speech," whispered Rusty. "What do you think that's all about?"

"I don't know," replied a worried-looking Scarlet. "But I'm sure we're about to find out."

The mood was sombre amongst the animals. Inside the pen, Rusty had waited patiently with Scarlet, struck with fear. Not so much for himself but for all the others now incarcerated with him.

What future lay ahead now for the inhabitants of the Great Wood? Then in the throng, much to his delight, he spotted his dear friends Rough and Archie who were standing outside the pen nearby. They were fine and he felt his spirits soar at the welcome sight. He waited till a guard had passed by and madly waved them over. At first, to his dismay, Rough had missed his signal. But then much to his relief the sharp-eyed Archie spotted him and they stealthily made their way nearer to the fence.

"So pleased to see you're okay," said Rusty in relief.

"Yeah, we're good," agreed Rough. "But what about you and the rest locked up like this?" he asked anxiously.

"We're fine, honestly, for now at least," Rusty assured him. He moved closer to the fence. "Listen, there's no time to waste. You need to get a message to Willard. I've tried to contact him as he instructed if I needed help. But I just can't get through. It's difficult to explain but my thoughts seemed blocked somehow," he said in desperation. "You need to let him know what's happened. He'll know what to do, I'm sure. And if you can retrieve the backpack too? It might help. It's at home."

Rough agreed in an instant. "Okay, Rust," he replied. "Leave it to us." Then, just as the sentry was returning, they melted back into the background.

The new regime had been busy and a hastily built platform had been constructed with timber by the beavers at sword point, outside the town hall. Chairs had been placed along its length with Slate, Oswald, Stone and six other commanders taking their seats.

"They're a surly-looking bunch, don't you think, Elder?" said Slate, sitting in the centre leaning into his advisor as he surveyed the mass of animals below.

"I'm sure your army will teach them to be subservient before too long, your majesty," Oswald sneered.

"My thoughts entirely, Elder," agreed Slate readily. "We'll soon whip them into shape, and we can always make an example of any troublemakers. You have to be cruel to be kind, don't you agree? Well, I've found it certainly works for me," Slate smirked as he gave a regal wave but received nothing but blank stares in return. "Elder, what do you think, do they fear me?" he asked unsurely.

Oswald sought to assure him at once. "It is obvious to all, sire. Fear and respect in equal amounts."

Slate liked the sound of that and stood at once to commence his speech, taking centre stage.

"Creatures of the woods," he began. "Today is a glorious day, for I have saved you from the tyranny of the reds. You will find I am a kind and generous king who rewards loyalty and metes out punishment in equal measure. The choice will be yours to take. You will of course be able to go about your daily business as usual and the only weapons you will be allowed to have will be to carry out your work.

"But under no circumstances are you to leave the wood without permission. And needless to say, but I'll say it anyway, there will be new taxes to pay for your protection and my prosperity, er I mean our prosperity," he blustered. "You will all be required to carry the correct paperwork saying who you are at all times. For those who cannot read, an image will be provided. But don't concern yourselves over such trivial matters, it is all for your own
safety."

He then stood on the very edge of the platform, to make sure all could see. "A word of advice. If you're thinking of law-breaking, even in the slightest way, I would strongly recommend against such folly. As you may have observed, I have with me my highly trained elite guard. Here too is my advisor, the Elder, who is a master of the old ways. A quick demonstration, Elder, if you please," he said before retaking his seat.

With that, Oswald stood and lifted his paw dramatically towards the heavens. Suddenly, the blue sky in an instant, turned black, followed by a crescendo of thunder, accompanied by a huge bolt of lightning streaking across the now illuminated sky. Oswald lowered his paw and the blue sky instantly returned. It was a clever illusion, but to all there it seemed very real.

Slate leaned over and whispered approvingly into his ear.

"Excellent trick there, Elder, one of your best."

He stood once more. "As you can see my advisor is all-powerful, so please don't upset him because he won't play nice."

Then he turned his attention to the captives in the compound. "Now listen carefully, you lot, it's not difficult to understand. You will toil freely for the grey cause or die. You will be tasked to work accordingly. My counsellor tells me he needs supplies for his needs from a nearby mine, so some of you will be set to work there for now, and the rest wherever is deemed necessary, for no pay at all of course. It will be a labour of love."

He then glanced at Stone.

"Now bring me my guests," he ordered, as Misfit and his fellow rats came onto the stage. "Ah, the rats. Which one is Misfit?"

"That would be me," Misfit said grinning from ear to ear.

"I believe you sent a message asking me to come and work alongside you?" Slate asked wearing a false smile.

"Yes, indeed I did," replied Misfit triumphantly. "I'm impressed with what I've seen so far and glad you took up the offer." He beamed. Slate's smile disappeared.

"Take up the offer? You're lucky I don't take off your head! Stone, seize them at once and take them away. You can worm your way back into my favour or join the reds!" he called after them.

As Misfit was dragged away in misery another came forward.

"Look," whispered Scarlet to Rusty in shock. "It's Ash!"

Slate looked mightily pleased. "Ah, Sir Ash, come join me by my side and bask in my glory. You've certainly earned the right."

"Yes, sire," replied Ash, giving a deep bow as he took a seat near the king. Rusty watched on in disbelief.

"As if I called you a friend, how stupid could I be?" he muttered under his breath.

In the crowd, Rough and Archie had heard enough.

"What do we do, Rough? What's the plan?"

"There's only one thing to do. Get to Willard like Rusty said. He'll know what to do."

"Yes, you're right, we have no choice. We'll go first chance we get," agreed Archie. "We'll show 'em!" the fox said defiantly.

CHAPTER TWENTY EIGHT

Over the next few days, the new regime started in earnest. Hastily drawn up identity papers were quickly issued out by the grey guard with regular spot checks carried out, and animals were stopped at random and asked to display them by the troops. Even the birds needed permission to fly, with the skies being patrolled by the carrion crows.

The red squirrels had been given tasks to do also. Some were ordered to cut down trees from the wood to make a more permanent compound to hold them in. Others were sent to work in the old mine. It could be extremely dangerous work as it had been abandoned a long time ago by the men who had tunnelled it years before, and in its neglected state the chance of a cave-in would be high. It was situated in an old stone quarry with high imposing red sandstone walls, and the entrance to the mine had collapsed, so the first task for the captives was to dig it out.

The work on the mine had begun under the watchful eye of the guards. The captive squirrels were given picks and shovels and had started to strengthen the tunnel entrance from first light.

Rusty and Scarlet were amongst the unfortunate work party and had toiled side by side all morning when a guard yelled out a new command. "Ten-minute water break, and not a second longer!"

It was baking hot and dusty work, so the work party of red squirrels gladly took their turn dipping a ladle into an old wooden barrel, filling their cups and quenching their thirst with the lukewarm water provided.

"Why do you think they've got us doing this? What do we know about mining?" asked Scarlet.

"I've no idea, but it must be of some importance to them for some reason," replied Rusty, taking his fill too. "But it's best to keep our heads down and stay out of trouble, until we can form a plan."

"I know you're right," she replied, "and with you still unable to reach out to Willard, maybe Rough and Archie will succeed and get help."

"Knowing them, they'll certainly give it their best shot," agreed Rusty, trying to hide how concerned for them he really felt as he drained his cup of its last drop.

"Drinks break over, back to work, you lazy lot!" the surly grey guard barked, cracking his whip menacingly. So they carried on working all morning clearing the collapsed entrance, toiling in teams, passing heavy baskets of rubble down the line and shoring up the ceiling with freshly cut timber. It was hard and heavy work, but by late afternoon the entrance was cleared and the mouth of the old mine yawned back at them like the mouth of a hungry toothless beast.

"Okay, good," the guard said peering into the pitch-black gloom, careful not to get too close. "I need two volunteers to go in to check if it's safe. You two, you'll do," he said picking out Rusty and Scarlet at random. "Get going, grab a lantern. And if you don't come back out, don't worry, I'll send two more in… to replace you!" he said throwing his head back and guffawing loudly. "Well, what are you waiting for?" he shouted impatiently.

Rusty and Scarlet, with a resigned look, picked up a nearby lantern, knowing refusal wasn't an option. But as they readied for departure, a small mole suddenly rushed forward wearing a steel helmet painted yellow, a worn tunic, and a bag strung across his shoulder. He was soon seen in deep discussion with the guard. After a moment or two, the guard broke away from him.

"You two, change of plan. You're to take the mole with you and do everything he says, or feel my whip across your backs," he ordered, as the mole came over to them.

"Hello you two, my name's Bookworm," the mole said quickly, his eyes squinting and blinking at them nervously as he spoke. "Now, please do as I ask. Health and safety is most important you know, you can't be too careful, even though this mine is safe," he insisted. "Well, at least I do hope so," he added, with an unsure scratch of his chin as he peered inside. "There's no time to waste. Come on, don't dilly-dally. Follow me in. We've got important things to do," said the mole, scurrying off into the dark of the mine, with a now bemused Rusty and Scarlet following closely in his wake.

"Keep up, then, don't hang about! That won't do, that won't do at all." He quickly bustled along, his voice echoing loudly off the old tunnel walls. Rusty and Scarlet, feeling insecure already, certainly weren't in the mood to hurry into the pitch-black hollow.

They noted that the wooden props that lined the wall and ceiling to prevent collapse looked quite unstable, with some now split and broken with the passage of time. However, they knew turning back was not an option either so they slowly edged forward with Scarlet holding out her lantern at arms-length by its handle. Its glow cast long eerie shadows on the high walls ahead, providing just enough light to see.

Suddenly, the mysterious mole had vanished out of sight and couldn't be seen at all.

"Where's he gone?" asked Rusty, mystified at his sudden disappearance. "How are we supposed to follow him when he vanishes like that?" Then abruptly the mole reappeared again out of the inky darkness wearing a puzzled frown, seemingly perplexed at their inability to keep up.

Scarlet then took her chance to speak up.

"I know you said to hurry along, but is this place safe? It looks as if it might collapse at any moment," she asked concerned.

The mole stopped and studied the surroundings whilst rubbing his chin, as if he was deciding what to do next. Noting his hesitation, she decided she'd like to know a little more about their odd guide. "Sorry we haven't even introduced ourselves," she said with a smile. "I'm Scarlet, and this is my husband, Rusty. You said your name is Bookworm?"

"What? Oh yes, names. No matter. I've got little use for them you see," the mole replied rapidly. "And yes, they call me Bookworm. It's not my real name. Oh no, my real name is…well, it's so dull that it's not even worth mentioning." Bookworm, is a moniker, a pet name if you like. Everyone calls me it, mainly because I always have my head lost in a book. I'm self-taught you see, and it seems to have stuck. So, there you go. "You're not from the island?" asked Rusty, not recalling seeing him before.

"Me? No, never been here before the other day. I arrived from what I believe you call faraway land; on the back of a carrion crow, you see. I've never flown before either, most

exhilarating," he said dancing a little jig of delight. He then leant forward as if sharing a secret. "I asked the crow, can I go again? But can you believe it? He just said 'No', and went off in a huff, the miserable thing. No matter. It was fun while it lasted."

Then he stopped, surveyed the scene one last time, and made a snap decision. "Yes, I've decided it's safe enough in here after all. I'll lead on at a slower pace. You slowcoaches can maybe keep up then, eh?" He chuckled to himself, and at once turned to head off.

"And yes, I've forgotten your names already. Told you I've no use for them at all," he said calling over his shoulder. "I've been told by my doctor that my head's too full of algorithms, equations and the like. You can't remember everything can y—"

"Excuse me for asking," interrupted Scarlet gently. "But what exactly are we meant to be doing in here anyway?"

"Oh, has no one told you? Oh, that won't do. That won't do at all. No matter. We're here to help my master, the Elder, to continue with his work." He turned to face them, and as he did his face lit up in a most peculiar way from the lantern held by Scarlet. He looked more mask-like than real in the half-light. He placed a paw to his pursed lip.

"Shush, I'll let you into a little secret. There's a piece of an ancient artefact buried in here, part of a sword placed here by the master himself for safekeeping," he began to explain.

"He left the island in quite a hurry a few years ago, I believe. And he's sent you here to find it."

"Why not come himself?" asked a confused Rusty.

Bookworm smiled. "Well, I'm his new apprentice, you see, and he said I'm to prove my worth. And if I do well, he will teach me all he knows," he said with an enthusiastic rub of his paws. "And believe you me he's extremely knowledgeable. And why are you here, you asked? Well, I'm afraid you two are the labour, you know, in case there's work to do. The odd rockfall to shift or other dangerous stuff, you know, stuff like that." He paused for a brief breath and then continued.

"Also, he's given me directions which I've learned by heart," he said proudly, looking really pleased with himself. Just up ahead we should come to a sort of crossroads," he said turning to peer into the gloom before moving off again.

"Oh, yes, here we are," he said after a few more minutes. They had arrived at a junction in the excavation, with tunnels veering off left and right. "This way," he said heading to the left with confidence before stopping. "Or is it to the right? Oh dear, I'm not good at names or directions it seems. Oh, this won't do. This won't do at all."

"Just take your time and think back to what the instructions were," Scarlet said patiently.

Bookworm's face then lit up. "No matter, it's fine, it's fine. What was I thinking? It's definitely right," he said finally making up his mind. "Come on, keep up. Don't dilly-dally! What could go wrong?" he said merrily.

"I'm thinking quite a lot," muttered Rusty as they both followed Bookworm, the little faith they had in him fading fast, as off they went into the unknown.

"Don't worry, shouldn't be too far now. Not far at all. At least, I don't think it is," said Bookworm unsurely, as they continued deeper into the mine. "Oh, and if you're wondering how I find my way so easily, don't worry about me I've no need of a lantern. We moles can see very well in the dark, and with my excellent sense of direction, we won't get lost once. Well, in theory that is," he added quickly, after having a slight stumble in the dark. "Oh, and did I mention? There are rumours of gold hidden down here too, though I'm not sure if that's true at all. Well, I'm not too sure of anything really if I'm honest," he admitted as he ambled along on his little legs.

"Do you think he really knows the way?" whispered Scarlet, getting more worried by the minute as they followed the shuffling mole down the dark tunnel.

"Who knows?" replied Rusty under his breath, not wanting him to hear. "I'm not really sure he knows what he's doing at all," he conceded with a tired shrug.

At that moment, the mine shuddered slightly and the timber beams creaked and groaned as if moaning and complaining about all the weight they'd carried for all these years.

"Oh don't worry about that, it's to be expected," said Bookworm matter-of-factly, just as they were covered in a cascading layer of dust, causing them all to cough and splutter. Once the air had cleared, Bookworm shook the dust off him, and carried on as if nothing had happened. "The excavation is rather old and movement in the infrastructure is not unexpected. Hopefully it won't have released any gases either. Some are toxic and others volatile and can even explode," he explained about the decaying condition of the mine, sounding completely unconcerned as if he was just discussing the weather. "With good fortune on our side I'm sure it'll be fine."

Scarlet hearing this decided she had heard enough and shot a concerned glance to Rusty before speaking her mind. "Bookworm, can I just say one thing? I'm not happy about being down here at all," she said tersely, getting more and more irritated by the scatty mole.

"Me neither!" snapped an irritated Rusty, his patience wearing beyond thin, as wiped the last residue of dust off him.

"Don't you think this is getting too dangerous and we should consider turning back?" insisted Scarlet earnestly.

But Bookworm was having none of it. "Oh, no, no, no. We go on because even though the Elder is oh so kind to me, I wouldn't like to fall out of favour," he bleated fearfully, with a tremor in his voice. "Returning empty-handed would be most unwise for all concerned." Then he seemed to brighten up. "And anyway, it's not too far now, I'm sure it's this way. At least, I think it is!"

"Come on," said Rusty begrudgingly, trying to keep calm and biting his lip. "What choice do we have anyway? The quicker we find this thing, the sooner we can get out of here."

After a few more minutes, which seemed more like an eternity, Bookworm stopped suddenly and his face lit up as if a light had been switched on in his head. He delved into his pocket and pulled out a large scrap of folded paper.

"Oh dear, why didn't you remind me I'd got a map? Or did I not say? No matter. I can't remember If I told you or not now," he said holding it up and starting to study it intently.

Scarlet couldn't believe her ears. "You mean you had a map all this time?" she asked dumfounded.

"And are you saying that we're actually lost down here?" asked an increasingly agitated Rusty.

"No, no, no, of course not. I told you, it was all memorised up here," he replied tapping his helmet. "And the map just verifies it. I've been counting our steps you see, and I've calculated precisely, with the given instructions I was given, that this is it."

"I don't understand, what is it? I don't see anything," said a bemused Scarlet, waving the lantern around.

"Oh, you can't see anything because you won't, will you?" he replied with a knowing grin. "What we seek is hidden on this very spot," he said looking really pleased with himself. "It's hidden in a chest buried beneath our very feet. Now tell me, did I remember to ask you to bring a shovel along with you?" he asked hopefully. Rusty and Scarlet both looked at one another, and then back at him, and shouted simultaneously.

"No, you did not!"

"Oh dear, no shovel to dig with. That won't do. That won't do at all. The Elder will be most displeased if I go back empty-handed, my apprenticeship will be short-lived for certain and I'll be sent back to the mainland in disgrace," moaned the miserable mole. "And as for you two, you'd be better off making a home down here in the mine. It would be much safer than facing his wrath!" Bookworm's shoulders slumped and he held his head in his paws, feeling dejected, with his head in his spade like paws looking close to tears.

"Look, there's no need to get upset." said Scarlet, now feeling sorry for him as it was impossible to stay angry with the crestfallen-looking mole. "We'll fix this, won't we Rusty?" she said giving him a gentle nudge.

"Er yes, of course we will. I'm sure we can find a way," he replied quickly, racking his brains to work out how to get a chest out of the ground without a shovel. "But wait a minute," he said brightening up, as a thought came to him out of the blue. "Aren't moles really good at digging?"

"Well, yes, you are correct, we are excellent excavators," Bookworm confirmed sheepishly. "But I have a delicate back you see. I've never dug a hole in my life. came his feeble excuse. "Unfortunately, of all the moles to bring along, you're stuck with useless old me, I'm afraid," he said still looking dejected. "Oh this won't do. This won't do at all," he groaned as his head sank deeper into his chest. And then his demeanour changed in an instant as he sprang back up lightly onto his feet. "Oh, silly me. No matter. I've just remembered what the Elder said to do once we reached the destination," he said grinning widely.

"I don't suppose you'd mind sharing this news?" asked Rusty, doing his best to keep his composure with the very trying, befuddled mole.

"What? Oh yes, now what did he say again? Once you've arrived, you just need to look up." And so, at the same time, all three did just that. Scarlet held the lantern up high and in the gloom they could just make out a grey cloth sack hanging from the ceiling. It was tied to a rafter by thick rope, just out of reach.

"Do you think you can reach up and undo that, Bookworm, if I lift you up?" asked Rusty.

"Yes, I suppose so.", it looks like a mooring hitch knot to me from here, but I'll need to get nearer to be sure," he replied, craning his neck to see. "Get me closer if you will. "

"Okay will do," replied Rusty, and

Rusty moved forward, grabbed Bookworm around the middle and lifting him up easily.

"Oh yes it's as I thought," he said examining the tie. "It's a quick-release knot, so if I just pull the tail it'll soon be free!"

And without any warning at all, he reached out and gave a sharp tug to the line of hanging rope and the sack cloth came crashing down with a big thump, narrowly missing everyone below.

"See? I told you I could do it," said a much happier Bookworm, totally oblivious of the near miss. Rusty put him down, relieved to see that no one was hurt from the sack, as Bookworm furtively delved into the sack. "You see the Elder is kind and fair." He beamed as he held up high in each paw a small pick and shovel. And so now, with the tools at hand to do the job, they set about their task with great vigour. It was decided that Bookworm would hold the lantern to light the way, as he freely admitted he was of little use for hard labour. So that left Rusty and Scarlet to dig.

Rusty took the pick and swung away to break up the ground beneath them, with Scarlet shovelling away the earth, until a hole had been made about half a metre deep. But there was still nothing to show for their efforts, so they took a short break.

"Are you definitely sure that we're in the right spot, Bookworm?" asked Rusty with an uncertain glance.

"Yes, I'm definitely sure," came the quick response. "Well, at least, I think I'm sure," he added with a thoughtful frown. "No matter. I never ever miscalculate. Though of course the law of averages means this could very well be the first time."

Before a now exasperated Rusty could harshly question his judgement, Scarlet decided she'd heard enough.

"If it's here, I'll find it!" she declared indignantly. Without any further hesitation, she got straight back to work with her shovel, and within a few seconds made contact with a loud thump as it hit a solid-sounding object.

"I think I've found something!" she declared, and began excitedly scraping back the soil by paw.

Slowly, surely, something came into view. With closer inspection, to their delight, what appeared to be the top of an old wooden chest came into sight. Seeing this, Rusty forgot his annoyance with the mole at once and immediately jumped in and joined Scarlet to help out, as they began to work together as one.

Before long, their endeavours had paid off handsomely, as they freed the large crate out of its pit and placed it down on the side with a bump. Now they could see the fruit of their labours. It was an old dark brown wooden chest with a metallic black hinge fastening down the lid, and secured with a large padlock.

"Oh, joy of joys! This is what we came for! Well done, you two. The Elder will be most pleased with our endeavours," Bookworm said in glee. Now over the moon, he did yet another little jig of delight. "There's no time to delay. Transport it out if you will. I'd help but of course my back would never forgive me."

Now with the lantern in hand to avoid trips and falls, Bookworm retraced their steps carefully as Rusty and Scarlet hauled the casket between them. Finally, and with great relief, they emerged back out into fresh air and they gratefully put down the heavy chest.

"You two guards, over here. Retrieve this for me, if you please," said Bookworm politely, as two soldiers ran straight over and heaved the box away.

Bookworm turned to face the exhausted couple once more. "Thank you for your help, whatever your names are," he gushed gratefully. "I certainly couldn't have done this without you! And now I've fulfilled my task I can fly home by hawk again with my head held high until I'm needed here once more!" He beamed. Preparing to leave, he said, "Please take care with your future endeavours, and who knows, maybe one day I will be able to return to the favour." Before turning and scurrying away with the laden guards following in his wake.

"Right, you lot, work duty over. Back to the compound or feel my whip!" yelled the burly sentry as the red squirrels fell into line and began to troop back.

"Do you think we'll ever see Bookworm again?" asked a tired-out Scarlet.

"You know what," replied Rusty thoughtfully, "I've got a feeling that somehow we will."

"Thank you so kindly, now please place it over there as I await the return of the Elder," said Bookworm to the two guards carrying the chest. They did as he asked and put it in the corner of the king's advisors' tent and then immediately left him alone.

"Well, that went even better than expected, and my ploy worked without fail," he said to himself. "Those fools didn't even realise it was I in their midst," he smirked, as he continued to admire his image. "Even though he has the beginnings of the foresight and should have sensed me, my powers are much greater, and I've blocked my real purpose with ease." He shows such weakness," he scoffed. "A mere novice of the old ways."

Glancing around, he checked to see he was still alone. Satisfied he was, he threw back his head and began to change. Dramatically, his whole body began to twist and contort and began to shrink in size, even his clothes altered too. In a few seconds he had shape shifted-back down to the size of a dormouse again.

Bookworm was no more, as Oswald the Elder had regained his true form. He then produced a key from a side drawer and went over to the chest, undoing the big lock and throwing back the lid with glee.

Inside was a long object wrapped carefully in a cloth covering. He reached in and pulled back the material to reveal his prize. It was half of an ancient sword, broken mid-way down the blade, its intricate designed golden handle gleaming back at him made a most welcoming sight. He had waited a long time to see the broken sword once more, having buried it himself many years ago deep in the mine for safekeeping.

Willard had ownership of the other half of the blade and refused to give it up, he mused. Thereafter followed a great battle. Oswald himself was exiled from the Brow by his very own brother over the fate of the riven blade. But he had returned and was now in raptures at seeing his half once more. "At last, we meet again," he gloated. "And soon the sword of Meriden will be whole once more. This I truly vow!" he said aloud, whilst wearing an evil grin.

CHAPTER TWENTY NINE

Back in the Great Wood everyone tried to stay calm and go about their daily business, but in these uncertain times it was difficult, to say the least. The grey guards now patrolled regularly and ID had to be shown immediately if stopped.

"Behave, or share the fate of the reds!" was the constant threat hanging over their heads.

It was another hot summer's day and barely a breeze was to be found as Rough and Archie took respite from the heat sitting in the cool shade of a beech tree casually eating handpicked fruit, drinking cold water, and doing their best not to draw attention to themselves.

"Any news of Rusty and the rest?" asked Rough between big bites out of a juicy red apple.

"Well, I sneaked down to the old mine yesterday and watched them all being taken back to the camp they've built," Archie replied. "They looked okay, I suppose, under the circumstances. And don't worry, no one saw this sly fox." He winked mischievously. Rough nodded approvingly whilst keeping one eye out for any new passing grey patrol.

"I snooped around today too, just to see what would happen," Rough admitted. "Acted as if I was doing my usual stuff, a bit of scavenging for fruit and scrap iron from the woods. The greys were everywhere though and I got stopped twice to show my ID. But it was fine, I showed them the paperwork and I could go on my way without too much bother. Don't know why they picked on me though. Not as if I look like trouble," he said with a shrug of his big shoulders, now gobbling down a handful of berries.

"I dunno, if I was a grey, I'd never let you out of my sight!" Archie laughed heartfully, which received a playful dig in the ribs for his trouble.

At that moment, two grey soldiers marched by, their pawsteps in unison., who completely ignored them. But the conversation was stilled until they were well out of sight. This was no time for complacency with both knowing any loose talk would be dealt with severely. Now satisfied they were gone, they continued their discussion again in hushed tones.

"Well, as agreed, I took a look around last night after curfew too, to check out their night patrols," confirmed Archie, careful to keep his voice down. "Managed to avoid 'em easily enough. They've got a bit cocky, if you ask me. There are less of 'em out at night thinking no one will dare venture out I reckon. But this wily fox doesn't scare easy!" He grinned. "Plus, they carry lanterns too. They stick out like sore thumbs. Nice of 'em to do that, don't you think? So much easier to avoid," he joked.

"Good job, Arch. You took a big risk there, mate," said an impressed-looking Rough. "But what do you reckon our chances are of avoiding them if we make our move at night?"

Archie gave a casual shrug. "I won't lie, it'll be tough." He then leaned in closer, just to be sure they wouldn't be overheard. "I heard it through the grapevine they've involved the rats – Misfit and his crew – to help keep the night vigil."

"Yeah, I've heard that too, giving them a chance to prove their loyalty," Rough replied in disgust. "Well, I'll tell you something for free, I bet they can't even spell the word loyalty, never mind show any!"

"Too right," agreed Archie, wearing his trade-mark grin but never dropping his guard once, furtively looking around for any sign of the enemy. "So, what do you reckon? We go tonight?" he asked.

Rough still finishing his fruit didn't need to give it any more thought and gave a slight nod of assent before whispering. "We'll meet under the willow tree near my sett, just after midnight."

Midnight duly arrived and the two met up as planned, unnoticed in the undercover of the night, and headed straight out towards the Maleficent Meadow. The evening was deathly quiet, which was most unusual for the Great Wood, with even the odd nocturnal creature banned from roaming under the new regime.

As they crept along, they were pleased to see there was no moon out tonight to bathe the world in its heavenly glow, and not even a star could be seen in the cloud-covered sky. They hadn't gone far when trouble suddenly loomed ahead. Bright lights could be seen spread out in a line coming their way like warning beacons on a hill, accompanied by distant shouts. They immediately recognised one as Misfit, his unmistakable whiny voice carrying far in the still of the night.

"Come on, we've been given a job, let's do this properly!" he shouted to his

The Battle for Badgers Brow

fellow rats, receiving a guttural grunt in return. As they drew ever closer, Rough and Archie froze, crouching down in the thickets hardly daring to breathe, hoping they would pass them by unnoticed. And then at once, from the opposite direction came another shout as four grey guards rapidly approached the rats.

"You lazy lot, have you covered much ground tonight?" yelled the leader of the troops dressed in the grey armour.

"Yes, Captain Dire, but there's nothing to report. All quiet," Misfit answered compliantly.

"Well, get a move on then, don't stand there gossiping!"

Dire snapped bluntly. "And any animal that's breaking curfew, detain immediately!"

Misfit saluted and gave the signal to move out, and much to the alarm of the hidden two, continued straight towards them. Archie nudged Rough and gestured over his shoulder.

"No time to waste, this way," he whispered. Rough agreed silently and they crept away as carefully as possible from the ever-advancing patrol. Edging away, the lights thankfully grew distant in the dark.

But a new problem now arose as they realised they were heading away from the meadow and in the wrong direction, towards the quarry instead. Then a sudden movement ahead, and at once they were caught in the glare of a relit lantern, the light momentarily blinding them as an ominous-looking figure now blocked their path. It was Misfit staring icily at them. And then he opened his mouth to speak.

"Nothing to see here, sector four all clear!" bellowed Misfit loudly, before stooping and giving them a firm warning. "I don't know what you're doing out here, but it's lucky for you I'm not a grey!" he hissed. "Now go home, you fools, before you're detected. They won't take you prisoner," he said his eyes darting nervously to and fro. "If they know I've not handed you in, I'm as good as dead too. Rebels don't last long. Now clear off!" Then he turned his back on them and moved away.

Rough and Archie looked at each other in utter disbelief thinking surely they'd been caught for sure. It made no sense. That was Misfit, he works for them! Why did he let them go?

But there was no time to process this new development as the sound of the searchers moving noisily through the undergrowth grew ever near. And then the shrill sound of a loud whistle pierced the air, like the cry of an attacking bird of prey, followed by the captain's voice calling out loud and clear, sending a cold shiver down their spines. They'd been spotted!

"Over there, two of 'em, don't let 'em get away!"

They looked up to see the lanterns moving in the dark growing in number.

All thoughts of stealth were now abandoned as Rough and Archie fled for their lives, desperately crashing through the brush. And then suddenly, to their dismay, they came to an abrupt halt, now confronted by the quarry's edge. Peering over the precipice into nothingness, Archie made a snap decision as their pursuers closed in. He grabbed Rough by the shoulders, looking him straight in the eye.

"We need to split up, meet back at the meadow," he said in desperation. "Good luck, mate," were his final words and before Rough could argue, he shot off. Archie knew what he was doing, buying time to save his friend and ran head-on purposely in to trouble. A grey trooper then stepped out as if from nowhere, and held him at sword point.

"Save yourself, I'll hold them off!" Archie yelled, and drew his short sword, taking up a fighting stance. The rest now caught up with the first, and surrounded him, grinning. Captain Dire then appeared from amongst them ogling his prey.

"What have we here then, a rebel?" he smirked, as Archie faced them, prodding here and there in an awkward attempt to fend them all off. Dire then yawned theatrically. "I'm not in the mood for taking prisoners, make an example of him. Finish him!" he ordered coolly.

The first trooper on the scene obeyed at once. Being much smaller than the fox, he leapt into the air, raised his sword arm to strike and swung it down in a vicious arc, aiming for a head strike. But Archie, having survived many a scrape back in the Great Wood read it easily enough and parried it away, knocking his assailant off balance. He then sidestepped, swung hard, and smashed the soldier hard on the side of the helmet with his blade, killing him instantly.

"Come on then, who's next?" Archie yelled defiantly, waving the blade to and fro. But his small victory achieved only one thing. Enraging Dire even more.

"Fools, take him as one!" he thundered, as Rough appeared on the scene.

"Nooo!" he screamed, as he looked on helplessly as the greys leapt into action, and Archie fell instantly under a barrage of blows.

Dire now standing over the stricken body of the brave fox drooled with pleasure at the gory sight, and then raised his head, grinning fiendishly.

"Give it up, badger. We'll make it quick like we did for him!" he sneered, as the greys advanced in a half-circle. Checking quickly behind him into the pitch-black darkness below, Rough realised he was cornered and there was nowhere else to go. As they pounced, he roared defiantly one last time.

"You won't take me tonight. For the freedom of the Great Wood!" came his final shout as he turned and threw himself off the edge, disappearing into the cold night air.

CHAPTER THIRTY

Dawn was breaking as Rough awoke with a start. Where am I? he thought, confusion filling his clouded mind. He blinked and opened his eyes, finding his vision blurred and out of focus. He lay still for a moment, and as his head slowly cleared, the awful memories of last night's ordeal came back to haunt him.

The meet up in the dark, being discovered, and then the brutal slaying of his friend Archie. His stomach churned at the thought, and despair washed over him like waves on a beach as the nightmarish image played over in his mind. But then he'd jumped, and now? He looked around to find himself lying in a thicket that had grown out of the side of the quarry wall roughly half-way down. What luck! It must have broken my fall, came the stark realization.

He then turned his head to see the quarry floor many metres below, knowing a drop from this height would prove fatal. Over in the distance, on the far side, he spied the old mine. The work would soon start again, he thought, as he noticed the sun rising higher in the early morning sky. And then, in the upper atmosphere, movement caught his eye. What appeared at first to be swirling black dots, like a swarm of bees around a hive, then became apparent as his vision began to clear.

To his horror he realised he'd seen the crow riders on aerial patrol. He now knew his situation was growing more desperate by the minute. He'd be spotted by any greys on mine duty or from above, sooner rather than later. No time to waste. If he was to survive, he had to move, and he had to move now. He had to get to Willard somehow.

"Come on, I can do this," he said to himself, even though he was balanced precariously in the outcropping bush. "This is for you Archie," he vowed, as he pulled himself up into a sitting position. As he did so, he realised how difficult getting away would prove as his back, injured in the fall, shot an excruciating pain straight through his very core.

"I need to move, and move right now," he said in an attempt to rally himself. He turned to look up and there, just above him, a possible way out, a paw hold jutting out of the escarpment. It's now or never, he thought, as the circling birds overhead seemed closer than ever.

Ignoring the searing pain, he twisted his battered body, reached out and grabbed the rock. Just above, he could make out another protruding part of the quarry face, and more ripples in the terrain further up too. This gave him renewed hope and with an almighty effort he pulled himself up, took hold and began scrambling slowly up the rock face.

"Don't look down, don't look down," he repeated to himself as he made painfully slow progress. The back pain was now worse than ever, but the thought of failure spurred him on. And then suddenly, a foothold broke free, sending debris spinning and crashing far below. He hung on now for dear life, pressing himself tight against the red sandstone wall. But somehow, he didn't fall and gaining extra purchase from sheer desperation, pushed on.

After what seemed an eternity, first one paw and then the other, reached out to grab a firm hold of the summit, and with one last Herculean effort he pulled himself clear and dropped thankfully to his paws, his head bowed in near exhaustion.

Gasping and fighting for every breath after such exertion, the world began to spin, and as he raised his head he groaned outwardly at the miserable sight before him. Standing over him head cocked to one side was a curious large black bird.

"Oh no, after all that, the crows have got me. I've failed," he gasped. Then he passed out.

CHAPTER THIRTY ONE

The following evening, the long victory banquet table, draped in a huge white tablecloth, was heaving, with the best bounty the island could offer. All types of steaming hot stews, lots of delicious pies, handpicked fruits and what felt like mountains of cakes, ready to be washed down with lots of piping hot tea.

They had been placed in a clearing in the woods with enough chairs to seat fifty. Slate sat at the top of the table with Oswald, Ash and his commanders plus a selection of the Grey Army chosen at random. Seated at the other end sat Misfit and his fellow rats, plus any other minions. The rest were made up of hand-picked Great Wood residents, most too afraid to say no.

"I must say, I'm most impressed, Elder, with the generosity of the local natives," remarked Slate, slurping noisily on his stew.

"Yes, sire, most generous," replied Oswald, trying his best not to look repulsed as the king always ate with his mouth wide open, showing the contents to one and all.

"Indeed, Elder, all they need is a gentle push in the right direction – or off the nearest cliff – like that badger last night!"

Slate roared, bursting into laughter, with all the table following suit. And of course, when he stopped, they all did too, as no one was stupid enough to out laugh the king. One poor unfortunate grey chuckled a little too long when all had gone quiet. Realising his mistake, he looked around wide-eyed in panic, before being roughly dragged out of his chair by a burly commander and thrown into the nearest bush for his perceived rudeness, which gained a satisfactory nod of approval from Slate.

"Oh yes, I did enjoy how Captain Dire told of his bravery. How he single-handedly dispatched the heavily armed fox," recalled Slate, now sipping noisily from a mug of tea. "And then, how he hurled the badger to his doom. That's a nice touch. I do so approve. Most impressive, he'll go far. But not as far as the badger! Hah. Oh, I do enjoy a good jest!" He smirked, followed by a big toothy yawn. "Now, Elder, I'm feeling bored – amuse me! A few of your parlour tricks will suffice. And make it snappy," he ordered rudely, with a dismissive wave.

"Of course, sire," simpered Oswald, inwardly seething at the king's slight of his prowess and his lack of manners. Then he took a deep breath in order to stay calm. Knowing what would please Slate, he looked down the table and picked out two grey soldiers at random. He was careful not to choose a commander, as that would be foolish, and he was nobody's fool.

He raised his paws and concentrated. At once, they both levitated out of their seats simultaneously, with a look of shock and disbelief on their faces, and at the same time, in the centre of the table a tray of cakes lifted too. The cakes then jumped up into the air and flew at them, splattering both. First one cake, then another.

Oswald then dropped his paws and they both fell into their seats looking utterly embarrassed, as the empty tray clattered down onto the middle of the table.

"Ha, ha, bravo!" cheered slate. "Oh, I do love a good food
 fight," and with that, pushed a cream cake into the face of the commander on his right!

"Well, what are you waiting for?" shouted Slate. "Food fight!" The rats all looked at one another, with Misfit shrugging his shoulders, before pushing a huge tart into Pitter's face. "Come on, join in or else we'll end up in a bush or over a cliff edge too," he added ruefully. And with that, the food fight started in earnest, with everyone pelting each other with cakes, and any other food at hand, of course none daring to throw any in the king's direction. Even Oswald had a cupcake hurled at him, but he just batted it away easily with a raise of a paw before it hit.

The king found it all hilarious and clapped his paws with glee and stamped his feet, loving every minute of the mayhem, with food flying through the air left, right and centre. But after a few more minutes, he suddenly tired of it and called a halt with a bored-looking wave. Everyone stopped flinging food around the table at once, with all the guests now dripping in food and goo.

"Oh, this is the best banquet ever!" ever declared Slate, grinning inanely. "Now, Elder, the finale. Fireworks! Oh, I do love a good display."

Oswald obliged at once by simply pointing up to the sky, and with a wave of his paw, the night sky was filled with crashes and bangs as pyrotechnics appeared in an array of reds, yellows, gold and slivers spreading across the sky in a brilliant illusion.

"Yet another of your best tricks, Elder. Excellent."

"Of course, sire, I'm only here to please," he replied forcing a smile, doing his best to hide his utter contempt.

Meanwhile, at the nearby compound, the captives sat resting after a long day's labour. They'd been fed only meagre rations and the aroma of the food from the banquet wafting over smelt delicious, as if they were doing their best to torment them. The four guards that were unlucky enough to be on duty, had spent their watch grumbling to each other at how they'd missed out, and how there would be nothing but scraps left for them at the end.

Then the fireworks lit up the velvety night in an impressive display of colour. Bright shapes emblazoned the blank canvas of the cloudless clear sky, leaving long glistening trails, accompanied by lots of bangs and whooshes.

Rusty stood watching with his arm around Scarlet admiring the fine display through the fence, momentarily forgetting how bleak the situation had become, as the young amongst the captives clung to their parents, open-mouthed in awe. And then suddenly as if from nowhere, a figure could be seen fast approaching them. It was difficult to see who it was at first, but to their astonishment it wasn't another grey guard that had joined them.

Now closer, they could see who it was. Standing on the other side of the fence was Ash. He looked around breathlessly, and then astounded them both by what he said next.

"I'm here to break you out!"

CHAPTER THIRTY TWO

"Well, hello, my friend. You've been at rest for quite a while now," said a softly spoken voice. Rough slowly opened his eyes to find he was in Willard's cottage lying on a mound of well-placed cushions. Willard himself was standing over him, peering at him through his small round glasses, perched on a foot stool, wearing a look of concern.

"Ooh, my head," Rough moaned loudly, placing one paw on his throbbing temple. "How did I get here?"

"You can thank the ever-watchful Chance for that," Willard answered affably.

Rough turned his head slowly to see Chance, with Izzy too in the room, smiling back at him, accompanied by the familiar sound of clattering coming from the kitchen.

"You asked how you got here?" Willard continued. "I think the answer is best coming from you, my friend," he said gesturing to the raven.

"Of course," Chance replied. He was usually one of few words, unless the occasion called for it. And this moment merited an explanation, so he began to tell all.

"I was out for a morning flight when I noticed on the horizon the crows acting oddly, circling in loops, so I thought I'd take a closer look. As I approached, flying low to remain unseen, the old sandstone quarry came into sight, and I noticed someone clinging to the side. I doubled back, and on closer inspection, I could see it was you, Rough. And then I realised the crows were ridden, and that surely meant trouble, so I landed out of sight. You were making good progress climbing out, so I waited patiently at the top. You made it up but collapsed from your injuries right at my feet, so my next move was to keep you from discovery, and out of sight. I broke away a few branches to give you cover, and flew to get help."

"So what happened next, how did I get here?" Rough asked still feeling light-headed.

"Well, that's where I come in," said Izzy. "Chance returned immediately to the pine forest and raised the alarm. Well, once I heard about your predicament, what choice did I have but to come to the rescue? So I jumped straight into action, gathered a team together and came straight over. As quickly as we could, we carried you back on a make-shift stretcher to Willard's place. Keeping to secret trails so leaving no chance to be followed, I may add," she winked. "Finally, Willard gave you some of his famed fix-all medicine and hopefully, you'll be as good as new soon!" she beamed.

"And rest assured, my fix-all heals all maladies," Willard promised with a light smile. "Now, Rough the badger, tell me what exactly is going on? Even though I fear I may know already. Start from the beginning and miss nothing out."

So Rough did just that, commencing with the invasion of the Grey Army, the captivity of the red squirrels, and the subjugation of the rest. Then the attempt to find help, the heroism of Archie and finally his leap of desperation. Willard listened solemnly as Izzy tensely paced up and down the room, taking in every word.

"That explains the rumours we've heard," she said. "Something odd happening in the south. We were about to come and see for ourselves but now we know the full extent. An invasion though? It's hard to take in," she said in disbelief.

"So what was foretold has finally arisen," Willard said forlornly. "And I am indeed sorry for the loss of your friend," he added with genuine remorse.

"Thanks, much appreciated, Arch was one of the best," replied Rough sadly. "He went down fighting to the last though," he added, with a melancholy smile.

A few moments of silence then followed as the gravity of the situation began to sink in. Willard stepped away and went to sit alone at a table to contemplate awhile, and gazed through the window at the forest outside lost in thought. After gathering his thoughts, he turned to them and spoke his mind.

"Archie was indeed most heroic and we must assure his bravery was not in vain," Willard began. "Therefore we must act at once, decisive action is needed if we are to turn the tide," he added gravely. "The greys have arrived, but surely not alone. I fear they are assisted with the aid of an old adversary, Oswald the Elder. I have felt his presence again recently and that explains my inability to contact Rusty, and not knowing of the threat. He must have blocked such thoughts from my mind. Of such deeds he is very capable," he concluded, with a worried frown. He then let out a huge sigh. "This Slate is a fool if he thinks he controls him, for he is treacherous, and much more powerful than he could ever imagine."

"Powerful in what way?" asked Rough, now beginning to feel a little better.

"In ways you cannot imagine," Willard replied ominously. "Long ago, he chose the path of evil and will not bow to anyone. Therefore, he must be stopped at all costs, for the lives of all who dwell on the Brow are at risk." Willard knew what was needed to be done.

"Izzy, Chance, take Screech with you and make haste," he said quickly. "Take this message to all who will listen. We're to raise an army of our own to right this wrong!" he cried, with a slam of his tiny paw on the table. "Tell them we have evil in our midst, and the invaders will not stop until they have vanquished all in their path. We need all the help we can muster as Oswald will not leave anything to chance. For he will surely wish to bolster their forces and reunite with an ally of old. An enemy that dwells only in the north."

Rusty stared at Ash through the gate of the dividing fence in total disbelief. "How can you stand there and continue to lie to us?" he seethed. "Why don't you just stop gloating? Move on and go back to your banquet, and leave us alone in peace!"

Ash stayed silent for now knowing actions would speak louder than any words he could offer. So he drew a sword from his belt, and swung it with all his might at the large padlock that secured the gate. It hit with a resounding clang, and the lock broke away, falling to the floor. The barrier swung open immediately. They were all momentarily stunned and no one made a move. Being caught by surprise by his deed, they weren't sure what to do next.

"Here, take the sword. Call it a show of good faith," said Ash taking a chance and tossing it straight to him, leaving himself unarmed.

Rusty caught it easily and stared back gripping the sword tightly, and Scarlet reading the anger in his eyes, for a fleeting moment thought he was going to strike him down. But something from deep within held him back. It was the foresight. It staid his paw long enough for his temper to cool, like water on a flame, and realise that Ash was not a threat. Well, at least for now. He then glanced in the direction of the guards.

"I don't see the sentries, where are they?" he asked sharply.

"Don't worry about them," Ash assured him, relieved his risk had paid off. "I gave them a night cap – a sleeping draught – they're out for the count." He grinned. "Now come on, there's no time to waste. We need to leave before the alarm is raised! Most are at the banquet but there are a few patrols out. I've found a cove along the shoreline to hide out in," he insisted, pointing towards the coast.

Rusty somehow knew he spoke the truth. He could sense it without any doubt, so he turned to his fellow captives in the compound and raised an arm. "There's no future here, only death. Come on, we're leaving!" he urged. "Grab the guards' weapons. We're getting out of here!"

CHAPTER THIRTY THREE

And so off they went with Ash leading the way along the shoreline. The night was cold but clear. They travelled fast, and luck was on their side as they met with no interference of any kind, the only sound to be heard was the waves of the sea crashing against the shore. After an hour's trouble-free trek, they came to the spot that Ash had promised would be waiting, as the cove came into view.

It was a small sheltered bay and was a safe refuge for now. As they filed thankfully into the shelter, Rusty pulled Ash to one side.

"You've delivered so far," he admitted, "but if you want me to believe you when you say want to help, you've got some
explaining to do."

As the escapees found suitable spots to rest and recover in the cove from their ordeal, Rusty and Ash sat down to talk.

"Go ahead, I'm listening," Rusty said patiently, as Ash cleared his throat and began to tell his tale.

"I was born in what you call faraway land," he began. "I'm an orphan, so I never knew my family and I was brought up in the military academy of the Grey Army. That's the only life I know. We were taught by a tutor, who said he'd ventured here many years ago. His name was Oswald, now risen through the ranks to become the king's advisor."

"Carry on," said Rusty, "I'm listening. "

"He taught us that the greys are superior to all, even to himself. 'I'm just a lowly dormouse here to serve' was one of his favourite lines," Ash recalled, quoting him directly. "He taught us about this island we could see from afar. This is where the aggressor lives, we were told."

"Meaning us?" Rusty asked, desperate to know more.

"Yes, exactly. 'The reds are our natural enemy and not to be trusted' were his very words. He had the king's ear by then and no doubt this is what Slate wanted him to say too."

A few metres away, Scarlet stood with Brick, observing them deep in conversation, just out of earshot.

"What do you think he's telling Rusty?" she said quietly to him.

"I don't know. But if it doesn't go well, I'll be first in line to finish the traitor off!" Brick spat angrily.

"Slate is the ruler of the grey squirrels and he rules with an iron fist," Ash continued to explain to Rusty. "He took control a few years ago by force in the battle of the steel mill, and it's not wise to cross him. He's always surrounded by his elite guard, and everyone bows to the king's demands or pays the consequences. His chief advisor, as you know, is Oswald the Elder, you may have seen him at the victory speech. My old teacher dabbles in sorcery and spells and can be very dangerous too," he added.

"Yes, I saw Slate and his advisor on the so-called victory day," Rusty answered ruefully. "And this Oswald, he has an apprentice, a mole named Bookworm. We met him at the mine too. Tell me about him," he requested, wanting to know as much as possible about the enemy.

Ash shrugged. "I don't know this mole so he must be a new arrival," Ash admitted. "I've been here for quite a while you see. I was sent ahead as a scout, to check out the area's strengths and weaknesses and report back. But shortly after arrival, I was captured by our friend Finnegan, and of course that's when we first met. And that's when things began to change."

Rusty hadn't taken his eyes off him for a second. But he still sensed the truth in his words and beckoned for him to continue.

"I now see it was all lies, everything they told me about the reds and the island are false," Ash admitted. "You befriended me from the start, and took me in as one of your own. Treated me like a brother, like family, in a way I've never known before." His head dropped, seemingly overcome at the thought. He stopped for a second to regain his composure and then continued.

"I've learnt how wrong I was and I'll never again judge a creature by the colour of its fur. Look, I wouldn't blame you for not believing in me, but I'll prove myself to you," Ash pleaded. "I've been trained in armed combat and if it comes to it, I'll fight by your side if need be."

Rusty smiled and said, "I believe you."

And with one look, Ash knew he meant it.

"Thank you, I promise I won't let you down," Ash replied gratefully.

"I know you won't," replied Rusty reaching out to him and placing an arm on his shoulder. "Now go get some rest, we need to sleep and form a plan at first light."

As Ash went to find a place to rest his head for the night, Scarlet came over to Rusty's side.

"Can we trust him?" she asked with a look of concern.

Rusty turned to her, pulled her close, and quietly replied. "Yes, we can, I'm certain of it. Don't ask me to explain why or how I know because I don't really understand it myself," he asked. She looked into his eyes and somehow, she knew he was right.

"I trust your judgment, but the others may need more convincing," she said, her voice tinged in concern as she glanced over at the brooding figure of Brick.

"I'll talk to the others tomorrow, leave that to me," assured Rusty. "But for now, let's get some rest."

The following morning, after a restless night, Rusty had risen early, woken by the stiff breeze blowing in from the sea. The sun was rising brightly heralding a new day, so he went with a few volunteers to forage for food. They found fresh fruit and nuts growing nearby and water too from a running stream, so a breakfast of sorts was distributed out. He made sure Brick came along too, and after a long discussion convinced him to give Ash another chance. He'd reluctantly agreed but had warned Rusty if he betrayed them again, it would be the last thing Ash would ever do.

They had found enough to keep their hunger and thirst at bay for now and after eating, Rusty went for a short stroll, paw in paw, along the water's edge with Scarlet.

"I've decided to strike out this morning and seek out Willard," he told her. "I just feel he'll know what to do. I've tried to reach him through thought again, as he asked, but for some reason I just can't," he said remorsefully. "And I know Rough and Archie went for help, but what if they somehow failed? I can't wait around for Slate to find us, I have to try."

"Well, count me in, I'm coming along too," said Scarlet bravely. "Someone has got to make sure you're safe." She grinned, holding onto him tightly.

"I never doubted for a minute you wouldn't," he said returning her smile. They then walked and talked a while, and agreed a plan of sorts. "I'll ask Brick to gather the watch together," Rusty suggested. "It'll be a dangerous task and so I'll ask for volunteers.

"So you're organising a mission," said Brick enthusiastically, later that morning back in the cove. "Well, count me in, especially if it means banging a few grey heads together!"

He grinned. "And it's unanimous, all the watch are coming along too," he added. "I've spoken to Chilli, Madder, Carmine and Cornell – they wouldn't miss it for the world.

"You're not going without me either," said Ash strolling over. "Sorry, I overheard you talking. I can help, I know how they work, you need me."

Brick said nothing but bristled at the thought. He consoled himself at the thought that at least he could keep a close eye on him.

And so it was decided that a small group would go for help, while most stayed in the cave, to stay safe and watch over the young and elderly, until their return.

Rusty led the way as they snaked up the pathway of a nearby hill, with Scarlet, Ash, Brick, Carmine, Madder, Chilli and Cornell following in line. They waved their goodbyes from its summit, and left with shouts of 'Good luck' ringing in their ears.

"This is the beginning of the resistance and the fight back against the greys. I can feel it in my bones," said an upbeat Scarlet, with renewed resolve as they headed away.

"I truly hope so," replied Rusty trying to match her enthusiasm, but inside he was deeply concerned, knowing the fate of so many relied on the fortunes of so few.

CHAPTER THIRTY FOUR

"What do you mean they have all escaped. How can this be?" Slate thundered, leaning forwards with fury written all over his face. His paws were gripping the chair so tightly his knuckles had turned white. If looks could kill, the unfortunate trooper who had delivered the news would be dead by now instead of being able to back away, deftly ducking as the king hurled his teacup, which went flying over his head shattering into a hundred pieces as he crept out of the king's tent fearing for his life.

"How could this happen?" he shrieked, his voice hitting a high-pitched crescendo which always happened when he was at his maddest, before turning his attention to Commander Stone. "I put you in charge of security and you've let them get away?" he bellowed; his eyes locked on Stone like a predator waiting to strike.

Stone knew he had to think quickly or he would be replaced. Or worse.

"Sire, I've got my best soldiers looking for them now, and the crow riders are out in force too. They can't have got far and will soon be captured, of that I'm sure."

"You'd better be right, Stone, or make a run for it too!" Slate snarled. "And while you're at it, round up the usual suspects!" Slate snapped, as he kicked over his footstool in temper.

"But, sire, there aren't any usual suspects," replied Stone nervously. "We've only been here a short while."

"Well, find some then! Do I have to do everything for you?" Slate screamed, his patience reaching breaking point. He then searched in desperation for his advisor. "Elder, Elder. Where's the Elder?" he yelled, wringing his paws in

The Battle for Badgers Brow

exasperation.

"I'm right here, sire," replied Oswald meekly. "At your feet."

"Oh yes, so you are, dormouse," said Slate dropping his gaze.

"I didn't see you down there. Well, you're supposed to be the clever one, advise me!" he snapped.

But just as Oswald opened his mouth to reply, a guard burst breathlessly into the tent.

"Your majesty, excuse my interruption but we've had a possible sighting of some of the runaways, by a crow rider."

"Sighting? Well, come on, speak up, stop dithering, spit it out, you imbecile!" growled Slate.

"Well, sire, he's sure he saw a small group of reds, and one of ours, a grey, heading north from the coast and reported straight back as ordered."

"See!" shouted slate wide-eyed with excitement. "Look what can be done when you actually get your paw out. And they must have one of ours hostage too, the cowards. Well don't just stand there, Stone, get the garrison together!"

"Yes, sire. Right away, sire," said a relieved Stone, rushing out of the tent just glad to get away. Once outside, he immediately called Captain Dire over.

"I want fifty troops ready to go at once!" he ordered. "Use the rats. Any sign of trouble, we can send them in first, as they're expendable."

"Yes, sir. Right away, sir," replied Dire, giving the two-fisted salute then rushed off to complete his task.

Back inside the tent, Slate still cut a frustrated figure, ready to explode at the slightest thing as Oswald watched on with unease.

"Now, Elder, where were we? Oh, yes. You were about to give me your counsel. Make it count, I can't have this. It's not good, not good at all," he fumed, shaking his head in disbelief. His eyes locked on him. "Elder, heads will roll if I don't get a satisfactory outcome, understood?" he threatened.

Oswald was now on his guard. "Yes, sire, of course," he said choosing his words very carefully. "I would suggest now we have a sighting of the fugitives, would it not be prudent if you led the charge? After all, they are greatly outnumbered, and think of the odes that will be sung in the honour of your great victory over the red scourge."

Slate sat back to digest the idea, and then his face burst out into a huge grin. "Yes, Elder, I do like the sound of that," he replied, his mood now lifting in an instant. "And who doesn't love a good ode, especially when it's about yours truly. And you're guaranteeing it won't be dangerous, and I won't be put in harm's way?"

"No, my liege, not at all. They are unarmed, desperate, and massively outnumbered. They are no match for the elite who will surround and protect you at all times. And as you know, I myself have a trick or two up my sleeve also," he assured him with a crafty smile.

"Very good then, Elder. I will listen to your guidance. After all, who doesn't love a good old-fashioned hunt, eh? And another thing, Elder. Use your gift to track him down. There's more than one way to skin a red."

Rusty and the rest had made good progress and as far as they were concerned had remained concealed, and managed to avoid any patrols. Then out of the blue, voices could be heard just up ahead. Rusty signalled for the others to stay back as he and Ash crept forward for a better look.

As they peered through the scrub, they could now see who the voices belonged to. Four grey troopers sat resting outside a tent on stools. Under the hot midday sun, they sat with their weapons and armour removed – for comfort from the heat – as they drank and ate their rations.

"So, what are the orders?" a burly grey asked, sitting with his back to them.

"We're to look out for the runaway reds," said another much smaller soldier, taking a big slurp from his mug before belching loudly. "So keep your eyes peeled. There'll be a big reward in this one, well as soon as we've finished our break," he said grinning, as the others chortled loudly, rubbing their paws together in anticipation of a big pay day.

Ash looked at Rusty and whispered in his ear, "Come on, there are only four of them, we can take them easily."

"No, wait, I have a better idea. It's something I've been waiting to try out."

The greys were just finishing their drinks and preparing to leave, when brazenly out of the bush Rusty strolled straight towards them.

"Oi, red, stop right there. I want a word with you!" demanded the burly grey, leaping up and grabbing his sword after spotting the intruder.

Rusty came to a halt just in front of him as the others remained seated, smirking and enjoying the show.

"Okay, red. What you doing out here on your own? Come here, little fella. Don't worry, I won't hurt you," said the burly grey as he approached Rusty, now towering over him. And then, in an instant and without warning, he swung his sword from left to right aiming straight at his head. But much to his bewilderment it passed straight through the red squirrel! Now unbalanced, he landed in a big heap, for this was not Rusty but his phantom self, a ruse he had been waiting to try out.

He'd practised quietly alone projecting his image and now he knew for sure it truly worked. The burly grey got to his feet, turned round, and realised he'd been tricked. To his dismay, his comrades had been taken by surprise and were being held at sword point by the fugitives they sought. Now humiliated, he eyed them angrily.

"You have two options," Brick said firmly.

"Oh yeah, and what are they?" the soldier replied doing his best to look brave, whilst weighing up the odds, which didn't look good.

"The easy option? Drop the sword. The hard option? Go through me. It's your call," challenged Brick.

The burly grey for the first time took a proper look at the big imposing red standing before him. He quickly decided he was outmatched and reluctantly let go of his weapon.

"Wise choice," said Brick. "You're not as stupid as you look. You couldn't be."

After relieving them of their swords, it didn't take too long to take some rope from their tent, and bind them around a nearby tree, and before you knew it, they were on their way again.

"That was a great trick you played there, Rust," said Ash. "It certainly would have fooled me."

"Thanks, it's the first time I've tried it on others too." He grinned. "Willard was right, I just needed to clear my mind and concentrate." But Ash had stopped listening, halting dead in his tracks and staring straight ahead.

They had reached a clearing in the woods just before the meadow and standing in their way was no other than Misfit, Pitter, Patter, Hugh, Hugo and Huw.

"Well, I'll tell you one thing for free." Misfit smiled slyly. "It doesn't take long to find you!"

Brick advanced at once, wielding the newly acquired sword taken from the burly grey. Rusty and the others had taken their pick too and must have looked an odd sight to the rats, now armed with the greys' swords and shields. Brick purposely picked out the largest rat amongst them – Hugo – and sent out a challenge.

"The bigger they are, the harder they fall," he warned as he stared him down.

"Woah, steady on!" cried Misfit holding out his paws. "There's no need for violence! We're all friends here, surely?" he whined, "Come on, let me explain our intentions, at least."

Brick came to a halt and turned his attention to Misfit. "You've got a minute, rat. Make it good or else I'll clear a path straight through you all, starting with you first," he threatened with a growl.

"Okay, relax. Stay calm and hear me out," said Misfit, trying his best to look convincing. "Look, as you know, we've never seen eye to eye," he said directly to Rusty. "But we've now got a common enemy in Slate, so that changes everything," he added, slowly approaching him. "I've had the misfortune to see him close-up and personal, you see, and believe me, he's as mad as a box of frogs."

"Yeah right," Brick retorted, not believing a word.

"I saw you at the banquet trying to cosy up to him too!" shouted Chilli accusingly over Rusty's shoulder, which gained a murmur of agreement from the rest.

"What, oh that? I was just using one of the oldest tricks in the book," Misfit said cunningly. "Weighing up the enemy, looking for a weak link. I got dragged away remember? Forced into working for them too. A bit like yourselves," he fibbed, along with his best attempt at a fake smile, which received nothing but another hard stare from Brick. Misfit saw this, gulped at the sight, but carried on. "Oh, where was I? Oh yes. Wondering how I found you so easily?" he asked, stopping a metre away from Rusty. "I took an educated guess you'd come this way. Well, I may have snooped on you before, when you crossed the meadow on this very route, but hey, that's another story!" He grinned. Then he came closer still. "And don't think you're in the clear. Oh no, the crows have done their job," he said pointing skywards. "There are around fifty or so of the greys heading your way right now too, led by Slate himself," he told them eagerly, knowing that would get their attention. And he was right. The news caused a stir amongst them all, because as far as they were concerned, they had remained unseen.

Misfit noted the look of surprise, and bolstered by, this continued on with renewed vigour. "Yeah, I know that's a lot of greys for such a small group of rebels."

"Just get on with it then. What do you want?" snapped Brick, becoming more and more irritated with the irksome rat.

"I'm getting to the point," Misfit answered.

"Calm down, will you?", which gained him Brick's fiercest glare yet. "We've had our rivalries but I suggest a truce," he went on, trying to ignore the big red. "We need to work together, it's the only way to get them off our island once and for all. Oh, and as a goodwill gesture I've even gone to your home, at great risk to myself I may add, to pick up the bag you're oh so precious about."

Pitter then produced the charmed bag and threw it over to Rusty who caught it neatly in mid-air. It felt like meeting with an old friend again, and he placed it gladly on his back.

"Now, for some good news," Misfit grinned. "The Maleficent Meadow lies ahead, and there was a recent fire caused by a lightning strike in the storm. My bet is you're heading to see the wise one again," he said with a smug-looking grin. "Well, the blaze cut a path straight through the middle of it, so we can be there in no time at all. Anyway, talk it through amongst yourselves, but you'd better hurry, they're on our tails, and I do mean literally." Misfit laughed and then sauntered cockily back to rejoin his fellow rats. Rusty and the rest huddled together in deep discussion.

"What do you reckon?" said Madder. "Can we trust 'em?"

"Do we even need them?" asked Cornell.

"I don't see how we have much choice. If what he says is true, they can't be far behind," reasoned Scarlet. "What do you think, Rusty? What do your instincts tell you now?"

Rusty felt the most assured he had in a while now being reunited with the bag. "There's one overriding thing I do sense about Misfit," he replied swiftly. "It's fear. It's all an act, he's not brave at all. He's a very scared animal. And it's not us he's afraid of."

The grey garrison had quickly been given their new orders by Stone and as they massed in formation, were told to split up. Half the troop had to remain behind to keep the Great Wood in check, the others were to follow the king in rounding up the runaways.

"Is there any more news of their whereabouts?" asked Slate impatiently to his nearest commander, as they set off in pursuit.

"No, sire, not as yet, but they can't hide forever. We'll flush them out," came the positive response.

"Excellent." Slate smirked as he strode confidently onwards, feeling secure surrounded by his elite guard on all sides.

"And you, Elder, does your magic not work? Does the main red elude you?"

Oswald scampering along by his side didn't want to admit that something was amiss. He'd blocked any attempt by Rusty to call out for help, but to his alarm it was he who was now kept from infiltrating Rusty's mind. He had failed, and this was a fact he desperately wanted to keep from the king.

"It's a matter of time, sire. Fear not, it is in paw," he answered. Deciding it was best to change the subject, he suggested another tactic. "We should take to the skies, my liege, to track them down. I advise a bird's eye view."

But Slate was having none of it.

"Oh poppycock, Elder," came the curt reply. "You know I'm not a keen flier and get travel-sick at just the thought of it. I'll do it as a last option, but only if I can't walk or be carried there first," he insisted.

At that moment, one of the advance scouts came hurtling through the woods.

"Your highness, I have news. We've found four of our finest guards gagged and bound. We've freed them and they've informed us that they were ambushed by at least twenty of the cowardly reds," he gasped. They fought bravely against the odds, but after a hard battle succumbed.

"Finest? And fought bravely?" sneered Slate. "Pah, not brave enough, otherwise how did they live to tell the tale? Have them arrested and taken back to camp in chains, I'll deal with them later," he said with a dismissive wave of his paw.

"Yes, sire, of course," replied the fearful scout.

"Do the cowards at least know which way the runaways went?"

"Yes, sire, towards a nearby meadow which lies just ahead."

Slate perked up at once at hearing this positive news. "A meadow, you say? How lovely! I do love a nice walk through a meadow especially at this time of year when it's in full

bloom. "

"But, sire, this meadow is—"

However, Slate wasn't listening and rushed forwards, brushing him aside to see for himself. Then as it came into view he stopped dead in his tracks, confronted by the huge barrier of thorns and bushes, the biggest briar patch he'd ever seen in his life.

"Oh dear," he said looking crestfallen. "This is most disappointing, this is not my kind of meadow at all."

"Your majesty," shouted an eager-to-please trooper. "I've found their tracks, they went this way!"

"Good job soldier, keep that up and you may even get paid," Slate sneered. "Right, you lot, lead the way," he urged his commanders. "First one to bag a red gets to keep his job! You too, Elder, keep up, don't lag behind. No one is irreplaceable,"

he said to Oswald, who was trailing in his wake.

"Indeed, your majesty," he replied, trying to keep pace. "I couldn't have put it any better myself."

CHAPTER THIRTY FIVE

And so it was decided Rusty and the reds would join ranks with the rats, at least for now, as Misfit led the way. He began to pick up the pace as they skirted around the perimeter of the obstacle of the impregnable looking thorn and brambles, known by all as the Maleficent Meadow. After a few brisk minutes, they made it to what he was searching for, a break in the wild thicket.

"Look this is it," he said indicating to a burnt-out and blackened gap in the formidable natural barrier. "I've been told it cuts straight through to the other side. Come on," he encouraged,

"there's only one way to find out."

The burnt-out passageway that lay before them, was at least twenty metres wide, and stretched off twisting and turning into the distance, so it was impossible to judge how far it actually went. Misfit, still out in front, was then joined by Rusty, as they all began to snake their way through the charred and scorched landscape.

"So Misfit, here we are on the same team for once, who'd have thought it?" Rusty said with a wry smile.

"I know, strange times, eh? But together is stronger, don't you think?" Misfit answered, doing his best to sound cordial. Rusty paused for a second before then asking a leading question.

"So you weren't tempted to work for the greys at all then?" he said, purposely testing him.

"What, Me?" replied Misfit, with an indignant look. "The thought never crossed my mind. What do you take me for?" he gasped, doing his best to seem aghast at the mere mention.

Rusty knew he was lying, the foresight told him so, and shut him down immediately. "I take you for someone who will stop at nothing to be on the winning side," he said scathingly, along with a withering glance.

"Oh, come on, if you mean furball that was just a game, but this is serious stuff," replied Misfit, trying to deflect his intentions. "When I heard you'd all been imprisoned like that I wanted to help out, but I knew I had to bide my time."

He considered telling Rusty of the fate of Rough and Archie, but the decision was taken from him as Rusty's attention now lay elsewhere. Up ahead, they could both now see that the seared passageway did in fact lead all the way through the meadow, and now in sight was a green foothill with Ursa's cave just beyond.

"Come on, it's this way to Willard's cottage!" Rusty exclaimed excitedly, knowing their destination was now in touching distance, and pushed the thoughts of distrust towards the rats to the back of his mind. For now, anyway.

The cottage was a most welcome sight to the group of fugitives, and Rusty in particular. He approached the familiar blue wooden door with a gentle knock.

"Come on in," came the ever-friendly voice of Willard from within. "I've been expecting you."

Rusty walked inside to see Willard sitting back in his old armchair smiling gently at him. "Willard, it's so good to see you!" he declared, rushing over to him to grasp his paw tightly.

"You too, my dear friend. You too indeed. Now I believe you've had a time of turbulence to say the least. Rough the badger has told all, so please, rest up and be seated," said Willard.

"Good old Rough and Archie, I knew they'd come through. Are they both okay?" replied Rusty, pulling up a chair, as the others waited outside.

Willard then looked crestfallen. "Your friend Rough the badger is fine, but unfortunately there is grim news regarding Archie the fox. He fell to the greys, but brave beyond all duty, I believe," he said solemnly.

"Oh no," said Rusty sorrowfully, holding his head. "Archie was one of the best and didn't deserve that." A feeling of guilt then washed over him, like a turbulent wave. For it was he who had asked them to go in the first place, and Willard, sensing this, reached out to console him.

"I sense your pain, my friend, but I'm afraid now is not the time to mourn," he said with a comforting squeeze of the paw. "I'm afraid there are more pressing matters at hand. There will be time later to remember the sacrifices that have been made, for the threat of the greys draws ever nearer."

Willard's demeanour suddenly changed, his expression now serious as he leaned forwards in his chair. "Now hear me out, for our situation is grave. Rough the badger, amongst others, has ventured out with a call to arms to any who will listen, to rally together to repel the invaders, and restore order. I have decided we are all to rendezvous beyond the swampland at The Vale. But now you must take heed before we depart to join them, and listen to what I have to say. I will be brief, for time is short, but it is most important that you learn more of the past, for its relevance may well influence the future."

"What I've feared has come to pass and my brother Oswald the Elder has returned, alongside the greys," he began.

"You mean the king's advisor, he's your brother?" Rusty gasped, looking astounded.

"Yes, indeed he is. But fear not, for we are brothers in name only. And be not surprised you failed to see that we are kin. His guise would have been well hidden by his powers," Willard explained. "Now, more of the past whilst we still have time," he said genially. "We lived and grew up on the isle together. But we did not share the same ideals, for it all ended in dispute, as he sought to reunite an ancient buried blade."

Rusty looked on wide-eyed in astonishment, and now realising the relevance, retold the episode of the mine, the dealings with Bookworm, and the unearthing of the casket on behalf of Oswald the Elder.

"That my friend is not the best news you can deliver, for that means he has retrieved his hidden half," Willard replied solemnly.

"So why is he so desperate to own this ancient sword?" asked a curious Rusty.

"Listen well and I will explain," Willard assured him.

"The weapon is a sword from a time gone by, known by man as the iron age. It's a sword of mystical qualities, a vessel made to hold and embody the ancient knowledge of the druids. They are holy men, who practise the magic arts, and the owner of the weapon would be able to access and learn the wisdom held within. It was forged in good faith by a master bladesmith called Meriden, centuries ago. Its purpose was to store, and therefore never lose, the canon of the druids for future generations to come. But a wise old head, a druid named Shelton, deemed it to be too dangerous to be held in the hands of only one, so he took it, broke it in two, and buried it two miles apart in secret locations.

But as Oswald grew older, knowing of its existence, he became obsessed with finding the two halves and reuniting them again. Believing his quest was in good faith, I helped him and searched the isle high and low until indeed they were both discovered. But I sensed a change in his intentions, an agenda of self-interest, and so I would not give up my find, and after placing it in a secret location, the battle lines were drawn.

He gathered an army and called on his allies, the she-wolves, and with the aid of another, made his advance. I too gathered together animals, but mine were of true worth. After a great battle he was defeated, and his punishment was to be banished, and never to return.

This was achieved, but his remnant was lost, until now." Willard took a breath, his faced now etched in concern, and then he continued. "And so he has returned, and surely his intent is to use the greys for his own end and finally reunite once more, the Meriden blade."

As Slate and the pursuing greys continued the chase, they too had now entered the barren stretch of burnt meadow hoping to catch sight of their prey, but as yet to no avail, and the king's patience began to wear thin.

"Is there any news of their whereabouts yet? Are you sure they came this way?" he spat out impatiently to the nearest guard.

"Yes, sire, their tracks are fresh, we are not far behind. The crow riders are due to report anytime soon," came the wary response.

"And if I may intercede, your majesty," asked Oswald timidly, as he hurried alongside. "I sense the presence of Willard draws ever near, and where he leads, I can easily follow, the foresight will show the way."

But Slate was less than impressed. "Hah. The gift that you promise will shortly be mine and never seem to deliver?" Slate retorted, with a withering sideways glance. "Well, I won't wait forever," he cautioned. But for now, you'd better put this gift to good use then, Elder, and make it snappy, for I don't suffer fools gladly.

"Of course, your majesty, and wise words as always, for neither do I," answered Oswald looking directly ahead to avoid eye contact, and hide his hidden loathing.

"And another thing, Elder, why did you insist that two of my troops bring along that casket you dug up?"

"Oh, that, sire, it's nothing," Oswald insisted. "As I informed you, it contains part of an aged broken sword, a mere amusement, too trivial for the likes of your royal self," he said, knowing this answer would stroke the king's large ego.

Then at that moment, as if on cue, one of the mounted grey crow riders dropped out of the sky and landed neatly just ahead. He swiftly dismounted his crow. and knelt down before Slate.

"Your majesty, I bring news from the aerial patrol."

"I can see that, imbecile, as you're right in front of my eyes!" came the scathing reply. "Well, hurry then, speak up, I haven't got all day. I wanted this over and done with by evening meal," he grumbled loudly.

"Yes, sire, the runaways have been spotted heading into a forest west of a bear cave, not too far from here."

"Not too far, eh? Excellent work, rider, you didn't take too long then in finding them. "

"One more thing, sire," continued the scout, looking to the floor, fearful to add the last bit of news. "They appear to have the rats in their group too,", which changed Slate's mood in an instant.

"What? They've taken the rats captives too? Is everyone around here incompetent except me? Am I surrounded by nincompoops?" he raged. "At this rate it will be roles reversed and they'll have us all locked up and I'll be bowing down to them!"

It was now mid-afternoon and the sun burned high in the sky like a red-hot cauldron, as the greys continued to follow the trail out of the meadow, climbing the hill, sweltering in the heat. Slate had long given up walking and was now being transported in a palanquin – his covered carrying chair constructed by the beavers. Four volunteer troopers, who had really been drawn at random by Stone, were instructed to carry out the task. Any thought of rest was out of the question and soon they found themselves weaving and sweating their way through the forest.

At long last, they arrived at Willard's cottage as Slate's troops gladly stood down, found some shade, took on fluids, and awaited the king's next orders.

"Undoubtedly, sire, this is the dwelling of Willard, but I do not feel his presence, he must have departed," said Oswald, confident he was correct.

"They may be still hiding in there. Who knows?" Slate remarked with a bored shrug. He turned to his commander. "Stone, knock on the door, will you? Oh, and no need for pleasantries, use an axe!" snarled Slate, standing well back and out of harm's way. "I do so hope you're wrong, Elder." He smirked, rubbing his paws together in glee at the thought of imminent bloodshed.

Stone duly obliged and picked out six troopers for back-up, took a large axe from one of them and approached the door. With one mighty swing, he smashed it open with ease. As the shattered door swung on its broken hinges, Stone peered in.

"You lot, straight in now. Make sure it's clear!" he commanded to the soldiers. "And take no prisoners!"

Without hesitation, the greys rushed in with weapons drawn, as Slate watched on eagerly hoping for an easy victory. But much to his dismay, he was about to be disappointed as after a few moments they filed out one by one reporting that it was indeed vacant.

"Your majesty, I sense they lack your valour and conviction for a fight and have fled with their tails tucked firmly between their legs," fawned Oswald.

Then came a shout from a trooper. "Over here, your majesty. The trail leads this way!" yelled a kneeling scout.

"Well, let's not wait any longer, daylight is burning and those reds won't dispatch themselves. A bonus to whoever gets me the first red pelt. So let's be after them!" roared Slate, paw pumping the air vigorously, which gained a hearty cheer of approval from his troopers.

Oswald gave him a sly glance. "May I suggest I delay here and give the cottage a thorough search? It may yet yield clues to their destination, or even their plans," said Oswald with a cunning smile.

Slate considered his suggestion briefly then responded. "Yes, I order you to do just that," said Slate dismissing him. "I don't need your counsel right now for I feel the end game draws near. We have them on the run, and I should be tucked up in my tent by nightfall with another conquest to my name," he bragged contentedly. "Go ahead, search the cabin. I'll leave you two guards to carry the plunder too as there must be valuables worth taking to help fill the royal coffers. Then join me forthwith with the haul," he ordered. Then he turned to look at him directly in the eye with a withering glare.

"Don't disappoint me and return empty-handed," he cautioned, as he waved his palanquin bearers away. "Begone. I've decided I'll take a little exercise and walk into battle now," he told them as they scurried away, before speaking to Oswald once more.

"I'll keep the casket you prize so much as an incentive," he sneered. "You can retain it on your return."

Slate then waved his troop on and took his usual place in the centre of the elite before turning back to hail him. "Failure is not an option, Elder, you'd be wise to remember

that," he cautioned and went on his way.

As Oswald watched them march on with the two troopers given the duty to stay with him standing by awaiting his orders, he discounted the king's remark immediately and turned his attention back to the cottage – his true intention for being here.

"Now brother, if I were you, where would I hide my part of the blade?"

Willard now hurried along towards The Vale, with Rusty and the rest following closely behind. To confuse their pursuers he used an old tactic he'd put to good effect in the past: weave in and out of the terrain, don't keep a straight path, and occasionally retrace their steps, so as to be more elusive, and hopefully confuse the enemy.

"Come on, this way, we must hasten, for I fear that they are not too far in our wake," said Willard in order to encourage them. Their route for now appeared safe enough and passed through lush green forest, with the thick canopy of the treetops giving them adequate cover from above.

"Do you think we've lost them?" asked Rusty, accompanied by a troubled look over his shoulder.

"I fear not, my friend. We can try to delay them but they will not give up the chase as their king would lose face, and my brother, as you know, has his own ends to achieve," Willard replied honestly. "But in our favour, they do not possess the local knowledge needed to traverse this way safely. My brother was born on this isle, this may be true, but our domain lay in the north and he rarely ventured this way," Willard explained. "So they will not be aware of the dangers that lie ahead."

Rusty knew this to be true. "Well, without Izzy we would certainly never have retrieved the herbs for the charm on our previous journey this way," he recalled.

"That is correct as it can prove to be most perilous," Willard admitted. "And your journey was also the beginning of a personal discovery too," he reminded him. "For this is just the beginning, and you have so much to learn. For instance, I have yet to inform you of your true ancestry."

This new information stopped a bewildered Rusty dead in his tracks. "'True ancestry', what do you mean by that?" he asked with a quizzical look.

"That, my friend, will have to wait as we have a more pressing matter at hand," Willard responded, as they left the relevant safety of the forest and saw up ahead, through the shroud of mist that enveloped it, the treacherous swampland that had now come into view.

Oswald surveyed the once tidy cottage of his brother Willard, now in disarray, with disappointment as so far, his search had been in vain.

"Go through it with a fine-tooth comb and look for any oddity," he'd demanded. "To be more specific, I seek a damaged blade, and take anything of value for the king," he'd said.

This was the order he had given to the two troopers when they had first entered the cabin an hour ago. The troopers, one of burly build named Drab, and the other, quite thin and scrawny, named Dull, had duly obliged, ripping open Willard's favourite armchair with glee, upending furniture, knocking over bookshelves and emptying drawers onto the floor.

Even the kitchen was ransacked with plates smashed and cutlery strewn everywhere, but to no avail. "Sorry, sir, you said to turn the place upside down but we've not found anything worth taking, or this broken blade," reported Dull.

"Actually, I think you'll find I said to be thorough and look for anything out of the ordinary too, but no matter," Oswald replied disparagingly. "Wait outside for further orders," he then snapped.

"Yes, sir, right away," said Dull, as they shuffled out to wait.

Oswald was left standing amongst the chaos of the once ordered cottage and was not happy at all, as he tried to second guess his brother. *What have I missed? Where could it be?* he thought to himself. *I know you, Willard, you'd hide it close enough to keep a vigil but not too obvious, and where you'd consider it safe too.* But he knew deep inside that the artefact couldn't be present in the home, as the foresight would have told him more by now.

Meanwhile, standing outside Drab and Dull were beginning to get restless.

"It's not here is it? This broken sword," said a moaning Drab.

"I know," replied an uncomfortable-looking Dull, too hot in his armour.

"Nothing worth taking either, I was hoping we'd fill our pockets, we've not been paid for months," groaned Drab.

"Yeah, me too, where's the plunder?" replied an unhappy Dull. "Plus, I'd like get a move on and catch up with the others, after all, this is supposed to be bear country and a cave was spotted nearby by too."

Oswald suddenly appeared in the doorway. "Repeat what you just said. Did you say there's a bear's cave nearby?"

"Yes, sir, well so the crow rider reckoned, just beyond the next hill," replied a worried-looking Drab.

"Oh, yes, I recall him telling Slate, I mean the king, the very same thing," said Oswald, his face lighting up. "Show me where this cavern lies, immediately!" he commanded, as a self-satisfied grin spread across his face. *A bear's cave. What better place is there to hide a thing of value?*

CHAPTER THIRTY SIX

Willard had not seen the swamplands for quite a while, and he'd almost forgotten how forbidding the wet land actually was, with its vastness of long brown and green reeds growing out of the treacherous-looking quagmire, shrouded in a heavy blanket of thick fog.

"Surely we're not going to go through that?" asked a dubious-looking Misfit, staring at the ominous marshland ahead. "That would make us even madder than mad King Slate himself," he complained loudly.

"No, don't worry, we've come this way before," explained Scarlet. "There's a route on the edge that's cut up into the rock side, it takes you safely around it. Izzy showed us the way, you just have to be careful."

"Is that safe? I don't like heights and it sounds a bit dangerous to me," said a worried Pitter, beginning to regret he'd come along.

"And how long does that take?" asked Patter. "After all, we can't afford to get caught. Is there another option?"

As they discussed amongst each other the next best move, Brick's attention was elsewhere. Up above, his keen eye had seen that the crows had returned, and he knew that meant possible trouble.

"Heads up, Rust, I don't like the look of that lot. Means we might get spotted and they'll report back," he warned.

"Yeah, you're right," agreed Rusty, peering up. That's not good at all. What do you reckon, Willard? Think they've seen us?"

"I can't rule out that possibility, but shall we give them something else to be concerned with instead?" he said with a mischievous smile.

Willard at once raised an arm and looked towards the horizon, as they all followed his gaze. At once, they saw a distant dark shape getting ever closer, and is it did, they could see it was a bird, with a huge wingspan.

"What is that? A bird of prey, an eagle?" asked Misfit, cupping his paw over his eyes to block out the sun.

The question remained unanswered as they could now see he was right, and as it came closer, it became obvious to all that it was a fearsome-looking white-tailed eagle, with its large hooked beak and talons hanging at the ready to strike. It got ever closer, and as they watched they could now see the crows in disarray, scattering and fleeing off into the distance, with the eagle giving chase, the hunters became the prey.

"Well, that went as well as could be expected," said a satisfied Willard. "It seems they fell for my optical illusion, even though it is but a mere trick of the light."

"You mean that big bird was a fake?" said an impressed Misfit, putting his arm around Willard's shoulders. "After all this is over, pal, you and I need to get together, and you can teach me a few of your tricks and schemes!" He grinned.

"Why? So you may eventually win this game of furball of which you so desperately desire?" he replied, shrugging him off. "Just to remind you, Misfit the rat, ours is but a relationship of necessity. To have a friend is to be a friend," Willard told him, which brought out quite a few loud scoffs. "But for now, we must make haste, for I feel our enemy draws near, and the crows won't stay fooled for long," Willard warned.

"Scarlet, if you will, please escort our party along the ancient step way to safety. Rusty, you and I have another task in hand, away from the rest for now. Oswald can sense us above all, as the foresight leaves an ethereal trail of which he can easily follow."

"So what are you suggesting?" asked a bemused Rusty.

Willard reached out to place a comforting paw on his arm. "You and I my friend have another path to follow. They play a deadly game and so we must match their every move. We will lead them a merry dance, of which one false step will prove their undoing."

He then turned to face the marsh head on. "For my friend, our course takes us on a different path. Through the very heart of the swampland itself!"

"You go in first," said a frightened Drab.

"No way, you go in first," said a scared Dull.

"What on earth is wrong with you? It's just a cave!" yelled an exasperated Oswald, as they stood dithering outside Ursa's lair.

"But, sir, it's not just any old cave, it's a bear's cave," said a panic-stricken wide-eyed Drab.

"Yes, sir, and he might just well be at home," agreed a frightened-looking Dull.

Oswald let out a huge sigh. "I will attempt to appease your fears on two counts," he replied, attempting to stay calm, but swiftly losing patience with the hapless pair. "Firstly, I would sense his presence. Secondly, you'll do as I ask because I gave a direct order! Or do I need to inform the king of your insubordination?"

Drab and Dull weren't sure what exactly he meant by that, but obeying orders was beyond doubt, so they both drew a big breath and edged towards the dark entrance but stopped at the mouth.

"Why have you halted? Did I give you permission?" barked Oswald.

"Well, it's so dark. Who knows what's in there?" gulped Drab, gawping into the gloom. Oswald had heard enough.

"Stand aside before my patience wears beyond thin," he ordered, as he marched sternly forwards. He bent down and picked up a loose stone from the floor. He closed his eyes and mumbled something inaudible to Drab and Dull, and then threw the rock into the cavern. As it landed it immediately illuminated, and gave off an immense light flooding the cave. It lit up the whole space immediately, and the glow stones entrenched in the stalactites above shone bright and clear.

Oswald looked up and immediately recognised them for what they were, and gave them his next orders. "Now you see, as I predicted, there's no bear at home. See the stones that glow on high?" he asked. "Take them for the king, he will surely value them greatly, for I have a more pressing matter at paw."

Now they could see that the cave was actually empty all thought of an angry bear melted from their minds and avarice now took over as Drab and Dull ran in, drawn by the sight of the gleaming stones.

"Look at these," said Drab. "They must be valuable."

"Yeah, too right," agreed Dull, with his eyes on stalks.

He then had a suggestion. "Here, I'll pick you up, Drab, on my shoulders. Then you use your sword to prise 'em off." As the two-foot soldiers went about their plunder, Oswald was lost in thought. He then stood completely still and began an ancient incantation.

> "Oh ways of old reveal to me,
> the sacred thing of which I seek.
> Take me to days of yore,
> reveal to me that which was hid so deep."

And then, before him, he could see a younger past version of Willard. He was furtive and ghostlike, scuttling by, dragging behind him a metal box and spade.

The Willard of old halted, looked around as if making sure he stayed unseen, and then made his way forward. At the rear of the cave, he dug away at the earth below his feet, and before long unearthed a hidden trap door. He then grabbed a handle, lifted the lid and placed the box inside.

Oswald smiled, he'd seen enough. He moved forward and stood at the exact spot Willard had been years before.

"You two, here now, I have a task for you," he ordered.

Before long, the three stood outside the cave with the unearthed box open in front of them. Having examined its contents, and finding the other half of the blade, the Elder was happy with their work.

"You have done well and I shall commend you to the king," said a delighted Oswald. "But your work is not done. Gather the stones you have taken as tribute to him, and place them in the casket too. And if you so wish, line your pockets with a few extra stones too. So be it, for I shall turn a blind eye," he said, along with a false smile as if being generous. "But the object in cloth that lies within the box is mine, and mine alone, understood?"

"Yes, sir. Of course, sir," Drab and Dull said as one, pleased at the thought of profit at last.

"You shall carry the chest back carefully and join the others, for I shall seek the king alone. Now begone, and do as I instruct," he commanded. With that, Drab and Dull piled the box high with the glow stones placed on top of the shrouded blade, and scurried off with it ready to rejoin the rest, leaving Oswald alone to his thoughts.

He stood motionless and cleared his mind. At that moment, a solitary hawk sitting in a treetop two miles away tweaked his head. His name was Talon. His master Oswald had called. He needed a ride so set off immediately towards him.

You're not as clever as you think, Willard, thought Oswald to himself. I've found your half of the Meriden blade so easily and so next time we meet, you shall thwart me no more. This finally ends, brother. For the power of the druids will be mine, and mine alone.

CHAPTER THIRTY SEVEN

As Scarlet led the rest away to climb the granite steps, Willard began to explain to Rusty what exactly would happen next.

"I have traversed these swamps many times before," he began to explain, as they stood side by side on the edge of the marsh. "I was first shown the way by an old friend, many moons ago." A faint smile crossed his face as he recollected the time from his youth.

"He was a frog named Ribbit. We grew up together as good friends, but we have not met for a long time as our paths went separate ways," he said with a trace of regret. "He knew this land well as his forefathers lived here for centuries before. He explained to me back then, that there lies one true path which takes you safely through the marsh, if you know how to find it," he added with a mischievous tap of the nose.

"So there's only one way. How do you know where to go?" asked Rusty, curious to know more.

"It is simplicity itself, you just follow the markers," replied Willard with a knowing smile. "There are rocks distributed throughout, each one marked with the footprint of a frog carved into it by my friend's ancestors as a gift. They are placed to guide intrepid travellers, to guarantee safe passage. But this secret is known only by a select few. Follow and do not deviate, and all is well," he added.

"Oh, I see, like following a trail of breadcrumbs?" said Rusty, beginning to understand.

"Indeed, but before we commence, as I have explained, where we go, Oswald will surely follow, as he can sense our aura."

"So he doesn't know about the markers then?" Rusty asked.

"No, for even though we are brothers, we are not alike in many ways. We had different interests and friends as we grew, so he and Ribbit never met, of that I am sure. But to prevail we must leave a false trail, to confuse our foe and gain valuable time. So you wait here a short while, my friend, while I do just that. And do not fear, Ribbit and I knew this swamp well."

With that, and before Rusty could object, Willard headed off, and without a backwards glance, disappeared into the swirling fog of the mire. Five long minutes passed by and just as Rusty was beginning to worry something was amiss, Willard reappeared from the marsh with a winning smile.

"All done, my friend, a route to nowhere is lain, and whoever follows is on a fool's errand, or worse," he said, indicating the path he had just taken. "But now, let us make haste, for I feel they are nearly up on us," he said with a worried frown.

"No doubt you will, my friend, as the gift bestowed on you grows ever strong. Now take heed and have no fear, follow me and all will be well," said Willard, as he again re-entered the swamp, but at a different entry point this time.

Rusty slowly walked behind him unsurely and slightly afraid at first, as the fog enveloped them both. As they moved forward, the tall marsh reeds all around him were at least four times his height, and a feeling of claustrophobia washed over him as if the narrow passageway of brown and green vegetation were closing in. He drew a deep breath, took a moment, and carried on. The damp squelch of the marshland under foot was disconcerting too, but the firm ground just below the surface gave him some comfort as Willard stopped to face him.

"There, do you see, Rusty? The first marker just ahead," he indicated to a nearby boulder.

Rusty could now see clearly, carved into it from aeons ago, four long frog digits neatly etched in the stone. He had never doubted Willard's wise words but seeing the first carving raised his spirits and urged him on.

Now the first check point had been reached, they could see the next one just ahead and as they slowly made progress, Rusty's confidence grew and his fear started to dissipate as his thoughts were now only of one thing. Reuniting with the others on the far side.

"So, tell me Stone, is there any news from my crow riders, have they not returned as yet?" moaned a fed up Slate, as he trudged on through the forest in his usual position in the middle of his troop heading directly towards the swampland.

"No, my liege, not as yet, but they do say no news is good news," replied Stone, in a feeble attempt to placate him. But knowing it probably wouldn't, he cringed as Slate duly exploded.

"What is that supposed to mean? No news is good news!" he bellowed. "I'll tell you what it means, it'll be extremely bad news for the crow rider general if he's not back soon! What's his name again?" Slate huffed.

"General Peck," replied a relieved Stone, pleased for once that it wasn't him that the king's anger was aimed at.

"Ah yes, Peck, I feel a demotion coming on. Hah, that'll ruffle his feathers, what say you, Stone?" Slate mocked with a sneer.

His commander, now hopefully sensing a mood swing, agreed with a half-smile and a slight nod when, much to his relief, came the distraction of a shout from the front of the column.

"Rider spotted, straight ahead sire!"

"Ah, it must be Peck, he's finally decided to give us the pleasure of his company," remarked Slate sarcastically as he hurried forward to see. But as they left the forest to be confronted by the swamp it wasn't the general waiting but his advisor, Oswald, who dismounted his hawk, Talon, and greeted him with a deep bow.

"Oh Elder, it's you. I do hope you bring a tale of success," he said mildly disappointed at not being able to give Peck a dressing down. Or worse.

"Yes, sire, I do." Oswald smiled genially. "The two troopers I had with me will soon be here with a chest full of precious stones that will surely swell the royal coffers greatly," he bragged.

Slate certainly liked the sound of that. "Oh goody, a treasure chest just for me? I do love new shiny things, maybe this day will turn out well after all," replied Slate grinning inanely, and rubbing his paws in anticipation.

"And the broken sword. Have you found that old thing too?" he sneered. "It is an odd fascination you hold for it. You do know if you asked nicely, I'd consider giving you one that's new? A very small one of course, dormouse size, to fit your tiny little paws," he snorted.

"Very good of you, sire," replied Oswald forcing a smile. "And you are too kind, my liege, but the old relic will appease me, for I have little need for new weapons of war."

"Oh dear," said Slate looking past him with a big sigh, now noticing the swamp for the first time. "Surely you can't tell me they went through that?" he asked in dismay.

"Sire!" called out a tracker on bended knee. "Some of them went this way!" he yelled, pointing out the route Scarlet and the others had taken.

But Oswald's attention briefly lay elsewhere as he sensed that through the quagmire, not one, but two trails lay ahead. "May I intercede?" said Oswald meekly, and then explained his findings to the puzzled King.

"You're saying they've split their ranks three ways, Elder?" he asked, looking bemused.

"Indeed, all the trails are true and undoubtedly they have split their group asunder," Oswald answered assuredly.

Slate perked up at the news. "They've gone their separate ways? Perhaps they've argued and are running for their lives. Well, if they know what's good for them they have," Slate remarked, surely sensing panic from their fleeing prey. But Slate also wanted reassuring. "Elder, advise me now and make it quick, we can't risk letting any of them get away. An example must be made of every single one of them," he said clenching his paws, determined to catch them all. "What course of action do we take? Hurry up, we haven't got all day. Those reds won't catch themselves!" he snapped.

"Sire, my counsel is as follows. We too must follow them wherever they go. And pursue them in each direction they have fled. Or risk losing some of them for good," came his stark warning. The truth then dawned on Oswald. "Sire, I now see the ruse for I know my brother well. Willard has surely left us an untrue path to follow."

Slate sat imperiously reclined cross-legged on a huge cushion with his feet resting on a padded foot stool, of which both had been carried on the back of an unfortunate trooper all the way here, now mulling over the new information he'd just received from Oswald.

"So, explain to me again, Elder," he said impatiently. "You're now telling me you suspect foul play and the devious reds are leaving a false trail?"

"Indeed, sire," replied a slightly embarrassed counsellor. "I have had time to give it more thought, my liege," he explained sheepishly. "My brother is a devious one. He is not to be underestimated, and there being three trails to follow, it's the only thing that makes sense." He stopped for a second to gauge the king's response, but Slate remained impassive and just stared ahead giving nothing away. He then sat forward and broke his silence, his eyes narrowed, fixed only on him.

"Are you telling me you've been outfoxed and I've hired the wrong brother to counsel me?" he hissed, along with his best glare.

"No, of course not, sire, it's just that—"

But Slate cut him off at once, not at all in the mood for feeble excuses. "Enough!" he bellowed. "I've heard enough! Prove your worth to me then, Elder," he instructed. "You need to match his cunning, step by step then," he sneered, before sitting back again and turning his attention to Stone. "There is no time to waste, commander, we must be up and after them at once. My orders are as follows: Stone, you are to take a dozen soldiers on one pathway through the marsh, and Elder, you are to take the other. The rest to follow the third trail. I of course will do the most important task of all and watch the rear, along with my personal guard," he said sitting back stiffly. "And you're to report back to me with your findings at once," he demanded.

Oswald and Stone looked at one another, and then back at the king, knowing his plan was ludicrous but not daring to disagree. "Well, what are you waiting for? Don't just stand there! Daylight's burning, those reds won't dispatch themselves you know!"

Oswald deliberated for a moment on which trail to take, before deciding that the one to his left had a more powerful aura, meaning it was surely the last one to be travelled, leaving Stone to take the other. Willard will have set the false trail first, he assumed. Stone, wanting to impress and set off first, gathered his dozen together promptly.

"You, you and you, take point and go in first," he ordered three unlucky troopers, choosing them at random.

"Yes, of course, sir," said the first in line reluctantly, before dating to ask a question. "Are we to wear our armour, sir?" he asked warily. "It's heavy, and may weigh us down," he added with a tremble in his voice, taking a sideways glance at the dangerous-looking swamp behind.

"What? Of course, you are to wear it!" came the angry response. "What if the cowardly rebels await in ambush in there? No more questions or you'll be court-martialled. You're here to be seen and not heard. Now get on with it!" Stone thundered.

The chosen three knew they had no choice but to obey, as to question an order was foolhardy to say the least, so one by one they edged into the swamp and were quickly swallowed up by the fog, as Stone and the others followed in their wake.

Stone edged his way slowly forwards, parting the reeds as he went, with his feet squelching in the most uncomfortable way, being sucked and dragged into the mire underfoot. It was hard going, but wanting to seem fearless, he pressed on regardless, also not wanting to lose sight of the soldier in front.

The fog seemed to be getting denser still, as they went further in. There was almost zero visibility now and this made him slightly disorientated. Suddenly, it dawned on Stone that it had been a few moments since he'd last set eyes on the trooper in front. And then all at once, from up ahead, he heard a gut-wrenching scream.

Just after Stone's group had disappeared into the quagmire, Oswald decided to move off too, but it was he who led the way, not an unfortunate trooper. This was not out of bravery, but of necessity as it was easier – the aura of Willard and Rusty was almost tangible to him. It was as if he could reach out and touch their essence, almost like a physical presence.

He'd only gone a short way when the first frog marker came into view, which pleased him greatly. Surely I'm on the right track, he thought to himself, and then seeing the next he now knew it to be true, and was about to return to Slate with the good news. But it was also then that he too heard the same ear-shattering scream, emanating through the fog, coming from somewhere to his right.

Stone stopped dead in his tracks and froze in fear. "What's going on?" he yelled, trying to hide the growing panic in his voice.

Then through the murk came the sound of loud splashing, as one of the bedraggled troopers fell sprawling into his arms.

"This is wrong, we've got to turn back, the other two are gone, sir!" he pleaded.

"Gone? What do you mean gone?" exclaimed a bewildered Stone.

"It's the swamp, sir, sucked them down in one, they stood no chance. They were there one second and gone the next. It's like they were eaten alive!" he cried, clinging onto Stone for dear life. "We need to go back. Please," he begged.

Stone could see the panic-stricken look in his eyes, and knowing he had no other choice, gave a command.

"New orders," he barked. "Make an orderly retreat." But his words fell on deaf ears as the others behind him had heard the cries of the lost troopers and the whimper of the survivor, and terror now gripped the ranks as they all turned and fled. This led to more frantic splashing and shrieks and wails, as the swamp took yet even more victims.

Stone now stood alone, and trying to belay his fears, took his time to get his bearings and slowly retraced his steps. After a few long minutes, he could see that thankfully his judgement had been correct, and he exited the mire more or less at the same spot he'd gone in.

He was met with the sight of Slate looking less than impressed, surrounded by his personal guard, and with two sorry-looking mud-splattered troopers gasping nearby.

"Ah, you're back commander. Most disappointing. With a name like yours I thought you may have sunk like a stone, like the ones you lost under your command!" he seethed. "And you seem to be without nearly all your platoon, it appears you chose unwisely," he remarked sternly. A worried Stone didn't answer, knowing the choice wasn't his at all, but thinking he may still pay a heavy price. Then he breathed a sigh of relief at the king's next words.

"You live for now, commander," he proclaimed. "But only because the

Elder has reported back with good news, that his was the true path. So dust yourself down and go again, what doesn't kill you makes you stronger, eh? And don't worry, the retribution the reds will pay will be worth the price." On hearing this, a relieved Stone was frozen momentarily to the spot.

"Well, come on then, Stone, snap out of your daydream. There's no time to lose, lead the way through," Slate said impatiently to his stationery commander.

"Yes, sire, of course, at once," replied a thankful Stone, who picked his head up and went to rally the troops.

"You are most forgiving, sire, and showed great lenience regarding his failure," fawned Oswald, once the commander was out of earshot. But Slate wasn't impressed at all.

"Poppycock, Elder!" he spat out. "I don't suffer fools, as well you know. I've let him live his miserable life for now. I've decided he can lead the charge, along with the bugler, when we meet the enemy. He has outlived his usefulness, and can die by all means then."

CHAPTER THIRTY EIGHT

Rusty and Willard exited the marshland, and they were greeted by the welcome sight of Scarlet and the rest, who had got there moments before.

"You made it then, what took you so long?" asked Misfit, making what he considered to be light-hearted banter, but all it gained him was a disapproving glance from Scarlet as his reward. She rushed to give Rusty an appreciative hug.

"You okay?" she asked him tenderly, noting the muddied state of his legs and feet.

"Always the better for seeing you," came his contented reply. "Any sign of the greys then Rust, did you lose 'em?" asked Brick, peering into the mist and listening out for pursuers.

"No sign of them, but I've got a feeling they won't give up that easily," he admitted.

"Indeed, this is true," agreed Willard. "They seek a final confrontation for their king. And I determine Oswald will only be content with outright victory for himself this time," he said solemnly.

"Well, if they're spoiling for a fight, let's give it to 'em!" roared Brick, which received a wide roar of approval. Willard's thoughts lay elsewhere now though, as his gaze settled on the imposing ravine that was next in their path.

"We must now press on to the proposed meeting point with great haste, at The Vale," he insisted. "The grassland itself lies beyond the canyon that is just ahead," Willard said, with an outstretched paw. "Some of you have passed this way before, but for the uninitiated, you must take heed to my words," he warned, as he peered at them over the top of his small round glasses. "The escarpment we must traverse has suffered erosion from the elements and is prone to collapse, and so we must therefore take great care. Stay close and as silent as possible, for any noise will reverberate and surely unsettle the environment within, and this could well prove our undoing." He then got ready to leave. "Enough talk for now, we must go and rally at the rendezvous," he insisted. Willard spun around and promptly led off in the direction of the gorge, as Hugo turned to Misfit with a look of confusion.

"What was that all about then?" he asked bemused by Willard's explanation and scratching his head, as the rest all fell in line and went after him. Misfit rolled his eyes with dismay at his stupidity.

"What he means is, keep the noise down or risk the lot coming crashing down on your head!" he answered abruptly. But Hugo wasn't impressed.

"Hang on a minute, Misfit. I didn't sign up for all this," he moaned, as he finally understood the dangers ahead.

"Me neither," moaned Pitter, as the rats halted and gathered round, grumbling amongst themselves.

Misfit spotting a growing dissent, decided to nip it in the bud.

"Fine, okay then, go back and face the greys on your own," he snarled. "I'm sure Slate would love your company, before he takes your head and puts it on a pike that is!" he added dramatically.

Hugo backed down immediately. "I was just saying Misfit, that's all, I didn't mean we won't go on," replied Hugo.

"Good, that's settled then, let's get a move on," replied Misfit, sensing he'd quelled any rebellion, at least for now.

As they entered the canyon, with Willard's words echoing in their ears, all around them the dangerous and forbidding surroundings were evident for all to see. The narrow and winding path way was strewn with boulders, large and small – a real reminder of past and recent falls –and one look upwards told them all they needed to know of their current predicament. The high ravine walls had a jagged cliff edge, which had huge sections clinging on precariously, like large birds of prey, ready to swoop down on them in an instant.

Below, on the canyon floor, Rusty followed just behind Willard admiring his bravery and fortitude, as the little dormouse marched gainfully on. Little did he know that Willard was far from happy, and he too felt extremely anxious, knowing one false step would almost certainly spell their crushing doom. But Willard knew from previous experience that he had to hide behind a mask of confidence in the knowledge that this would spread conviction through the ranks, and help them complete their mission. And there was no one more content than he when at last saw the exit of the canyon come in to sight, and the wide-open green space of The Vale, beckoning towards him like a long-lost friend.

General Peck, had as far as he was concerned, a long and distinguished career behind him. He'd fought bravely in battles on the mainland, including the taking of the steel mill from the rats and mice, which helped put Slate on the throne. At the time he'd been just a lowly ranking crow, but helped to form an alliance with the greys, and form the squadron of crow riders. This was one of his proudest moments, and swiftly rising through the ranks he became general, meaning he remained riderless in order to orchestrate the rest.

On a day-to-day basis he had little to do with the king, and he was sure Slate didn't even know him by name, but this suited him well, as he was in sole charge of the squadron and was revered by those who mattered to him the most. His crew.

But now he feared his well-earned reputation was lying in tatters as he was the first to take flight from the huge eagle that had come upon them, and then, in an instant, mysteriously vanished from sight. He sat forlornly, head down, high in the treetops on a branch, filled with self-pity. Luna, one of his flight crew members, landed neatly by him on a lower branch. On her back, sat a grey rider, but he sat silently as Luna spoke to him, the etiquette of the crow riders being the bird addressed the general first.

"General Peck, I bring news from the front," Luna said clearly, and in an efficient manner.

"What is it?" replied Peck wearily. "Has the king won the day without us?" he sighed.

"No, sir, not at all, sir," she went on. "I took the initiative and followed my training and went to do a reconnaissance, just in time to see the army enter, and disappear into a huge swampland. "This caught Peck's attention, and he lifted his bowed head to hear more.

"Go on rider, you have my ear," he replied.

"Yes, sir. As I said, they disappeared from view, so were completely unaware of my presence."

"You mean the king will be unaware of our absence?"

"Yes, sir, absolutely. The reed bed is much too high to see above."

Peck was listening intently now, hoping to perhaps salvage something from this so far wretched day.

"And also, sir," she continued, "a scout from the north has reported on a known accomplice of the renegades – an owl going by the name of Screech. He has been gathering together any bird wiling to join him against the king, and is reported to be heading this way."

This news delighted Peck as he now felt rejuvenated, and saw a chance for redemption. "Tell me, rider, what is your rank and name?"

"Private Luna, of flight company two sir," she replied smartly.

"Well, Luna, you are now promoted forthwith to captain, for your excellent sterling work," he said with a grin, now feeling his circumstances had taken a turn for the better. Relieved, he gave his next command.

"Get the squadron ready to fly, immediately, with these precise orders. We have a new mission. To take out this Screech and his cohorts, and to prove our worth, once and for all!"

CHAPTER THIRTY NINE

Slate waited impatiently for his troops to emerge from the swampland, having flown over it in mere minutes. He had informed Oswald he would take the hawk, and after dismounting Talon, sat on a rock waiting. Drumming his paw on his thigh, they began to appear from the marsh one by one, soiled and muddied. Some were covered head to toe in slush and slime, led by a mud-splattered Oswald, as the rest appeared at the same time descending from the granite steps.

"Ah, Elder, so good of you to join us. You found your way through finally I see. Not too taxing I hope?" he said with a crafty grin. Then he took note of the bedraggled troop that followed behind, exiting the misty mire, and his smile turned instantly into a frown.

"No, sire, the trail was clearly marked, and no more were lost to its treachery," Oswald replied wearily, whilst shaking a large deposit of sludge from his feet, much too close to Slate for comfort, and certainly to his distaste.

"Just make sure you keep that filth to yourself will you, Elder? You know I like to look pristine and at my best at all times," he said, with a look of undisguised disgust. "I have an appearance to keep up, and you know I abhor anyone who is slovenly," he said loftily. A fuming Oswald wanted to say, I defy anyone to come through that filthy swamp unsullied, but bit his tongue and did his best to remain outwardly calm, as Slate continued to drone on.

"Also, I have kept your hawk Talon busy. He informs me that their tracks are fresh, and led off into the canyon beyond. Surely victory is but a short step away. What say you, Elder?"

"It was never in doubt, sire, for the reds are no equal to your cunning," he replied through gritted teeth, trying his best to sound sincere.

Slate then turned to his bedraggled-looking commander, with a look of contempt.

"Now, Stone, try to make yourself look presentable, will you?" he said, looking him up and down in dismay. "We greys do have standards to keep up, you know. It sets us apart from the wretched locals," he added sniffily. "And once you've achieved that, Stone, prepare the advance for the final march to glory, and use the bugler," he demanded. "I want him to lead the charge, along with yourself. The sound of his horn will surely strike fear into the hearts of the enemy."

"Yes, sire, I'll do as you command," replied Stone, as he slowly trudged away, wiping the mud from his armour as he went.

Oswald, in the meantime, had been viewing the canyon ahead with a growing concern. "Sire, may I advise a more subtle approach? The terrain ahead looks most unstable, and so I advise caution. They may even wait to ambush us in a trap," he warned, spying the narrow passageway and high forbidding walls, identifying them as an ideal place for a surprise attack.

"Poppycock, Elder," Slate blustered. "They wouldn't dare. And if we dither any longer, they will surely get away. Have faith, Elder, when have I ever been wrong before?" he bragged.

"Never is the answer you seek," replied Oswald, dumbfounded by his arrogance.

"We'll catch and dispatch the red scourge and be back for evening meal, you'll see," predicted Slate.

Whilst the king had been talking, Oswald's attention again lay elsewhere, but this time his gaze fell on the wooden chest containing the first half of the Meriden blade found in the mine, being held onto by two large grey soldiers, under orders not to let it out of their sight. And now a devious plan began to form in his mind.

"May I request that I re-join you again shortly?" he asked, trying to seem dutifully. "I can take Talon and find the two who bring the treasure chest from the bears cave, and hurry them to your side. I'm sure you will be delighted with the spoils they bring. And the stones within are known for their good fortune. And fortune favours the brave," he added slyly.

"Oh really. Good fortune? And the brave. eh? Oh, I do like the sound of that. I feel another ode coming on, written about yours truly," replied Slate, puffing out his chest, as his eyes filled with greed at the thought of the riches and fame coming his way. "Yes, I give you permission to go. And do hurry them along, as I do so wish to see my prize," he added excitedly, happy at the thought of swelling his coffers.

"And once you have achieved this, you may have your broken blade. I have held it back as promised, as your reward for pleasing me," he grinned, pointing out the wooden chest. With that, Oswald bowed, spun around, and immediately mounted his hawk, taking to the air in an instant.

"The final piece of the puzzle is falling into place," he scoffed, as he flew away, feeling the moment he had waited for finally drawing near.

As a young grey cadet led the column of troopers into the eerily quiet high-walled canyon, he'd never felt prouder in all his life. He had always wanted to be a bugler, just like his father before him, and it had been a great honour to be chosen from a select few, to become the official bugle cadet of the Grey Army.

The bugle he carried had been passed down from father to son, and had last been used in action by his father at the famous battle of the steel mill. He'd practised lots on the parade ground, and at home with an occasional friendly scold of, "Keep that noise down", from his loving mother, but this was his first active duty. Proudly puffing out his chest, he took point in the column with his arms swinging in a steady parade ground rhythm, bugle at the ready, awaiting the order to sound the attack.

High up above, in the narrow slice of sky visible, he'd noticed the crow riders fly by, and wondered if his friend Luna was up there, keeping a watchful eye on him as she surely was. He then glanced around to see that the rest were looking nervously at the uneven terrain and softly whispering to each other in frightened tones. But he wasn't scared at all, as his father had taught him, "Lead by example, and show no fear".

As he rounded the next corner, he excitedly saw an open space, and spied, against a back drop of emerald green field, the enemy not far ahead waiting in line.

Then a shout came from near the rear. It was the unmistakable whiney voice of the king himself.

"Enemy ahead!" he yelled. "Bugler, sound the charge!"

This was the moment that the bugler had trained for all his life. He put the bugle tightly to his pursed lips and blew out as hard as he could. Oh, what a joyful sound it makes, he thought, as it echoed loudly off the high stone walls. But that was when a moment of jubilation changed in an instant to one of despair, as the once serene landscape immediately changed to turmoil, as amongst a most deafening din, the whole world seemed to come crashing down around their heads.

Moments before the reckless charge, Rusty, Willard and the others, paused for a breath, and took time to take stock of the situation in The Vale. It was a lush open meadow, full of wild flowers, with a forest to each side. The ravine they had just exited was directly ahead and to their rear, lay the chasm to which Finnegan had fallen to his doom. The bridge was still broken, leaving no way across.

"So what happens now? I say we make a stand and fight for it. We can't run forever," said Brick, bunching his paws defiantly. However, Misfit wasn't happy.

"I don't know if you've noticed, but we're a bit outnumbered; just a handful against an army, and we're not even all armed. I say we move on, head for the trees and take cover. It'll give us time come up with a plan," suggested Misfit, pointing to the woodlands. A grumble of agreement echoed round from the other rats.

But Scarlet tried to rally them. "You're forgetting one thing, the call has gone out to take up arms, and meet here at The Vale. Surely, help is on the way. Isn't that right, Willard?" she asked, trying raise their spirits, and renew hope.

"Indeed, it is true, and I am sure it is but a matter of time before the call is answered," Willard replied readily.

"Well, time is one thing we're running short of, 'cos I don't know about you but I don't see anyone here but us," retorted Misfit dismissively.

"And I'm betting no one's coming either," said a worried-looking Patter, glancing around for the support he was sure wasn't on the way. It was then they all heard the faint blast of a bugle horn, echoing from the canyon beyond.

"Well, that's made up our minds for us," said Rusty, his ears pricking up to the sound. "They're here, it looks like Brick was right," he said to them all, gripping his sword tightly. "We have no choice; we stand and fight!"

But just has he finished speaking, they all heard the unmistakable tumultuous sound of a rockfall, accompanied by clouds of billowing smoke, emitting from the ravine itself.

The bugler froze in his tracks. Everything around him seemed so unreal. The scene unravelled around him in seemingly in slow motion, as if time itself had decelerated. The noise was a deafening crescendo all about him, and as he watched wide-eyed in horror, a huge boulder fell just behind him, landing with a crashing thud. It was a direct hit, crushing two unfortunate troopers beneath its weight.

"Run for your lives!" came an echoey shout from another, as a trooper pushed him out of the way, only to be engulfed under a shower of rocks before his very eyes. Then from somewhere deep within, he recalled words of advice from his father echoing to him from down the years.

"In moments of crisis, son, fight or flee. Doing nothing is the option of only a fool." As everything around suddenly sped up to real time, his natural instincts of survival took over, and heeding his father's words, he found himself hurtling out of the chasm of dust and chaos as fast as his legs could carry him.

At last, the bugler left the scene of devastation behind, falling to his knees, choking and gagging for air. And as he did, another dropped next to him, covered in dust, shaking and coughing too. He turned his head to see which miserable trooper had managed to escape the devastation and join him. But it was not a fellow soldier crouched over next to him gasping for air, but the king himself, turning to look directly at him, through terrified streaming eyes.

Rusty and the rest couldn't quite believe what they'd just witnessed as the chaotic scene unfolded before them. The twenty or so grey troop who escaped being entombed, lay in disarray, with half their company surely perished, and left behind under a mountain of rock and soil.

"Only fools rush in, eh?" smirked Misfit as he stood enjoying watching the Grey Army in turmoil.

"Let's rush 'em now," suggested Hugo eagerly. "Don't give 'em time to regroup," which gathered a resounding cheer from his the now emboldened rats.

But Willard's thoughts lay elsewhere. "I think we may yet have a more pressing matter at hand," said Willard, his attention focused not on the ill fortune of the Grey Army, but to the forest edge. "For I fear a new danger is upon us."

They all followed his gaze to the trees, but nothing out of the ordinary could yet be seen.

"What are you taking about? I don't see anything," questioned a puzzled Misfit.

But Rusty felt alarmed too. "No, Willard's right, I sense another threat also," agreed Rusty, his heightened senses enhanced by foresight. And then, suddenly movement could be seen, deep in the forest. A group in the shadows coming their way, as the sound of undergrowth being hacked down grew ever closer. As the newcomers broke cover, it became apparent who they were.

Padding towards them came ten heavily armoured large wolves, their glaring yellowed eyes visible under their steel helmets. They all brandished swords or axes strapped to their belts and carried round shields on their backs, along with an air of menace. The largest wolf in the middle stopped, raised a gloved right paw, and they all came to a halt immediately. The wolf then spoke.

"Ah Willard, we meet again on the battlefield, but this time the outcome will be different, I promise you that!" the wolf growled, before taking a step forwards clear of the pack. "Hear me now, all of you, for I will not repeat myself!" the wolf boomed. "I am here on the bequest of my ally, Oswald the

Elder, to aid the king known as Slate, and the army of the greys. You must be Rusty and the renegades," the wolf growled, now staring directly at them. "I have heard of your escape, as I have ears everywhere. Now hear my name and quake in fear, like so many before you. For I am Anubis, queen of the she-wolves of the north. Hear me now. Lay down your arms at once, renegades. Or die. The choice is yours."

Slate, still on his knees, felt a large shadow cast over him, as he looked up through blurred eyes, to see the large she-wolf, standing over him. The wolves came from the north of the Brow. In their community, it was the females who went to war and being soldiers of fortune, would fight for a cause. At the right price.

"I take it you are the king," guessed Anubis correctly. "As unlike the rest, you wear no armour."

Anubis was a fearsome-looking creature. The biggest of the wolves, her grey fur adorned with impressive armour, her head, mostly covered in a round steel helmet, her bright yellow eyes seemingly stared straight through him.

Slate, his vision now clearing, was taken aback initially, at the fearsome sight of the huge wolf before him. But he quickly gathered his thoughts. Being a born survivor, he knew now was not the time to show any kind of weakness. So feeling he needed to take the upper paw in front of his troops, he rose quickly to his feet, dusted himself down, and addressed the dominant-looking newcomer, with as much confidence as he could muster.

"Oh yes, you are the hired paw, the wild wolves of the north the Elder sent for," he said disparagingly. "Well, I am King Slate. You may now bow," he said, with his nose in the air.

Towering over him, Anubis leaned in closer, nose to nose, and hissed at him through gritted teeth. "Queen Anubis bows to no one, you'd do well to remember that!"

A chastened Slate, visibly shaken, immediately shrank back. She straightened up and gave a half-smile, her tone now changed at his perceived deference.

"As you know Oswald paid for our services in advance, and paid well too, so we will fight alongside you and honour our contract. And it appears I came not a moment too soon," she said glancing disapprovingly at the remainder of the greys, as they struggled back to their feet. "I was told your troops were elite, but it looks like I was misinformed," she scoffed at the sight.

Before Slate could protest, the sound of wings came from above and Talon dropped out of the sky, ridden by Oswald, who landed before them. He had the wooden chest from Ursa's lair, strapped to the rear of the saddle, and immediately dismounting, picking out the two nearest troopers.

"You two!" he barked, "grab the chest and bring it to your king, now! "he ordered stiffly. They both did as they were told, and scurried over to set about their task with vigour. Oswald strode over quickly towards the mighty wolf. "Queen Anubis, we meet again," he said, greeting her warmly. "It's been too long."

"Yes, I agree, for this day of reckoning is overdue, and I finally get to take revenge on your wretched brother – and get paid handsomely in the bargain too," she said, grinning broadly.

As the two troopers burdened with the chest hurried over, Oswald turned to Slate.

"My liege, here is the booty as promised," he said, as it was deposited by the guards at the king's feet. Oswald flung open the lid, to reveal the glow stones in side. "The precious rocks, as promised."

Slate immediately forgetting the catastrophe of the last few moments, made his way over and grabbed a handful of them. He ran them through his paws, as they danced in the sunlight, much to his delight.

"Elder, you have done well," he said greedily. "These beauties will be a fine addition to my trove."

"I am here to please you, sire, so may I now receive my reward?" Oswald asked meekly.

"Reward? Oh, the riven blade. It was carried by two of my elite, it's yours if they survived." he said, waving him away.

But Anubis was getting impatient. "Slate, may I remind you, we have a battle to fight!" she growled.

Slate immediately forgot his loot, as the thought of victory once more crossed his mind. That, and bloodshed. "Oh yes, of course, let's not dilly-dally, there's fun to be had," said Slate straightening up. With a wicked look in his eye, he turned to address his troops. "Now where is Stone? Don't tell me he's not here," said Slate, searching for his commander amongst the remainder of the Grey Army. "Oh, where is he? I didn't give him permission to die," he moaned.

"Sire, I'm here, alive and well," replied Stone, appearing from their midst, unharmed.

"Excellent, you survived. Now rally the troops and ready them for battle!" Slate commanded. "It's time to quash this rebellion once and for all!"

Across The Vale Rusty watched with the rest, as the opposition began to fan out in a line. The wolves, led by Anubis, on one flank to their left, and the greys, headed by Stone, on the other. Slate and Oswald stayed well back at the rear.

"Willard, what do I do? I need your advice," asked Rusty, as he felt the others now looked to him for leadership.

Willard smiled and answered him softly. "This is your, time my friend. Your destiny has led you to this place to be the figurehead of the rebellion. You need to stay strong, and assemble and ready them for what lies ahead." He then leaned in closer. "Have, faith Rusty, draw strength from your forefathers, for I feel your day has come, of this I am sure. And above all, speak from the heart." A determined look then crossed Willard's face as he readied himself for what he needed to do next. "As you set about your task, I will prepare to face my brother, for I know he will show his final hand."

Rusty drew a breath and stood in front of the rebels, addressing them all. "We need to ready ourselves and stay as one," he began, as all eyes now fell on him. "We've come this far and I'm proud to take a stand with you, to defend what is precious to us, our freedom. This island is our land. We won't let it be taken from us, so we must fight for what is right. To defend the weak, unite the strong, and win the day. We may be outnumbered but I for one will go down fighting. Who will fight with me? Say aye!" he roared.

"Aye! Aye! Aye!" came the shout, all buoyed by his inspiring words.

Brick then came forward. "Those with a sword, step up to fight; the rest stay back until we fall, then take our place," said Brick. As he turned to face the enemy, he was joined by Rusty, Scarlet, Misfit, Ash, Cornell, Hugo, Pitter and Patter with swords at the ready with Madder, Chilli, Huw and Hugh standing by ready and waiting to take their place.

"Nice speech there, Rust," said Ash, as he came to stand by his side. "Not so sure about the going down fighting bit, though," he added with a grin. Across The Vale, the sound of the cadet's bugle horn pierced the air as the Grey Army began their steady advance. And as they did, all at once, a volley of arrows flew through the air, just falling short at their feet. Taken by surprise, they stopped in their tracks, as Rusty and the rest followed their gaze to see where the projectiles had come from. And to their astonishment, they were greeted by a sight that made their spirits soar.

CHAPTER FORTY

A great cheer now filled the air as Izzy, Tricky and ten more pines, bows at their sides, strode towards them from the forest. Once in range, with a signal from Tricky, they dropped to a knee and formed a line ready to strike if the enemy dared to advance again.

"Is this a private party or are we all invited?" Izzy quipped as she joined them to cheers and much back slapping.

"Here you are, we have weapons to spare," she said as a few of the pines ran forwards carrying a trunk, flipped the lid, and handed out swords and shields to grateful paws. Then following in their wake came the unmistakable figure of Rough, crashing breathlessly through the underbrush, beaming widely.

"It looks like we got here just in time, I wouldn't want to miss the fun of joining Rusty and the renegades!" he shouted jovially, as he wrapped his big arms around Rusty and gave him a huge hug.

"Rough, I'm so pleased to see you mate," said Rusty, grinning widely and returning the embrace gladly.

"And what's this renegades tag? It's the second time I've heard it today," he asked with a bright smile. Rough smiled back.

"That's the word in the woods, up in the north. How the renegades escaped, led by fearless Rusty the rebel. You're a legend mate," he beamed. "And I must say, it's certainly helped swell the ranks, see for yourself," he said, gesturing over his shoulder as yet more arrived. Rabbits, hares, foxes, stoats and more. Some were grateful survivors of Finnegan's den, wanting to repay the debt, others just wanted to help to repel the invaders. But all had one thing in common. They were armed to the teeth and ready to fight.

The Battle for Badgers Brow

"You see what I mean," said Rough, as they all banded together. "I didn't need to ask twice, they all wanted to do their bit."

Suddenly, Ursa the bear came into sight, his huge frame ambling towards them, gaining the biggest cheers of approval of all. "Just point me in the direction of trouble and I'll do the rest!" he roared.

Across The Vale, the greys watched on in dismay as they felt the balance of power shifting away from them as the opposition ranks grew in number, and became agitated as they awaited new orders.

"Elder, what is this? You didn't inform me they have archers, and a bear. Why don't I have a bear?" whined Slate.

"And reinforcements too? We haven't even had chance to kill any yet! Elder, advise me," he wailed pathetically. But to his dismay his advisor seemed distant, as if in a trance. "Elder, pay attention, this is no time to daydream!" he screamed. But his cry was in vain, as the Elder's thoughts were elsewhere. He'd laid out the Meriden blade still clothed and in two in front of him, staring across the battlefield, his eyes defiantly fixed on Willard. They were locked together in a mental battle of wills.

"Desist brother, for this time you will lose once and for all," he spoke directly to him, through the power of thought. "Join me," he implored. "Think about it, we can rule this isle and more. For we are kin, and our bloodline spans the centuries. Once the blade is riven no more, the power and knowledge locked within will be unleashed, and we can be unstoppable!"

Willard grimaced, and then replied. "You know Oswald, this cannot be," came the unsatisfactory reply. "You too know the truth, for the Meriden blade was parted for all eternity, its wisdom too much for one to hold, and we must obey the lore of our ancestors," he implored.

"So be it brother!" Oswald spat out venomously. "You had your chance. Once they have fought their petty squabble, I will reunite the blade and make you rue this very day.

"Sire, sire, the troops await your orders!" came a shout from the frontline to a bewildered Slate, lost for words, with his advisor still unresponsive. He felt a surge of panic rising over him, and a quick decision was made.

"New orders?" he blurted out. "Isn't it obvious? Advance at once and slay them all, you fools. Make an example of them and take no prisoners. Leave not one rebel alive to tell the tale!"

"You heard the king!" yelled Stone. "Bugler, sound the charge. Glory for the greys!"

As his bugle rang out again, the greys could hear the defiant response it received, as the cry of "Renegades! Renegades! Renegades!" rang out in their ears. The battle for Badgers Brow had truly now begun.

CHAPTER FORTY ONE

As the two opposing sides began to face off far below general Peck too had combat on his mind. He searched the skyline incessantly for a first sighting of the enemy, particularly the known associate of the renegades, Screech the brown owl, but to no avail. He and his crow riders knew that in ariel combat the element of surprise could help win the day so they remained as high as possible, keeping the sun at their backs in tight formation. It didn't take long before the waiting game paid off as coming in below them from the north, in a flying 'V' formation, their quarry was sighted.

Screech led them in flanked by four wild geese, two at each side. The general was now filled with exhilaration as this was exactly what he had been waiting for, a chance for redemption, and by all accounts an easy target too.

Without hesitation, Peck gave the signal, a simple nod of the head, to tell them to draw their sabres, the weapon of choice for the riders. Now at the ready, Peck made the crow rallying call with a loud caw, caw, one swift movement, and a fold of his wings, began to dive-bomb his opponents, leading the attack. Dropping out of the sun, with it behind them, the foe beneath would be struck without prior warning. They won't know what's hit them.

"Go out and seek those who will listen and heed the call", Willard had said, and so Screech had done what his dear friend had asked, and gone out to spread the word. But much to his amazement, the tale was known in abundance and Rusty and the renegades, and their fightback, was already becoming folklore. One white dove had said to him, "It's a small island, and news travels fast."

And so, the call to arms to join the resistance was made easier, as animals, even those without combat training, had heard of their subjugation and didn't want to share their fate. Screech met up with Rough and Ursa and sat through the night deliberating, and a two-pronged attack was deemed the best tactic to use.

It was therefore decided as the ground assault began, Screech would take to the skies to take on the crow riders in order to prevent them entering the fray below. They all knew aerial dominance could be key to the outcome. A name was needed said Rough, for the new squadron. It needed to be heroic, something memorable, and to inspire the cause. And that's how the name the Freedom Fighters was born.

Aerial tactics were then discussed, and after much debate, all finally agreed that the brown owl's approach would have the best odds for success. Screech's plan was simple and in two parts. If it were roles reversed, what would he do? He'd launch a surprise assault from on high with the sun at his rear.

And so now as they approached in the low flying 'V', it was time to put the plan into action. Screech waited until what he considered to be the pivotal moment as they spied The Vale directly below. He at once abruptly changed flight path, swiftly turning to the right, with the geese going the opposite way. It worked better than he could have ever hoped for as the incoming riders, right on cue, hurtled by, filling the void they had just vacated, completely missing their target.

Now the second part of the plan came into force, as the rest of the newly formed Freedom Fighters, who had flown a short distance behind staying just out of sight, joined the fray. They were led by a wily old hawk named Tempest, his name was given to him, so he claimed, due to the stormy weather on the day of his birth. Screech and the slow-flying geese had been the bait to draw them in, but now came the speedy fighting birds of prey, consisting of six hawks, two kestrels and a falcon, closing in, with loud shrieks being their battle cry. They swooped on to their startled targets, talons drawn, and avoiding the wild swings of the cutlass.

Tempest was the first to strike, pulling an unfortunate grey from his saddle, and avoiding his desperate cutlass swings, let him go and he fell screaming, condemned to his fate. Peck turned out of his dive, he realised he'd been out manoeuvred. He saw the melee taking place to his rear, as the battle raged, steel against claw. His squadron now embattled and losing more riders, the tables now turning quickly, he knew he had to begin a quick counter-attack, or face certain defeat.

"Captain Luna!" he yelled to the young recently promoted crow rider, flying by his side. "Lead the charge into the thick of them, and cut them down!"

"Yes, sir," she replied immediately, and joined by two more, quickly returned to the fight.

"Right, where are you, owl?" fumed Peck, trying to pick out Screech amongst the combatants. "Try to make a mockery of me, eh? Well, it's time for you to pay the ultimate price!"

CHAPTER FORTY TWO

"Archers, take positions!" came the order from Izzy. The pines immediately ran to the fore, and in a well-practised drill, took the knee, and drew back their bows, aiming skywards. Now in line in front of the renegades, they held their position and awaited the next command.

"Wait," she said, gauging the distance, arm held high. "Wait."

The Grey Army striding purposefully forwards drew ever closer, so near you could see the fire in the eyes of some, and fear in the eyes of others. But Izzy was ready.

"Fire!" she ordered, and with a drop of her arm, they let fly. With that, a volley of arrows arced up into the air.

They then fell down, towards their intended targets.

"Incoming, raise shields!" barked Anubis, and the she-wolves lifted them as one. The barrage of arrows pinged and bounced off any armour it found, and a few, who didn't have the luxury of possessing shields, fell to the ground wounded or worse. Stone then gave the order to engage.

"Charge!" he thundered. As he ran forwards roaring them on, the cadet's bugle again pierced the air, with the pines taking aim, and firing again. Their job done for now, they then fell back as Rusty led the renegades.

"Attack!" he shouted, rushing bravely towards the grey line, in an attempt to push them back.

As the two opposing ranks charged at one another, Brick picked out an opponent. He had one rule in a fight, choose the biggest opponent. The largest grey in his sights was Stone, so Brick headed straight for him, sword at the ready, closing the distance fast, and without warning, swung down hard. But Stone was experienced, for this was not his first fight, far from it, and read the strike easily and blocked it with his sword. He hit Brick flush on the jaw with his bunched gloved paw. This stunned Brick and knocked him momentarily off balance, before quickly recovering.

"Come on, is that all you got?" Brick roared defiantly and hit out again, but this time his blow was evaded easily, as Stone gingerly dodged away.

Stone then made his move, but this was parried with a deft shift in balance from Brick, knocking the blade to one side. He then immediately counter-attacked and lunged forwards, and this time his aim was true, as Stone staggered back badly wounded.

Nearby the bugle player stood around dumbfounded, as his father's words again resonated in his head. "Fight or flee," he had told him, so choosing the former, pulled a short dagger from his belt, and braced to face the enemy head on, as Stone teetered towards him, holding his side.

"What do you think you're doing, young cadet?" he gasped, through laboured breath.

"I'm going to fight," the bugler said determinedly.

"Oh no you're not, fall back. That's an order," rasped Stone, and grabbed him before he could protest, dragging him to the rear.

On the opposing flank, Anubis led the charge of the howling she-wolves, and were nearly on top of the renegades, when she saw through the corner of her eye a huge figure appear. It was Ursa, lashing out in a towering rage, sending three of the she-wolves crashing to the ground immediately. Anubis now maddened at the sight of her fallen comrades flashed her sword in a downward arc, striking the big bear across his chest, making him roar in pain.

But to her alarm, instead of causing serious harm it intensified his anger. He struck Anubis with a large swing of his right paw, breaking her breastplate in two, and sending her up in the air and into a crumpled heap, as Ursa, now ignoring her, battled on.

The pine martens, feeling emboldened at the sight of the fallen Anubis, took on the remaining wolves. Due to the wolves' superior size, they had to swarm them like angry bees, with at least three pines to each wolf, attacking from all angles with their short swords. The wolves fought their tormentors back, swinging wildly at their nimble foe, but were much slower in their unwieldy armour, and the pines wore them down, their many blows now taking their toll. Izzy was there in the thick of it, and used her speed to great effect, bravely helping to put one wolf down, with a high leap and a head strike to the top of the helmet, splitting it in two. But the remaining snarling wolves fought back fiercely, with casualties now being taken on both sides. The battle raged on all fronts, as the sound of clanging metal rang out loudly and clearly across The

The Battle for Badgers Brow

Vale, alongside the cries of the wounded. Rusty, Scarlet and the remaining renegades, fought on in ever fierce pockets of combat with the greys, with no quarter being asked or given.

Rusty now battled one on one with a grey, each attacking and defending with equal vigour, both giving their all, but then, with a final lunge, he sent the grey falling to the ground. Yet another appeared, and leapt screaming wildly, weapon on high, taking his place, catching Rusty off balance. Sensing the danger, Scarlet leapt into action and screamed madly. She intercepted the threat, and with deadly accuracy, finished him in quick fashion. Rusty acknowledged her quick thinking with a nod, as there was little time for much more, and the struggle went on.

Ash, fighting by Rusty's side, had proved his worth time and time again, his sword working tirelessly, and never backing down. Rough, at his other shoulder, was right in the thick of it too, fighting for all he was worth.

"This is for Archie. Rough by name, rough by nature!" he bellowed sword in paw, scattering greys before him, as if cutting down hay for harvest.

Skirmishes were abound, as Carmine, Chilli and Madder fought with valour, alongside Misfit and the rats, all doing their utmost. However, the bigger, stronger greys on this front, were beginning to get the upper hand. Misfit watched on in dismay, as Huw fell by his side, and through gritted teeth fought on aggressively, and beginning to slowly force them back.

Slate had ogled at the life and death struggles playing out in front of him, as his emotions ranged from joy to despair. After what he deemed early success now changed, as the tide seemingly began to turn against him.

"Elder, tell me this is going to plan, and we're lulling them into a false sense of security? You know I never like to lose at anything," he wailed. Then in an instant, his mood changed from despair to anger, as the reality of defeat stared him in the face, and so he turned on his advisor. "Act now imbecile, or the blame will lie at your door!" he warned.

Oswald having watched on silently with morbid fascination at the grim scene before him, gave Slate a final look of disdain. "I have listened to your snivelling whine for the last time!" Oswald snarled. "You thought you ruled over me? Well, think again, oaf, for your purpose has now been served."

With a deft raise of Oswald's paw, Slate was lifted up into the air with his limbs flailing comically.

"What are you doing, you fool? Put me down immediately!" he cried, as he floated helplessly above the ground.

"As you wish, sire!" shouted Oswald, and with a flick of his arm, sent Slate flying over the battling greys, dropping him in the thick of it unceremoniously at Rusty's feet. He fell to the floor with a thud cowering, his paws hiding his face as he peeked out and bleated pathetically.

"Don't strike me, I'm defenceless! Don't hurt me, I meant you no harm."

"Of course you didn't, and you'll make a fine prisoner too!" replied Rusty brusquely. He grabbed him roughly by the collar, pulling him close to him and spun him around. His arm was across Slate's chest using him as a living shield. The injured Stone saw this, and now infuriated, shouted a warning of his own.

"Hands off the king!" He stormed forwards, and in desperation, raised his sword and lunged at Rusty.

Ash was the first to react to the danger of the onrushing Stone, and threw himself between them, his sword raised in an attempt to block the strike, but took the blow himself. A stricken Ash then fell to his knees, head bowed as if in prayer, as Rusty braced for the impact. But it never came, as Stone was cut down by the quick-thinking Brick, and fell motionless to the ground.

The two sides, seeing the king now captured, halted their struggle. Oswald, observing from the rear, had seen enough and decided to finally act. Before him lay the two pieces of the blade, still wrapped in sack cloth. With just a quick gesture, the cloths unravelled easily, revealing what had lain inside for so long. The broken sword of Meriden.

The battle below had gone on mostly unnoticed in the sky above by Peck, as his only thoughts now were on the combat his corps faced and his own agenda – to take out the brown owl. But he could see to his utter dismay that his original plan was lying in tatters, as the hawks swooped and dived in turn, with the crow riders valiantly fighting back, mostly in vain, blade against claw. And then he spied his target, Screech himself, and raced towards him. Being riderless, his task was meant to just command, but this had become personal, and he felt he had to intervene, even if it cost him his life.

Tempest, the hawk captain, had already formulated a plan beforehand, and his team had used it to deadly effect. It was to single out a crow on the perimeter by attacking in groups of two or three. This led to an inevitable panic as the bird tried to evade them, and that was when the trap was sprung, because yet another hawk lying in wait, dropped from above and finished the job.

Captain Luna had followed her orders to the letter and struck back continuously with venom, even causing a hawk to fall, but now could see the situation had become desperate, as her comrades were picked off one by one.

"Luna, are you injured?" she heard, and turned to see a desperate Peck had joined her side.

"No, sir, but we can't win this, we need to fall back and regroup."

"Agreed," replied Peck, "but not before we kill their leader – the owl. With me now!" he ordered, and flew off in the direction of Screech. He knew his only chance was to strike swiftly and from behind, and avoid the owl's claws at all costs. Luck appeared to be on his side, as his opponent didn't spot his approach, and he was therefore able to slam into him at great speed, using his beak to full effect, raking deep into the owl's back.

Screech had in fact not seen the crow's approach, and as the pain of the assault registered, he cried out and immediately changed direction to see his assailant. But this was when Luna too joined the attack, her crow rider leaning in, and slashing with his cutlass across the owl's outstretched wing. Screech felt the pain sear through him but managed to pivot, grab and unseat the rider, and hurl him from his seat. But as the grey began to fall, he lashed out desperately one last time, again hitting home, before disappearing, falling from view. Peck, now seeing his enemy badly wounded, joined in with renewed vigour.

"Now to finish you off!" he yelled, as he went again on the attack. But this time Screech was ready, and as Peck struck out with his beak, he turned in mid-flight to the crow's horror. Screech grabbed hold tightly, and embedded deeply, with both claws, into his attacker's torso. As they both now stared defiantly into each other eyes, they began to spiral down, together locked in a deadly embrace as they fell to earth. For them the battle was over.

CHAPTER FORTY THREE

"Indeed, you are a thing of beauty," declared Oswald, as he revelled in the sight of the ancient broken blade lying on the grass before him. Meriden had obviously been a master swordsmith and taken great care in his work. The handle itself was decorated in an intricate gold and garnet design, with the blade pattern welded from iron and steel rods. It lay there gleaming in the sun, as if it had only been forged yesterday, showing off its wondrous rippling pattern, which ran throughout its length. It had been snapped in two at the mid-way point in a clean break, many centuries before, but now lay together for the first time in aeons, nearly as one.

"And now my moment of destiny has arrived," he gloated as the riven blade did as he asked and levitated up before his outstretched paws, like a puppeteer pulling his strings. He closed his paws together and the sword did the same, again becoming as one. As it joined together, it emitted a bright flash of light, which flew across The Vale, making all there present shield their eyes. This was immediately followed by a large boom coming from within the vessel, resembling a clap of thunder, the sound waves rippling out far and wide, causing most to nearly fall over in its wake. Oswald now revelled in the situation.

"Good, I have your attention!" he bellowed, as every eye was now transfixed on him. "Take heed and hear me out, for now my time has come. For it is said only one is destined to wield the sword of Meriden, and receive the truth which lies within."

He then reached out and grabbed its man-sized handle, as it shimmered and glowed in mid-air. It began shrinking and reducing in size before their very eyes, until it became the perfect fit for a dormouse to hold. He then raised it triumphantly up in the air and roared.

"All bow down before me, for a new age has begun. Behold, for the reign of Oswald the Omnipotent has begun!"

CHAPTER FORTY FOUR

Oswald had never felt such joy in all his life, as he stood triumphant, the sword he had sought for so long now intact. He held it aloft triumphantly, sending an unspoken message to all present.

Lay down before me.

Then as he stood arm on high and head held proudly back awaiting their adulation, from behind him came a strange whisper. It was man babble but Oswald understood every word.

"Welcome oh seeker of the truth," the voice gently said.

"What, who's there?" asked Oswald, as he spun around to see who had spoken. But there was no other to be seen as he stood quite alone. Rusty, watching on mesmerised along with the rest, leaned in towards Willard.

"What's happening. Why is he talking to himself?" he asked, watching the odd actions of Oswald, seemingly holding a conversation with no one but him.

"Witness this my friend," Willard answered knowingly. "For he now takes the test."

A woman's voice, this time in front of him, whispered to Oswald in a warm and pleasant manner. "What name do you go by?" she asked sweetly.

"Oswald, my name is Oswald the Elder," he found himself replying to nothingness, as they all continued to watch on in silence at his strange antics.

"We must know if you are worthy," they said in unison, speaking as one. "Do you seek the truth?" the strange voices asked.

"Yes, I do," he replied in earnest. "Tell me the truth. Tell me all, and tell me now," he said excitedly, gripping the blade tightly. And again, the man spoke in his ear, but this time his tone had changed from friendly to hostile.

"Well, Oswald the Elder, your answer is false. Therefore, we find you most unworthy," came their damning verdict. The voices then abruptly stopped. And that was when he felt the searing pain. He opened his eyes in horror to see the sword burst into flame, from tip to tail. It was much too hot to handle, and he let go of the burning weapon in agony, turning away from the throng, wringing his hands and crying out in anguish as it fell to the floor. And as it did, the flame extinguished straight away, and the sword expanded immediately to its original man-size shape.

The assembled all watched on astounded at the strange scene playing out before them. The Elder, now with his back turned, moaned in pain as the sword hissed and cooled at his feet. Rusty, stunned at the scene that had played out before him but sensing the end game drew near, turned to Brick and pushed Slate firmly into his arms.

"Here, keep hold of our friend Slate, will you?" he said forcefully.

"With pleasure," Brick replied, and grabbed him tightly, with his arms pushed up high behind his back.

"There's no need to play rough," Slate bleated, which just made Brick give him a quick extra twist of an arm to shut him up, making him yelp out loudly.

Anubis now back on her feet, had been watching the proceedings with great interest too. "Fall back!" she ordered to the remaining she-wolves, with a sweep of her gauntlet. They obeyed at once backing away from the renegades, taking their wounded and fallen with them. The few greys left standing leaderless and vulnerable, looked around in bewilderment. Not one commander was left standing, and the king had been taken prisoner, leaving them lost. The bugler, seeing their dilemma, took the initiative and made a quick decision.

"We need to withdraw. That way we can live to fight another day," he suggested.

Knowing they were defeated, they took his advice and slunk away, much to the dismay of Slate, who now felt deserted by his own kind, still locked in the powerful grip of Brick. Rusty now free of Slate, bent down to Ash and put his paw gingerly under his head.

"Take it easy, you're going to be fine," he said tenderly.

"Did we win?" replied Ash softly, his eyes half shut, gripping Rusty's arm tightly.

"Yes, we did Ash. They've retreated, and you helped win the day."

Ash smiled weakly, and then replied. "Like I said before," he gasped. "You treated me like kin. You're all the family I've never known."

Rusty, sensing his friend was weakening, leaned closer still. "You are my brother, now and forever more," he promised solemnly.

Ash smiled for one last time, released his grip, closed his eyes, and gently slipped away.

Anubis, seeing them all in disarray, decided now was the time to make her move. She marched towards the stricken Oswald and the fallen sword. He looked up in confusion at her approach, still smarting from his burns, not quite believing what had just occurred, as his well-laid planned plans lay in tatters.

"What's the matter, dormouse?" she said, grinning from ear to ear. "Was it too hot to handle? You're obviously undeserving and not fit to hold a weapon that was surely forged for royalty. Out of my way!" she snarled, pushing him aside. She then bent down and picked up the blade, easily holding it aloft, as it again changed size, this time to fit a wolf. "All hail queen Anubis!" she roared, as the three remaining wolves all howled in agreement.

Then she too heard the same questions that Oswald had heard from voices again unseen. "Yes, tell me the truth," she replied willingly, her eyes widened in awe, admiring the magnificence of the fine blade in her grasp. "And look, it is a sword fit for a queen!" she screamed in ecstasy, now swinging it back and forth through the air, in front of her with delight. Then at once, a flame burst out of the blade, creating an arc of burning light across her front, as she swung it wildly.

"Aaaarghhh! What trickery is this?" she screamed as the ancient sword turned into a bright orange inferno, scorching her too, causing her to let go. She dropped to her knees in anguish, as the flame went out as it cooled, burning the blackened earth before her.

Willard had seen enough and moved to Rusty's side. "My friend, we have lost some that are dear to us today," he said, reading the sorrow in Rusty's eyes. "But now is not the time to grieve, as we must secure the victory."

Rusty acknowledged him, knowing deep inside he was right. "So what happens now?" he asked unsurely.

Willard didn't answer, just raised a paw, and the sword of Meriden lifted and flew towards them, stopping and floating in front of him.

"Now, have no fear my friend," encouraged Willard. "Grasp the blade, for the legend says all that lies within awaits for one that is righteous. And my friend I believe that one is truly you."

As the wondrous blade, glistening in the late afternoon sun hovered before his eyes, Rusty felt so unsure. Was Willard correct? Is he truly the one able to unlock the swords secrets? Meanwhile, Slate marvelled at the gleaming blade, so close he could almost reach out and touch it.

So this is what that cunning Oswald had yearned for all

along! he thought to himself, admiring it through envious eyes. And seeing it up so close, how magnificent it really was, he now desired it for himself.

Sensing Rusty's indecision, he craned forwards and made a devious offer of his own. "If you've got doubts about this weapon, I don't mind handling it," he said, trying to sound sincere. "Give it to me, it does look dangerous, and in the wrong paws who knows what may happen. Just look at that fool, he's certainly had his paws burnt," he scoffed.

Willard, hearing every word, gave him a withering glance and signalled to Brick to pull him away.

"Are you ready to try now, my friend?" he asked, sensing his hesitation. Rusty still doubtful, turned to Scarlet for her advice as he always did in times of need. She read in his eyes his indecision, and so reached out to him.

"I trust in Willard and I know you do too," she said gently.

"So do what needs to be done." She gave him a tender kiss. Now, with Scarlet's blessing, he reached out slowly and grasped the handle tightly with both paws. At once the blade shrank down in size, as if it were made just for him. Then before his eyes a falling leaf from a nearby tree froze, suspended in the air, as all around him did too. He then heard a strange voice of a man, whispering quietly in his ear.

"Welcome, oh seeker of the truth," he said. And then a woman spoke too.

"Tell me, what name do you go by?" she asked sweetly.

"Rusty, my name is Rusty," came his calm reply.

"We must know if you're worthy," they both said together. "Do you seek the truth?"

"The only thing I seek is to help others," he replied honestly. There was a moment's silence and then the man spoke again. "Your answer is worthy, therefore so are you."

In an instant, a blast emanated from the sword itself, and blew outwards creating a ripple in the air. Like a stone thrown in a pond, it created a circle of air which expanded all around him, and as it did, The Vale and everything in it changed completely.

Rusty felt now like he was in a dream, and found himself standing by a group of strangers – men and women – standing in a clearing of a mist enshrouded wood. They were dressed like no one he'd ever seen before. They all had long robes and cloaks and wore their hair long, and were standing together in a circle in deep discussion. Then one left the group and approached him. He had a kindly face and a warm smile.

"Welcome traveller, we have been awaiting your arrival for some time," he said amiably. "Do not be afraid, for we wish you no harm, for we here are all the same." Rusty was left speechless as the man talked on. "You are called Rusty, that I already know. Well, I go by the name of Nat-Jos. And I will now explain the reason why we are gathered here today," he said.

"We are druids, one and all. Our practices and teachings span the centuries, knowledge and wisdom gained through the passage of time. But we know that man may come, and may even go, and therefore it has been decided, after much discussion, that as a safeguard we have placed all we know into a singular vessel, so that our wisdom may never be lost, and kept safe for generations to come. And so we called the best swordsmith in the land Meriden, who forged what you now hold," he went on. "We knew in a time of turbulence, for the good of all, our wisdom could become unlocked. It seems that time has come, so clear your mind and listen well and begin to learn, for what is ours is yours too".

"Rusty's head then started to fill with whispers and voices, speaking in ways he didn't understand, in an ancient tongue. Just then, another figure came towards him from the group, this time his face was etched in concern.

"Heed the warning, stranger. You must stop this at once. I am Shelton, and my truth is beyond doubt. The knowledge held within is too big a burden for one to bear, for it can only lead to desolation and despair. The sword must be broken, and kept apart for the sake of all. I vow I will do this, and promise until my dying breath that I will fulfil my vow!"

He was then dragged away by two other Druids, still protesting. "You know not what you are doing, it must be split asunder. Whoever holds the blade will be cursed!" And then abruptly, Rusty was back in the present day, as the leaf from the tree again began to fall, and all around reawakened. But now he felt confused, different somehow. His senses were magnified, his eyes picking out the smallest detail, every colour a vivid glow.
His hearing also intensified, enhancing each and every sound.

"Are you okay?" asked a concerned Scarlet. "Look, your eyes, they've changed."

Rusty was unsure what she meant, and then he caught his reflection in the steel blade of Meriden, and to his astonishment, his eyes now glowed a bright red. Then his ears pricked up, his improved senses picking out a hushed conversation held by Anubis to a wolf.

"I still want that blade, take it for your queen," she hissed.

The three remaining she-wolves silently agreed and began a stealthy approach. With a lift of one paw, a wolf was thrown to the ground. Then, with just a look from him, another became unable to move, her feet stuck as if fastened down. But the last remaining wolf unperturbed, still advanced. But Rusty was ready. He stamped his foot on the ground and a shock wave flew out towards her, singling her out, and knocking her down, as the rest looked on in awe at this new show of power.

Anubis, knowing now it was pointless to continue, gave the order to retreat. "I've seen enough deception for one day," she snarled, as her wolves, now free to move, joined her at her side. She then looked to Oswald and growled once more. "Again, you shame us with defeat. If you hadn't paid early, you'd pay with your life. Now never cross my path again!"

And with that, she led the she wolves away without pausing, or even giving a backwards glance.

Oswald watched on in despair as he saw his schemes unravel before his very eyes. Slate, still detained by Brick, observed with renewed interest as the wolves moved away.

"Elder!" Slate then shouted across the field. "You're fired!" He then turned his attention back to Rusty. "Rusty, I believe it is your name?" he asked sneakily.

Rusty gave him a hard stare.

"Well, Rusty, it's your lucky day, and I'll again repeat my offer. "You're hired! I know a winner when I see one. Let's forget the last few days. Call it our little disagreement. Come work for me, what could go wrong? Shall we shake on it?" he said grinning inanely, holding out his scrawny paw.

Rusty had heard enough and more than anything wanted him gone. "I'm saying this only once. You're defeated. Get off my island while you still can. And take your troops with you!" His eyes narrowed and glowed even brighter still, now burning with real menace. "Do I make myself clear?" He then held up the glowing blade in front of Slate, so close the point nearly touched his nose.

"Of course, of course," said Slate recoiling immediately. "We'll depart, never to return."

"Let him go, Brick," Rusty then said. Brick didn't need asking twice. He roughly pushed Slate away, causing him to stumble to the ground. An embarrassed Slate then picked himself up, dusted himself down, puffed out his chest, and then called out for help.

"Stone, where are you?" he cried. But then he saw his commander lying still nearby. "Oh dear, he's dead. Never mind. What's your name, Private?" he said to the nearest trooper.

"Charcoal, sire," came the smart reply.

"Well Charcoal, it's your lucky day, you're promoted to commander. Call in my crows for immediate departure."

"Yes, sire," he said in delight, and gave the signal for the crows to land.

As the few surviving birds joined them, Slate saddled Wolfram and took to the air. Now free to go, he hurled one last final insult.

"You and your renegade scum can keep this accursed island, but I will leave you a final message!" he warned.

His attention then turned back to Oswald. "As for you, imbecile, you're still fired!"

And with that took off and disappeared out of view.

CHAPTER FORTY FIVE

The renegades, with Slate now defeated, were left with a feeling of mixed emotions. Elation because the battle was won, and sadness at their losses too. But now their spirits were raised as a familiar face they presumed lost, came slowly towards them, and a small cheer broke out as Screech hobbled into view.

"Screech, are you okay?" shouted Izzy, as the pine martens, seeing him hurt, rushed forwards to help him.

"I've seen better days," he replied with a weary smile.

"It seems I do everything around here, including crash landings," he added with a wince, as one wing hung by his side, in an odd position. "But I'm sure with a bit a rest from the kitchen I'll be just fine," he joked half-heartedly. Screech was then helped by the pines to sit down on a nearby log, as Willard rushed over to his injured companion.

"It is so good to see you again, my old friend." He beamed, which was returned in kind. "And it seems you have been in the wars too," he added, examining his wounds with concern.

Willard then took a vial of clear liquid from his pocket, and after removing the stopper, handed it to Screech. "Here, just a few drops of my fix-all elixir on the tip of your tongue, along with a little rest, will surely have you back on your feet in no time at all," he promised. "And once you have partaken, I shall administer to the needs of the others who are injured too." Screech gladly took the medicine, took a few drops, and then handed it back to him. Willard scuttled away to see to the needs of others who sought help, knowing he was surely on the mend.

The Battle for Badgers Brow

Willard soon found willing hands to join him as Scarlet, Rough and the others who were uninjured helped to tend to the wounded, making his task so much easier.

Meanwhile, all this time, Rusty had stayed unmoved, his eyes still a burning red, fixated on Oswald across the meadow, who now stood glaring defiantly back at him. After administering yet another dose, Willard noticed this and with a worried look hurried over to his side.

"Tell me, my friend, what is it you see?" he asked.

Rusty replied at once, never taking his eyes off the Elder. "I sense that he isn't finished, and the battle isn't yet over," Rusty answered defiantly. But then self-doubt crept into his mind. "Why me? What makes me so special? Why do I not burn when holding the blade like the others did?"

Willard gave a knowing smile. "The vision of the druids you had was also revealed to me," he began to explain. "You now know the origin of the sword you wield but there is so much more to learn, so listen well, my friend. For now, the time has come. I needed to know you were ready for the truth and now I feel indeed you are. So listen well while I reveal all."

Rusty still watching Oswald intently was desperate to know all, so continued to listen as Willard resumed.

"The druids were wise and holy men, and one power they possess is reincarnation," Willard began. "This is a rebirth of the body, be it man or beast. This is why we have the gift of the foresight. You, Oswald and I, for we were druid too, and now are reborn again."

Rusty had never been more astounded in his life. "Really, you mean I'm like them?" Rusty asked in astonishment, never taking his eye off Oswald for a second. As the truth hit home, he had a sudden revelation. "So that's why he knows and desires the sword so much. It's all making sense now, I suppose," he admitted, breaking his vigil for a second.

"Indeed, my friend, and there is still so much for you to learn. I mentioned reincarnation to you. Well in your vision you met a previous incarnation of yourself. For you see my friend you are born again, renewed in your current form. In your past life you were the druid Nat-Jos and—"

At that moment, Oswald, seeing Rusty distracted, decided to act.

"Willard, you had your chance to join arms with your brother and you rebuked me!" he yelled. "We could have risen up together, and helped heal this broken world that man has tried to destroy with his weapons of war. But would you listen? No! They call you wise. Well, I call you a fool!"

Rusty, still reeling from the revelations he'd just received from Willard, again locked eyes with Oswald, as Willard responded.

"Leave now, Oswald, for your day is done. The blade is with its rightful owner and will never be yours, so I say to you. Once and for all. Begone!"

Now Oswald was enraged. "How dare you threaten me!" he thundered, with an angry shake of a paw. "You would not listen; therefore, I challenge you to face me for one last time in a battle of the beasts!" "What does he mean, a battle of the beasts?" asked a puzzled Rusty.

"There is little time, but I will try to explain," replied Willard quickly. "We druids may change form at will, for we are shape-shifters. As you heard, Oswald has challenged me to duel, and I cannot refuse, for the situation will be fraught with danger and he will attack regardless. It is a fight that will be short-lived, because to change form and battle as he wishes expends a lot of mental energy. Now, my friend, I must accept the challenge for it is for me to do, and to do alone."

Willard then moved forwards bravely before Rusty could protest, as Oswald strode towards him too. Willard then stopped abruptly and crouched down. His body started to shake and tremble, and then he threw back his head and let out a huge primeval roar, as all around him shrank back. He then began to change, to grow rapidly, his once tiny body now expanding hugely outwards. His once slight frame now massive in comparison, made up of muscle and sinew, encased in a golden coat of armoured mail, his now huge head, framed in an impressive mane of fur. Again, he roared and reared up, now all claw and fangs, no longer a simple dormouse but a fearsome cave lion of old.

Simultaneously, Oswald grew upwards and outwards, rapidly now to the size of a horse. He too, an image of brute force, his muscular frame impossible to ignore. He wore impressive armour too – the colour of silver – and let out a loud guttural roar of his own, both were now making the sounds of animals that had not been heard on this isle for centuries. For Oswald had transformed into a snarling Smilodon, a large sabre-toothed cat, his huge jaws agape showing his large deadly fangs.

And then, without warning, they pounced at one other, like the release of a pair of tightened coiled springs. And so, the battle of the beasts began.

As the renegades watched on in awe, the two beasts of old attacked each other, claws extended, jaws widened, their fierce wild eyes fixed only on each other. And then with an almighty collision, they crashed into one another, coming together snarling, biting and scratching, each trying to hurt his opponent and gain an upper hand. To all there watching on, the noise was tremendous. The sound of claw on armour almost ear-splitting, the raw show of bestial savagery an awesome sight to behold.

The huge sabre-toothed cat lashed out in an attempt to maim, but hit the lion's body armour with a thunderous blow instead. The cat then quickly spotted an opening, as his connection knocked his opponent off balance. He quickly opened his jaws wide, hoping to sink his huge tusk-like fangs into the lion's neck for a killer blow. But the lion rolled to one side at the last second and hit out with a claw of his own, raking the side of the large cat's face, making him back off, roaring and hissing with pain.

Rusty and the rest stood by and watched in amazement and disbelief at the spectacle of raw primal power playing out in front of their very eyes in this brutal contest. Misfit near the front leaned over to Pitter beginning to enjoy the clash, now in a mischievous mood.

"We've got great ring side seats don't you think? It's a shame we didn't bring nibbles," Misfit joked, causing Pitter to laugh out loud. "I'll put a wager on the lion," said Misfit, the turn of events bringing out the rogue in him. "A week's supply of food."

"You got it, I'll take the cat," replied Pitter with a grin.

"And may the best dormouse win," Misfit answered playfully.

The cat stayed back still reeling from the facial wound. He then countered and appeared to lunge again for the neck, but at the last second feinted and dropping his head, bit the lion fiercely on his right front leg. Gripping ever tighter, he shook his head violently to and fro, growling ferociously, biting down hard. It was now the lion's turn to roar with pain, and in an attempt to break free, he snapped his jaws, biting and hitting home, making the cat let go. But now the lion was truly hurt and backed away limping badly.

"No!" yelled Rusty loudly, fearful for his friend and mentor. "You can't lose now!" The lion heard the shout and glanced over to reassure him, but the cat took advantage of the distraction and charged again. Lowering his armoured head, he pounded the lion in his side, sending him sprawling to the ground. The lion at once stood back up shakily on all fours and snarled and roared back defiantly, but you could read the hurt pain and desperation in his eyes.

CHAPTER FORTY SIX

"Now tell me, Commander Charcoal, do you feel a bit chilly at all?" asked Slate, posturing and rubbing his arms furiously.

"Er no, sire, it's summer and I'm not cold at all," came the confused reply.

"Hopeless, truly hopeless, you just can't get the staff," moaned Slate, shaking his head in disappointment at the answer. Slate then looked around their landing site in the Great Wood and picked out a familiar-looking trooper nearby.

"You, yes you!" he hailed loudly. "Is that Commander Stone I see before me, or do my eyes deceive me? After all, I could have sworn you were dead. Are you a ghost come to haunt me?" Slate asked with a frown.

"No, sire, I am no spirit, he was my brother," came the strait-laced reply. "I'm Sergeant Pumice, sire," he answered.

"Tell me Sergeant, do you feel chilly?" asked Slate again, this time briskly rubbing his paws together, and blowing into them theatrically.

Sergeant Pumice, knowing the best way to gain favour with the king was just to agree with him, no matter how odd his behaviour may seem, bowed and replied instantly.

"Yes, sire, extremely chilled," he lied.

Slate was immediately impressed. "Charcoal," Slate said abruptly, pointing straight at him.

"You're demoted. Pumice, you've shown initiative, you're now my new commander." Charcoal bowed and gave Pumice a withering glance, before backing off grumbling to himself.

"What are your orders, sire?" asked Commander Pumice, pleased as punch at his unpredicted new promotion.

"My orders are simple. Take the troops and burn this wood down to the ground," sneered Slate. "Now that should definitely warm things up nicely!" he added, before chuckling with glee. "And hurry, we leave for the mainland immediately.

"Yes, sire, of course, sire," said Pumice, bowing and scraping as he started shouting out the new orders, leaving Slate alone to his thoughts of revenge.

"If I can't take this place for myself, I'll destroy it. I said I'd leave them a final message. And this will be one they'll never forget!"

The two great beasts started to circle each other now both wounded, but neither was willing to give ground.

"Yield to me now, brother," Oswald snarled, his face filled with rage. Seeing his brother seemed to be injured more seriously, he gambled that he'd surrender. "You're wounded, you'll never defeat me now. Submit and I promise to let you all go unharmed."

Willard was certainly hurt badly, with his leg bleeding profusely, but he snarled back defiantly at his tormentor. "I will never give in. It is a fight to the death, remember?" he retorted bravely.

Seeing the situation was becoming desperate, Izzy leaned into Rusty with a quickly thought-out plan. "Let my archers send a volley into the cat," she urged. "I know he wears armour, but we'll see how he likes that!"

"On my signal." Rusty nodded. "But let me try something first."

Izzy went to ready the pines as Rusty moved forwards, his eyes glowing brighter still, like the burning embers of a red-hot fire. Rusty hailed the cat.

"Elder, back down, you've caused enough trouble for one day!" he warned. The cat turned and stared back defiantly, his large yellow eyes brimming with hate, and hissed a manic reply.

"And what's a lowly red squirrel going to do against the likes of me?" he cried scornfully, before letting out an almighty roar.

Rusty stood tall and didn't reply. Listening to his inner self, he instinctively threw his sword arm skywards. The sword glowed even brighter now, and from its tip a beam of light flew upwards to the heavens. Then suddenly, a flash of bright lightning burst from on high and zig-zagged down, hitting the ground right in front of the giant cat with a tremendous bang, making him jump back in alarm.

"That was no illusion," Rusty warned. "The next one won't miss. Now, archers, take aim!" he ordered.

Izzy raised her arm and the pines stood in line; arrows aimed ready to fire.

With all the exertion of shape-shifting into a great cat, Oswald was now exhausted. Knowing he was beaten, the beast hissed and growled for one last time and started to slowly retreat. With each step he took back, he started to shrink and change and revert back to the size of a dormouse. Now back to his original form, he looked to the skies and called out once more.

"Talon, to my side!"

Within seconds his hawk landed neatly next to him. He climbed aboard gingerly wincing with pain, and with one last scowl, took off without another backwards glance.

"Where to, my master?" asked Talon, as they headed skywards.

"Just get me away from this accursed place," he groaned, humiliated.

Now the danger had passed, Willard began to return to his normal self too, and returned to a dormouse again, he fell back exhausted.

Scarlet rushed immediately to his side.

"Are you okay, Willard?" she asked, greatly concerned for the brave dormouse. "You fought so well," she added, putting a comforting arm around him.

Willard looked back at her through weary eyes. "I will be fine, I am sure," he said. "Though being in a big cat fight is tiring work indeed," he said with a wry smile.

Rough then came bounding over to help, fix all in hand.

"Here you are, it's your turn to be healed. Take this. There's just enough left for a little fellow like you," said Rough with a smile, holding the vial out to him. And as he did, there came an urgent cry from Izzy.

"Everyone, look! You need to see this."

They all then turned to see what she was pointing at.

A huge plume of black smoke could now be seen rising menacingly on the horizon. And it was coming from the direction of the Great Wood.

"No!" shrieked Scarlet in alarm," that looks like our home is ablaze!" They all looked on in despair as the black plume billowed up high into the summer sky, like a smoke signal foretelling a message of doom.

"We need to hurry back if it is the Great Wood!" said Rough urgently. "Fight the fire the best way we can."

"But we'll never get there in time," said Izzy. "It's half a day's march at least."

A quick-thinking Willard got up from his resting position, feeling a little better as his elixir quickly coursed through his tiny battered body. "Rough the badger, I have a possible plan, but first of all I will need the aid of Screech."

"Did I just hear the mention of my name?" said the brown owl as he made his way over, eager to help.

"We need to reach the Great Wood as quickly as possible, therefore we will need the service of your feathered friends," Willard began to explain.

"Not a problem, I'll call the Freedom Fighters right away," replied Screech desperate to assist.

"And please inform the rest, for those who can, need to ride. It is not only the Grey Army who can take to the air when the need arises.

Willard's plan was soon put into action as there was no time to waste. Tempest and the rest of the birds had landed, and after a short discussion, riders had been allotted, as Rusty and Willard made final arrangements too. It was decided that those who could, would fly, whilst Rough and Ursa would trek back, aided by the ever reliable Tricky to act as guide. Chance the raven would stay behind for now to patrol the skies over The Vale as a precautionary measure, just in case a treacherous foe dared return.

Willard sat astride Screech with Rusty, Scarlet, Izzy, Misfit and the rest doing the same astride a bird of their own. The renegades who remained behind tended to any wounded who still needed help and put to rest any who had fallen at the side of The Vale.

Willard gathered them all together for one last time. "Thank you all who rallied to the call today!" he called out.

"For you were all brave beyond doubt. My fellow foxes, rabbits, stoats and more, I salute you all. As for now, we will part our ways, but remain forever in your debt."

"Once a renegade always a renegade!" came a shout from a stoat, which gained the greatest cheer of all.

Willard then sat up straight on his mount. "Now, all those who ride, take to the air!" he cried. And with that they ascended quickly, and were soon out of sight as Rough readied to go also.

"Well, we'd better make tracks too," he said to Ursa and Tricky. "We can't let them grab all the glory," he quipped in an attempt to brighten the mood, but secretly thinking, *I just hope we aren't too late*.

Rusty and the rest of the renegades hung on tightly as they flew fast and low over the trees. His ride was Tempest the hawk, and as they grew closer, were now in no doubt it was the Great Wood that was ablaze. The acrid smell of burning wood filled the air, as Willard flew alongside Screech. Looking down they spied animals of all kinds running from the ferocious blaze, as orange and red flames, like red-hot tongues, devoured all in its path and Willard was sure who the culprit was.

"This has all the hallmarks of Slate. Are there no depths of depravity to which he will not sink?" he spat.

"I know, I sense it too," agreed Rusty angrily.

Now directly above the blaze they began to circle in hope of spotting a good place to land. Then Scarlet saw movement down at the beach, and signalled them to follow. As they closed in, they could make out the families and friends from the cove, stretched out in a line into the sea, passing each other buckets in a vain attempt to put out the fire.

Seeing this, they swiftly landed and Scarlet, with the aid of the pines, the rats and the rest immediately ran to help with their valiant efforts. Rusty and Willard watched on in frustration, knowing their desperate efforts would not be enough as the blaze raged on, being fanned by a stiff sea breeze.

"My friend," said Willard turning to Rusty. "It is time for you to act and use the power entrusted to you."

"But what do I need to do?" asked Rusty, not sure what action to take.

Willard then placed a firm paw on his arm. "With the help of the Meriden blade, you must call on the elements. It is the only way to halt this. You managed a single bolt of lightning to help defeat Oswald. You must now call up a great storm. This is the route to take to engulf the flames. But I must warn you. It will take up all your inner strength; your very essence to summon up such a force of nature. It will come from the very core of your being, therefore, such action will be taxing and fraught with danger," Willard warned ominously.

Rusty looked at the scene of devastation unfolding before him and knew he had no choice. "If it's my destiny to save the Great Wood then so be it," he said defiantly.

Willard let out a huge sigh. "Indeed, this is true. But you must know this. If I could trade places with you, my friend, I truly would," replied Willard solemnly. "Now time is of the essence. You must clear your mind and call on the wisdom of the druids to guide your way. To do this, concentrate with all your might," Willard instructed him.

Rusty nodded, took a deep breath and closed his eyes. Again, he felt removed from all around him as his head was filled with the incantations and the sounds of ancient chants. Then an unseen voice spoke out clearly to him, through the mists of time.

"Heed me, Nat-Jos. Trust your instincts and let the blade of Meriden empower you. For I am Pen-Am, your companion, for now and ever more."

The voice faded and Rusty opened his eyes to see his sword arm lifted, as if having a life of its own. It then started to glow an incandescent glow so bright, all present had to turn away. At once, a shaft of light burst from within the sword itself, and shot a bright beam into the cloudless sky. The upper atmosphere immediately above them changed, and the darkest storm clouds they had ever witnessed rolled dramatically in. The sky was now a thick blanket of cloud, so dense it blocked out the sun. A huge streak of lightning then shot across the sky, followed by a great clap of thunder. Then came the rain.

The Meriden blade now felt as if it had multiplied by ten times its original weight. Rusty began to weaken now by its burden, as if being drained of life itself. And still the rain fell. Huge drops cascaded down, the heaviest rainfall they had ever seen, the downpour so hard they could hardly make out the animal standing next to them. But it now began to have the desired effect. The raging fire began to hiss and cool, the once black clouds turned to grey, as the monsoon-like deluge began to slowly extinguish the flames.

The storm still raged on above, the thunder and lightning filling the whole sky with a stunning display of nature's work. But Rusty was tiring. He fell to one knee, the sword now the heaviest thing he'd ever lifted in his entire life. But still he held on, orchestrating the events above, not wanting to let go.

"Just a little longer," he gasped. "I've got to hold on."

And then suddenly, it was over.

"Look!" came a shout. "He's done it. The fire is out!"

And to the great delight of all present it was true. Then the storm abated, its job now done, giving way again to blue skies once more, amid cries of jubilation.

As the cheers subsided the sound of sobbing filled the air. It was Scarlet, tending to Rusty, cradling his head in her arms. She looked up and simply said through a veil of tears.

"He's not breathing. He's gone. I've lost my Rusty."

CHAPTER FORTY SEVEN

The mood had turned from joyous to sombre in an instant, as their euphoria quickly disappeared at the sight of Scarlet and the stricken figure of Rusty, lying in her arms.

"Willard, is there nothing you can do? Maybe your fix-all medicine, can we try that?" Scarlet pleaded.

Willard approached her with a heavy heart and tenderly put his paw on her shoulder. "My elixir won't help this time for he is too far gone for that," he said sadly. He paused to gather his thoughts for a moment before speaking again. "There is a possible course of action I can follow, but you must lay him down and step away for me to proceed, as it may prove dangerous," he reasoned.

Scarlet, trusting him completely, placed Rusty's head gently down and backed away. Rough came over to comfort her as the rest of the renegades gathering silently around. The Meriden blade still glowed brightly in Rusty's unmoving grip, as Willard stood over him eyes shut, concentrating.

Willard felt himself instantly removed from all those around him. Voices of the past could now be heard faint and inaudible at first. And then a voice he knew and hadn't heard for an age called out to him.

"Pen-Am, it is I. Do you seek me out after all this time?"

"Yes, Shelton. I beseech you, for you are wise. Tell me, how do I retrieve a companion who has felt the power of the Meriden blade, and in doing so, their spirit has been lost to the realm?" Willard asked of him. The answer was instant.

"The use of the blade carries with it a heavy price. And that price must always be paid in full."

After a brief pause Shelton spoke again, giving hope this time.

"Old friend there is a way. The only course to take is to bisect the blade and release that which is held within. But this act does not guarantee success. If the spirit does not find a host, it will be lost to wander the Earth, alone for all eternity."

The risk was great but Willard knew if he was to save Rusty, he had no choice but to try.
"I understand," Willard answered determinedly. Shelton then spoke for the last time.
"Heed my warning. Keep the blade apart forever more. For not doing so will ne'er end well. Farewell my old friend, may your endeavours bear fruit, for you now know the right and true path to take."

The voice of Shelton then went silent as it vanished completely.
"Thank you, I know now what needs to be done," Willard replied with new resolve. Emboldened, he opened his eyes once more and raised his paws up. At once the sword released itself from Rusty's grip and levitated upwards, in front of Willard's outstretched arms. It at once started to change, its glow now fading, and then expanding outwards, back into its original length, a weapon made fit for a man. Willard then with paws faced out, moved them apart in order to break the blade, using the power of foresight.

He felt as if he were pushing against an immovable force on each side, like trying to move mountains, but he persisted regardless. And then it happened. The blade began to quiver and shake, ever so slightly at first, but still remained stubbornly intact. But he didn't give up. Grimacing with the strain, he pressed on with all his might but still the sword stayed as one.

He looked down at his stricken friend and this pushed him on to double his efforts. With one last almighty try, it split back into two pieces with an almighty bang as the broken blade stayed hovering in mid-air in front of him.

Suddenly, vapour came streaming out of the two broken pieces, like a wisp of white smoke. It joined as one, twisting and turning like a ribbon streaming in the wind, and as this happened the broken sword at once fell to the ground. The wisp then began, with snake-like movements, weaving in and out of the renegades. Each of them watched open-mouthed in awe as the strange vapour twisted about them and moved to the next, as if to investigate what and who they were.

It now came to Scarlet and did the same, swirling around her from tip to toe, briefly stopping in front of her eyes, but seeming unsatisfied continued to move on. Finally, after going around them all it stopped as if deciding where to go next, and then turned in the direction of Rusty. The serpent-like vapour moved through the air before stopping directly before him, and then came to a halt over his fallen figure. The strange wisp stopped. It was above him, bobbing like a cork at sea, a fraction from his face, as if deciding if this is what it had been searching for all along. As if now satisfied its search was over, slipped silently and easily inside Rusty's mouth as the renegades watched on transfixed, not sure exactly what would happen next, just hoping that somehow Willard had succeeded. But Rusty remained still. Nothing changed; there was no sign of life at all.

"Come on Rusty," urged Scarlet, "please come back to me." A few moments past in silent vigil and then Scarlet's eyes widened as she saw his chest begin to rise and fall. She leapt to his side and softly lifted his head just as his eyes fluttered open. His eyes no longer crimson, he broke out into a light smile as he saw her loving face looking down on him.

"What happened?" he asked looking around confused. "Where am I? Is the Great Wood saved?"

Scarlet then held him close as more tears, this time of happiness, filled her eyes as a happy Willard crouched nearby.

"Thank you, Willard. Thank you so much. You saved him," she said gratefully.

"Saved me, how?" asked a bewildered Rusty. "Have I missed something?"

Willard then reached out to him, so pleased he was alive. "As I explained, my friend, what was needed was fraught with danger. Your brave deed nearly cost your life. Your life energy, your very essence was consumed by the Meriden blade and left you spent. You had nothing left to give. By breaking it back into two pieces, your life force was released and returned to you," Willard explained with a smile.

Rusty turned to see the blade broken, lying in two pieces on the ground next to him. He turned back to Willard. "Shelton was right. I've felt the sword's might for myself. The wisdom, the power, it's all-consuming, it's too much for one to bear," he answered wearily.

"I believe you are indeed right, my friend," Willard replied readily, and he had now come to a final solution. "I suggest, with your consent, that I take the blade away with Screech and rebury it again in secret locations so that no one can be tempted to re-join that which is best kept apart."

"Agreed," said Rusty immediately. "It's the best way. And then finally perhaps the island can return back to some kind of normality." He got unsteadily to his feet with the help of Scarlet, and holding on tightly she spoke to them all.

"We've got lots to do. First of all, we need to head off and see who needs our help. We animals of the Great Wood are a close-knit community and we look out for each other. And we showed the greys what can be achieved when you come together as one. So let's go and rebuild and reclaim what is ours. Let's get this done!"

As she finished, they all broke out into a round of applause as she gave Rusty a longed-for kiss. "Oh Rusty, I'm so proud of
 you," she said squeezing him tight.

"Without you, I'm nothing," he simply replied, giving her a tender kiss on the cheek.

Willard then intervened. "You have been through a torrid test, my friend. May I suggest a little pick-me-up?" he said with a smile, as he handed over the very last drops of fix-all.

Willard and Screech were now alone standing over the broken blade.

"Screech, my old friend, we have a pressing matter of our own at hand – to put the blade back in the ground where it rightly belongs. May the secret of its placements stay forever a mystery that remains unsolved."

CHAPTER FORTY EIGHT

Rough and Ursa had begun to make their trek back to the Great Wood ably led by Tricky, and so far, much to their delight, it had gone without incident.

"Follow me, folks, I've done this journey loads of times," she told them cheerfully as she nimbly descended the granite steps on the edge of the swamp, seemingly not at all concerned about the great height. "And don't worry, I'll make sure we get back safe and sound," she added with a cheeky grin.

Rough and Ursa being less agile than her, followed as quickly as they could, which in truth wasn't very fast at all, but they did their best to keep up as they descended the steps in her wake.

As the afternoon wore on and now in the lush forest beyond the swamp, Tricky decided they needed to get a move on and pick up the pace.

"Come on, let's hurry along now," she urged. "We don't want to be in these parts when the sun goes down, now do we?"

"Er, any particular reason for that?" asked a now nervous Rough, not liking the sound of that one little bit.

"Oh it's nothing really," said Tricky lightly. "It's just that these parts at night are occupied by bats. Really odd, big bats."

This made Rough more anxious than ever. "When you say 'big', how big is big?" he asked, getting more worried by the minute.

"Oh, big enough to carry you and me off if they wished," she said with a carefree smile. "But not Ursa, oh no, for he's much too large for that. But there's nothing to worry about. If we get a move on, we've got plenty of daylight left to get back before dusk," she said as she skipped along in front.

"What does she mean nothing to worry about?" whispered Rough to Ursa, as they hurried after her. "I don't fancy being a giant bat's midnight feast!"

"It'll be fine, I'm sure badger isn't even on their menu," replied Ursa grinning broadly, before roaring with laughter.

"Oh, and one more thing I forgot to mention," Tricky went on. "Legend has it they are witches' familiars, super natural assistants, and do all their bidding. Which is stuff and nonsense of course, just tales of the wood. But again, it's all good. Nothing to worry about, I'm sure. We'll be home before you know it. You'll see," she said brightly.

On hearing this, Rough's thudding heart skipped a beat.

"Witches! Oh, that's just great. This journey just keeps on getting better. Not only do they want to eat you for dinner, they work for witches too? I know it, I'm heading for a witch's cauldron!" Rough groaned.

And then, Rough being Rough, the mere mention of food completely changed his mood as only one thought now filled his mind. His next meal. "I don't suppose anyone brought along anything to eat?" he asked hopefully as his stomach let out a loud growl.

But before anyone could answer they heard a huge clap of thunder and saw lightning streak across the distant sky, in the direction of the Great Wood. Through a clearing in the trees, they could now see the dark storm gathering and the black plumes of smoke slowly turn to grey, and then finally dwindling away.

"Great stuff. Looks like that rainstorm has put out the fire!" enthused Tricky.

"Must be something to do with the enchanted blade I presume," guessed Ursa correctly, pleased at the sight.

"Yeah, you're probably right," agreed Rough, his spirits now lifted by the new developments. "Let's just hope not too much damage has been done. Come on, let's get going," he urged.

"We will still need to help out."

With the knowledge that the fire was probably out and their assistance would surely be needed, they doubled their efforts moving quicker than ever through the forest.

Then suddenly Tricky raised her paw and abruptly came to a halt. "Listen, did you hear that? I'm sure I heard voices," she said, much to Rough's alarm.

"It's not the witches, is it?" he asked anxiously.

They stood still for a second just to be sure, and then the voices could be heard again. In a clearing just ahead, they could now see four grey troopers come into view having a heated discussion amongst themselves.

"Well, if you're so clever, then you lead the way!" said one loudly with an angry shove.

"Well, it's you who's got us lost in the first place," replied the other pushing him back.

"It's not my fault we got lost in the swamp," said the first.

Then a third spoke up who seemed to be their senior. "You two, I've heard enough squabbling for one day. I'll have no more or you'll be on report, got it?"

"Yes, sir," the first replied sheepishly.

"Good," he said curtly. "Now we've set traps for any reds that are stupid enough to come this way. So now we will head back to the main camp before we get accused of desertion by the king. Have I made myself clear?"

"Yes, captain," said the second, but a listening Rough wasn't happy at all.

"Did you hear what they said? They've laid traps," he said quietly, as a deep frown crossed his face at the thought of their treachery. And then he made a snap decision.

"We have to capture 'em. Make 'em tell where they all are."

"Well," said the captain, "I'm sure it's this way," he finally decided. "We'll head in the direction of that smoke. Judging by the sun that's due south, so it must be right." He was then startled by a voice to his rear.

"Excuse me, are you lost by any chance?"

The greys all whirled around at once to see who had spoken, as Rough strolled casually towards them, as if he hadn't got a care in the world. He then stopped short of the captain who answered him sharply.

"So, you know the way around these parts then badger, do you?" he snapped.

"Yeah, of course. I know these woods like the back of my paw. I'll tell you what," Rough continued, "ask nicely and I'll show you the way."

This had the desired effect on the captain. To rile him up. "I think not! You who will be doing exactly as I say regardless!" said the captain tersely, as he quickly drew his sword.

Rough smiled casually as Tricky then stepped out behind the greys with her bow aimed directly at them with Ursa by her side, growling menacingly. Hurtling around, the sight of the huge bear and the archer was enough for the four startled greys to know the game was up, and one by one dropped their weapons to the floor and raised their paws in the air to surrender.

"So, what do you want then, badger? Maybe we can strike a deal?" said the captain, trying his luck. But Rough was in no mood for bargaining.

"Shut up, you're lucky I don't let my friends loose on you. What kind of animal leaves traps for another?" he snapped.

"Here's what's going to happen next. You're now our captives; you're coming with us. But first show us where these snares are and maybe we'll let you live. And no tricks. My friend hasn't eaten all day and he certainly looks hungry to me."

Ursa, then on cue, reared back onto his hind legs to his full height and roared loudly. The captain had seen enough.

"Okay, we agree," he said visibly taken aback. He then addressed the troops. "You lot, how many traps are there set?"

"Half a dozen," came the reply from the first.

"Show them where they are. Well, don't just stand there. Do it now!"

"Yes, sir. Of course, sir," he replied.

With their weapons now confiscated it took just over an hour for the troopers to point out and disable all the traps as Rough, Ursa and Tricky watched their every move.

"Did you see the looks on their faces," laughed Rough to Ursa,

"when I suggested you might eat them?"

"You mean you were joking," replied Ursa merrily. "I quite fancied a grey squirrel feast!" he boomed before laughing his deep laugh.

"Well, that's the last of them, all done," declared Tricky as the last snare was dismantled. "Nasty little spring-laden traps they were, too, shame they didn't set off their own."

She then glanced up at the setting sun. "We must get a move on," she insisted. "It's almost dusk."

"My cave's a short distance away," said Ursa. "We could always spend the night there, set out at first light," he offered.

"Okay, good idea, we'll do just that," said Rough, thankful at the thought of sanctuary.

So off they went in single file, with Tricky taking point as usual.

The sun was now sinking below the horizon, and the once well-lit forest now had an eerie feeling as darkness slowly closed in. Suddenly, out of the gloom, they heard what sounded like the fluttering of huge wings beating in the air.

"What was that?" asked an unnerved Rough. They all came to a halt as Tricky stared dead ahead. Directly in front of them, a huge dark shape appeared blocking their path, seemingly hanging from a low branch. They couldn't quite make out in the half-light exactly what it was at first. And then suddenly it stretched out its huge leathery wings for all to see. A wide-eyed Rough was frozen to the spot and gulped loudly, not quite believing his eyes. For before him was the largest bat he'd ever seen in his life.

CHAPTER FORTY NINE

They all stood stock-still as the huge bat seemed to hang there for what seemed like an age unmoved. Around them, they could hear the unsettling sound of the beat of more wings, flapping and fluttering somewhere high above in the dark treetops. And then the great bat in one swift movement, flipped off the branch and landed up right on its feet. It leant forward onto all fours, tucking back its wings, resting on long gnarled clawed fingers, watching them through big black round inquisitive eyes. It had a quiff of blond spikey hair atop its large head, between its long, pointed ears, and its brown furred body was covered in a close-fitting black vest. It had short muscular legs with its huge clawed feet protruding out. The bat then came towards them, still on all fours, more of a swagger than a walk.

And then it spoke.

"Aaaah, now let me introduce myself," the bat said in his slow distinctive drawl. "I'm Isaac. My friends call me Zac. But you may call me Isaac," he sneered. He then looked up. "And just so you know, I'm not alone. My cohorts are up high, watching you, watching me, watching you," he said with a sly grin. He strolled up to Rough. He was easily twice as tall as him and stood a metre away, looking him up and down.

Was he trying to scare him? Rough wasn't sure. Though uneasy, he didn't want to show it, and did his best to stare back.

"I know what you're thinking. "Naaah, these ain't bats. Bats are teeny, weeny flying rodents," he said holding out his claws close together to demonstrate the size of a normal bat.

"But I can assure you, we are. Very much so." He grinned showing off his set of large fanged teeth. "And yes, we're bigger than your average bat. Much bigger. A gift you may say from our benefactor, who knows the odd spell or two," he chuckled.

He then continued to strut casually on past Rough and Tricky before coming to a halt in front of Ursa. "Oooh, a bear," he cooed. "I like bears. Never seen one for real before, only heard of 'em," he admitted. "So you're a first. And my, you're a big one," he said looking up at him, as Ursa was three times his height. "You're probably thinking nothing to worry about, I'll just squash you with one claw, aren't you bear?"

Ursa didn't answer, his expressionless face unable to be read. He just let the bat do the talking. For now.

"Yes, you could crush me, I'll give you that," Isaac conceded. "But I have to warn you. I bite!" He then showed off his fearsome sharp fangs once more.

"A bite from me can even make someone as big as you sick," he said before continuing to saunter down the line around past the last shaking grey, and headed back up again. "Now tell me. How is this going to go down. Good or bad? Your call. Now me, I'm a happy camper and would prefer a happy ending. But hey, I'm not you. Thankfully," he smirked.

He then made his way back up to Rough and looked him dead in the eye. "You look kind of intelligent-looking for a badger. Tell your group you're all coming with me. I've got someone who'd love to make your acquaintance. Our benefactor. She doesn't like strangers on our patch, you see. So you'll have some explaining to do." He then leaned further in; his squat nose almost touching Rough's snout. "Like I've said, you're coming with me either the easy way or the hard way, it's your call. Me personally, I would choose the first 'cos I like an easy life. Tell you what, you've got a little time decide, it's all the same to me."

He then turned and strolled back to the tree he had leapt from and leant against it, his large unblinking round eyes staring blankly at them. Rough turned to the others to quickly decide what to do. "There's only one thing for it, we fight our way out," he said quietly. "Whoever makes it, get back to Rusty and warn him about these bats."

"Now, now folks, time's running out."

Tricky then leaned in and whispered urgently. "There's a better way. You've got to trust me on this one," putting her hand into a hidden pocket and pulling out a small silver round ball. "When I say 'Now!', all cover your eyes, and when I say 'Go', we run."

Rough knew the time was up. "We're with you," he quickly agreed, speaking for them all.

"Okay folks, I'm coming, ready or not," announced Isaac. "And I do hope I'm still a happy camper with your answer."

Tricky then made her move. "Now!" she yelled. She then threw the ball up into the air and it landed at the big bat's feet, as they all followed her lead and covered their eyes.

"What's this?" said a bemused Isaac eyeing the object curiously. "You want to play ball?"

The object Tricky had thrown then exploded with a large bang! A big flash of bright light immediately illuminated the gloom, like a huge firework exploding.

"Aaaarghhh!" screamed Isaac, clutching his eyes, turning away. "What's this trickery? I can't see!"

Tricky then took the initiative. "Run!" she shouted. "Go, go, go!"

They didn't need telling twice, and pushing past the blinded bat, quickly disappeared into the bush, running for their very lives.

CHAPTER FIFTY

And so they fled. They now crashed through the undergrowth with only one thought in mind. Run. Tricky led the way, followed by Rough and Ursa, with the greys taking up the rear. She gave the occasional fearful glance over her shoulder to spot any potential pursuers, but so far thankfully there were none. When they'd got far enough away from the bat they stopped to take a breather.

"Think we lost 'em?" asked a breathless Rough.

"Who knows, but we need press on regardless," gasped Tricky. Then somewhere out there in the dark came the awful sound of beating wings, getting closer and closer. "Come on, let's go!" she urged. So again they ran.

The captain of the greys had never been so afraid in all his life. He'd often been on a hunt on the mainland, which he quite enjoyed. But now the hunter was the hunted, a feeling he didn't like one bit. Terrified, he now found himself near the rear of the group and saw movement fleetingly in the corner of his eye. Then a large shape dropped out of the dark canopy above. He ducked in fear as a huge rush of air shot over him and he heard the sound of an impact as the trooper further back was plucked up and carried away, kicking and screaming into the night. He felt then like he was in a waking nightmare as another trooper, just behind him, attacked from the side this time, was whisked abruptly away, suffering the same awful fate. He turned to see the remaining trooper looking scared witless.

"Captain Dire, do something," he pleaded. "Please save me!"

But Dire didn't listen, his attention lay elsewhere. Looking over the shoulder of the hapless trooper he saw a bat swooping in fast, claws extended, ready to take another victim. Dire reached out and putting his paws firmly on the soldier's shoulders, pushed him backwards into the path of the incoming bat, as he dropped down into a ball. The bat obliged by taking the easiest target and grabbed the stumbling grey and lifted him off into the night wailing, his legs and arms flailing wildly.

Dire now in a blind panic turned to see in utter dismay Rough and the others were nowhere in sight. Where are they? he asked himself, now so scared he could hardly breathe. It was deathly silent. And then a noise startled him – a rustling from the bush. He scanned the dark avidly in abject fear. But it was no bat. It was Rough. And he looked angry.

"So it's you," he snarled. "I thought I recognised you but it was dark. Then I heard him call out your name. It was you who killed my friend Archie the fox that night back in the Great Wood!" he spat venomously.

"Look, I'm sorry for that. But all's fair in love and war. You know that, right? Just take me with you," begged a tearful Dire, "before they come again." But lucky for him Rough was not looking for retribution.

"Shut up blubbering and come on. You're our prisoner. You can be dealt with later," replied Rough gruffly. And then he suddenly stopped talking and looked up. Dire followed his gaze and found himself staring into the doll-like eyes of the huge bat hanging upside down above him, as he was grabbed and whisked away in an instant, leaving Rough standing quite alone.

Rusty and the rest of the inhabitants of the Great Wood had been busy and now gathered around outside the old oak tree to rest, as night fell eating a late meal after a hard day's toil.

"Well, it could have been a lot worse I suppose," Rusty said to Scarlet, sitting back full to the brim.

"Yes, you're right," she said snuggled up close to him taking a sip of her tea. "Although, we did lose half of the woods to the fire," she admitted sadly, "but we've made a good start and pulled together."

"I know," Rusty replied, "and you were great at organising temporary homes for the ones who'd lost everything," he said in admiration.

"Thanks," Scarlet said with a smile. "But it's the least I could do."

Izzy came over to join them, sitting next to Scarlet. "I've spoken to the beavers and they've promised to cut fresh wood at first light to start the rebuild. It'll be a joint effort too as we pines can build tree homes in no time at all," she added cheerfully, before happily tucking into a hot pie.

"That's great to hear," said Rusty, but seeming a little distant.

"What is it, dear?" asked Scarlet. "I know that look, you're worried, aren't you?"

"It's Rough and the others, they should be back by now," he admitted. "There must be something wrong. I can sense it."

"I'm sure they're fine," insisted Izzy. "They've got Tricky with them, she's one of the best, believe me."

"I just hope you're right," he said quietly.

CHAPTER FIFTY ONE

"What do you mean you've lost them?" spat Isaac into the faces of his two fellow bats.

"Dunno, boss," said one, "they jus' done a runner."

"Yuh, boss," said the other. "Like he said, jus' scarpered." Isaac was far from impressed.

"They can't have just vanished, you idiots. We're bats. I'm not sure if you've noticed. But we're good in the dark!" he screamed in frustration. He took a step away to regain his composure before speaking to them again. "You two, you need to relax, use your senses," he said seeming much calmer now. "The night is but young. You've caught up with some of 'em, the rest ain't got far, and we love a good night hunt. Ain't that right boys?"

"Yuh, sure do, boss," they both agreed submissively.

"No, let's get that right, we love a good night FEED!" he sneered, before bursting into hysterical laughter.

Not far away, hiding below an outcrop of rocks, Rough, Tricky and Ursa had listened to every word. They stayed motionless, until they heard the swishing of wings signalling they were surely alone. Tricky peered out to confirm it, and crouched back down again.

"They've flown," she whispered.

"Good," Rough replied. "And great job earlier. What was the exploding ball thing you threw to get us away?"

"Oh, that. I call it my Tricky dazzler. It's a little something I put together. I like to experiment, you see. They don't call me Tricky for nothing," she added with a mischievous wink. "It worked well don't you think?"

"Yeah, it was great, don't suppose you've got more with you?" whispered Rough hopefully.

"No, sorry, only the one. They're a bit temperamental, you see. Kept together they have tendency to go off on their own accord."

"Okay, no problem," Rough replied hiding his disappointment. "But we can't stay here any longer, they're bound to find us."

But Ursa had a solution. "Agreed," he said, "but we aren't too far from my cave. Once there, we can defend it from attack easily. I say we leave for it now. They seem to attack from behind. I'll watch your backs and take the rear."

So with a hastily made plan formulated, they made a start for Ursa's lair, staying low, keeping to the shadows and before long the cavern loomed in the distance.

"Their it is," said Ursa, pointing across the half-lit meadow. "I see it," replied Rough. "Slight problem though, no cover. We'll have to make a run for it."

"Told you, I've got your backs," reminded Ursa. "Go first, I'll follow."

And so off they ran, heads down, racing towards the safety of the cave. They got about halfway across when again they heard the beating of wings, drawing ever closer. Then the three bats loomed out of the darkness behind them, closing in fast. Ursa, hearing the danger, stopped and turned to meet them head on. Isaac signalled the attack and the first bat dived in, but Ursa was ready and easily batted it to one side with a strike of his paw, sending it hurtling to the floor. Ursa roared defiantly as the two other bats swooped and turned to start the next pass. At this point, Rough reached the entrance of the cave, throwing himself inside, followed closely by Tricky.

They turned to see Ursa having fended off one bat, charging towards them, seeking refuge from the others. He was in touching distance of the cave when Isaac dropped on him out of the darkness, biting him firmly on the shoulder. Ursa howled with pain and then knocked him away, before stumbling inside exhausted, as the bats landed lining up in front of the cave mouth.

"Woooaaah now I see why such a rush. Nice cave, I approve," said Isaac peering inside from afar. "Could do with maybe a little mood lighting, but hey,

you can't have everything," he sneered. "Tut tut, looks nasty. But he'll be fine. Oh no he won't!" he hissed. "You see, I'm afraid the bite of a bat like me won't end well. Give up now, I'll provide a cure. Don't give up, well let's say don't bother making him breakfast."

A few tense minutes had passed by as the two groups eyed each other warily. Rough gave a concerned glance to his side to see the injured Ursa had sat back on his haunches, looking up with a tired smile.

"Are you okay, Ursa? That bite looks painful," he asked, before making his way over for a closer inspection of the nasty-looking wound.

"I'm sure I'll be fine with a little rest," he replied wearily. "Just keep an eye on those three out there for me, will you? After a short rest I'll be up in no time to sort them out," he said with a sigh. Tricky took note of the conversation but never dared to take her eyes off the bats at the cave edge, bow readied at her side.

"Well, hello in there," said Isaac, as he paced up and down, hunched on all fours outside the cave mouth. "Time's a ticking, you know. And that bear looks mighty sick to me," he said, studying Ursa with an empty soulless stare. "Oh, and where are my manners? I didn't introduce my cohorts to you," he said indicating the others.

"To my left is Eli. He's one of the best, even if I say so myself." With the introduction the bat duly bowed. "And to my right, meet Gideon. What can I say? One of a kind. He'd do anything for you. Well, he will for me," he sneered evilly, which gained another bow from Gideon.

They were dressed identically to Isaac, but slightly smaller in frame and height, with the same round dark empty eyes.

"What's the plan now, boss?" asked Eli with a sly grin.

"Well, it's up to our new friends here," Isaac replied loudly enough so all would hear. "We've got all night, but I'm not so sure about the bear. He looks mighty sick to me. I'm pretty sure he's seen better days," he smirked, seeming to enjoy every moment of their predicament. He faced the cave mouth again. "Are you ready to give up?" he asked. "Come out, I'll go easy on you," he suggested. But his offer fell on deaf ears. "I'll tell you what. As a show of good faith, we'll take a step back, give you some breathing space. We wouldn't want you to make any rash decisions now, would we?"

Isaac then moved away and gestured the others to close in. "Listen you two," he said quietly. "We'll call their bluff, get them to give up. They won't know we can't cross the threshold of a new abode without an invite."

"Plus be back before dawn boss. Don't forget that," reminded Gideon, trying to be helpful.

"Of course I know that," Isaac snarled impatiently. "The bear should be near the end soon anyway. That should hurry them along nicely. They'll be ours soon enough. A fitting gift for the benefactor."

"So what happens now?" asked Tricky, bow in hand, still on her guard. "Take a look at Ursa. He's taken a turn for the worse," she said gravely. Rough turned to Ursa who was now lying on his back with his eyes closed taking quick shallow breaths, as panic now filled his thoughts.

"I don't know, I need time to think," replied Rough, now feeling the pressure on him, knowing time was running out. After a few moments of silence, he spoke again.

"I just don't get it," he said after thinking it through. "If I was them, I'd rush us, get it over and done with."

Ursa then cried out in pain with anguish etched across his troubled face.

"He's getting worse," said Tricky anxiously. "I say we try to battle our way out. At least if we go down, we go down fighting," she said gamely.

"You're right agreed Rough. He won't last the night.

He then turned to her and smiled. "There's one thing Tricky I'd like to say before we go to fight. If I could choose someone to go into battle with, I'd struggle find any one braver than you."

"Thanks, Rough," she said proudly. "That means a lot.

And I've got the Great Wood wrestling champion with me too," she said with a grin. "What else could I wish for?"

"Two times champ, I'll have you know," said Rough, smiling before clenching his paws tightly.

"Well, that's even better then," she grinned, before steadying herself in a fighting stance too. "Are you ready?" she said gritting her teeth. "Let's do this!"

She drew her bow ready to let fly. And then, just as they were about to begin their charge, the night air was again filled with the beating of wings. But this time they didn't belong to any bat, as Screech landed beside Isaac and the others. And then an even larger bird, a giant eagle owl, much bigger than Screech, appeared at his side, towering above the startled bats. The huge rusty brown owl then just glared at them through intense bright orange eyes, set deep into its feathered facial disc, its prominent tufts of ears twitching to and fro, listening for any slight movement. And then it spoke, in a deep commanding voice.

"Begone you creatures of the night, or regret your decision to stay!" the giant owl thundered.

Isaac, then as if awoken from a bad dream, shrieked with alarm. "Owls, owls, oh how I hate owls!" he cried and immediately spread his wings and took off, with the others following too. But he left with a final warning. "You've not seen the last of me!" he wailed, as they fled rapidly into the night.

Rough and Tricky watched on in sheer delight at the welcome sight of the three large bats retreating into the night. Now gone, their attention returned to the owls that had come to their rescue. But instead of two owls standing before them there was now only one. Screech. The eagle owl was no more, as a smiling Willard now took his place, having shifted back to his true self.

"Willard, it's you. I should have known," beamed Rough. "But how on earth did you find us?"

"You can thank the paw of fate and our friend Screech for that, my badger friend," replied Willard with a smile. "Listen well for I will briefly explain. The great fire was put out and we were returning from a task regarding the Meriden blade. Our flight path took us back over The Vale where the ever-vigilant Screech spied a casket that had been abandoned. On closer inspection, it was found to hold the glow stones of Ursa. We were returning them to him when we spied the bats aligned outside his lair. We then hid out of sight and watched and listened, enough to learn of your dilemma. And knowing they feared owls the most, I knew what would do the trick to best scare them away. Now I heard the lead bat say Ursa was sick?" he asked seeing Ursa clearly for the first time.

"Yes," replied an anxious Tricky. "It's from a bat bite."

"Oh dear, that is not the best news you can deliver, for a bite from an accursed bat can be very serious indeed," said Willard with a frown. Screech, please head back to the cottage, if you will, and bring an extra-large bottle of my fix-all elixir as quickly as possible."

"Of course, at once," he replied, and knowing time was of the essence, immediately flew off in the direction of their home.

"Now let me take a look at our friend, Ursa the bear," said Willard, and made his way over to his side.

Ursa was now motionless lying on his back, his eyes closed tightly and breathing in deep laboured breaths. Willard made a mental note of his condition and then inspected the bite. He could see two deep wounds on Ursa's right shoulder, where Isaac's fangs had dug in deep and decided it needed immediate attention.

"He's in a deep sleep which is to be expected when bitten by a bewitched bat," was his diagnosis. "And it is a slumber, that if not dealt with correctly, will be one from which he will never awaken." First things first. The bite will ulcerate if not cleansed and dressed. So we need clean water to cleanse it with," he said as he continued to examine the wound. "Also, we will need to apply a poultice of special herbs. Time is short and so we must make haste to assure of a good outcome."

"There's a fresh water supply, a stream nearby," Tricky said, desperate to help. "I'm sure Ursa must have a bucket I can use to fill. I'll go now if you like?"

"If you will, that would be most helpful," agreed Willard. "I know where the herbs required grow locally,"

he continued, "so Rough, if you will, stay and watch over our ailing ally whilst I depart to gather that what is needed."

He then went to rush off but stopped as another thought occurred to him. "If Screech returns in my absence, please administer the full pot of fix-all," and as he spoke the sun began to rise on the far horizon, beginning to bathe the Brow in its golden glow. "Ah, good news," he said with a smile. "Dawn is breaking and so a return of the bats is most unlikely."

"Great stuff," said Tricky, buoyed by the welcome sight of the new day. "Now let's get going. We've got a bear to save."

Screech had arrived at the cottage but was outraged at the sight that greeted him. The once pristine home was now in disarray, as he saw the damage Oswald and his cronies had inflicted in his search for the broken blade.

He approached the once stout blue wooden door with dismay to see it swinging from its hinges. It fell open easily and once inside, he groaned inwardly at the act of vandalism inflicted on their once tidy home. The room had been trashed with everything upended, and even Willard's favourite armchair had not been saved from attack, with its cloth shredded and torn. But he knew now was not the time to deal with the damage, that would have to wait, as he hoped he could find what he had come for.

He went into the upturned kitchen to see his precious pots, pans and crockery strewn all over the floor. He again ignored this upsetting sight, went over to the sink and bent down to a small cubby hole which lay underneath, behind a small hinged door. The door was shut still, so had it been missed? He grabbed the small round knob positioned in the middle and pulled, and the door dropped forwards on two hinges.

To his joy he could see a large untouched large brown bottle with its cork stopper still in place. It remained intact. "Great, the fix-all is still here," he said to himself as he scooped it up. He then went back into the sitting room, and picking up a satchel bag that had been thrown to the floor, put the bottle in it and placed it carefully over his shoulder, and headed to the broken front door and took one last look around.

"I do everything around here," he said to himself forlornly, "even all the repairs," closing the damaged door behind him and left.

Willard made his way into the woods knowing exactly where to look and which herbs he was searching for. He'd made a list in his head consisting of exactly what he'd need. Ginger, turmeric, dandelion, eucalyptus and cats' claw were all on it. He knew he had no time to waste, so immediately he'd shape-shifted into a brown hare, the swiftest animal on the Brow, and hurriedly began his search. He knew he dare not fail, as the fate of the big brown bear hung precariously in the balance.

Screech wasn't the first to arrive back at the cave as Tricky had returned minutes earlier, laden with fresh water from the nearby running stream.

"I've got it!" Screech declared triumphantly, holding the bottle of medication up high. "How is Ursa, any change?"

"No," replied Rough anxiously. "He's not improved at all, he's still in a deep sleep."

"Well, let's see if this fix-all can help, it's certainly done the trick for me on more than one occasion," said Screech hopefully. "Rough, Tricky, lift his head and I'll do the rest," he asked. They duly obliged, with one on either side, and with a huge effort lifted the heavy bear's head in to an upright position. Screech then leant forward and taking the top of the bottle, gently poured the elixir slowly into the sleeping bear's open mouth drop by drop, until it was empty. Just as he finished a voice came from over his shoulder.

"It appears I have arrived just in time." It was Willard, now back to a dormouse, clutching the sought-after herbs. "Screech, has the medicine been administered in all its entirety?" he asked.

"It certainly has," replied Screech, tipping up the empty bottle to demonstrate. "Down to the very last drop."

"Good, very good. And now for the wound. I see we have fresh water now too," remarked Willard, pleased with the efforts made by all. He then made another request. "Now I will need clean cloths also to dress the wound." On hearing this, Rough jumped up willing to do his bit.

"Ursa's bedroom is at the rear of the cave and he has clean clothing there. I saw that when I was searching for the stones.

I could get some and bring them back," he suggested.

"Very good, that should suffice nicely," said a pleased-looking Willard. "But to help light your way, make use of this," he said as he held out one of Ursa's glow stones in an upturned paw and then gave it to Rough.

The stone shone, a bright yellow, immediately lit up in a lantern like glow. "I have enhanced its power to emit more light with a simple spell. Therefore, it will glow brightly, and long enough for you to retrieve that which is needed," Willard explained, as Rough admired the bright shining object in his grasp. "In the meantime, I will busy myself. I need to grind down the herbs I collected into a paste, to apply on the bite."

Rough nodded and proceeded into the gloom of the cavern, his path now well-lit by the bright yellow light of the stone, illuminating enough for him to easily make his way back to Ursa's alcove. He quickly got there, and as he entered sure enough, just as he remembered, sitting on a side cupboard, was a pile of neatly folded clean clothes. He took a handful from off the top, put them under his arm and was just about to leave when something glimmering in the light cast by the stone caught his eye.

It came from in a nook in the wall, in the corner of the small room. He made his way over to investigate and reached inside the small hole with one paw and pulled out the object that lay within. He then held it up to the light in an attempt see more. He could now make out that it was golden in colour and was flat and long, just bigger in length than his own paw. Around the edge it had what seemed to be small red precious stones, glistening like shiny cut glass. He wasn't sure what it was he held, but one thing was for sure, he'd never seen anything like it in his life. So curiosity got the better of him and he decided to bring it along with him.

I'll just ask Willard what it is, he thought to himself. He is sure to know, and I'll put it back afterwards. He headed back towards the exit. As he approached the cave mouth, the stone he held began to dim back to its normal light, and much to his delight, he could see Ursa was now sitting up smiling, and seemed to be more himself.

"Ursa, how are you feeling, mate?" he asked, placing a friendly paw on his giant shoulder. Ursa let out a relieved sigh.

"Oh, a little groggy, but Willard tells me I'm on the mend," he said gruffly. "It's down to you all that I'm okay, so I'm forever in your debt," he added with a thankful smile and content that the stones had been returned to him. But then his expression then changed from calm to angry in the blink of an eye. "But if I ever see that bat again he'll wished I hadn't," he growled fiercely.

"Now that sounds like the Ursa we all know and love," grinned Rough. He then handed over the clothes he'd taken to Willard for him to use. "We have taken a few garments in your stead to dress the wound," Willard informed Ursa. "I do hope this is agreeable."

"It's fine," replied Ursa. "Whatever it takes to help me feel well again."

Willard nodded, and now happy to continue, tore a few strips off the clothing and then dipped into the water bucket provided by Tricky. He then dabbed and cleansed the wound thoroughly and then once dried, added the herb paste he'd ground down with rocks he'd found, and applied it directly on to the wound, before binding it tightly in a fresh clean bandage. "You will need to keep this poultice in place for a day or two, and then you'll be as right as rain."

"Thanks again," said the grateful bear as he began to slowly regain his strength as the medicine coursed through him.

Rough then held out a paw. "Oh, there's one more thing, I found this strange object back there too. It was sort of stuck in a hole in the wall. Being a nosey badger, I decided to bring it out and ask exactly what it is." He then held up the find for all to see.

Ursa knew it straight away. "Beats me," he said with a shrug. "I was digging up some roots over by Goat Bridge, way on the other side of the island, some time back. It was there, just buried in the ground. I clawed away at the soil and it caught my eye, so I just brought it back and never gave it another thought."

Willard stared at the piece transfixed. "Please, let me examine it closer," he asked.

Rough placed it down on the ground in front of Willard, as it was much too big for a dormouse to hold. Willard leaned in, and after a close inspection looked up to speak. "Where did you say you found this, was it at Goat Bridge?" "Yes," Ursa replied. "It's like nothing I've ever seen before. I just liked it 'cos it's shiny and unusual."

Willard gave him a knowing glance. "Well, I can tell you with some certainty what this is," he began to explain. "This is a cheek plate of old, which would fit on the side of a man warrior's helmet," he said pointing to the side of his face. But if my judgement is indeed correct this is no every day find, but one of great worth. For it surely belongs to no ordinary helmet," he said as they all now hung on to his every word. "For I believe it to be a part of none other than the lost helmet of the child king of Badgers Brow."

And as Ursa recuperated Willard began to tell them more of the ancient wonder.

"Legend has it that around 1,500 years ago, during the time of the Anglo Saxons, which was the name given to some men at the time, a great king died in battle. He was known for his wondrous helmet of gold, which he wore into many battles on the Brow, to strike fear into the hearts of his enemy, and it always helped him to remain victorious. But for a reason known only to him, into one battle he did not wear it, but another in its stead. His decision is said to have brought him great misfortune, the battle was lost, and he was killed. His lone heir, his son, was only twelve years of age at the time, and even though he was of tender years, he became king.

The old king's golden helmet was smelted down and a new helmet of gold was made, big enough to fit a boy king, and again good fortune came with it. But the helmet was stolen by thieves in the night, never to be seen again. The boy grew into man and searched high and low but it was never found. It was an unhappy reign, and it was said due to the missing helmet that the new king's misfortunes lay. Legend dictates if the charmed helmet was again discovered the new owner would then be crowned true ruler of the island, and good fortune would surely follow."

Rough being a forager was enthralled with the tale. "Wow, who'd have thought this island had so many secrets? With an enchanted sword and a lucky helmet of gold, who knows what else is out there?" he said excitedly.

"Indeed, the isle has a rich tapestry of history, woven through out," agreed Willard. But his mind now strayed away from the golden find and back to the appearance of the strange bats, and what that might mean with growing unease.

CHAPTER FIFTY TWO

As the morning sped by turning quickly into noon, a concerned Rusty tried to keep himself busy to keep his mind occupied, helping out in the Great Wood as best he could. He knew it was going to be a big undertaking in the aftermath of the huge blaze as large swathes had now been lost to the fire, the pungent smell of smouldering wood still filling the air, a constant reminder that there was so much to do. It was a scene of hustle and bustle as all around him the local inhabitants all pulled together as one, hurrying to and fro. Some, like the rabbits and hares, helped clear away the debris, while others, such as the pines, worked alongside the beavers, the carpenters to help build new tree homes, with everyone helping out and doing their bit.

But Rusty was still worried as Rough and the others still hadn't returned. So he put all his thoughts into his work now sawing freshly cut timber, as Scarlet worked away by his side.

Suddenly, he heard a commotion coming from nearby. He looked up then from his task to see a most welcoming sight. There they were at long last, Rough and Tricky trudging towards them from out of the woods, accompanied by whoops and cheers from happy well-wishers, pleased to see them too. Rusty and Scarlet immediately stopped what they were doing and rushed over to greet them.

"Where have you been? I thought you'd got lost," he yelled, as he approached smiling.

"No, we just went by the scenic route," quipped Tricky.

"And met a few local characters along the way," laughed Rough.

They then began to fill Rusty and Scarlet in all about the escapade with the sinister bats, and how Willard and Screech had come to the rescue. And also to explain that Willard sent his apologies but would call later in the day to help in any way possible, with Screech and Ursa, as he was busy preparing more of his fix-all elixir, and the that others had pressing tasks too.

After eating a hearty meal and after lots of catching up, Rough and Tricky set about helping out the best they could as they went off to help the pines and beavers. Tricky nimbly took to the tree tops to assist in building the new high-top homes, whilst Rough got busy fetching and carrying the heavy timber that was needed, when he was halted from his toil by a hearty shout.

"Hey, Rough, long time no see!" Rough turned around from his labour to see another badger standing before him. It was his cousin Graham. Burly in build just like Rough, he was dressed ready for work in an old worn tunic, and greeted Rough with a warm smile and a hearty pawshake, obviously pleased to see him.

"Graham, what are you doing in these parts?" asked Rough, surprised by his visitor.

"Well, as you know, I live quite a distance away, but I'd heard rumours and hearsay you'd got trouble here in the Great Wood," Graham began to explain. "And when I saw the smoke, I knew that meant there was no time to waste. So, I made my way over as quickly as possible, and here I am to help in any way I can."

Rough was obviously delighted to see him. "That's great to hear Graham, 'cos if there's one thing we need right now, it's as much help as possible."

"Yeah, and I'm in no rush to leave too. In fact, I'm thinking of moving and finding a place here in the Great Wood to call home," he said looking around.

"That'd be great to have you as a neighbour," said a pleased-looking Rough. "I'd like that a lot. I could even help you dig out a new sett," he offered. "There's plenty of room where I live at Rough Close, and I've been known to be quite good at the odd dig too," he said proudly.

After Rough introduced Graham to the others, Scarlet gave them all news that was music to their ears.

"We're planning a big meal later in thanks for all the hard work that everyone has put in," she told them all.

"Will there be blackberry crumble?" asked Rough wistfully. "You know it's my favourite."

"Of course there will be, it's all in paw," she promised. "In fact, our old friend Roy has been out all morning collecting fruit, and will be baking pies before you know it. I'm sure he'll be back soon enough," she added hopefully.

"That's good news, everyone in the Great Wood loves Roy's world-famous crumble," said Rough. "Especially yours truly," he beamed, licking his lips in anticipation.

The old friend that they both spoke so fondly of was a friendly field mouse. He was a great baker too, or so he'd tell anyone that would listen. Roy had been a cook all his life and made many a dish, but blackberry crumble was definitely his speciality. He'd set out first thing that morning donning his favourite tweed flat cap and his most comfy tunic, knowing there was lots to do as everyone would be famished after working so hard. He'd set out early, because there's one thing he didn't want and that was to be followed. His world-famous crumble, or so he'd tell anyone who'd listen, needed the juiciest blackberries and only Roy knew the place in the Great Wood to find where the best luscious fruits grew. He was very precious about its location, and he wouldn't share his secret spot with anyone. Some of the youngsters of the wood had tried to follow him on various occasions in the past, but he was much too clever for that, losing them easily along the way. He now left Briars Road and headed down towards Tiddlers Pond, as he had done countless times in the past, carrying the biggest bucket he could manage.

When he reached the pond, so called because of the small fish that made it their home, he stopped and checked all around to make sure he wasn't being followed. Once assured of this he then continued on his journey. Next, he headed up towards yet another pond. This was known by all as the fifty-metre pond, and it was home to much bigger fish.

Again, he stopped and scanned all around looking for nosey snoopers. Now sure the coast was clear he stopped to pick up a fallen twig that lay at his feet. He had a peculiar habit of writing his name in big letters in the mud by the side of the pond. Self-taught by reading the odd man book, he wrote 'ROY', always in large capital letters as if marking his territory. Not the best idea when you are being secretive, but he was a creature of habit and had always done it, so why change now? So he did just that and satisfied with his handiwork moved on.

Roy wasn't sure how anyone could know for sure that the pond was fifty metres deep. He'd been going up there for years and it had always gone by that name, but it was a mystery that remained unsolved. He then had one last look around and now perfectly sure no one was about, he then bent down into a small gap in a nearby thicket and dipped in through the small space.

And there it was, what he considered to be the best blackberry bush on the whole of Badgers Brow. He got straight down to work, and soon filled the big bucket he'd brought for the juicy treats. He knew it would take quite a few journeys to and fro to collect enough of his secret fruit, but it was worth it to keep the knowledge of its location to himself. He then started to head back and soon found himself on Briars Road again when coming the other way he saw a close neighbour of his, Melvin the mole.

"Hello Roy, been off blackberry picking again?" he asked cheerfully.

"Yes, I'm making crumble later, and everyone's invited." Roy beamed proudly.

"You know what," continued Melvin, "the best spot for blackberries is up by the fifty-metre pond. If you stoop down, its hidden behind a big bush." Roy was astounded and annoyed in equal amounts.

"Oh, I didn't know that," he said trying to hide his irritation that Melvin actually knew his secret spot.

"Yeah, I go there all the time," he replied with a smile. "And you know why it's called the fifty-metre pond, don't you?" Melvin asked. "It's not how deep it is, it's the width," he said sticking out his arms to demonstrate.

Roy looked back and just smiled. I've been going up there for years and didn't know that, he thought to himself ruefully.

"See you later for a piece of your world-famous crumble or so you keep telling anyone who'll listen," said Melvin, as he left with a cheery wave.

Well, who'd have guessed that? Roy thought to himself as he continued on with his precious load. After all these years the mystery of the fifty-metre pond was finally solved.

The evening came along swiftly, and after everyone had worked so hard in the Great Wood they were all ravenous and ready to eat their fill. Various tables had been put out with seating all around in the big clearing of the furball pitch which previously, not too long ago, Slate had held his now notorious victory banquet.

Everyone brought something along to share and the tables were full of sumptuous delights, including of course Roy's world-famous blackberry crumble. At one table sat Rusty and Scarlet alongside Willard who had now joined them with Rough, Tricky, Izzy and Ursa seated too.

"I'd like to make a toast," Rusty announced, standing up to raise a teacup to a now hushed gathering. "Here's to all in doing a great job of defending the island against the grey invaders," he began. "They tried to divide and conquer us, but in the end failed, and through staying as one, we won the day."

"Hurrah!" came the cheer, along with rapturous applause.

Rough then stood. He waited for calm and then solemnly said his piece. "And let's not forget the brave sacrifice of the fallen. Archie, Ash and all the others who went down fighting and gave their all for our freedom. Let's make sure we never forget their sacrifice and bravery," and raised his cup in tribute too. For all it was now a short time of reflection, as they discussed amongst themselves the highs and lows of the past few weeks.

As the night wore on a more celebratory mood now filled the air, and even the odd song broke out as spirits began to lift, along with hopes of a brighter future.

Roy the field mouse, as promised, had kept himself busy all night long going to and fro, and now returning once more pushing a heaving trolley of delicious delights. "Would anyone like more crumble?" he asked, walking by with lots more freshly baked crumble. "It's world-famous you know," he said, to anyone that would listen.

Rough immediately put his paw up. "Over here, Roy, please," he said with a hungry look in his eye. Roy decided he would have a little fun and tease him.

"But surely you've had enough," he said playfully. "I realise one helping is not enough, and two is just right, but more? Surely not."

"Roy, your crumble is amazing and I'm sure my belly can squeeze in one more slice," replied Rough, drooling at the thought.

Roy just smiled. "If you're sure? Two helpings is normally just about right," said Roy still kidding him, before cutting off a big piece.

"Definitely sure," replied Rough eagerly. "After all, I'm a growing badger, you know," he replied, before joyfully rubbing his belly. "Everyone knows that. And if I could only ever have one food for the rest of my life, it'd be your world-famous blackberry crumble."

"Well, that seals it then," said Roy, beaming widely at the glowing endorsement. "You can have as much crumble as you like," at which all within ear shot burst into laughter.

Roy placed down the hot treat and went off happily to dish out more, feeling exceedingly pleased with himself.

"Well, my friend," said Willard to Rusty, as they sat back later on a nearby log, satisfied by the mouth-watering feast, "you've certainly been on a voyage of discovery in the last few weeks, have you not?"

"I know, it's a lot to take in," replied Rusty, still taken aback by the recent events.

Willard gave him a knowing look before continuing. "Your life as changed beyond all recognition now you know you're no ordinary creature of the woods," Willard began to say. "Your future, your destiny, it is yet to be fulfilled, for your true self has now been awakened, for by wielding the blade of Meriden, the experience, the power, it will have changed you forever."

Rusty knew this to be true. "I know, the fact that I'm not just Rusty, an ordinary red squirrel of the Great Wood, and to find out I was once a druid too, well, that will take a long time getting used to," he freely admitted.

Willard then reached out to him. "You have now learned your ancient name of Nat-Jos, let's not forget that too," Willard reminded him.

Rusty had a burning question he'd been waiting to ask.

"So tell me," he said turning to him. "Were you there in my vision of the druids?"

"Indeed, I was, my friend. For my name of old is Pen-Am, and our paths have intertwined throughout the centuries," Willard confirmed.

Rusty just beamed. He'd known deep inside that their connection was special, and this just confirmed it.

"My friend, in this life you are still young," Willard went on. "But as you mature, your powers will grow. Maybe one day you'll be known as Rusty the Wise. I do hope so," he smiled wistfully.

Rusty smiled too at the thought, and then spoke once more. "This island of ours holds so many secrets. The Meriden blade, Finnegan's den, the abandoned mine. And then there's the piece of the gold helmet you found in Ursa's cave, Rough told me about. I can't wait to see that," he said excitedly.

"All in good time, for I have left it in the safekeeping of Screech," Willard replied. "But for now, listen well, and I will tell you how the charmed helmet came to be."

Screech too had been busy. He'd promised to join Chance and the rest of the Freedom Fighters, who were out on a newly arranged aerial patrol of the island, once he had fulfilled his task. He'd spent all day at his home the cottage, fixing it back up again as best he could. He hadn't mentioned its sorry state to Willard as not wanting to upset him, but now sitting back he felt better about things.

He'd put everything back in position first. And to his delight found lots were fixable. He'd next stitched together Willard's favourite chair with needle and thread until it was nearly as good as new, and put anything beyond repair outside at the back. Now it's time to relax a while he thought to himself, and settled down in front of a roaring log fire feeling quite content and began to doze off. A few hours passed and he awoke with a start as he heard a noise. And there to his astonishment stood Willard.

"Oh, you're back," said Screech, stretching out with a big yawn. "I didn't expect you till morning. I've been meaning to tell you the cottage needed some attention too," he said, with a look of concern.

"Oh we'll soon fix that, don't concern yourself," said Willard reassuring him. "I don't suppose the kettle is close to warm, is it?" Willard asked in hopeful anticipation.

Screech leapt up immediately. "Don't worry, consider it done, I'll make tea because—"

"I know," chipped in Willard with a smile, "you do everything around here."

Screech then sloped off into the kitchen with a little grumble to himself.

"Oh screech!" Willard called after him. "Where did you place the cheek plate? I'd like to examine it further."

"Oh, it's in the bottom drawer of the cabinet, next to the fireplace."

"Why, thank you. Oh, yes, of course, there it is," replied Willard from the living room.

Screech continued to make the tea as a nagging doubt crossed his mind. Willard was surely not due back till tomorrow, he'd said so himself he recalled. Screech put down the kettle and went back into the living room to ask. But Willard was gone.

"Willard, Willard, where are you?" he called out, but there was no reply.

He then noticed the front door was ajar. That's odd, he thought, I'm sure I shut that. He walked over and opened it to peer outside just in time to see Willard shape-shift into a huge black she cat. She then turned and smiled evilly at him.

"Thank you for the gift, owl, most gracious of you," she hissed with menace. "And don't think to follow, as I never travel alone." She then slinked off into the night gripping the gold firmly between her teeth once more.

"Oh dear," said Screech to himself. "That wasn't Willard at all. What on earth have I done?"

He hardly slept a wink all night, worried about what to tell the real Willard on his return. He decided he couldn't sleep by dawn so he did what he did best, keeping busy by doing the housework and baking delicious cakes. Mid-morning came and he was sweeping the porch as Willard came walking up the path.

"Good morning, keeping busy I see," said Willard with a cheery wave. "I do hope breakfast is not too far away?"

But Screech didn't reply, and Willard could sense straight away something wasn't quite right.

"Screech, you seem concerned but whatever it is, I am sure tea and cake will help sort it out."

So shortly after they sat on the porch, with the aforementioned tea, Screech busily explained exactly what had happened the night before. "Well, before we go on, let me say it is not your fault, the blame is laid entirely on the doorstep of the thief itself," said Willard comforting his friend. "You did say a black cat?" he went on.

"Yes, a large black she cat," replied Screech, now feeling less at fault and a little better after hearing Willard's comforting words. But Willard himself was now concerned.

"That in itself is not good, not good at all," he said with a frown. "For this can only mean one thing. Someone who I thought had perished a long time ago has surely returned. For it can only be the work of one. Delilah the Devious, for she is a sorceress. A witch of the highest order.

CHAPTER FIFTY THREE

"Now remind me again, Gutterpress, of my glorious victory on the Isle of Grey," said Slate pompously, his back to his scribe, staring out of a side window of the old steel mill at the distant isle, as the sun sank in the distant like a red-hot disc fashioned by a blacksmith, being dipped in the sea to cool.

"Yes, sire, of course, sire. Nothing negative, always positive, as always," the scribe grovelled before clearing his throat and then reading out what he had transcribed.

"You landed on the island and most of the inhabitants were there to greet you and laid flowers at your feet, in homage to their new benevolent king," he began.

Slate was immediately impressed. "Yes, I like it so far, go on," he remarked with a self-satisfied grin.

"A few of the reds were rebellious, and became fugitives known as the renegades. But soon you had them on the run, tracked them down with ease, and had them cornered."

"Go on, tell me more," Slate urged him. "For after all, this is the exciting bit."

"And then you met in the great battle of the Valley of Doom. You led the charge of the Grey Army, and fought valiantly with little losses, leaving the renegades begging for mercy."

"Yes, this is good, very good indeed. You've even got me convinced this is what actually happened." Slate grinned.

"Now, hurry along, dolt, what happens next?" he said, impatiently rubbing his paws in anticipation.

"After a wonderful victory, the islanders declared you king of all that can be seen, as was foretold, and they held a huge victory banquet in your honour.

"Was there lots of cake? Oh I do love a good cake," asked Slate, licking his lips and imagining the scene, still staring across the sea.

"Yes, sire, mountains of cake," added Gutterpress wearily.

"Oh excellent, I do like the sound of that. Now tell me, what about the fire, how do I explain that?"

"You were crowned king in a great ceremony and they lit huge bonfires in your honour, which could be seen for miles around. You then left for the mainland to rule forever from across the water," explained Gutterpress, hoping his work was acceptable.

"Excellent. Oh, I do love a happy ending. And do make sure all this gets given to my minister of misinformation, Bliss, immediately, and sent out to the masses for their consumption as soon as possible," ordered Slate, as he then finally turned to face his scrivener. And as he did, he jumped back in shock.

"Yikes! What on earth are you wearing this time?" he shrieked, aghast at the sight of his scribes latest multi-coloured tunic.

A sheepish-looking Gutterpress said, "It was a present from my mother," desperate to not look embarrassed.

Slate just shook his head in utter disbelief. "Is she colour-blind? Do you glow in the dark?" asked Slate, still taken aback. "Does your mother actually dislike you?" he added in sheer exasperation. "I suggest next time you shop for yourself," was his final advice.

"Yes, sire, of course, sire," replied Gutterpress timidly as he went back to scribbling away. "I'll finish my work then, sire," he said head bowed, feathered pen in hand.

"Nothing negative, always positive. As always."

Later, as Slate was ready to retire for the evening, there was a loud knock at his bedroom door. He was immediately unimpressed.

"What is it, it's late!" he bellowed. "I was about to get my beauty sleep. Oh, come in, I suppose," he grumbled loudly. "But it had better be good."

A grey servant then opened the door and came shuffling in, visibly shaking, followed closely by Commander Pumice.

"Well, come on, imbecile. Don't just stand there quivering. Spit it out!" spat Slate.

"There's someone to see you, sire. He seeks an audience, says it will be most beneficial to you," answered the quaking servant, looking at the floor. Slate said nothing and just stared at him annoyed. The servant now more nervous than ever gulped and then spoke again.

"He awaits just outside and asked me to show you this. The servant then held out something that gleamed in the candlelight in his shaking paws. It was the stolen golden cheek plate. Slate's eyes at once lit up with greed.

"Oh, I say, I do like the look of that. It's fantastic," said Slate, as he took hold of the golden piece. "What exactly is it, serf?" he asked, as he turned it in his paws.

"I'm not sure, sire, but the visitor awaits on the outer wall," replied the servant edging away meekly.

Pumice then stepped up. "Shall I see the intruder off?" he asked, now at Slate's side, hand on sword.

"No, you fool, I need to hear what he's got to say!" snarled Slate, his interest now piqued by the golden piece.

"But be right by my side nevertheless, and strike at once if I give the sign."

"Yes, sire," replied Pumice, as they edged slowly forwards together. But Pumice was slightly bemused.

"Er, excuse me, sire," he asked nervously. "What exactly is the sign?"

"Oh, I don't know," Slate declared impatiently. "Perhaps if I shout 'Kill the intruder' and then stand on my head. Will that suffice?" fumed Slate impatiently. He then gave Pumice a glare as if to say 'Shut up, you fool", and then continued to edge forwards again side by side.

But Pumice had another question. "Shall I lead from the front, sire?"

At this Slate blew his top. "From the front!" thundered Slate coming to a halt. "You'll watch my back too!"

"But how am I supposed to do both at once?" blustered his now confused commander.

"How am I supposed to know?" yelled Slate, flinging his paws in the air in exasperation. "You're the bodyguard. Guard me! Now get out there and see who it is," he ordered, finally losing his patience.

But before Pumice could obey the door swung open of its own accord, and to their alarm a huge bat stood there, his shoulders so wide they filled the frame. The bat then spoke.

"Pleased to make your acquaintance," the fearsome newcomer hissed, as they both took a step back. "Now let me introduce myself," he drawled. "My name is Isaac. My friends call me Zac. But you may call me Isaac."

Pumice bristled at the perceived insolence and went to draw his sword, until Slate intervened. "Stay your paw commander!" he ordered, placing an arm across him. "Let's hear this, err, Isaac, out. My name is King Slate," he announced haughtily to the bat. "Ruler of all you can see. Now tell me, what is the reason for your visit?" he asked curtly, not letting on he was quite afraid.

Isaac stared back at him momentarily through dark unblinking eyes, before answering him. Uninvited, and unable to enter otherwise, he stayed in the doorway. "I'll be brief, King Slate," he said in his slow drawl. "I have a proposition for ya, from my mistress. Her name is Delilah. See the golden piece?" he said nodding to the cheek plate. "Well, let me tell ya something for free. It's old, and belonged to the helmet of a king long gone."

"And what's that got to do with me?" asked Slate, nose in the air, doing his best to sound brave.

"Well, ya see, Slate. Sorry, I mean King Slate," he said quickly correcting himself. "It ain't no ordinary helmet, ya see. It's charmed, and the owner of such a prize would be sure to receive good luck and prosperity."

The bat had now certainly got Slate's attention.

"Go on, I'm listening," he said, eyeing the piece now with renewed interest.

"Well, here's the thing," the bat continued. "My mistress ain't interested in it at all. She's only got one thing on her mind. Revenge against the one known as Willard. So here's the deal. She's watched you from afar the last few weeks with great interest. And now wants a pact, for mutual benefit. Once the winter's done, come next spring, you return to the isle with your grey muscle and back her up. Help her achieve her aim and you get to keep the helmet. Deal?"

Slate paused for a moment to deliberate on his answer. "So you're telling me she'd just give it away?" he asked, finding it hard to believe.

"That's right," replied Isaac. "In her words it's nothing. She just wants payback."

"Tell this Delilah, I'm in," said Slate at once. "But I'll keep the gold you brought tonight as a down payment," he added with a grin.

"Agreed," replied the bat. "I'll report back to my mistress and will return to see ya soon to make the plans."

With that, Isaac immediately spun around, and with a beat of his mighty wings disappeared into the night.

But Pumice was far from happy. "Your majesty, tell me you don't trust the word of this bat," he said anxiously.

"Of course not, you fool," said Slate, again admiring the ornate piece. "But if there is a lucky helmet of gold fit for a king, who better than yours truly to wear it? Oh, and I've got unfinished business too," he said, turning to glare back across the water towards Badgers Brow. "To get rid of that meddlesome Rusty and his renegades once and for all."

CHAPTER FIFTY FOUR

Today it was decided would be a day of rest all for all the residents of the Great Wood. After all, they had been busy all week working extremely hard to rebuild what had been lost in the blaze, and so it was agreed by all to take a break. Rusty and Scarlet had no real plans for what to do with their free time, but a late-night visit from Screech the night before had now determined what they would do with their day.

They both rose early and then made their way to Rough's sett to make an unannounced morning call. Rough's home was just a short walk from the old oak tree they called home in a turning, just off Briars Road. The leafy lane was known as Rough Close, a name chosen by Rough himself. The sett itself was neatly dug out of an embankment on the side of the Close, and stood out from amongst the other setts by its distinctive red wooden door. But it had now been a few minutes since their arrival and they had begun to think no one was home.

"Rough, are you there?" asked Rusty once more, after knocking firmly for the third time on the stout red door. There was no answer, so just as they were about to give up and walk away the door then swung open as Rough stepped out with a big stretch and a yawn.

"Morning Rust," he said sleepily. "It's not like me to be up this late. I must have slept in, must be all the long hours I've been putting in lately," he said with another yawn and a rub of his eyes. Now fully awake he then looked slightly perplexed to notice Scarlet standing there too. "Is there something wrong?" he asked knowing it was unusual for both to call so early in the day.

"Morning to you too, mate," Rusty replied brightly. "No mate, not really," he assured him, and then began to explain. "The reason we've called so early is that Screech came calling late last night. He said Willard would like to meet up with us all as soon as possible, to discuss what he called a pressing matter. He suggested he'd bring Willard over later, but they've been busy fixing up their cottage after an unwanted visit from the greys before they fled, so I said we'd call on them instead to hear his news, and give them a hand to help fix it up too. Just wondering if you're free to come along too?"

"Yeah, course I am, mate," Rough replied readily. "I've got nothing planned. Hang on, I'll just get ready. "

"That's great news," said Scarlet with a bright smile. "We can fill you in with what we know along the way."

It had turned out to be another nice day on the Brow. Overnight rain had now made way for better weather as the warm summer sun rose in the sky as the trio cheerfully headed off together down the tree lined road side by side.

"What do you reckon Willard wants then?" Rough asked, whilst busily munching on an apple he'd brought along.

"Well, I'm not entirely sure if I'm honest. But I have to admit I've felt uneasy the last few days," Rusty admitted. "A sense that something's not quite right."

For the last few nights, he had been restless again with a feeling of foreboding washing over him. He knew it was the foresight reaching out to him, a sensation he had now become used to. Not wanting to worry Scarlet and get the repairs done, he'd put it to the back of his mind, but after the visit by Screech he knew it couldn't wait, and now was the time to act.

As they continued to make their way down the leafy lane after much chit chat about this and that and nothing at all, Rough now appeared troubled.

"I've got something to ask," he said turning to Scarlet.

"Go on what is it?" she answered with a smile, pretty sure she already knew what he was about to say.

"I don't suppose there was any mention of dinner when we get there? I've missed breakfast and I'm starving already," he said, patting his belly looking slightly sorry for himself.

"Don't worry mate, I'm sure Screech will rustle something up, I know you can't function properly on an empty stomach," teased Rusty jovially.

Rough grinned happily. "Yeah, I know. I'm a growing badger. Everyone knows that. And after all, we've got to get our priorities in order. Once we've eaten, we'll have plenty of time to hear what Willard has got to say," replied Rough, happy at the thought of an upcoming feast. Now in high spirits, he decided it was time for a bit of fun. "What is needed in uncertain times, as everyone knows in the Great Wood, is a bit of badger good luck," he declared.

"You know, to bring good fortune."

He then immediately skipped behind Rusty, before deftly reappearing again at Scarlet's side.

"Come off it, Rough, you know I don't believe that it's actually true," scoffed Rusty with a grin.

"Of course it is," replied a wide-eyed Rough in mock disbelief. "It brings you loads of good luck. Like having me as a friend for example," he said chuckling loudly which brought gales of laughter all round. The three good friends then continued on their way with lots of light-hearted banter, all content in the knowledge that whatever it was that lay ahead, they'd do what they always did. Face it all together, as one.

Rusty and friends (and foes too), will be back for more adventures soon in:

The Quest for the Gold of Badgers Brow

ABOUT THE AUTHOR

LA Roberts was born in Stoke-on-Trent. He began writing in 2018, and has contributed to Doug Weller's 'Six Word Story' and 'CrimeBits: 100 Opening Gambits for Great Thrillers & Linked Mystery Puzzles' chosen by Lee Child. He lives and works in Stoke-on-Trent and 'The Battle for Badgers Brow' is his first novel.

Printed in Great Britain
by Amazon